STILL HIDDEN
The Still County Thrillers
Book 4

LAUREN STREET

STERLING & STONE

STILL HIDDEN

Chapter One

Rita stared at the public awareness posters on the elevator wall siding: HPV vaccine; Naloxone protocols; Alcoholics Anonymous meetups.

Each word fell apart before her eyes until they were mere rows of letters arranged by color and style and size. And otherwise meaningless.

The elevator door slid open.

Otto's ward.

A handful of night nurses managed the midnight hours. She passed Larissa, who gave her a wordless nod devoid of a smile.

Rita entered Otto's room.

He was no longer intubated and the ventilator turned off, and his breath shook like a rattle. Shallow and uneven, it echoed against the walls. Beside him sat Cash, his shoulders hunched as he leaned his elbows on his knees.

At the sound of her footsteps, he lifted his head. His eyelids were puffy and red. "Rita." Seeing she wasn't a nurse, he got up. But didn't approach.

Rita stared at him. "Two hours ago, I thought you

were dead." Her voice was barely a whisper. Then her gaze shifted to Otto.

Her father.

He looked the same as yesterday—wizened, white, his skin paper-thin.

"He's peaceful," Cash said. He stepped back as she approached the bed. "You can moisten his lips with the sponge." He indicated a cup of water containing a small blue sponge on a plastic stick. "I just did it a moment ago."

"Thank you," Rita said, though she was looking at Otto. She threaded her fingers through his. Purple needle-pricks dotted the back of his hands, and his fingernails were turning from yellow to black.

Cash fisted his hands around the back of the chair he'd been sitting in. "Here, have a seat. I was only staying till you got here."

"I appreciate you being here with him," Rita said, taking a seat. The vinyl upholstery sighed as if it too grieved the man departing in the bed. "But don't feel you need to go."

"I don't want to be an intrusion."

Rita scoffed, her gaze still locked on Otto. "Are you kidding me? You've been sleeping under his roof with me. He'd want you here." She paused, chewing on her lip. "I'd like you here."

Cash's strong hands slid over her shoulders. "I'm happy to be here."

Rita watched Otto breath, his nostrils flaring with each intake. Two dry and hairless black holes.

"Has he been awake today?" she asked.

"They said he's come and gone out of consciousness," Cash said. His grip tightened on her shoulders. "I've been telling him you're coming."

Rita squeezed Otto's hand. "I'm here, Dad. Otto. It's me. It's—"

Otto's face twitched.

Rita came out of her chair. "Dad!"

Then his face froze again, his breath like a wind shaking an old barn.

She twisted around to look at Cash. "Did you see that?" Her voice felt tight. "He smiled. Did you see?" She cleaned over Otto again, clutching his hand to her chest. "Dad, it's me."

Otto's eyelids fluttered, then flew open. "Honeybee—"

Then his hand went still in Rita's.

"Dad?"

But Otto's eyelids didn't twitch.

His nostrils didn't flare.

Without his ragged breathing, the room had become solemnly silent.

"Dad." She gripped Otto's hand tighter; it too was still strong, despite all he'd been through in his final years. "He can't be dead. Not yet. I just got here. Call the nurse, Cash."

Instead, Cash's hands moved over her back, pulling her into an embrace. Reluctant, she released Otto's hand and leaned into Cash.

But she felt stiff against him. "Call the nurses," she said, her voice sharper than she intended.

Cash dropped his hands. "Sure."

Rita sat back in the chair and picked up Otto's hand again.

Footsteps sounded behind her. She turned to greet the nurse. But it was Jason.

"Jason," Rita said, her voice cracking. "He…"

Jason walked towards her. "I'm sorry, Rita." Moisture

glistened in his eyes, and he held his arms open. "Would you like a hug?"

Rita paused. Shrugged, Then nodded. But he'd already pulled her into his chest. His neck smelled like Otto's, the same soap-bars stocked the trailer as the bathrooms in the house.

"He held me, too," she said.

Jason was silent for a moment. "Otto?"

Rita nodded, her cheek chafing against his uniform. "Yeah. After Lisa's body had been found." She leaned into him. "His shoulder had felt so strong. Even though he was dying."

Jason squeezed her. "Otto was always a real strong soul." He chuckled. "Apple doesn't fall far from the tree."

Rita let out a shuddering breath. "He was trying to tell me something."

At the arrival of more footsteps, she lifted her head and looked over Jason's shoulder. Larissa approached, followed by Cash.

"Sheriff Jonas," the nurse said, passing Rita on a beeline for the bed.

Picking up Otto's hand, she checked his vitals.

Then she swept a hand over his eyes, lowering the lids, and confirmed Otto's time of death. But the words, like those on the posters in the elevator, broke apart into pieces of sound that pelted her ears.

"I beg your pardon?" Rita said.

"I said I'm going to step out now, Sheriff Jonas." Larissa gave Rita a sad smile, her demeanor softened by lack of urgency. "You are free to stay as long as you need to. When you're ready to go, let us know down at the nurses' station when to expect body collection."

Her throat tightening further, Rita nodded, and Larissa took her leave.

Rita turned to Jason. "Thanks for coming by."

"Of course," Jason said. "Otto was a mentor to me, in many ways." He picked up Otto's hand and stood by the bed for a moment in silence. Then he laid down Otto's hand and gave Rita another hug before leaving the room.

When he'd gone, Rita looked at Cash. "Body collection." She shivered. "This isn't work, Cash." She chewed on her lower lip. "How'm I gonna do this?" She ran her hands through her hair. "Any of it?"

"By accepting help," Cash said.

"Thank you," she said, giving into a smile. "But I have no idea about Otto's funeral plans."

Cash smiled back at her. "It's okay. Otto's arranged most of it."

Rita blinked. "What?"

"Yeah," Cash said. "When he was diagnosed terminal, he took care of business. He's got everything booked through Still Waters Memorial Services."

"I didn't know any of this," Rita said.

"It's okay, I got it," Cash said, pulling out her phone. "You don't need to worry about any of this."

"But…" Rita said, reaching for the words. "How come you know this and I don't?"

Cash knit his brow. "Know what? About his funerary plans?"

"Yeah," Rita said, her chest tight. "I'm his kid."

Cash ruffled her hair. "You're also the sheriff in town. And Otto knows something about that. I'm sure didn't want to burden you."

Rita let out a breath. "I guess so."

Cash pulled her in for a quick kiss. "Come on, Rita, we both know you don't like guessing. So don't start thinking dark thoughts about Otto. He loved you and there's no mistaking that. Not like my— well, never mind. The same

5

way I know that man made his funeral plans, I know that man loved you."

Rita nodded, swallowing back a tidal wave of emotions. "I need to go to the bathroom."

Unable to bring herself to use the toilet in Otto's room, she marched down the hall to the public one. She barely had time to lock the door behind her in the accessibility bathroom before she doubled over the sink and threw up.

Bracing her hands on either side of the ceramic sink, she reviewed what she'd eaten in the past forty-eight hours. Not that this felt like any food poisoning she'd suffered before.

She washed out her mouth with cold water, then the sink with hot, all the while calculating the days.

"Fuck."

She tore off some paper towels and wiped her face, then the sink. Then stared at herself in the mirror. They were careful.

Sort of.

Sometimes.

It was hard to track the details when small-town, grown-up life threw a sucker punch or two.

"Fuck."

She stayed for a moment, dropping her gaze to the sink and staring into the drain. A black hole of uncertainty. She stayed for a moment, not wanting to return to the room.

What the hell was she going to tell Cash?

Inhale.

Exhale.

She washed her hands again, patted her cheeks, and retied her bun. Then she stepped into the hallway.

And caught sight of Ruby Joe leaving Otto's room.

Chapter Two

"I just saw Ruby Joe leaving," Rita said, walking into Otto's room. Her eye snagged on his body, lying in the bed as though asleep.

"She was in town," Cash said. "Someone told her Otto was here, so she stopped by."

Rita looked at Cash. "In the middle of the night?"

Cash glanced at Otto. "Extenuating circumstances."

"Yeah, but it's not like her to be in Casper at this hour."

"She's not married to The Shaft," Cash said with an edge.

Rita frowned. "She didn't stay long."

Cash gave her a look. "What do you expect?"

Rita shrugged. "That she'd wait to see me."

Cash mirrored her shrug. "Yeah, well, it's the middle of the night."

Rita bit back a comment. "Did you call the funeral home?"

"I left a message," he said. "Recording says they'll be ringing me back soon to start the process."

7

"Thanks." Rita wanted to reach out and hold his hand. But something stopped her, and she bunched them into her pockets. "I appreciate that."

"Of course," Cash said, his eyes lingering on Otto. "Have you let Mary Lou know?"

Rita chewed on her lip. "Not yet."

Cash took out his phone again. "I'll give her a call."

"No thanks," Rita said. "I'd like to do it. But not from his room." She looked around at the pale gray walls and the medical equipment and the lowered blind across the window. "I'll be back in a minute."

Out in the parking lot, Rita needed five minutes to breath.

Why hadn't she told Cash?

Her fingers itched for a smoke. But that wasn't a habit she indulged anymore, pregnant or otherwise. She consciously dropped her tense shoulders.

Inhale.

Exhale.

She paced the stalls, walking the white dividing lines as though proving her sobriety. Five minutes later, her heart rate felt normal and she called Mary Lou.

"Rita."

"Mary Lou," Rita said. Though she couldn't bring herself to say anything.

"I understand," Mary Lou said. "You still at Casper hospital?"

"Uh-huh," Rita said.

"I'm coming right away. Sing him a song while you wait."

"Huh?" Rita said. "Like a lullaby? I don't know any songs. Except Christmas ones."

"While you're waitin' on me," Mary Lou said, "tell him: 'Til we meet again, may God bless you.'"

"The King?" Rita asked.

"It sure ain't ABBA," Mary Lou said. "It's how Elvis closed his shows in 1977."

Rita promised to deliver the message and hung up. Then she put her phone in her back pocket and returned to Otto's room, walking on wooden legs.

"Mary Lou's coming," she said, entering the room.

Cash stirred from dozing in the chair beside the bed, as though Otto himself were merely taking a nap.

"You can leave if you like," Rita said. "Mary Lou will stay with me until the body transfer."

Cash shook his head. "I ain't goin' anywhere right now. Hell, why would I?" He ran his hands over his head. "Anything can happen."

Rita gestured to Otto. "Look at him. Nothing's going to happen how."

Cash shook his head. "I mean earlier. About thinking I was dead. Why'd you say that? What happened tonight?"

Rita drew a breath. "Max Bannister tried to kill you."

Cash popped out of the chair. "What?" He padded his chest. "How?"

"By setting fire to your house."

Cash's eyebrows shot up. "Jesus, why the fuck would he do that?"

"Apparently, he was jealous. Thought his ex, Heather, had left him for you."

Cash's cheeks colored. "That's bullshit."

Rita gave a stiff shrug. "Maybe. All the same, he had a thirst for vengeance and lashed out. Marcus Dwyer paid the price."

"Shit. Marcus…?"

"Died in the fire."

Cash shook his head in disbelief. "Fuck, Max is mad. You catch him yet?"

"Matter of fact, we did," Rita said. "But—"

"Jesus Christ," Cash said, pulling her into his arms. "Thank God."

Rita gave a wry laugh. "When you'd get so religious?"

Cash put his lips close to her ear. "Must've been when you saved my life."

"Not sure I did that."

"Sure you did. Bannister can't hurt me now, can he? Not when he's in custody."

Rita pulled away. "Er—about that…"

Cash gave her a look. "Yeah?"

"Our prisoner escaped, thanks to that crooked cop your dad hired."

Cash crumpled his brow. "Crooked cop?"

"After David's murder, Thomas planted a dirty cop at the SCSO."

Cash's eyes widened. "No shit? Vee Logan?"

"That's the one," Rita said.

"This is fucked up." Cash tapped his teeth together. "You know I have nothing to do with any of this, right?"

Rita nodded. But she wasn't sure she agreed. "I know. You're just Tom Gabriel's kid."

A muscle tensed in Cash's jaw. "Just 'cause he raised me, doesn't mean I'm caught up in this shit."

She forced a smile. "I understand."

"You know I'm nothing like my father," he said, the flush in his cheeks deepening.

Rita's smile faded as she approached the bed. She touched Otto's cold hand, his skin like an autumn leaf. "Once upon a time I would have said that about myself, too."

An unsettled silence bled into the room.

"Jesus, listen to us," Cash said, coming to stand at Rita's side. He laid his hand over both hers and Otto's.

"Dragging on about my dad, while yours is lying right here."

Rita softened and laid her head on his shoulder.

Cash's shoulder softened, too. "Anything can fucking happen in a night, huh?"

Rita's thoughts returned to her uterus. "That's for fucking sure."

Cash grunted. "Arson's fucked up."

Rita other hand drifted to her belly. "This whole 'life' thing's fucked up."

He stiffened beside her. "Death isn't fucked up. Though I'll admit it's damn hard to take, the first time."

Rita lifted her head. "I've seen a lot of cadavers in my profession, Cash."

"I know, I know," Cash said. "But this isn't work tonight, is it? It's family." He rolled his shoulders. "It's not the same."

Rita exhaled. "You're right. Nothing's the same. Not now."

Chapter Three

Rita watched the funeral attendants roll Otto's body out of the room from her perch in the chair, curled tight in a ball, not a squeak from the vinyl. On the other side of the room, Cash leaned against the wall, reading on his phone.

"Good night, Miss Jonas, Mr. Gabriel."

Rita inclined her head, the first movement she'd made in a while. Funny how she'd sat still for so long. She was accustomed to being the one asking the questions and making the decisions.

Cash pushed off the wall and walked towards her when Mary Lou burst into the room, her silver hair flying free of its typical beehive. Carly hovered in the doorway.

Rita uncoiled from the chair. "Mary Lou. Carly."

Mary Lou hugged Rita close. "Hope you don't mind Carly coming along. She drove, on account of my poor eyesight at night. She's a bit of a night owl, that one."

Rita shook her head. "Of course I don't mind."

"Good," Mary Lou said, still holding tight to Rita. She swung her head in Cash's direction. "Cash, you get on over to Otto's place, considering yours now is cinders. You can make the arrangements with the funeral home, and I'll take care of Rita."

A muscle twitched in Cash's jaw, but he only said, "Gotcha." Then he gave Rita a peck on the cheek. "See you back at your dad's place."

Rita nodded, unable to find words.

"You're looking tired," Mary Lou asked. "Have a seat," She patted the vinyl care and Rita sunk into it. "You want a cola? Coffee?"

Rita rubbed her eyes. "I want a magic carpet so I can sleep all the way back to Still."

Mary Lou laughed. "I'm impressed at your sense of humor at a moment like this."

Rita gave her a wry smile. "So am I."

"All right, we'll get you organized to get out of here. Now, has anyone told Helen yet?"

Rita stiffened. "No. And I'm not volunteering to do it."

"I'll go up to psych," Mary Lou said, "and have the nurses inform her." She bustled towards the door, where Carly leaned against the frame. "Carly, why don't you help pack up Otto's things?"

Then she left and Carly drew closer. "Hi, Rita."

She crossed to the cupboard and found a plastic hospital bag inside. Then she started to pack Otto's personal effects: pants, shirts, socks, underclothes, shoes, keys, wallet.

"Reminds me of prison," Carly said. She glanced at Rita, blushing. "Not that I've spent many nights in the pen."

"Thanks for driving Mary Lou," Rita said.

"She told me lots of stories on the drive over," Carly said, closing the cupboard door. "She was a real good friend to your dad." She set down the bag and sat on the now-vacant hospital bed. "She's been a good a friend to me, too."

"Glad to hear it," Rita said. "Mary Lou's the unofficial town Welcome Wagon, so consider yourself welcomed."

Carly laughed. "Guess that makes me an official resident of Still."

Rita gave her a look. "Whatever floats your boat. I can't imagine it's much of an improvement over Beaumont. But seeing as we're all glad to have you around, I'm glad you like it well enough to stay."

Carly smiled, but more to herself than at Rita. After a moment she said, "Is it true? Is Jeff really dead?"

Rita nodded. "It was sudden. And overly quickly. Did Mary Lou tell you what happened?"

Carly nodding, a tear slipping down her cheek.

"We've both lost someone we loved, in a way," she said, wondering how Carly's eyes could shed tears for an abusive husband, while Rita's eyes remained dry for her father.

"How are you doing?" she asked.

Carly blew out of breath. "A little annoyed, to be honest."

"Oh, yeah?" Rita asked.

Carly's fingers picked at the sheer on the mattress. "I always thought I'd feel relieved to be rid of Jeff for good. But instead I feel kind of upset." She shook out her shoulders. "I don't want to feel like that."

"You were married for a while," Rita said. "And co-owned a business. That'll lead to a lot of complicated feelings."

Carly sighed. "Yeah. You're smart not to have gotten married, Rita."

Rita pulled a face. "'Smart' isn't a word that I've heard used to describe my avoidance of matrimony."

"Well, at any rate, you get to decide everything about your life. *Everything.*"

"Yeah," Rita said, touching her belly again. "All my decision."

A chime sounded and Carly checked her phone. "Mary Lou says she's done upstairs. I'll tell her we'll meet her in the parking lot, if you're ready to go."

Rita nodded and got up. "Ready."

Carly messaged back, then picked up the plastic bag of Otto's belongings.

In the doorway, Rita took a last glance. "There's a good chance work will bring me by this hospital room again."

"It ain't a big county," Carly said.

Rita sighed. "But it'll always be the room where my dad died."

Carly made the sign of the cross. "Amen."

Then they walked out of the room, taking the last of Otto Jonas' remains, his body and spirit already vacated.

Out in the parking lot, Mary Lou was already leaning against Carly's green hatchback, reading her phone. Carly unlocked the car and Mary Lou settled Rita into the backseat.

On the drive back to Still, Rita's head lolled on the edges of sleep, Carly and Mary Lou's voices sounding distant though they were mere inches away. When Carly missed the freeway exit, Rita stirred from her reverie.

"It's all good," Mary Lou said, "Carly's driving you to my place."

Rita rubbed her face. "Why?"

"So you can stay with me that's why," Mary Lou said, her silver hair like a halo.

"Or you stay with me, of course," Carly said. "At your place. I'm sorry, that sounds weird."

"I'm going to stay at Otto's," Rita said.

Mary Lou and Carly exchanged a look. "I'm not sure that's a good idea."

"Why?" Rita said, with a note of exasperation this time.

"You were sleep-talking back there," Mary Lou said.

"No I wasn't," Rita said.

"How d'you know? You weren't the one listing to you."

"Because I wasn't sleeping," Rita said.

Mary Lou sighed. "Look, there are a lot of memories in that house."

"I know," Rita said. "I grew up in it." She leaned over to point through the windshield. "If you take that left," she instructed Carly, "you can double back to my dad's place."

"Okay," Carly said, taking the turn. "But what Mary Lou said—it's why I don't want to go back to my house in Beaumont. Even with no chance of Jeff coming around." She glanced at Rita in the rear-view mirror. "I've never slept so good as at your place, Rita."

"See?" Mary Lou said. "You'll sleep like a baby at my place."

"I don't like being watched by so many copies of Elvis," Rita said. "Especially the velvet ones."

Mary Lou let out a gasp. "That doesn't deserve a comment."

"This is my dad's place," Rita said, showing Carly where to turn.

Carly rolled the small hatchback onto the gravel drive, past the trailer, and parked in front of the house.

Mary Lou twisted in her seat. "You sure you don't want company? I could stay here with you. I recall Carole always keeping a nice guest room."

Rita gave her a look.

"You're right. It's been a long time since Carole's been in this house. I'm sure Helen kept a nice guest room."

Rita scowled harder, then scrambled out of the back seat. Overhead, a spray of stars glittered like silver dust.

"I'm fine," she said, gesturing towards the trailer on blocks. "Jason's here, if I need someone."

Mary Lou got out of the passenger seat to join Rita in the driveway, her hair the same shade as the stars. "Let me at least see you inside."

"Thanks for being here for me tonight," Rita said, accepting her arm. "Nothing's going to be the same now."

"Nope," Mary Lou said. "Happens every time someone leaves this place. Otto. The King. Jesus."

"I'm not sure my dad deserves the company of those two greats," Rita said, allowing Mary Lou to lead her up the porch steps.

"Oh, shush with that," Mary Lou said, slapping the back of Rita's hand. Carly followed them up the steps, bringing the plastic bag of Otto's items.

After putting everything inside, Rita accepted a hug and kiss from each of them, then closed the door.

Silence.

And the lingering scent of Otto's life: his instant coffee; his laundry detergent; the stale pong of cigarette smoke.

And the fact of his death hit her as hard as though he'd suddenly embraced her. She put a hand on the closet door to steady herself. She was tired. And quite possibly pregnant.

Admitting the first thought to be true, she kicked off her shoes and shuffled towards the stairs.

A colorful flash caught her eye. She peered through the shadows into the living room. A tower of Otto's birthday presents in bright, metallic paper flickered in the moonlight. All of them unopened. But not one of them from Rita.

She gripped the banister and planted her foot on the first tread.

Chapter Four

Rita bent over the toilet and barfed.

Goddammit, she'd just brushed her teeth. She dabbed her lips dry with some toilet paper, then dropped the wad in the toilet and flushed.

Rummaging through the bathroom cabinet, she found an almost empty bottle of Listerine. Something about the bottle didn't look quite right; its label had missed the most recent update to the logo. And the stamped best-before date had faded into oblivion.

She uncapped it, sniffed it, then swilled a mouthful and spat.

And then stuck out her tongue to cool it, taking several deep breaths. It seemed that with age, the mouthwash had grown more potent.

Sighing, she regarded her reflection in the mirror, wearing pajamas, her hair standing on end. It was increasingly imperative that she buy a pregnancy test. But there was no way she was going do it in Still. She should have done it in Casper, at the anonymous hospital pharmacy.

Rita returned to the guest room, where she checked

her messages. But the battery was flat; she'd forgotten to charge her phone last night. She plugged it in and returned to the bathroom to take a shower.

After she dressed in a T-shirt and jean shorts, she turned on her phone to find a cascade of messages. Word about Otto had gotten around.

She flicked through the list of missed calls, recognizing all the contacts except one. She dialed her voice mail and listened to the message.

It was from Tom Gabriel's lawyer: "Hello, Rita, this is Alan Crenshaw. I'd like to talk at your earliest convenience. Please let me know the best time."

Rita deleted the voice message and ignored the others. Then she swiped to read the text messages.

The first, which was Mary Lou's, read: *Do not come in today.*

Setting down the phone, Rita blew out a breath. If she didn't go into HQ, what would she do? Otto was on ice. Cash was making arrangements. Carly would still be sleeping.

She got up and crossed to the window. Jason's Kia was gone. Everyone was doing something but her. Except Otto, she supposed.

Inhale.

Exhale.

Mary Lou was right: Rita didn't really want to be alone. Not in her dad's house. And once, Carole's house too. And for nineteen years, Rita's childhood home.

But maybe Mary Lou was also right that Rita needed a break from the office. She walked downstairs, not daring to peek into the other rooms she passed, as though Otto's ghost occupied every last one of them.

And she didn't even believe in ghosts.

Rita most felt Otto's presence in the kitchen, where his

grocery list hung on the fridge, and his phone charger sat on the counter, and his jar of instant coffee never changed brand, and he kept his collection of souvenir ashtrays. She rolled her shoulders, shrugging off the memories.

But despite scavenging the cupboards for ingredients that weren't off-putting, breakfast was an immediate turnoff. A dry rice cake might have offered some appeal. But as Otto had never taken up eating them (unsurprisingly), the pantry provided no solutions.

Rita decided to go for a walk.

In the foyer closet, she found a souvenir ballcap from a Y2K police jamboree and some Coppertone which rivaled the Listerine's age. She slapped on both and headed outside.

The August sun blazed overhead, casting long shadows across the gravel driveway. Rita adjusted the cap, pulling her short ponytail through the opening in the back. A light breeze carrying the faint scent of sagebrush cooled her neck and coaxed her out of the shade of the verandah.

She headed down the driveway, then along the rural road that ran parallel to the freeway. The distant roar of traffic flowed past like a river, blending with the whisper of wind blowing through the grass.

She'd often walked these routes as a kid. But once getting her driver's license, she couldn't remember having done it since. She definitely didn't remember the pavement being this cracked when she was little. A lot of frozen winters had passed between then and now.

To accommodate the spring snowmelt, deep ditches were cut into the shoulders. Here, clover and yarrow grew, filling the ditches with flowers, though their colors were dulled by a skim of summer dust. Although every ten to twenty yards, bright goldeneyes and Indian paintbrush stood out.

As the sun climbed, the shadows shortened. Heat waves shimmered on the pavement and in front of the distant rolling hills.

Rita stepped off the hot pavement, onto the shoulder, and fanned herself for a moment. Why hadn't she brought a water bottle?

A fly dove at her neck, trying to steal a sip of her sweat. She swatted it away and started walking again—

When a sudden rustling in the bush brought her to a halt. Out of the corner of her eye, something massive moved. Her breath hitched as a bison emerged from the foliage.

Its dark eyes locked onto hers. Rita's heart hammered in her chest. The bison continued to watch her, its moist nostrils flaring.

Rita took a breath of her own as the world seemed to shrink, closing the distance between them.

The bison snorted, a low rumble that rippled the air between them.

Rita backed away. "Hey there, fella, I didn't expect to see you out here."

The bison stood still for another few seconds, gazing at her with a wary intensity. Then it turned with another snort and lumbered into the meadow, swaying the tall grass.

Rita waved. "Nice meeting you."

For a while she stood watching the great beast until it disappeared into the landscape. Fresh sweat prickled the back of her neck, and the buzzing fly returned. She swatted it away and stepped off the shoulder, back onto the weathered pavement.

And walked the rest of the way into town.

Chapter Five

Rita walked into The Bighorn Bean, thirsty as hell.

"Good morning," Skyler said with her usual merriment. Her hair was a vibrant shade of lemon.

Rita blinked at her. "You're blonde."

Skyler laughed. "Sort of. I was going more for 'sunshine.'"

Rita tried for a smile. "Well, why didn't I say that?" But the joke fell flat.

Skyler knit her brow. "You okay?"

Rita nodded. Then shook her head. "My dad just died."

Skyler's eyes widened. "Oh, my God. I'm so sorry. Is there anything I can do for you?"

Rita shook her head. "No, though I appreciate the offer."

Skyler smacked her palm against her forehead. "Oh my, God, I'm such a dummy." She spun and grabbed a box off a shelf, then a clean pair of tongs. "Muffins. That's what I can do. I can give you muffins."

Rita managed a genuine smile. "Got any maple pecan today?"

"For you, I got extra." Skyler filled a box and handed it to Rita.

"Thanks," Rita said, opening it at once and taking out a muffin. "I'm kind of famished. I walked into town."

Skyler blinked at her. "No shit? All the way?"

Rita nodded, swallowing the mouthful of muffin. But it didn't go down as smooth as she'd hoped. She returned the muffin to the box. "I needed to clear my head."

"Then I'll grab you a chilled bottle of water, too," Skyler said, crossing to a mini fridge. "On the house."

"Thanks," Rita said, accepting the damp bottle and cracking the lid. "I saw a bison. While I was walking."

Skyler's eyes sparkled. "Cool. Where?"

"Along this quiet section of road, out by my dad's place."

"I've seen antelope locally. But no bison."

"Me too," Rita said. "I didn't know there were any around here. Must've come through from Wilkins State Park. Or Pathfinder Refuge."

"I'm going hiking down that way for couple of weeks," Skyler said.

"Nice," Rita said. "You're not thinking of closing shop, are you?"

"No way," Skyler said with a wink. "Gotta make the best of the end of the tourist season. I found someone to take my shifts, and she's been learning to make your usual just the way you like it, Sheriff."

Then she went to make Rita's usual, while Rita tapped her card against the terminal to pay.

Two minutes later, Skyler handed Rita a to-go cup. Then Rita headed outside, balancing the box of muffins.

For a moment, she stood on the sidewalk, first looking

up the main street one way, then the other way. The river birches along the boulevard were already turning yellow, their display challenging the sun's brilliance. And Skyler's hair, for that matter.

Jaywalking, Rita crossed the two lanes to sit on the vacant bench, which had been donated by the Bledsinoe family some years ago.

On the back of the bench, a memorial plaque commemorated the deaths of Dean (twelve years ago) and Dorothy (six years ago), who together had run the local post office for a combined forty-four years.

She rapped a knuckle on the plaque. "Say 'hi' to dad for me." Then Rita lifted the muffin box lid, willing her mouth to water. But no such luck.

She hazarded another nibble of candied-pecan encrusted muffin top (the best part). But it tasted pasty, as though Skyler had swapped out flour for sawdust.

Movement across the street caught Rita's eye. Mary Lou emerged from the SCSO and headed up the block. Rita waved, but Mary Lou paid her no mind, marching directly for The Bighorn Bean.

A shadow flickered in the window of the coffee shop; Skyler hovered, watching through the glass. Then she withdrew her bleached head as Mary Lou entered the front door.

"Hm," Rita said, considering the situation odd. Mary Lou drank almost exclusively her own home-made iced teas and lemonade. Rita regarded her muffin again. Then put it back in the box with a burp and lowered the lid.

A minute later, Mary Lou emerged from the café carrying a disposable coffee cup. She glanced both ways, then crossed the street towards Rita.

"Fancy seeing you here," Mary Lou said, approaching the bench.

"Yeah, fancy that," Rita said. "Something going on at the station?"

"Oh, no, not at all," Mary Lou said. She sat on the bench. "Don't you worry about anything. I was only taking a break away from desk, that's all."

"Bullshit," Rita said. "That coffee was waiting for you."

Mary Lou flattened her lips. "I called in my order."

Rita wrinkled her nose. "Skyler called you."

Mary Lou waved a hand, studded with costume rings. "Oh, what does it matter who called who?"

"She made you a coffee on the house so you'd come out to check on me."

Mary Lou frowned at her. "She was worried."

"Why?"

Instead of answering, Mary Lou took a sip.

"Why?" Rita repeated.

Mary Lou grunted. "Is that your best interrogation tactic?"

"I want to know why Skyler thought I needed checking up on."

Mary Lou glanced around. "Well, you *are* hanging out on the Bledsinoes' bench—all alone. And hell, your dad just died. She thought you might need someone to talk to." Mary Lou cleared her throat. "Besides the Bledsinoes."

"I'm not talking to the Bledsinoes," Rita said. "Much. I don't believe in ghosts. Besides, you told me to take the day off."

Mary Lou patted her hand. "It's good you're taking some time off. But I reckoned you'd take that time with Cash." She cut her eyes to Rita. "After all, the man's house burned down last night."

Rita scoffed. "And my dad died last night."

Mary Lou patted Rita's hand. "All the more reason for

the two of you to spend some time together." Then she sighed. "This isn't a pissing contest, Rita."

Rita matched her sigh. "I know you're all not used to seeing me at loose ends. But I'm fine. Really. You can tell Skyler. And Cash, if it helps."

Mary Lou flared her nostrils. "All right, all right, I'll come clean."

Rita raised an eyebrow. "About what?"

Mary Lou fluttered her eyelids. "I'm not here because you're sitting on a bench all alone."

Rita blinked at her. "You're not?"

Mary Lou shook her head, one hand on her beehive to stabilize it. "This is serious. Skyler called me because she said you put a muffin back in the box."

Rita laughed. "So she's a detective now?"

Mary Lou puckered her eyebrows. "Well, it's awfully out of character for you."

Rita sighed. "That's for damn sure." She opened the box again and offered the muffins to Mary Lou. "Want one?" She pointed to the lower left corner. "I ate some of that one."

"I can see that," Mary Lou said, selecting the muffin on the top right. "And I'm not even a detective."

Rita laughed again and took another sip of water.

"It's not a crime to check on you, Rita. Grief's a complicated thing." Mary Lou bit into the muffin, spraying crumbs. "When my mom died, I didn't eat anything but Kraft Dinner and pepperoni for six months."

"That's terrible," Rita said.

Mary Lou nodded. "But don't worry, it'll pass." Then she bit off the remainder of the muffin's crown. "So what are you going to do today?"

"I don't know," Rita said, draining the last of her water. "What's going on at the station?"

Mary Lou flicked a bit of pecan from her lip. "Don't ask. Me and Jason got everything handled."

"What about Walter?" Rita asked.

Mary Lou hesitated. "He's requested a leave of absence. Of course I'll deny it. I hate to do it, but I'll tell him this afternoon."

"No, no," Rita said. "Let Walter take it."

"But we're short of hands. And you need bereavement leave."

Rita shook her head. "I'll be fine. Otto's death was expected, in a way. But Adrian's wounds? That's different. No parent should go through what Walter and Winnie have."

Mary Lou put an arm around Rita's shoulders, giving her a sidelong hug. "Sure, I'll let him know." Then she released Rita and took another bite of muffin. "Make sure you take care of you, too."

"I will," Rita said, pushing up from the bench. "But I can't leave Jason hanging out to dry. Not after what happened with Vee." Then she pushed up from bench and set her empty water bottle next to the box of muffins she'd left on the bench. "And when he's still recovering from that GSW."

Mary Lou got up too, gesturing to the box on the bench. "If you're leaving the rest of those here for Arbuckle, you really are going through it."

"Don't think I'm going to eat them," Rita said. "And Jason doesn't need any more muffins. Ruby Joe told me I give him too many as it is."

"You're just like Otto," Mary Lou said, as they crossed the street. "Always looking out for others."

Rita shrugged. "I've always just wanted to help."

Mary Lou smiled. "The lemon doesn't fall far from the tree."

"I remember Otto working through birthdays and Christmases," Rita said as they arrived at the station. They paused at the bottom of the front steps. "And other times he kept working when he was injured or ill."

Mary Lou gave her a look. "That don't mean you have to follow in his footsteps."

Rita bit on her lip. "Not entirely. But crime doesn't care about the calendar. And in a small town, there ain't much back-up."

Mary Lou squeezed her arm. "Just as much backup here in Still as anywhere. Just looks different, that's all. Like old friends. Or trusted mechanics."

Rita indulged her with a smile. "I really don't need you dropping hints, Mary Lou."

Mary Lou winked. "Oh, these ain't hints, Rita. I'm pointing out clues to the evidence."

Chapter Six

Rita walked into her office, the low summer sun through the slatted blinds tracing a pattern of bars on the floor. Her office might look like a prison cell, but she was here by choice.

Wasn't she?

The usual stack of paperwork sat on her desk. She shoved it aside and pulled out the chair to sit down.

And noticed a cat hair. She picked it up. Tawny gray on one end and silver on the other. She got up and walked back into the bullpen.

"I found one of Ted's hairs."

Folding her arms, Mary Lou rolled back from her desk. "You want it entered into evidence?"

Rita took a moment before answering. "I actually just want to hold him. Maybe cuddle him for a little while."

For a moment, Mary Lou looked at her. "Can I get a record of you saying that?"

"Nope."

Mary Lou grinned. "Sure, though he's settled in quite nicely at my place."

"Unlike Vee," Rita said.

"Don't mention her," Mary Lou said.

"Okay, I won't," Rita said. "Where's Jason?"

"He's out running a speed trap near the highway," Mary Lou said. She indicated a sizeable stack of rainbow-colored file folders. "If you're bored, I've got some paper-work you could do."

Rita grimaced. "I've got my own paperwork, thanks."

Mary Lou smacked her lips. "That's right, you do."

Rita headed back to her office, shutting the door. Sitting at her desk, she checked her voicemail. The only notable one was from was from Hunter Green, asking her to return his call.

Rita sighed, then picked up the receiver and hit the preset dial for the DA.

He picked up on the second ring. "Rita, you're calling from headquarters. Aren't you on bereavement leave?"

"I'm down two cops, Hunter. You do the math."

For a moment he was silent. "I apologize about saddling you with Officer Logan."

"I need to know if I can trust you," Rita said. "Are you in Thomas Gabriel's pocket as well?"

"We don't need to talk about this now, Rita. Not if you don't want to. I left that message to talk before I'd heard about your dad."

Rita's shoulders stiffened. "This is as good a time as any, Hunter."

"No, it's not," he said. "You need to take some time to yourself. I'll send you a prospective list of officers to choose from."

"Thanks, I'll watch out for it," Rita said, then hung up before Hunter could offer more condolences.

She turned to the stack of paperwork. A sunbeam

shone across it, cutting the top page in half. One side in sunshine, the other in shade.

She supposed Otto had arranged his desk here to catch the morning sun. He'd always enjoyed it at the breakfast table, too. And it had never occurred to her to rearrange the furnishings when she'd moved into the office.

Pushing back in her chair, she got up and removed the phone, stack of paperwork, and pile of junk from her desk, stuffing it on top of the filing cabinet. Then she put her hip against one end of the desk and shoved with all her strength. It slid a foot and a half, exposing four dark squares on the floor where the sun hadn't bleached the linoleum.

She rotated the desk to put the sun at her back, rather than facing the window. Next, she transferred the pile of things on the filing cabinet back to the desk. Then set her shoulder to the filing cabinet and slid it into the far corner, where the sun never reached. She was tired of touching the hot metal drawers in the afternoon. Of course she'd have to get up from the chair if she wanted to fetch a file. But since everyone said it was important to take frequent breaks, she figured she was setting herself up for improved longevity.

The door popped open, and Mary Lou entered.

"For the love of Graceland, what's going on in here?" She glanced around the room, beehive wobbling. "Wouldn't it be easier to just grieve?"

Rita shook out her arms. "It feels good."

Mary Lou frowned. "What? Disturbing dust bunnies? What'd they ever do to you? If this is what you do when you're mourning, I'd be happy to bring in the damn cat for a cuddle."

Rita wiped some sweat from her brow. "I meant, it feels good to move my muscles. To use my body instead of my brain." Rita shoved the filing cabinet another few inches, its metal rims squealing as they scraped across the floor. "Or my heart."

Mary Lou's frown deepened. "And God forbid that."

Rita frowned back. "God forbid what?"

"Using your heart."

"Ha, ha," Rita said, not laughing.

Mary Lou folded her arms. "You know your father had things arranged a certain way."

Rita stiffened. "What's that got to do with anything?"

"Just sayin' there was a reason for the way things are around here," Mary Lou said. "He was thoughtful, that way. Never did nothin' without intention."

Rita's half-sister, Lisa, crossed her mind. "Everything was intentional, huh? Well, he's gone now."

"Oh, Rita," Mary Lou said, clucking her tongue, "listen to yourself. Now that Otto's gone, don't throw him out so quickly."

"I only wanted the sun at my back," Rita said. "I was tired of the glare in my eyes."

Mary Lou grunted. "Well, then maybe you'll be able to get some paperwork done. Without all that glare."

Rita threw her a look. "Pushing papers isn't really my style."

"Well, you can push around furniture all you like, Rita Jonas, but you can't push away your feelings."

Rita stiffened. "Noted. Now what is it you wanted, Mary Lou?"

Mary Lou cleared her throat. "Report came in from Frenchie."

"Who's Frenchie?"

"Franklin Garstang. He lives about ten minutes outside of town, on a run-down acreage."

"Hoarder?"

"Not so much as a recluse."

"What'd he report?"

"A UAP."

Rita blinked. "A UAP? What's that?"

Mary Lou nodded, her beehive bouncing. "Unidentified Aerial Phenomena."

"Oh," Rita said. "Like a UFO."

"Well, yes," Mary Lou said, "but that's not the term used now."

"Okay," Rita said, "UAP sighting, huh?"

"Apparently one's been circling his house."

"Oh, yeah?"

"And he wants something done about it."

"He does?"

"Like, yesterday."

Rita shook her head. "Sorry, I don't do UFO calls."

"UAPs," Mary Lou said. Then she drew herself up. "And yeah, we do."

"We do?"

"State policy."

Rita laughed. "You're joking."

Mary Lou pursed her lips. "Nope."

Rita stared at her for a heartbeat. "Well, what am I supposed to put on the paperwork?"

Mary Lou frowned. "You don't *do* paperwork, remember? I always do it for you. And in this case, there's a form."

Rita blinked again. "A form for UFOs?"

"UAPs." Mary Lou smiled. "And all's you need to do is fill it out. Easiest peasiest paperwork ever."

"All right, all right," Rita said, "I'll fill out the form." She spread her hands over her father's desk. "So how many of these UAP sightings did Otto deal with?"

"Back then they were called UFO sightings." Mary

Lou tapped on her lip. "And since I've been here, must have been half a dozen reports come in. Every few years we hear some rumblings. But Otto never processed any of 'em."

"Why not?" Rita asked.

"'Cause he was like you. He didn't do UFOs."

Rita spread her hands. "See?"

"So I gave 'em to Walter."

"Why?" Rita asked. "He some kind of expert?"

"Nah," Mary Lou said. "I just knew it would wrinkle him up real good."

Rita laughed. "You got Frenchie's address for me?"

Mary Lou slapped a Post-It on Rita's desk. "He's expecting you ten minutes ago."

Rita pushed away from the desk. "All right, I'll head over there now."

"You're not wearing a uniform."

"You said he's a recluse. An oddball."

Mary Lou folded her arms. "I didn't say that."

"Okay, I surmised it," Rita said. "Must have been the talk of UF—UAs, or whatever they are. So why's he called Frenchie?"

"Dunno," Mary Lou said.

Rita crossed to the door. "That's not like you, not knowing something about someone in town."

Mary Lou cocked her head. "True enough. But Frenchie's always been a bit of a mystery."

"Don't think we'll find much of a mystery here," Rita said. "It's probably a new flight path over his house. There's more air traffic every year."

Mary Lou gave her a skeptical look. "Good luck, Sheriff. I hope he sees your point of view."

Rita gave her a look. "Isn't there something important you should be doing?"

"Sure. Paperwork. Or I could finish rearranging the office." Her eye glinted. "I'm not sure it's good for you to be moving all this furniture. Grief ain't the only thing you're dealing with these days."

Before Rita could answer, Mary Lou breezed past her though the doorway.

Rita paused to take a breath.

Inhale.

Exhale.

Then she passed through the bullpen and headed out the back door of the station. She popped the door of the cruiser, let out the waves of hot air, and dropped into the driver's seat.

But before tuning the ignition, she had a call to make.

Chapter Seven

Rita parked at the curb a block up the street from Merritt Drugs.

A teenage girl walked towards the cruiser, wearing a black ankle-length overcoat despite the heat of the day. Even her artfully applied goth makeup hadn't melted.

Rita lowered the window as Edith Mae approached.

She rested her forearms on the top of the car door and passed Rita a small cardboard box. "This is some news."

"It's not news," Rita said, taking the box. "That's why you're doing this for me, discreet-like. It's the opposite of news, basically. It's a secret." Then she looked down at the box Edith Mae had handed her. "Lidocaine?"

Edith snatched the box from her hand. "Oops, sorry about that. I actually paid for that one, since they keep it behind the counter."

"What's the lidocaine for?"

Edith Mae pulled up her jacket sleeve, in which Rita caught a glimpse of some lip liners or eyebrow pencils (presumably both, since Edith Mae clearly used both in abundance), and displayed her forearm to Rita.

Inked into her skin was an intricate outline of a forward-facing bison, framed by a wreath of sagebrush and wildflowers, topped by a crescent moon.

"I'm getting color tomorrow," she said, pushing out her chest.

"Nice," Rita said. "Wyoming is definitely a state to be proud of."

"It's bison I like," Edith Mae said, turning her forearm to admire it. "Not that I've ever met one."

"What do you like about them?"

"They symbolize strength and resilience."

"Cool," Rita said, looking closer. "I met one today."

Edith Mae's eyes widened. "You met a bison *today*?"

Rita nodded, still unsure if she'd seen a mirage instead. "I think so."

"Wow." Edith Mae rolled her jacket sleeve back down. "That's cool." Then she fished around in her jacket until she found another box. She passed the pregnancy test to Rita.

"Thanks," Rita said, dropping it into the console and snapping the lid shut, as if everyone on the street had x-ray vision through the vehicle. "I owe you one, Edith Mae."

"I'll remember that," she said.

Rita grinned. "I know you will. Oh, and I'd appreciate you not saying anything to Jason."

"'Course not," Edith Mae said. "I'm a vault."

Rita winked. "Presumably that's why you know how to pick one."

"You're funny," Edith Mae said. "Like Otto was."

Rita's breath caught. Then she asked, "Do you want to come to his memorial service?"

"A funeral?" Edith Mae nodded. "For sure. I might be on codeine. You know, because of the ink." She pulled up her sleeve again. "That's a big fucking tat."

"Must be quite an investment," Rita said.

"Yeah. My artist ain't cheap. But I've figured out how to save a lot of money on clothes and hygiene products and shit like that."

"Yeah, I bet," Rita said. "You can find the details for Otto's service in the weekend paper."

"Okay, I'll be sure to pick one up," Edith Mae said. "What should I wear?"

Rita glanced at her floor-length coat. "Um, something black."

Edith Mae's liner-laden eyes rolled upwards. "Hmm. I can probably make something work. Or pick up something in Casper."

Rita frowned. "Could you not? What if you get picked up by Casper? Then you won't make it to the service, and I'll be distracted by saving your ass."

Edith Mae crinkled her nose. "Okay, I'll figure it out."

"Wear that," Rita said, wagging a finger at her coat. "Thanks again, Edith Mae, I'll see you around."

Edith Mae stepped back from the Honda and onto the curb. "See you around, Sheriff." She gave Rita a salute. "And anytime you need me, I'm here for you."

Rita saluted back, then drove out to Frenchie's address.

Ten minutes later, she didn't feel any closer.

"Frenchie, you live way the fuck out of town." She glanced around. "I wouldn't want to be stuck out here in a snowstorm."

A shadow caught her eye, and she leaned forward to peer through the windshield. A kestrel reeled overhead.

She returned her eyes to the road. "Mary Lou said it would be a ten-minute drive. But Frenchie, you're at least twenty minutes out."

Even as Rita said it, she remembered Mary Lou drove

a Harley. For her, Frenchie's probably *was* ten minutes out of town.

Rita's gaze drifted again. Though not to the sky, but to the rolling grasslands, a patchwork of purple-peppered serviceberries and yellow rabbitbrush and silvery-green sagebrush. But there were no bison here.

At last Rita spotted Frenchie's unmarked driveway, finding it only thanks to Mary Lou's scribbled note to look for the dented traffic cone in the ditch.

Which was enormously helpful, given the GPS seemed to be struggling as much as Rita's cellular signal. And if she hadn't known to look for an orange traffic cone, Rita might have missed it altogether since it had clearly been driven over, its peak now sheared off, giving it the appearance of an infant's training potty.

She turned the cruiser onto Frenchie's driveway, which consisted of two dirt ruts with a tall hump of grass growing between them. Cottonwoods and ponderosas bordered either side, their trunks surrounded by dense clusters of sagebrush. As the cruiser rolled up the driveway, the long fronds of grass pinged against the oil pan, creating a mesmerizing tempo.

Rounding a bend, she came upon a sudden gate across the drive — no, not one, but two — which prevented her from advancing. Several signs fixed to the gate warned trespassers against prosecution, dangerous dogs, and being recorded on camera. Although there was no evidence of cameras. Or a dog.

Rita pulled out her phone to call Frenchie. But the call failed.

"Shit."

She leaned into the cruiser and radioed Mary Lou. "Mary Lou, my cell phone keeps dropping out."

"What'd I tell you?"

"Can you call Frenchie and let him know I'm here?"

"Ten-four."

Rita waited five minutes, the wind whispering through the cottonwoods. And then another sound—

Honeybee-bee-bee.

Rita shivered. She didn't believe in ghosts. It must have been the *kree-kree-kree* of the kestrel. She craned to look at the cobalt blue sky. A foot scuffed behind her, and she whirled, coming face to face with a specter of Otto—

The light shifted and the shadows moved. The man looked nothing like Otto, beyond his faded blue jeans, checked cotton shirt, and brown and gold ballcap. Though Otto had never been a Cowboys fan.

"Pistol Pete," Rita said, pointing to his cap.

"You a Poke?"

Rita nodded. "Sure. Actually, today I saw…"

"Yeah?"

Rita cleared her throat. Why the hell was she going to tell this stranger about the bison?

"I saw a kestrel," she said instead.

The man shifted. "They're all right, too. Clean up the vermin 'round here."

Rita nodded. "I'm sure." She extended her hand over the gate. "I'm Sheriff Jonas."

Ignoring her hand, the man adjusted the brim of his cap. "Don't look like it."

She pointed to the jamboree cap on her head. "I'd taken the day off, to go for a walk. But your call came in, and it sounded urgent."

"Urgent? It's about damn time someone showed up. Been callin' you lot more'n' once, you know."

"It's been a busy stretch for us," Rita said. She opened her palms to him. "But I'm here now to have a look around the property. You're Frenchie, yes?"

The man grumbled something under his breath, then opened the first gate with a crank. The second one he opened manually. Waving her in, Frenchie motioned for her to drive up to the house.

"Hop in," Rita said, indicating the passenger seat.

"No thanks, Sheriff." Frenchie turned away and loped towards the cluster of outbuildings. "You go on ahead, I'll see you up at the house."

Rita rolled the cruiser up the dirt track, mindful not to push too hard on the pedal and douse Frenchie in fumes as she passed.

She wasn't sure which of the three single-story buildings was Frenchie's house, each having the same sloped shingle roof and nondescript door, so she pulled in between two of them to park. She turned off the engine and got out.

A minute later, Frenchie scuffed up to her. He flapped a hand towards Rita's chest. "If we're gonna talk, you gotta take off that thing."

Rita stiffened. "If you're referring to my T-shirt..."

"You got one of them cameras on you," Frenchie said, his jowls reddening.

Rita paused, working out Frenchie's meaning. "Are you referring to an officer's body camera?"

He folded his arms. "Damn right. I ain't lettin' you put me on tape."

"No camera," Rita said with a smile, "seeing as I'm not in uniform." She held up her cell phone. "Although I would appreciate being able to record our conversation, seeing as you have a lot to say. That is, if it's all right with you?"

"No, it's not all right with me."

"Right, you don't like recordings," Rita said. She

42

mimed using a pencil and pad of paper. "D'you mind if I write some notes?"

Frenchie stared at her. "You plan to write down what I say? Why?"

"Makes it easier to fill out the paperwork," Rita said. "That's all."

"Paperwork?" Frenchie asked. "You submitting reports to the G-men?"

"No, it's to assist our file-keeping at the office. To make sure I record all the facts straight."

Appearing to like her answer, Frenchie relaxed his shoulders. "And do these records stay in the state of Wyoming?"

"Yes, sir," Rita said. "Nothing we talk about even needs to ever leave the county."

Again appearing pleased, Frenchie gave a sharp nod.

"Not that I understand how the SCSO's response to an alien arrival could surpass the country's," she said.

"Because we folk out here are wild and independent," Frenchie said.

"Forever West," Rita said.

Frenchie gave her an appraising look. Then he huffed like a horse. "Okay, I'll tell you everything. But d'you think we could talk in code?"

Chapter Eight

"I'm not very good at codes," Rita said. "But I use a special kind of handwriting that only I can read. Ask any of my staff. None of them can decipher it. It's why I don't do paperwork."

Frenchie narrowed his eyes at her. "You don't do paperwork?"

Rita shrugged. "I tried, for a while. But every time I fill out a form, no one can understand the information." She shrugged. "So I don't do it anymore."

He lowered his brows. "Ain't that part of your job?"

"Yes." Rita glanced over her shoulder, then leaned into Frenchie. "So don't tell anyone, okay?"

He gave a pert nod. "I won't tell no one if you won't tell no one."

"Tell no one about what?" Rita asked.

"About the—" Frenchie paused. "Oh, wait. You're doin' it, ain't ya'? Not talkin' about it to no one."

"Talking about what?"

Frenchie's face lit up. "Ah ha, that's my conspirator." And he punched her in the upper arm.

Rita rubbed her bicep. The septuagenarian was stronger than he looked. "Not your conspirator."

Then she returned to the cruiser and dug though the glove box for a notepad and pen. A hard crust of ink had dried on the ballpoint. She broke it off and scribbled a series of circles to get the ink flowing.

Then she looked up at Frenchie and smiled. "Can you describe the UAP, Frenchie?"

"Say what?"

"The unidentified thing in the air," Rita said. "What did it look like?"

"Well, how the hell should I know?" Frenchie said. "It was dark."

"Anything you remember will be helpful," Rita said. "For the paperwork."

Frenchie screwed up his face, thinking. "It had lights."

"That's helpful identification," Rita said, "seeing as it was dark. Anything else?"

"What else do you want?"

"How many lights?" Rita asked.

"Dunno," Frenchie said. "It was moving fast."

"When you say it was moving fast," Rita asked, "did it make any sounds?"

Rubbing his neck, Frenchie thought for a moment. Then he said, "Nope. Don't think so. Though my hearing ain't so good."

"Where did you see them?"

He flicked a finger, pointing past the buildings into a clearing. "There." His finger moved in an arc. "And out by the outhouse." He pointed again. "And way over by the fence line."

Rita followed the path of his finger. "Do the lights always circle the property?"

Frenchie shook out his shoulders. "They ain't circlin' the property. They're damn well circlin' me."

"And why do you think that is?"

"They're coming to take me, that's what."

"Take you? Why?"

"Because they took Ma."

Rita chewed on her lip, trying to work out the logic. "And that's why they're coming for you?"

Frenchie pushed up the cap of his visor and stared at Rita, wide-eyed. "It's only a matter o'time before they get me, Sheriff. I can't stay indoors forever."

"You certainly can't," Rita said. She pointed to the building directly behind him. "Is that your house, Frenchie?"

He shook his head. "No, on account of the coons."

"Coons?" Rita repeated, trying to piece together the puzzle.

"Yeah, they surprised me, too, turning up like they did."

She squinted at the roof, noticing patches where the shingles had caved in. "Looks like they moved in a while ago."

"Yup," Frenchie said. "I seen a few generations raised up, by now. Been a lot of years since the coons arrived and Ma disappeared."

Rita's pen scratched across her notepad. "Are you saying the coons took your ma?"

"Jesus Murphy, not the coons," Frenchie said, with a note of disgust. "They took over the building."

Rita wasn't sure if his tone was directed towards the raccoons, or her. "Okay. So if the coons didn't take your ma, who do you think did?"

Frenchie glanced up at the sky, then pulled his brown and gold brim lower. "*They* did, of course."

46

Rita pointed to the billowing clouds. "They did?"

He nodded. "Aye."

Rita raised an eyebrow. "Are you referring to extraterrestrials?"

Frenchie thumped his chest. "How the hell should I know? Half the time you folks say it's military operations. Though them folks over in Sedona say it's fairies. All's I know is, whoever took Ma — and wherever they're hiding her — she's bein' held against her will. And because I know it, they're coming for me, now."

"You think the military's coming for you?" Rita asked, her pen flying to keep up. "Or fairies?"

"Jesus Murphy, ain't ya' listening? I'm telling you, them same lights are the ones that showed up the night Ma left. Course those ones were bigger. And low to the ground. And blowing up a shit-ton of dust."

"To clarify," Rita said, "it's the lights that took your ma?"

Frenchie grimaced. "More'n forty years ago."

Rita gave him a somber smile. "I'm sorry for your loss."

Frenchie looked skyward again. "She ain't gone forever, Sheriff. Otherwise them lights wouldn't be back."

"And you think these lights that took her are the same lights you saw last night? Even though they're high in the sky, instead of low to the ground?"

Frenchie set his jaw. "They're high in the sky, all right, Sheriff. And like I already told Mary Lou, it ain't only last night they appeared. Or the night before last. I been seeing 'em out every night, now for a while."

"When did they first reappear?" Rita asked.

Frenchie adjusted his ball cap. "I don't notice the date so much, Sheriff. I run my farm by the moon phases."

"Fair enough," Rita said. She looked around at the

scrubby pastures and broken-down fences. "What do you farm?"

Frenchie gawped at her. Then snorted. "You really ain't from these parts, are ya?"

"I came in from New York," Rita said. She gestured towards the metal-roofed buildings. "So which one is your house?"

Frenchie pointed in the opposite direction, towards a smaller outbuilding that looked more like a goat's shed with a metal roof. "In there."

"No coons?" Rita asked.

Frenchie ran his tongue over his teeth. "I shot 'em all."

Rita gave him a tight smile. "Well, that's reassuring."

"You want a look around the place?"

Rita shook her head. "That won't be necessary."

"It used to be Ma's house," Frenchie said.

"Oh, yes?" Rita made a note of Ma Senior.

Frenchie nodded. "You know she disappeared more'n once."

"Oh, yes?" Rita asked, continuing to take notes. "What happened?"

"Every now and then, the lights would roll through the mist, waking me up in the night. I'd hear voices. First laughing. Then protests. Then the dust-clouds would rise, and when I was brave enough to come away from the window, the lights retreating into the darkness, I'd find Ma had gone too."

"But she came back?" Rita asked.

"Sometimes days later. Sometimes weeks."

"Where did she go?"

Frenchie shook his head. "She never said. Only said the things they did to her."

"Who, the aliens?" Rita asked.

Frenchie shrugged. "Or the G-men."

"What kinds of things?" Rita asked.

Growling, he lowered his bushy gray eyebrows. "Sexual things."

"I see," Rita said. "Has anything unusual happened in your life lately? Perhaps regarding your health?"

Frenchie screwed up his face to think. "I had a backed-up colon for a while."

Rita refrained from making a note. "Any head injuries?"

"I know what you're getting at, Sheriff," Frenchie said. "But I ain't lunatic. I know what I saw."

Rita gave him a slight smile. "Of course you're not lunatic. But various health conditions can cause us to see lights. You may want to ask your doctor about that."

Frenchie scowled. "Don't got no charlatan doctor."

"Well, that's good then," Rita said, closing her note-book. "In the meantime, since these lights have been a frequent occurrence, perhaps you'll consider some added security measures."

"Ain't putting up no damn cameras around my place," Frenchie said. "I'm already tryin' to escape all them eyes on me."

"Doesn't have to be security cameras," Rita said. "Could be automatic lights. Sprinklers. Maybe a dog, like the sign says."

"Used to have a dog," Frenchie said. "Then it up and disappeared."

"Did the lights take it, too?"

"Nope. My friend did. Took Digger to fix up its hind legs. But he never came back with him."

"I'm sorry," Rita said. "You've suffered a lot of loss, Frenchie."

"Aye," Frenchie said. "That's why I deserve to have Ma come back. Instead of them taking me away, too."

"I'll see to it that no one takes you away, Frenchie," Rita said. "This is your home."

"That's for damn sure," he said. "Now you go on and do your job, Sheriff, and tell that lot to stay away from me."

"I'll do my best," Rita said. "But I don't have the aliens on speed dial. Or the G-men."

Frenchie growled, then turned on his heel and stalked towards his place.

Sighing, Rita turned in the other direction to go search his property.

Chapter Nine

Rita picked her way through the strewn lumber and scrap metal, sending up a spray of dry grass seeds. She stopped abruptly before a small hole, about a foot in both diameter and depth. Frenchie had mentioned a dog named Digger.

She stooped to examine it. Hard edges indicated the blade of a tool, rather than an animal's claws. But what was it for?

Rita stood and scanned her surroundings: More junk in the grass; a copse of boxelders and aspens, bookended by ponderosas; a rail fence (in need of fresh paint) running the perimeter of the property.

A section of the fence was newer, piecing off a corner of Frenchie's lot. A bushy laurel hedge ran inside the fence line, although it failed to hide the monstrous house rising above the greenery.

She looked down at the hole again. Why here? And why hadn't it been refilled? Especially considering it was a sizeable tripping hazard. She shuddered to think of Frenchie coming out here for a car bumper and spraining his ankle. Because a cell phone couldn't be counted on.

Nor could it be counted on that Frenchie even owned a cell phone.

She glanced behind her. Frenchie still watched her from the window. She gave him a wave and continued.

A few paces onward, Rita found another hole. And a few paces beyond that, another. She followed them from one to the next, as though connecting dots to discern a hidden design.

But the holes revealed no particular pattern.

She sighed and walked back to the cruiser, giving Frenchie (still at the window) a wave as she passed. He inclined his head, then came out of the building to follow the cruiser as she rolled down the drive.

After passing through the two gates, she watched in the rear-view mirror as Frenchie closed them behind her. At the bottom of the drive, rather than turning left to head back into town, she turned right.

Fifty yards up the road she turned right again, this time onto an asphalt drive marked by two concrete lions instead of a busted traffic cone. She rolled up the smooth driveway, either side lined with trimmed boxwood, and parked in front of a three-door garage.

She walked up the path to the front door and knocked. Then she rang. When there was no answer, she got back in the cruiser, left, and continued south along the country road.

But it dead-ended shortly thereafter in a thick bramble of young cottonwoods. Pulling a U-turn, Rita headed back the way she'd come, passing the mansion behind the laurel hedge, then Frenchie's place.

On the other side of the road, she passed a property with a For Sale sign at the foot of the driveway. A bright flash of movement, like a kite, caught her eye; a butter-yellow bed sheet dried on a clothesline. Someone must be home.

She pulled onto the shoulder in front of the house and took out her phone to text Jason.

Can you meet me at an address?

Can you give me fifteen? Or are you in danger?

Not in danger, Rita texted back. *I'm in shorts and a T. Need you to make me look official. It's about a UFO. They might not take me seriously in a ballcap.*

We call them UAPs. And they might not take you serious, period, Jason messaged. Then he sent a laughing emoji. Rita put away her phone with a smile.

Then she lowered the window and the seat-back to rest while she waited. She exhaled, thankful for a chance to catch a breath after trudging around Frenchie's hazardous property.

Moreover, she was damn tired lately. She rubbed her face. She thought mothers were supposed to be tired *after* the baby came.

She took the pregnancy test out of the console and looked at it, turning it over in her hands. She had time to take the test, while waiting for Jason to arrive. But where would she pee? In the ditch?

She groaned and returned the box to console. She'd have to wait a little longer. At that point, her thoughts ceased, as she drifted off to sleep.

What seemed like only a few seconds later, a horn tooted. Her eyes fluttered open to see Jason idling in the SCSO truck.

"Thanks for coming," she said, blinking her eyes into focus.

"This house here?" he asked, pointing to Irene's driveway.

"Yup," Rita said, "the place with the sign."

She started the ignition, then did a U-turn and pulled in behind him. She shut off the ignition and joined Jason on the stoop. On either side of the door sat a large pot of petunias that appeared to be as immune to the heat as the small, rectangular lawn within the half-acre property; a caring hand had watered the immediate environs of the house, while the rest of the land was as yellow and dry as Frenchie's junk-filled fields.

Rita raised her knuckles to knock when Jason gave her a sidelong glance.

"Do you feel official enough?"

Rita's hand paused in mid-air. "With two cars in the driveway, just to ask about a UAP? Definitely. Even with the jamboree hat."

Jason grinned at her. "It's cute. It's vintage."

Rita let her hand drop. "Cute isn't what I was going for. And it's not vintage. It's from 2000."

"Anything older than twenty years is vintage," Jason said.

"No, it's not," Rita said. "That's retro."

Jason shook his head. "Not a chance. Look, you can always tell them you're under cover."

Rita blinked at him. "Then I wouldn't be under cover anymore."

Jason shrugged. "Guess not. But it would explain the lack of a uniform."

"Hey, no guessing," Rita teased. "Now let's get this over with."

"How long we gonna be here?" Jason asked.

"We'll be out of here in five minutes," she said.

"Is that a promise?" Jason asked.

Rita winked and knocked on the door.

A high-pitched dog bark echoed inside the house. A

minute later the door slowly opened by a woman in her eighties, her hair dyed purple. A Pomeranian pranced around her ankles. Then it tried to nip Jason's.

"Don't worry about Baxter," the woman said, gathering the dog into her arms, "I'll put him away in the laundry room."

Jason smiled. "I imagine most folks living out here have a security dog."

The woman chuckled. "Not Baxter. He's scared of everything. And the most dangerous thing out here is shooting stars."

Rita smiled at the pun. "I'm Sheriff Jonas and this is Deputy Perry with the Still County Sheriff's Office. Er— I'm not wearing my uniform today, but we'd like to ask you a few questions about your neighbor, Frenchie."

"Certainly," the woman said, as though she'd been expecting the request. She smiled. "I'm Irene Wilcox." She opened the door wider and shuffled backwards. "Come on in, Sheriff Jonas and Deputy Perry."

They entered the house, and a pong of lemon-scent hit the back of Rita's throat.

She suppressed a cough as she took in the framed display of needlepoint on the wall: big-horned antelope; a grizzly bear; grouse; gray wolves.

Having cleared her throat, Rita gestured to the display. "Nice work."

Irene beamed and hugged Baxter closer. "It's like a gallery, isn't it? One of them fancy art ones. My daughter hung them all for me. She's real smart about things like that. Now you go on through to the living room, now. I'll put Baxter away and fetch the strawberry iced tea."

Then she and Baxter shuffled forward across the foyer and disappeared into the kitchen.

"Smells clean in here," Jason said, lifting his nose. "You wouldn't know there's a dog."

"Febreze," Rita said. She sniffled. "I might sneeze."

They found their way into the living room and Rita stopped short in her tracks, breath caught.

A bison stared back at her. Tire took a sharp breath.

Inhale—

"Impressive needlepoint," Jason said, peering over the back of the sofa to admire the massive woven tapestry hanging on the wall. A brown bison stood on a grassy knoll, with the state flag rippling behind it.

"Thank you, Deputy Perry," Irene said, walking into the room. She carried a tray with a glass pitcher containing an iced russet drink.

"You made that?" Rita asked, studying the animal.

"I used a loom for that one," Irene said, setting the tray on the glass-topped coffee table. Then she shuffled around to finger the weaving. "I wove real bison hair into it, right here, in its beard."

Rita leaned closer to look. "Where did you get bison hair?"

"Out walking in the wilds. In the spring, they like to rub up against the junipers and willows to slough it off. When my daughter was a teenager, I was taking her hiking up Yellowstone way. We took a few treks up there. Collected what I could every time and got enough to do this here part, just under his chin."

Rita ran her fingers over the bison's tufted beard. "It's prickly."

"These are the guard hairs," Irene said.

"You have many talents, Irene," Jason said. "Needlepoint, houseplants…"

"Strawberry iced tea?" Irene said, picking up the pitcher on the coffee table. "It's one of my specialties, too."

"Thanks," Rita said as Irene passed her a glass, then one to Jason. "I've never had it."

"Of course you haven't," Irene said. "I'm the only one in these parts that makes it. My gran down in Alabama taught me."

Rita tool a sip. An explosion of full and earthy flavors surprised her. "Delicious," she said.

"Best way to use up the strawberry leaves at the end of the season," Irene said, beaming. She poured a glass for herself and sat in a coral-pink wingback armchair that reminded Rita of a scallop's shell. "Have a seat, Sheriff Jonas, Deputy Perry."

Rita sat on the sofa, which was unexpectedly firm as if it'd recently visited the upholsterer's for an injection of foam. Jason remained standing by the window, sipping iced tea and admiring some pale pink and purple African violets in a plant stand.

"Did you do all these needlepoints?" Jason asked, draining his iced tea.

Irene gestured to some handiwork hanging above the fireplace mantel. "That's my mother's. She liked ducks quite a lot."

"That's definitely a lot of ducks," Rita said, studying the needlepoint canvas which was three feet in length.

"There's three hundred of 'em," Irene said.

"Ducks?" Jason confirmed.

"Birds," Irene said, smacking her lips. "There's a few geese in there, too, plus a kingfisher on that tree and a blackbird in the rushes."

"You counted them?" Rita said.

"My mother did," Irene said.

Then she swung her finer, crooked with arthritis, towards a glass frame hanging above the flat-screen TV standing upon an old entertainment unit that was deeper than required. The stitches formed a portrait of Boy George in electric shades of magenta and lime.

"That one's my daughter's. Though she did it quite a number of years ago now."

"A family tradition," Rita said, swallowing a burp. She finished the last of her tea to clear the acidic burn at the back of her throat. "How nice."

"It's very bright," Jason said. "I like the colors."

"That's them synthetic dyes they use now. Neon, they call them." She gave Rita a benign smile. "Do you do a handicraft, Sheriff?"

Rita shook her head. "Nope. Never had time in New York." And then something made her add, "But my mother sewed."

Jason gave her a look and tapped his watch.

"How nice," Irene said. "What did she sew?"

"Um," Rita said, thinking back, "aprons. Nightgowns. Curtains. I think she was good at it. When she finished a project."

Irene smiled. "That's nice. Though a shame you never took it up."

"She tried," Rita said. "But I think I was a poor pupil. She often lost her patience with me."

Irene found that funny. "Mothering and teaching are not the same thing. I'm going to move to my daughter's in Beaumont, and I'm hoping it'll work out, after all these years on my own."

"I'm sure there's a lot of upkeep you have to do around the place," Rita said. "Must have to be fairly independent living this far out of town."

"That's for sure," Irene said, bobbing her purple head. "Sometimes, in the winter, we don't get plowed for a few days. That's why I appreciate my neighbor Frenchie so much. He got all sorts of little machines over at his place."

"We'd actually like to ask you some questions about Frenchie," Rita said. "Deputy Perry will take notes."

Accordingly, Jason moved to take out his notebook.

Irene nodded, then smacked her lips. "I'll do my best to tell you what I know," she said. "But I can't imagine why you'd want to check up on him. He's a real good man. Always taking care of us neighbors."

"How do you mean?" Rita asked.

"When it snows, he's out in his tractor clearing my drive. Like I said, we don't always get plowed. In the spring, he woodchips all the branches that came down over winter. He's also got one of them lawn aerators. He ain't got no lawn, but he's got this machine and drives it over my grass twice a year." Irene waved her claw-like hands towards the window. "It's real green, isn't it?"

"Looks great," Jason said. "Lush."

"Real lush," Irene said. "But them folks across the way, though"—she moved her hand along—"they put that grass seed down on a construction site. Nothing but hard-packed dirt filled with cigarette buts and screws. They've tried to get that lawn going more than once, but it always dies off. Only fix for that is a load of cow manure." Irene paused to giggle, sounding almost child-like. "But I can't imagine that going over well with the missus in the house."

"Do you mean the new house next to Frenchie's?" Rita asked.

Irene inclined her head. "That's the one."

"Do you know the owners of that house?" Rita asked.

"New bank manager and his wife. What's their surname…?"

"The Slaney?" Jason said.

"That's right," Irene said, "the Slaney."

"Did Frenchie subdivide his lot?" Rita asked.

"Sure did," Irene said. "He had hernia surgery last

year. Needed some money, so he cut off a little corner of his acreage."

"Some of Frenchie's neighbors," Rita said, "have been noticing some lights in the sky lately."

"You mean satellites?" Irene asked. "I hear some folks is real upset about cellular towers too."

"I mean unidentified lights," Rita said, proceeding with caution.

"Oh," Irene said with a smile, "you mean the UFO that flies on over Frenchie."

Rita swapped a look with Jason. "That's the one," she said. "Have you seen the lights?"

"Nope," Irene said. "I go to bed with the sun."

"Has Frenchie told you anything about them?" Rita asked.

Irene puckered her lips. "Just that some spacecraft's been following him around."

"Have you known Frenchie a long time?" Rita asked.

"Sure have," Irene said. "We're the last two old-timers on the block." She paused to swallow some iced tea. "Frenchie might be odd, but he sure ain't crazy."

"Well, it's very kind of Frenchie to pitch in around the place."

"Sure is," Irene said. "Done it for years now. Ever since my Ernie had his stroke and couldn't get round so easy." She gave a sad laugh. "Now it's me that don't get round so easy. My daughter's always warning me I'm gonna trip over Baxter. That's why I'm going to live with her." She held up her hands. "Arthritis."

"I'm sorry for your condition," Jason said. "I expect arthritis makes needlepoint difficult."

"Makes it impossible," Irene said. "It was needlepoint that made my hands like this in the first place." She rested them on the coral armrests. "I've made my peace." She smiled. "That's the blessing of age. All the time in the world to make peace with your past."

"Wise words," Rita said.

Irene's eyes flashed. "Funny, that's what Frenchie always says. 'Wise words.'"

"Thank you for your time," Rita said. She passed Irene her card. "If you think of anything else about the UFO sighting, I'd appreciate you calling."

"Have a good afternoon, Irene," Jason said, putting away his notebook. Then he gestured to the plant stand. "By the way, what's your secret for the violets?"

"Southwestern exposure," Irene said.

"Ah," Jason said, as though receiving sage spiritual advice.

Rita set her empty glass on the tray. "Thanks for the refreshment," Rita said. Then she tipped her chin, inhaling the air. "What's that lemony aroma?"

"Furniture polish," Irene said.

Rita half-smiled to herself. Of course she couldn't identify the scent; furniture wax was not something Carole would have used in their household. If anything, the furniture was covered in water rings. Or rather, vodka rings.

Irene smiled again, her eyes twinkling. "Glad you came by, Sheriff Jonas. Deputy Perry."

Jason added his glass to the tray, which Irene then picked up.

"Have a good afternoon," she said. Then she turned and shuffled back to the kitchen with the tray.

Before heading for the front door, Rita stooped and pulled out the basket beneath the glass coffee table and took a quick peek at the needlepoint inside. The mesh was half filled with a pattern. At the top, it looks to be fairly neatly done. But farther down, the threads were poorly mixed, their hues a jumbled pattern lacking uniformity of tension.

"Must be hard to say goodbye to the things we love," Rita said.

Jason glanced at her. "Like a parent?"

Rita tucked the basket back under the coffee table. "Like handicrafts."

Then she and Jason let themselves out of the house while somewhere in the back of the bungalow, Irene cooed to Baxter.

As she and Jason walked back to the vehicles, Rita sighed. "Didn't find anything out there, aside from recipes and gardening tips."

"Maybe that Frenchie's a harmless old gentleman?" Jason said. "Sounds like a nice guy."

"Maybe," Rita said. "Or maybe Irene's as crazy as he is, and we've mistaken her collusion for assurances."

"They're both harmless," Jason said, walking back to the SCSO truck.

"You know him?" Rita asked. "Frenchie?"

"Not me," Jason said. "But my oldest sister bought some car parts from him, one time. She only had nice things to say. Likes to give a deal. Says he likes to stiff the taxman."

Rita cocked her head. "That sounds like Frenchie."

Back in the cruiser, she waited a moment before starting the ignition, hoping that aliens might swoop down and scoop her up. Then all her problems would be solved. Maybe.

But when nothing of the sort happened, she drove back towards town, taking her time on the country roads.

Then she pulled onto the highway and kicked up her

speed. A compulsion to get out of sleepy, UAP-infested Still pumped through her veins.

New York.

She was already on the I-25. Not long and she could be on the I-80. And then the I-90. And the I-95 after that.

All she'd have to do is turn left...

Chapter Ten

But before Rita could make the choice between heading back to Still or continuing onto New York, her phone rang. She pulled onto the shoulder and answered it.

"Hello, Miss Jonas. This is Dustin Ashbury from the Still Waters Memorial Home. I'm calling to find out when would be a good time to discuss the matter of your father's death?"

"I can come now," Rita said. "You're at the corner of Galland and Hilliard Street?"

"Correct," Dustin said.

Rita thanked him and hung up, then drove the ten blocks and pulled into the parking lot, passing a white wooden sign with black lettering. She parked the cruiser in a row of stalls opposite the shingled building. For a moment, Rita sat in the driver's seat, feeling queasy.

Inhale.

Exhale.

Then she got out and walked up to the entrance of the funeral home. On either side of the door, flowering shrubs filled a garden plot. She pulled open the wood-panel door and stepped inside. Dim pot-lights cast halos of light on the cream-colored walls of the foyer.

A woman wearing a periwinkle sweater set and pearls sat at a reception desk. She looked up, giving Rita with a serene smile.

"Good morning, Sheriff Jonas. I'm very sorry for your loss." She stood and came around to shake Rita's hand. "I'm Allison. Dustin, the undertaker, is expecting you."

Rita shook her hand. "Thank you, Allison."

"I'll take you back to him now," she said.

Rita followed Allison down the corridor, passing a large showroom which contained several velvet- and satin-lined caskets on display, until they arrived at an office. The door stood open.

Allison swept a hand for Rita to proceed. "Here's Dustin."

Rita stepped into the office, plush carpet underfoot.

A man about three decades younger than Allison got up from a cherrywood desk and extended a hand. He also wore a serene expression, and a charcoal suit.

"Miss Jonas, welcome. Allow me to offer my condolences at the passing of your father. My name is Dustin, and I'll be helping you with your father's funerary arrangements." His voice was like distant thunder further dampened by the room's soft furnishings.

Rita shook his hand. "Thank you. Is Otto here?"

Dustin seemed taken aback by the questions. "Yes, his body has arrived from the morgue at Casper Hospital." He paused, then said, as though sensing Rita wanted more: "He's downstairs, in the freezer."

Nodding, Rita sat in one of the two cream-colored armchairs opposite his desk. On the desk lay a file folder bearing Otto's name. "You can call him Otto when speaking with me, if it's easier."

"Very well," Dustin said. He consulted the paperwork in the folder, then folded his hands. "Are you familiar with your father's — I mean, Otto's — final wishes?"

"Not entirely," Rita said. "I hear he made most of his own arrangements."

"That's true," Dustin said. "Would you like to read the documents for yourself, or have me review them for you?"

"I appreciate if you would summarize," Rita said.

Dustin nodded. "Your father — Otto — he elected cremation."

"Sounds about right," Rita said.

"Which is scheduled for tomorrow."

"Okay."

"And he's prepaid for an urn."

Rita raised an eyebrow. "Very organized."

"Very. Would you like the ashes delivered to your home? Or would you like to pick them up here, after the memorial service?"

Rita's chest tightened. "Are we having a memorial service?"

Dustin's gaze softened. "It would be appropriate. He would have wanted it." Fiddling with the file folder, Dustin cleared his throat. "He's given us a playlist of songs."

"For the service?" Rita asked.

"Some for the service. Some for the reception."

"A reception, too?" Rita inhaled. "I'll pick up the urn at the service."

"Regarding the service, will that be held here, or have you chosen another location?"

"You mean like a church or a garden?"

"Yes," Dustin said. "Often families around here choose their family farm. And of course, we have a lovely chapel here for public use."

"Here," Rita said. "I'm — we're — he isn't religious.

Er, *wasn't*. He used to say he didn't have to uphold the Lord, because he was upholding the Law."

Dustin gave a slight smile. "Not to worry, we're very familiar with planning a secular memorial service. You'll be delivering the eulogy?"

Rita's mouth went dry. "Yes."

"There's a podium in the chapel you can use, with a mic. It's all very straightforward."

"Okay. Thanks."

Dustin opened a leatherbound day planner. "Which day are you thinking?"

Rita paused. "I haven't given the service any thought. I've been very busy at work."

"I understand," Dustin said. "We recommend seven to ten days after your loved one's passing. It allows for family to grieve in private before making travel arrangements. Allison can schedule him in as you see fit."

"Great," Rita said, her voice feeling hollow, like an urn.

Dustin passed her his business card from a stack in a brass holder. "Regarding Otto's obituary, you can download a template from our website."

Rita stifled a burp. "Okay."

"Then email it to us, and Allison will submit it to the papers. You can also let her know which ones. I would think Beaumont and Casper as well?"

Rita took his card. "Yes, please. He worked with several of the retired cops in Casper."

"Excellent. If you could please send us the obituary within the next forty-eight hours, it can get into the weekend papers. Your father was a notable citizen in the community. Even though he'd been retired for, what, nearly a year? — folks in town still think of him as the sheriff."

"How flattering for me," Rita said. "Although I

suppose his death will likely make it clear that I've been holding that position for a while now."

Dustin's smile faltered. "It can take some folks a while to change. Especially in a small town. I'm sure that's hard to get used to, being from New York."

"I'm originally from Still," Rita said. "And I'm still here." She laughed bitterly. "Still here. Get it?"

"Sure do," Dustin said. "I'm a born-and-raised flat-lander, too. The land always calls us back here."

Rita shifted. "I don't know about that. I came back to town for Otto. Because he was in poor health."

"Sometimes death can be especially disruptive to the life of a first responder."

"That surprises me," Rita said. "Because I think I'm desensitized to it."

"It can be shocking when it touches close to home. And isn't consigned to the job."

"That's what my boyfriend said," she said.

Dustin nodded. "It's good to talk through our grief."

Rita squared her shoulders. "You don't need to do this. I debrief with my team."

Two red spots bloomed in Dustin's cheeks. "I'm only sharing because I lost my dad, too. I grew up in this business, hiding in caskets when I wasn't supposed to. Or worse, stuffing my cousin into one and closing the lid. That was worthy of double the trouble. Although mostly my sister was to blame for that one. Anyway, when my dad died, I was too grief-stricken to take on the business, as he'd willed for me to do. My mom — that's Allison — did both her job as bookkeeper, plus the job of funeral director for two years, until I was ready."

"Your family sounds very close," Rita said.

Dustin blushed a little deeper. "My sister's the embalmer. I operate the crematory."

"Your father must be proud," Rita said. "And may I say, I am sorry for your loss, as well—" She broke off with another burp. She covered her mouth with her hand. "Pardon me, I'm not feeling very well."

"It's common to feel unsettled at the passing of a loved one," Dustin said. "Grief often manifests physically."

Acid bubbled up the back of Rita's throat. "I don't think this is a death issue."

Dustin gave her a quizzical look. "You're looking pale, Sheriff Jonas."

Rita nodded and stifled another belch.

"There's a bathroom near reception." Dustin got up from his desk and came around to her side. "It's on the right-hand side, just past the showroom."

"Thank you," Rita said, slipping from the office.

She hurried down the hallway and locked herself in the accessible bathroom. Then spun around and puked in the toilet.

For a moment she stayed bent over the bowl, gripping its sides, willing away the spins. But still the room tilted.

She stayed in place for another few heartbeats before pushing off from the toilet and washing her hands till they were pink. Then she washed out her mouth and cleaned her face.

"This is it," Rita said to her reflection. "What's the point in waiting any longer?"

She took the pregnancy kit out of her pocket and read the instructions. Three minutes and the mystery would be solved. If only it were so with criminal investigations.

She pulled down her pants and peed on the stick.

Inhale.

Exhale.

She set the stick on the edge of the sink and checked her phone to pass the time.

There were several messages from Mary Lou. And some from Cash. Even one from Carly. But she couldn't bring herself to read any of them.

With two minutes remaining, she paced the bathroom.

"You must think I'm crazy, Dad," Rita said. But then, because she didn't believe in ghosts, she paced the remaining minute in silence.

Then she checked the stick.

Chapter Eleven

Rita stared at the stick, the taste of strawberry-flavored vomit still on her tongue. She pushed away from the sink and chucked the test wand in the trash.

Inhale.

Exhale.

Then she scrambled to retrieve the stick and put it back in her pocket.

"Jesus Christ," she told her reflection, "I don't want to be dealing with this."

Her reflection filed to offer advice.

Rita hung her head. "Shit."

On the bathroom was everything to assist recovery from crusty snot and teary splotches: tissues; rosewater towelettes; peppermint face-mist; vanilla hand lotion. She washed her hands. Then her face. And declined the vanilla moisturizer, since her stomach was already bucking against the potpourri of garden scents.

She exited the bathroom and returned to the foyer. Dustin leaned against the reception desk, chatting to his mother. He looked up as she approached.

"How are you feeling, Miss Jonas?"

"I'm fine."

"I brought you some refreshment," he said, passing her a thin can of sparkling water.

Rita took the can and went to sit in one of the olive armchairs in near the door. "Thank you," she said, "I'll feel better once I'm hydrated." She cracked the tab and took a long swallow, washing away the acidic residue in her throat. "I walked into town this morning and it was hotter than I realized. I forgot to bring some water."

Dustin gave her a sympathetic smile. "It can be difficult to remember the basics, when we're knocked sideways by loss. But it's in these liminal times surrounding a death that it's especially important to manage the matters of life."

She crinkled her nose at him. "You're doing it again — grief counselling."

Dustin gave a small laugh. "Can't help it," he said. "I'm an undertaker."

"Everyone expects me to be bereft," Rita said. "But Otto was terminal. We knew what was coming. It's why I was here."

"Some of us cope with grief by masking our emotions."

"I don't think Otto masked his emotions," Rita said. "It's only that he was obviously prepared for what was coming. Like you said, he'd made a playlist and a payment plan. It must have been so hard to know his death was coming." She paused to blow out a breath. "And yet, I'm glad he had the foresight to plan so much for himself." A bitter laugh escaped her throat. "God knows I didn't know him well enough to make a playlist."

Dustin cleared his throat. "I wish I'd known what my father wanted, more specifically. The way Otto left these notes." He unbuttoned his charcoal jacket and put his hands in his pants pockets. "You'd think, being in this business, I would have known. Would have remembered to ask. Sure, I knew to order in a Batesville, 'cause they were clearly his favorite. But his favorite songs to play?" He shrugged. "Well, everyone likes Pachelbel's 'Canon in G Major.'"

"Is that one of Otto's choices?" Rita asked.

Dustin cast up his eyes to think. "I recall pop songs on the list."

"That surprises me," Rita said.

Dustin shrugged. "I'm pretty sure they're all retro."

"I guess I'll wait for the service to find out," Rita said, placing the empty can on a side-table. "And usually I don't like waiting. Or guessing."

Dustin laughed. "Have a good afternoon, Sheriff Jonas."

"Thanks for the arrangements."

Dustin inclined his head. "It's my pleasure."

Rita paused on her way out the door. "I don't find myself saying that about my job too much."

"No?"

Rita sighed. "And yet I must find pleasure on the beat, mustn't I? Otherwise why would I do it?"

"To follow in his footsteps?" Dustin asked. "Because it's what you're used to? The funeral business tends to be a family one. So I know what it means to be born into your vocation. And get this: My surname is Ashbury. You now, like ashes to ashes and dust to dust?"

Rita laughed. "What a pun to be saddled with."

"Mom insists they didn't do it on purpose." He threw her a look over his shoulder. "Isn't that right, Mom?"

Allison looked up from the desk, smiling, and gave them a small wave.

Dustin turned back to face Rita. "Growing up, the kids

called me Dusty-ass Ashbury. My sister thought it was hilarious, but seeing as her name is Holly, I called her Holy Ashes."

Laughing, Rita got up from the chair. "Cute nicknames."

This time the funeral director laughed. "Cute?"

Rita shrugged. "Dusty-Ass isn't very vulgar. Not like my moniker at WLEA."

Dustin gave her a good-natured look. "Spill."

"Romeo India T'n'A."

Dustin smirked. "That's a good one." He straightened his face and his tie. "It was nice chatting to you, Rita. Thanks for stopping in to take care of matters at the end of your day." They moved towards the door. "We'll be in touch over email. Take care."

"Thanks," Rita said as Dustin pulled open the door for her.

Rita returned to the cruiser. For a few minutes, in the lot, she sat behind the wheel.

Inhale.

Exhale.

Then she turned the ignition and pulled out.

On the way back to the station, she passed Lisa's Place. Her gaze followed the name Lisa written in cursive script, lit up and hung over the main entrance to the newly constructed townhouse complex.

Then her gaze dipped lowered, noticing a slender figure with a familiar face and a brand-new look. She pulled the cruiser to the curb and idled, lowering the passenger window.

She leaned to the side and waved through the window. "Arbuckle!"

"Hi there, Sheriff," he said, approaching in a navy-blue uniform with an Apex badge. "Mary Lou told me 'bout your dad." He put a fist to his logoed chest and bowed his head. "Sorry to hear it. He was a good man. Always did right by me."

Rita nodded. "He always liked you, Arbuckle."

He grinned. "That pleases me to hear, Sheriff."

Rita looked him up and down. "Nice uniform."

Arbuckle hooked his thumbs through his belt loops. "Got myself a job."

"Congratulations." Rita read the badge over his left chest pocket. "You doing security?"

"Yep. I'm auxiliary. I thought, security's ain't nothin' but standing around watchin' shit all day. Or in this case, all night. And I do that as it is. So I thought, why the hell not?"

Rita shrugged. "Why not? How many shifts have you got?"

"I come in Friday and Saturday nights. Residents' association wants two of us on weekends. And I cover a few odd shifts like this afternoon, to cover someone's sick leave."

"How do you feel about working for Apex?" Rita asked. "Given their history with Lisa and everything?"

Arbuckle rolled his shoulders. "They're trying to do better with this place. And I don't want to carry hate in my heart. Besides, Apex is gonna own the whole goddamn town soon anyway."

"The Ashburys over at the funeral home are holding out," Rita said.

Arbuckle nodded. "Good to hear."

"Goodnight, Arbuckle," Rita said. "Have a good shift." Then she pulled away from the curb and headed to the station.

She parked the cruiser beside her Honda and yanked off the jamboree ballcap. Digging her nails into the scalp, she ran her fingers through her hair. She needed a hot shower and a long sleep. It had been one hell of a day, from Arbuckle wearing a uniform to UFOs on the outskirts of town, from planning a funeral to crossing paths with a bison.

Not to mention finding out she was pregnant. Again, she took a moment to breathe.

Inhale.

Exhale.

She could do this. She'd dealt with some fucked-up shit in New York. Not bison or UFOs, but character-building shit all the same. And she was sheriff of this town.

She was Otto Jonas' kid.

She got out of the cruiser and walked through the back door into the station, determined to complete the damn form about Frenchie's UAP and call it a night. Because this day couldn't possibly get stranger.

Until it did.

Rita stopped short and stared the woman seated in the foyer: Hair neatly styled; makeup heavily applied; manicured hands folded on her lap.

The woman smiled, her lips twice as full as Rita recalled. Then she opened them to speak.

Rita breezed past her, retreating from the foyer and storming into the bullpen.

"What the hell is Carole doing here?" she asked Mary Lou, her voice louder than she'd intended.

Then, without awaiting an answer, she stalked into her office and slammed the door.

Chapter Twelve

Rita tripped over a chair, forgetting she'd rearranged the furniture.

"Fuck!"

She picked herself up from the floor, rubbing her hip.

The door opened and Mary Lou looked in. "Was that question directed at me?"

"Well, it wasn't directed at Carole," Rita said. "I have nothing to say to that woman."

"When did you last speak to her?" Mary Lou asked.

"Hell, I don't remember," Rita said. "I didn't even know if she was alive or dead."

"Yikes," Mary Lou said, with a shake of her head. "Like a bridge over troubled water."

Rita gave her a look.

"What?" Mary Lou said in defense. "It's my favorite of the King's covers."

"I'm not mending fences with Carole right now," Rita said. "I've got my dad's affairs to put in order."

"No, you don't," Mary Lou said. "Otto took care of

everything. I already told you, this is a time for your feelings. Not busy work."

"Fine." Rita shuffled through the papers on her desk,
pretending to organize them. "You figure out what to do
with Frenchie's UAP. And Carole."

"Fine," Mary Lou huffed, "leave me your notebook
and I'll fill out the form. But what the hell am I supposed
to do with *her*?"

Rita shrugged. "I don't care."

"I can't put her in the cells. And I'm not having her
move in with me, like Vee. We all know how that turned
out."

"Well, then maybe you shouldn't be so trusting of Ted
either."

Mary Lou glowered. "You're changing the subject."

Rita stopped shuffling papers to blow out a breath.
"Look, just tell her to go away, all nice. Like you are."

"I already tried that."

"And what happened?"

Mary Lou shrugged. "She took a seat in the foyer."

Rita shrugged. "Then write her up for something.
Loitering?"

Mary Lou scowled. "That would be *your* job. And she's
your mother."

"She's dead to me."

Mary Lou scoffed. "So you're an orphan now, is
that it?"

Rita blinked at her. "Huh?"

Mary Lou tsk'ed. "What's wrong, Rita? You don't seem
like yourself."

"Of course I'm not myself. My dad's just died. "

"Yep. And you've still got one living parent. Perhaps
this isn't the time to shut her out."

"Shut her out? You think I'm shutting *her* out? Do you

know my history with that woman? Oh, wait — of course you do. You know everyone's business. Well, then, you should know exactly who's been shutting out whom for the last how many years."

Mary Lou slipped her arm around Rita's shoulder and coaxed her to sit on the edge of the desk. "That lemon that fell from the tree? Don't let its juice turn sour. You're going to need someone to talk to these days. So don't you go shuttin' me out, y'hear? It's not easy burying a parent, especially when you got no siblings. Er — no more, God bless Lisa."

Rita nodded. But she wasn't able to speak for a moment.

Mary Lou let the silence be, her arm softening against Rita's back.

After a moment, Rita pulled the test wand out of her pocket and passed it to Mary Lou.

Mary Lou's arm tightened again, then her other one encircled Rita and pulled her into a hug.

"Goodness-golly, child, congratulations," Mary Lou said into her ear, clearly trying to control her level of excitement so that Carole didn't overhear. Then she pulled away and held Rita at arm's length. "Who's the father?"

Rita glared at her. "That doesn't deserve an answer."

"Well, have you told Cash yet?"

Rita cut her eyes at her. "Of course not, because I don't know if I'm going to keep it."

"I see," Mary Lou said. "Well, how far along are you?"

"I don't know," Rita said. "I just looked at it today. I need to consult my calendar. Maybe six weeks."

Mary Lou's eye shone with moisture. "Did — did Otto know?"

Rita shook her head. "No." Then she gave a stilted laugh. "Took the test at the funeral home."

"Oh, Jesus," Mary Lou said, with a laugh. "Can I do anything for you?"

Rita thought for a moment. "I'd appreciate it if you'd write the obituary. You probably know best, all the important milestones in his career."

Mary Lou dabbed at her tears and nodded. "You're right."

"Thanks," Rita said. "I think he'd like that."

Mary Lou nodded. "I reckon you're right."

"Also, could you please call Marnie to change the locks at Otto's place?"

Mary Lou gave her a level look.

"You know … in case Carole still has keys."

Mary Lou bobbed her beehive. "I'll give her a call." Then, "How did it go out at Frenchie's?"

Rita crinkled her nose. "I didn't really know what to look for. Never investigated extraterrestrials before."

"Anything unusual?"

"A bunch of empty holes in the ground. But otherwise, there was a ton of crap on the property … car crap, scrap crap, nature crap."

"He's been living off the grid before it became a trendy thing to do."

Rita blinked at her. "It's trendy to live off the grid?"

Mary Lou waved a hand. "Oh, poo! You're from New York; you wouldn't understand."

"I understand that Still County is as far off the grid as I get," Rita said. She sighed. "So d'you know how he pays his property taxes? I'm not sure he's farming anything out there besides conspiracies."

"Nope," Mary Lou said. "Never known him to have a job."

"Speaking of jobs, guess who got a new one?"

"You don't play guessing games."

Rita stuck out her tongue. "Humor me."

Mary Lou sighed. "Stu?" Then she cocked her beehive. "Or Vic."

"Probably. But I was thinking of Arbuckle."

Mary Lou raised an eyebrow. "Now *that* is new news around here."

"He's a security guard over at Lisa's Place."

Mary Loo gave a nod. "Good for him."

Rita matched her nod. "Weekend auxiliary."

"Nothing stays the same," Mary Lou said. "Just when you think you know a thing, it changes."

Rita felt for the pregnancy test in her pocket. "It's been a hell of day. I'm going to go home to bed." She pushed off the desk and crossed to the door. "Good night, Mary Lou."

"Goodnight," she returned, her voice the softest it had been all day. "Remember, you can take off the day tomorrow and this place'll still be standing."

Rita laughed as she walked through the bullpen.

A shadow shifted and Rita paused. She'd forgotten about Carole, still seated in the foyer.

She stood up. "Rita—"

Rita flinched. Then quickened her pace and headed for the back door.

"Rita!" Carole said.

But Rita was already running down the back steps, into the parking lot.

"Fuck," she said, sliding into her Honda.

On the drive back to Otto's, her stomach kept churning. Hands shaking, she pulled over, unbuckled, and opened the car door.

She'd barely taken a step when she threw up. Strawberry bile splattered across the dirt, staining it pink.

Rita wiped off her lip.

Inhale.

Exhale.

Then she got back into the Honda and pulled into the lane.

She barely remembered the drive out to Otto's. She pulled into Otto's driveway. Jason's Kia wasn't back yet. The stars were out, though. She and Mary Lou had stayed late. And she hadn't eaten anything.

Inside the house, Rita kicked off her shoes, then grabbed a bag of low-sodium potato chips from the pantry. She ate a handful while trudging upstairs, but they were stale.

She stuffed the rest of bag in the bathroom trash-can, then stripped off and showered, letting the vomit, the sweat, and the stress of the day disappear down the drain.

Five minutes later, Rita emerged, her skin the same shade as Irene's strawberry iced tea. She patted herself dry with one of Otto's ancient brown towels, then padded to the guestroom in bare feet. She drew the blind and collapsed on the mattress.

Inhale.

Exhale.

Then Rita pulled the cover over her head and fell asleep.

Chapter Thirteen

Rita woke to the sound of her phone ringing. Rubbing her eyes, she picked it up. Mary Lou.

"I'm sleeping in," she said. "I'm mourning, remember? I like to do it in the morning."

"I know," Mary Lou said. "But we've got a dead body."

Rita groaned and pushed up to sitting. "Really? Today?"

"Jason's already at the scene," Mary Lou said.

"Does that mean I can go back to sleep?"

"It means I already let you sleep late, before I called," Mary Lou said. "And if you want book off bereavement leave, then fill out the paperwork. But if you want to pitch in like you say you do, you'd better go assist."

Rita sighed. "So where's the body?"

"Parkland Elementary School, but don't worry, it's not a kid."

"Thank God," Rita said.

"I've already contacted Casper Forensics," Mary Lou said. "They might be there before you, at this rate."

"Ha, ha," Rita said with a yawn. "I'm on my way."

She showered and dressed, and went downstairs to find Marnie in the foyer, drilling out the lock on the front door.

"Marnie, I didn't hear you come in. I was sleeping like the dead," Rita said, then wished she'd used another turn of phrase.

"Well, then I'm glad I didn't wake you," Marnie said. "I'm just about to start the back door."

"Thanks," Rita said. "And can you please take a look at the window locks to make sure they're in working condition?"

"Consider it done," Marnie said. "And I'm sorry to hear about your dad."

Rita gave her a nod. "Thank you." Then she slipped past her and walked down the porch to her Honda.

As Rita drove into town, she passed the Still Haven Inn, now a blackened heap of timbers while insurance investigations were underway.

Arriving at Parkland Elementary School, she parked the cruiser in the staff lot and walked towards the strips of yellow tape sectioning off the field. In the center of the area sat a dark blue Chevy Cavalier. The backside of Jason protruded from the driver's door.

Rita headed out across the field, tire treads barely recognizable in the dry, dusty weeds. As she approached, she could detect the stench of death. As she walked up to the car, Jason pulled his head out of the interior.

"Hiya," he said. He looked about as well as Rita felt.

"Haven't seen one of these for a while," Rita said. "I think they stopped making these things around the time you were born."

"You're mistaken about that," Jason said. "But it's true that this car has to be at least twenty-five years old."

"This where the body is?"

"Yup. Several neighbors saw the car this morning, but

Joanne called it in." Jason pointed to a woman sitting dog on a bench by the gymnasium. "Though she couldn't provide a plate number. Never got close enough to be able to read it. I haven't talked to any neighbors yet that actually approached the vehicle."

Rita noticed several onlookers leaning against a chain-link fence running along one side of the field. "Why'd everyone else ignore it?"

"They all thought it was a school-kid prank."

"This is an elementary school," Rita said. "Every kid here is younger than thirteen. And it's the middle of the summer. Somehow, I don't think they're driving donuts around the soccer field."

"No donuts," Jason agreed, "but this car's been baking like one of them solar ovens. None of the windows were lowered."

Rita raised an eyebrow. "Usually when someone wants to dispose of a body, they expose it to nature."

"On the plus side, forensic evidence might be preserved," Jason said. "I was the one that found the keys in the ignition and popped the trunk."

"How fun for you," Rita said.

"You think it smells bad now? Shoulda been here when I first opened 'er up."

Rita's stomach pitched. "I can imagine."

Jason went an even whiter shade of pale. "Actually, I'm not sure you can. Come on, have a look for yourself." And he led her around to the trunk.

Rita followed on leaden feet. She wished she was back in her bed. Jason lifted the trunk. Rita buckled over and barfed.

"At least that didn't taste like strawberries," she said, dabbing her lips with the back of her hand. She straightened and glanced at Jason. "I hope I didn't splatter you."

Jason pointed a few yards away. "My puddle's over there. I could smell what was coming, so I got ready to run."

Rita nodded and braved another look in the trunk.

A man lay coiled and contorted in the tight space, his cheeks and lips eaten away into a gaping hole, revealing a shredded mass that once might have been a tongue. Burn marks sprawled across his hands and down his arms, where the remnants of his sleeves had been devoured by something potently caustic.

Rita looked at Jason. "What the fuck?"

Jason swallowed. "That's exactly what I said. After I vomited."

Rita nodded. Then burped. And vomited again, this time several paces away.

Clearing her throat, she returned to Jason's side. "What about ID?"

Jason bent over and pointed into the back of the trunk. "I can tell there's a wallet in his back pocket." He straightened and glanced at his watch. "Forensics should be here soon."

"Mary Lou run the plates yet?" Rita asked.

Jason nodded. "Vehicle belongs to Trevor Bachman."

"Looks like you covered all the bases, Deputy," Rita said. "Good work."

Then she stole another glance in the trunk. "Trevor, Trevor, Trevor ... what are you doing driving around with a dead body in your trunk? And where are you now?"

"Likely on his way to Dakota or Alberta," Jason said. "Probably hitching."

Car doors slammed in the school parking lot. Rita glanced over her shoulder to see the head of Casper Forensics, Tilda Keating, and the Chief Medical Examiner,

Dylan Bruce, walk across the parking lot, carrying their kits.

Rita gave them a wave.

As Tilda approached, she set down her kit and opened her arms. "Rita, I am so sorry to hear about your dad."

Rita accepted the embrace. "Thanks."

Tilda released her. "But you're not on bereavement leave?"

Rita gestured towards the Chevy, where Jason and the medical examiner were standing over the trunk, chatting. "These are special circumstances."

Tilda gave her an understanding nod. "No doubt. All the same, it's hard to lose a parent."

Rita sighed. "It's even harder to have one show up in town unexpected. For some reason, that's rattled me more."

Tilda met her eye. "Your mother?"

Rita nodded.

"You never talk about her," Tilda said.

"Nope," Rita said. "Because as mothers, you two are nothing alike."

Tilda's gaze softened. "Hang in there, kid."

"Thanks," Rita said. "Do you want to be my mother?"

Tilda laughed and ruffled Rita's hair.

"You're going to mess up my bun," Rita said.

"You look like hell already," Tilda said. "Like you slept on it."

Rita nodded. "Because I was sleeping. Very recently."

Tilda slapped her shoulder. "Then you should do some more of that, huh?"

Rita shrugged. "You're probably right, Mom. But I'd like to stay until we ID the body."

"Working on that," Bruce said, now dressed in a Tyvek suit and bent over the trunk. "We've got a wallet."

Tilda opened her kit. "Time to suit up."

While Tilda tugged on a Tyvek coverall, Rita pointed to a dark patch on the ground. "That's my puke over there." Then she pointed the other way. "And that's Jason's."

"Got it," Tilda said, tucking her hair into the hood.

"And I got your ID," Bruce said, walking over. His nitrile-gloved hands opened a wallet and showed a photo ID in the name of Trevor Bachman.

"That's the owner of the car," Rita said.

Bruce took a closer look at the idea. "The dead guy?"

Rita nodded. "Can you positively ID him?"

Bruce returned to the trunk and held the card close to the corpse's face, while Tilda moved into take photographs. "Despite the corrosion and hemorrhaging, I'd say this man is the same as in the photo."

"So how'd he end up like this?" Rita asked, rhetorically.

Bruce looked grim. "Ingestion of a hazardous substance."

Rita rubbed her belly. "My guts feel hazardous, too." Then she turned away to vomit again.

Chapter Fourteen

"Trevor Bachman's got a nearly clean slate," Mary Lou said over the line. "Only mark against his name is a single ticket for a California roll."

"Hm," Rita said. "How does a guy with only one traffic violation end up in a trunk like this?"

"That would be your job to find out," Mary Lou said with a note of confidence Rita didn't feel.

"Can you find me the details for the next-of-kin notification?" She asked. "I'm gonna talk to the witness now, so you can text me the details."

"Ten-four," Mary Lou said and hung up.

Rita walked back over to Jason, Bruce, and Tilda, who stood conversing a few feet behind the Cavalier.

"We're gonna take the body *in situ* to Casper," Bruce said, as she joined them.

"Flatbed's coming to hoist it," Jason said.

"And I've called in some more people for a ground sweep," Tilda said. She gestured toward the greenbelt that stretched behind the field. "This is one big-ass field."

"Yup," Rita said, rocking on her heels. "Lots of space out here in Still County."

"I'll do door-to-doors," Jason said. "Though half the neighborhood's been out here all morning watching me." He pointed. "Look, there's even more of them now."

Rita craned to look around his shoulder at the crowd gathering along the fence. "Shit," Rita said, "I should go tell them to move along. But I'm not having the best week on the job."

"I'll do it," Jason said. "I don't mind telling them to move along, all polite-like." Then he pointed to the children's play equipment, where the witness was now sitting on a swing. "Joanne moved into the shade."

"I'll go talk to her," Rita said. "See you dogs later."

Then she walked across the field towards the playground equipment.

Joanne, about sixty, sat on a swing, gently swaying to and fro, her feet planted in the gravel. A red curly-haired dog lay next to her, its head in his paws. It lifted its head as Rita approached, her shoes shifting in the deep pebbles.

"Hi, Joanne. I'm Sheriff Jonas. Thanks for calling in the vehicle."

Joanne nodded her silver bob. "Sure thing, Sheriff. Looked suspicious when I saw it, so I didn't let Bertie off the leash, like I usually do." She paused to waft a hand towards the field. "During the school holidays, I come to run him in the fields."

"What made you think the car was suspicious?"

"'Cause it didn't make no sense," Joanne said, crinkling her brow. "What the hell was it doin' out there, middle of the field, at six-thirty in the morning on a Thursday in August?"

"No doubt," Rita said. She sat on the empty swing beside her. "Did you recognize the vehicle?"

"Nope. Not from the neighborhood." Joanne swung her hand the other way, to indicate the row of houses opposite the school. "Only the twelve of us addresses down this way, then the road dead-ends. Traffic's controlled out here by the school zone, so I tend to notice any new folks in the area."

"Have you noticed anything else that's suspicious?"

"I see suspicious folk often enough at the school, but I figure out most of them are harmless enough."

"Oh, really?" Rita said. "What sort of suspicious activity have you noticed?"

"Me and Bertie came across a mushroom picker once, asleep in the middle of the field. I had a hell of a time waking him, and when I did, he insisted I was the Easter Rabbit. Another time a couple kids were sleeping in the back of a van. Well, they weren't really sleeping, if you know what I mean. But I knew so one was camping in the car, because the windows were done up tight. And it wasn't a mushroom picker 'cause it ain't the season. Too dry."

"I recently learned they can be found in the mountains at this time," Rita said. "Have you seen other suspicious vehicles? Some of the neighbors mentioned kids playing pranks."

Joanne nodded. "Sure. Couple years ago the graduating class from the high school towed their principal's care over here, and his wife's — who's the librarian here at Parkland — over to the high school."

"Creative," Rita said.

"Yeah, well, Chester's nephew was the mastermind behind it, 'cause he had access to a tow truck, don't he?"

Rita gave an obliging nod. "Thanks for answering my questions, Joanne, and keeping Bertie out in this heat. Enjoy the rest of your day."

Joanne managed a feeble smile. "Thanks, Sheriff Jonas.

I'm looking forward to having a bath. 'Cause when the breeze changes direction — well, it's an odor I ain't gonna forget. And I feel like I have to wash it off of me."

Rita passed her a card. "Please call me if you think of anything else."

As Joanne collected herself, Rita returned to Jason, who was conferring with Tilda about the ground sweep.

Rita touched his shoulder. "Got a minute?"

He stepped away from Tilda. "Sure."

"I'm gonna go do the NOK," Rita said. "Thanks for staying at the crime scene. Hopefully we'll get some more hands, soon. Hunter is sending a list of officers to temporarily fill in for Walter."

"You think that's a good idea?" Jason asked.

"I know it's hard to trust Hunter's referral," Rita said. "That's why I'm going to choose from a list of candidates this time. Do my own background checks, if I have to."

"Okay," Jason said, sounding unsure.

"You know what?" Rita said. "You should be the one who chooses."

Jason looked at her. "Yeah?"

"You're gonna be working with this officer the most. Your input's going to matter in the review process."

Jason brightened. "That makes sense."

Rita slapped his shoulder. "See you later. Good luck with the flatbed." Then she raised her arm to wave at Tilda and Bruce. "Thanks, I'm heading out now."

"Hold up," Tilda said, jogging over, head-to-toe in Tyvek.

"See ya, Rita," Jason said, stepping away.

"What's up?" Rita asked, as Tilda nudged her several more paces out of earshot of Jason and the medical examiner.

Tilda's eyes narrowed. "So how far along are you?"

Rita stiffened. "What are you talking about?"

Tilda laughed. "You're talking to the head of forensics."

Rita frowned. "So what's your hypothesis, Head of Forensics?"

"It's not like you to barf. You found a guy with a severed head and didn't barf. I've seen you attend autopsies, then eat a meatloaf."

Rita tilted her chin. "I've barfed before at a crime scene."

"Sure. You and I both pitched out biscuits at that Alcova Lake accident, when we'd contracted salmonella at that diner. But this isn't food poisoning."

Rita eyed her. "It's not, huh?"

"Your boobs are bigger."

Rita looked down at her chest. "They are?"

"Half a cup size at least," Tilda said.

"Jesus, what else do you notice?"

"Your breath stinks."

Rita frowned. "That's because I was half asleep when I dragged myself out here. I forgot to brush my teeth."

"Then you should go back to bed." Tilda counted off on her fingers: "Changing hormones, increased blood production, lowered blood sugar, low blood pressure—"

"I'm trying to be discreet about this," Rita said, bugging her eyes at her.

"It's all good," Tilda said, I won't mention it again. "But if you need a doctor—"

She motioned for Rita to pass her the phone. She did, and Tilda opened the web browser and navigated to a doctor's webpage.

"If you need an appointment, let the practice know I recommended you."

"Thanks," Rita said. "I appreciate the support."

"Of course," Tilda said. "Becoming a parent is overwhelming enough, without the added overwhelm of losing one."

Rita tried to think of a response. But her head hurt. She gave Tilda a weak wave. "I got to go do Trevor Bachman's NOK. Then get back to help Jason."

"Or have a nap," Tilda called out after her.

Chapter Fifteen

Rita rolled along the curving street in Apex Hills, scanning for Trevor Bachman's address at thirty mph.

Each two-story vinyl-sided house was a look-alike to its neighbor, in varying shades of gray. No architectural details of any kind defined one address from the next; only its number affixed to the skinny pillars (these werecat least painted in an array of unique colors) propping up the miniature front porches, seemingly more decorative than functional. Compared to the Slaneys' mansion next to Frenchie's place, the houses in Apex Hills looked like dollhouses.

Rita found Trevor Bachman's address and slowed the cruiser. A neon, decaled moving pod stood in the front drive, like an alien spacecraft landed amidst the homogenous houses and minivans. Rita pulled onto the narrow strip of asphalt and parked behind the fluorescent cube.

A strip of orange lettering suggested that Rita, *Make a Move with EZ-Pod,'* followed by a purple toll-free number.

"Someone else leaving town," she said to herself.

"Maybe it's an omen that I should move back to New York."

But instead of driving to New York, she got out of the cruiser. On the front lawn was a pile of outdoor plastic children's toys marked "free."

Rita walked up to the front door and knocked. A jumble of children's shoes lay strewn across a doormat, and a fountain of petunias sprouted from an elephant-shaped plant pot.

A woman wearing a ponytail answered while bobbing a baby. Its head matched the size of each of the woman's breasts, as if she were juggling three watermelons.

She swallowed, looking over Rita with a wary gaze. "Yes?"

"Mrs. Bachman?"

The woman nodded. "I'm Shannon."

"I'm Sheriff Jonas," Rita said. "May I come in to have a talk?"

The woman shifted the baby to her other arm and pulled a lock of hair out of her eyes. "It's Trevor, isn't it?"

"Er, yes," Rita said, surprised at Shannon Bachman's preparedness.

Nodding and stepping back, the Shannon pulled open the door. She turned to bellow over her shoulder.

"Ma!"

A woman with sandy hair bustled into the foyer, stepping around a tower of cardboard boxes.

With one look at Rita, she gathered up the baby. "I'll take the boys out back." Then she bustled out as swift as she'd come.

"Benny, Corey! Get your trikes!"

"Busy morning around here," Rita said.

The woman wrung her hands, looking lost without the

baby. "We're getting ready to move." She motioned for Rita to follow. "Come on through to the kitchen."

They pushed through a swinging door.

"Coffee?" Shannon asked.

"No thanks," Rita said, passing up the offer of a stool. "Already filled up this morning."

She glanced around the corner of kitchen cabinetry into the adjoining living room. A forest-green sofa and cherry-wood coffee table were barely visible beneath what appeared to be the entire inventory of Toys "R" Us.

"Sorting toys for the yard sale?"

"Huh?" Shannon said. "Oh, you mean the junk on the front lawn? That's free for anyone who can use it."

Rita pointed. "I meant the toys in the living room."

Shannon gave a weak laugh. "Oh, that's the daily fall-out of having two on the go and one already picking up bad habits."

Rita's mouth felt dry. "They make that mess ... every day?"

Again, Shannon laughed, this time her voice stronger. "Of course. They're kids."

Rita forced a laugh. "It's not even noon."

Then she gave Shannon a warm smile.

And swallowed.

"Mrs. Bachman—"

Rita paused, noticing a framed photograph on the mantelpiece. She thread her way across the living room to retrieve a silver frame and returned to the kitchen.

She handed it to Shannon. "This is your husband, Trevor?" Rita asked, having recognized the man from his driver's license. He had been handsome, his eyes and smile open and trusting, before he'd swallowed poison.

Rita's voice caught. "You both look very happy here."

Shannon ran her thumbs over the two faces trapped

beneath the glass. "That's our wedding day," she said with a smile. But her jaw trembled.

"Let's have a seat," Rita said, gesturing to the kitchen table.

Without a word, as though again prepared for what Rita was about to say, Shannon slid onto the L-shaped breakfast bench. She hugged the framed photograph to her chest.

Rita took a seat on the other side, adjacent to her. This was the worst part of the job. Definitely worse than autopsies.

Inhale.

Exhale.

She cleared her throat, then met Shannon's eye. "I'm sorry to inform you, Shannon, that Trevor is dead."

A second of silence passed.

Then Shannon let out a wail, dropping her head onto the table to cry.

For a minute, Rita sat beside her, calming her own movements and breath. Then she got up, took a glass from the drying rack, and filled it at the sink. She tore off a sheet of paper towel and returned to the bench.

After a few minutes, Shannon took a shuddering breath. Rita passed her the glass of water and paper towel. Shannon dabbed her eyes with the towel, then drank half the cup of water.

"I knew Trevor was lying."

Shannon's sobs returned, then subsided a minute later.

"Lying about what?" Rita asked.

"I knew the chemo wasn't working. He said it was. That's why he was doing another round. He said it'd buy him another year or two."

"Trevor was undergoing chemotherapy?" Rita asked.

Shannon blinked at Rita. "Yes."

"And you don't think it was working?"

"Of course not. He looks like a ghost, doesn't he?" She pulled the frame away from her chest and regarded the couple. "I have a reoccurring nightmare about our bed turning into a coffin."

"That sounds very distressing," Rita said.

"Is he still at the Casper hospital?" Shannon asked.

"No," Rita said. "His body was found here in Still."

"Here? In Still?" More tears flowed from Shannon's eyes. "Does that mean he didn't make it to Casper for his session today?"

"No," Rita said.

"Then — was he — was he in pain? His Advance Directive outlines all his palliative preferences. I'm his Power of Attorney, but no one called me to discuss palliation."

Rita cleared her throat. "I'm sorry to inform you, Shannon, he died of unnatural causes."

Shannon's mouth fell open. "Not cancer?"

Rita shook her head. "No. We—"

"We knew the Cavalier was a bit of a junker, but Trevor had been replacing lots of parts. One of the CV boots was dodgy. And the tires are bald. But we didn't think they were that bad."

"Trevor died of a toxic substance."

Shannon's red eyes widened. "An overdose?"

"Possibly poison," Rita said. "We haven't ruled out foul play."

"Foul play? Poison? What are you saying?" Shannon's voice trembled. "Are you suggesting murder?"

"An autopsy is scheduled. I'll let you know when I know more."

"The chemo makes Trevor confused," Shannon said, gripping the framed photograph. "Maybe he mixed up a bottle of something he wasn't supposed to. Or a medical error. Sometimes the wrong meds are given to the wrong patient. Or the wrong dose."

Rita softened her voice. "I'm sorry to say, his body was found in the trunk of his Cavalier."

Shannon let out another wail, dropping the frame and burying her hands in her face.

"I'm sorry to ask you these questions," Rita said. "But when did you last see Trevor?"

Shannon sobbed for another minute, then cleared her tears enough to say: "Last night. When we went to bed."

"What time was that?" Rita asked.

Shannon thought for a moment, wiping her face on the paper towel. "Maybe eight? He went to bed before me because he had to get up early this morning. I gave the baby one last feed at nine, then joined him. He was already asleep."

"What was his reason for getting up early today?"

"The chemotherapy session in Casper. He leaves before the commuter traffic gets heavy."

"What times is that?"

"He usually goes by five. Gets his breakfast at the hospital cafeteria."

"Did you see him leave in the vehicle this morning?"

"No, I was still sleeping."

"So you couldn't be absolutely sure he left by five?"

Shannon stiffened. "Er... no."

"And he went alone?"

"Always," Shannon said, again stiff. "Of course I offered to go with him, like I always do. But Benny's cutting a tooth, and Corey's hell on wheels. Trev didn't think my mom could handle all three on her own."

"I'm glad she's here for you and the boys now," Rita said.

Shannon sniffled. "Yeah. She's been coming around most days, ever since Trevor was diagnosed terminal."

"How was he last night?"

"Now that you mention it, he seemed a bit on edge. But he was always a bit anxious before chemo."

"Do you know of anything else that's been on his mind?"

Shannon took a sip of water. "He's been tense for weeks. But that's understandable, right? He's in so much pain all the time. And his condition is terminal. Neither the cancer nor the chemo have been kind to him. He tried counselling at the church, but that didn't help. It all just seems horribly unfair."

"I'm sorry for his suffering. And yours." Rita forced a smile. "Will your mom be able to stay overnight with you?"

Blowing her nose, Shannon nodded. "Yes, we have a hide-away bed in the living room. She stays over lots. Like when the baby has a fever, and the boys or Trevor need care, too." She blew out a shuddering sigh. "What would any of us do without our moms, huh?"

"Mm," Rita said, noncommittal. "Goodbye, Shannon. I'll be in touch when I know more."

Shannon sniffed and nodded. "Okay."

Rita got up and moved towards the front door. "In the meantime, could you or your mom please send the station a list of contacts for Trevor?" She passed Shannon her card. "I'll ask Mary Lou at the station to watch for your email."

Shannon took the card. "You mean like his buddies and family?"

"Exactly," Rita said. "And anyone else you think it might be important to talk to. Did Trevor have a falling out with anyone?"

Shannon's face hardened. "If you mean did anyone

hold anything against Trevor, I don't think so. He was always helping out folks. Never said a bad thing about anyone. A real Good Samaritan type. But if you're asking if he had a bone to pick with anyone…" Her voice cracked. "Well, I can tell you one name: Apex."

Rita cringed. *Shit.* She forced her face to remain calm.

"Thank you, Shannon," she said. "Reach out for anything. Anything at all, okay? And I'll be in touch as soon as I know more."

Rita returned to the cruiser and sat behind the steering wheel, breathing. She glanced up at the house. Visible through the front window, Shannon's mother cradled her while the boys orbited around them.

Rita's heart contracted and she dragged her gaze away, to settle on the neon moving pod. A different line of orange letters assured Rita that *Moving with EZ-Pod is a* box-office *hit!*

Rita took out her phone and texted Jason: *NOK done. Stopping at Apex. Back soon.*

Then she called the doctor's office in Casper that Tilda had recommended.

"I'm sorry, ma'am, we're not taking new patients."

"That's not what my colleague, Tilda Keating, mentioned," Rita said. "She was sure I'd get an appointment."

There was a moment of silence, then the tapping of a keyboard.

"Miss Keating is Dr. Roseberg's patient," the receptionist said. "I'll schedule you with Dr. Roseberg, too. Does 7:45 work? She can fit you in before her other patients."

Rita felt her shoulders relax. "It works great."

Chapter Sixteen

Recognizing Rita, the guard at the Apex gate waved her through. She parked in front of to the modern glass building, the facade newly repaired since Helen had shot it up with a handgun.

Rita got out and entered the tiled foyer, which contained more potted plants than people. Another security guard gave Rita a familiar nod while the receptionist, Ginny, gave her a wave. Then Ginny pressed a button at her desk to call the elevator. By the time Rita walked up to it, the steel doors slid open to welcome her.

Rita stepped inside and rode to the top floor, where the executive offices were located. Ken Saunders now occupied Boyd Farmer's former office. She rapped on his door.

"Come in?" came a deep male voice.

She opened the door. "Nice digs," she said, appreciating the view of the rolling hills and distant mountains through the window. "Are congratulations in order?"

Ken moved some papers around on the desk. "Position's still temporary. I just needed some space to work."

He shrugged his massive shoulders, clad in a royal-blue sports jacket. "You know, to stretch out and work."

"I inherited a dead man's office too," Rita said. She waved a finger towards Ken's face. "What's the scratch on your face? Another late-night meet-up at the reservoir?"

Ken flushed. "Had a disagreement." He forced a laugh. "You should see the other guy."

"Well, I'd put a little baby oil on that," Rita said, "if you don't want a scar. But then, maybe a scar's the look you're going for. You're a tough guy."

Ken straightened in his chair, which looked nowhere near big enough. "To what do I owe this meeting, Sheriff?"

"I've just done an NOK for an Apex employee. Trevor Bachman."

Ken's fingers drifted past his scratch. "Sorry to hear that."

"It's sad that he's so young." Rita said, studying Ken.

His broad face reminded impassive. "Cancer's a senseless killer."

"Hm," Rita said, neither in agreement or disagreement. "When did you last see Trevor?"

Ken shrugged again. "Weeks ago. A few months, probably."

"Can you please look up when he officially went on leave?"

"He's not on leave," Ken said. "He's not even an employee anymore, actually."

Rita paused. "So that's why the family's moving?"

Ken nodded. "Can't live in the company housing if no one works for the company. In fact, it's been a bit of a problem getting them out of there."

"No doubt due to Trevor's medical needs and his wife caring for three children under age five," Rita said, cutting him a look. "Did Trevor quit? Or was he fired?"

"It was nothing personal," Ken said. "His whole department was shut down. He worked in one of the chemical labs."

"You remember him well," Rita said, "for not working in Human Resources."

Ken straightened his jacket. "It's part of my job to do escorts."

Rita's eyebrows shot up. "Escorts? What does that refer to?"

Ken frowned at her. "I walk out the employees, if there's a Personnel Optimization."

"Say that again?"

"Personnel Optimization?"

"Yeah," Rita said. "What the hell does that mean?"

"It means that the research project he was working got discontinued, and the resources in his department where being redirected into a new project."

"And so Trevor was redirected to unemployment?"

"It was his choice," Ken said. "Personnel Optimization offers two options: a new job at equal or lesser pay, or a payout."

"What's the payout?" Rita asked.

"Four weeks wages."

"That's it?" Rita asked. "For termination?"

"It's not termination, it's optimization. Most employees choose the new job."

"So why didn't Trevor?" Rita asked.

Ken blinked at her. "Well, I don't know. I just walked the guy out."

"There must have been a reason he turned down the job offer," Rita said. "Can you look it up?"

Ken tapped on his keyboard. "A copy of his Letter of Offer is in his file." He clicked the mouse to open the document, then read the screen for a moment. "He was offered a waste disposal job at a lower pay scale." He read for another few seconds. "Also the option to be a delivery driver, providing he got the right training and license."

"In other words," Rita said, "he got the short end of the stick. Did he take any medical leave during his employment term here?"

Ken sighed and tapped some more keys. "This is a lot of questions about a guy who hasn't worked here in a while."

"He's deceased."

"I'll have the company send a card."

"He died under suspicious circumstances."

This time Ken's eyebrows shot up. "What?"

"His body was found in the trunk of a car at Parkland Elementary."

"Jesus," Ken said. He turned back to his computer screen. "I'll email you a copy of Trevor's employment record."

"Perfect," Rita said, "I appreciate that."

But in everything in her gut told her a snarl of red tape would prevent Ken from actually sending any records or answering any further questions about Apex real estate properties or their employee benefits packages.

"In the meantime," she continued, "if you think of anything to tell me, you know what to do."

Ken nodded. "Can't think of anything."

Standing, Rita smiled. "But if you do…"

Ken forced a smile of his own. "You bet, Rita. Sheriff Jonas."

"Have a good day, Ken."

Then she walked out of his office, rode down the elevator, and exited reception with a final wave to Ginny.

Outside, warm sunshine bathed her face, and the

breeze carried the scent of dry sagebrush. And for the first time in days, Rita didn't feel nauseated.

Chapter Seventeen

For a moment, Rita sat in the cruiser, looking up at the giant red A-P-E-X running along the roofline, unable to shake the feeling that Ken was holding back.

She pulled out her phone. A text from Cash — he wanted to talk. Her thumb hovered over the keys. Then she called Mary Lou instead.

"Is Carole still there?"

"Nope," Mary Lou said. "And nope, I ain't got no idea where she went."

Rita made a noise in her throat.

"Otto's obituary is done," Mary Lou said.

"Already?" Rita said. "Thanks."

"He'd written one a few years back. In case anything ever happened to him on the job."

Rita paused. "And you knew about this?"

"Of course," Mary Lou said. "If anything happened to him, I'd be the one sending it into the paper, right?"

"But you didn't say anything to me?"

"Well, who knew if it was any good? I had to read the damn thing first."

"Was it?" Rita asked.

"It was fine," Mary Lou said. "Short. Simple. Concise."

"And somewhat morbid," Rita said.

It was Mary Lou's turn to make a noise in her throat. "Morbid? I'd say it's practical. Your father was a practical kind of guy."

For a moment, Rita thought in silence. Then, "Do you think I should write one?"

"What, write your own obituary?"

"Yeah," Rita said. "In case anything happens on the job?"

Mary Lou blew her lips like a horse. "Oh, go on, now! So do you want me to email you Otto's obituary?"

"Could you please send it directly to the funeral home?" Rita asked. "Care of Dustin Ashbury?"

"Don't you want to read it first?" Mary Lou asked.

"Not really."

"All right, then, consider it done. By the way, Marnie gave me the code."

Rita paused. "Code?"

"For the lock. Marnie's moved into the new millennium. Says she only installs keyless-entry deadbolts for residential jobs these days. The override key is on your kitchen table, along with the bill. The code to get in is 1-6-0-3. Which is obvious, I suppose."

Rita's breath caught in her throat. "Obvious? I was going to ask you how Marnie knew?"

"Everyone knew Otto's favorite number," Mary Lou said.

Rita's mouth went dry. "Otto's favorite number?"

"He damn well used that number for nearly everything. His locker downstairs. His lottery ticket picks. But I'm sure you can change it easily enough if you like."

"No, no," Rita said, "it's perfect. That number is my birthday. March 16th."

Mary Lou let out a whistle. "Well, I'll be damned. So it is."

"I'm headed back to the crime scene now," Rita said. "I'll see you later at HQ."

"Ten-four," Mary Lou said, hanging up.

Rita started the ignition and pulled out of the Apex lot. When she arrived at Parkland Elementary School, Trevor Bachman's Cavalier was in the process of being loaded onto a flatbed. She parked the cruiser in the lot and headed across the field.

"Nearly done here," Jason said as Rita approached.

Rat eyed the tow truck. "All the big toys are out today."

Jason rubbed at the sweat under his collar. "Now that the car's up, Tilda's organized to cut away the sod under the vehicle."

"But I don't imagine I'll find much there," Tilda said, approaching. She'd peeled off her Tyvek and packed up her camera. "The ground looks untouched. I suspect this is a body dump and not a murder scene."

"When Tilda's finished," Rita said to Jason, "you can release the scene."

"Ten-four," Jason said. "I'm going with the flatbed to Casper, to keep continuity of the Chevy. Haven't had time to get to the door-to-doors."

"No problem," Rita said, "I'll go canvas for witnesses."

Parkland Elementary School stood at the end of the road, backing onto a broad green belt of birch, though the leaves now shimmered like yellow coins in the late summer conditions. Across the street, a row of two-story bungalows, built some sixty years ago, lined the block, their views of the school partially obscured by quivering aspen, not yet bedecked in fall colors like their brethren. Only the last house had a clear sightline over the school and into the field beyond.

Rita stepped off the sidewalk and made her way up the path to the front door.

A woman in her sixties answered the door. "Hello?"

"Good afternoon, I'm Sheriff Jonas," Rita said. "Have you heard about this morning's incident?"

She pressed a hand to her chest. "Oh, yes, the whole street was aflutter. Len from next door let me know about the car out in the field. I walked over sometime around eleven."

"I noticed several bystanders," Rita said with an edge. "Did you chat with your other neighbors about the event?"

"Oh, yes," she said. "We figured it was drugs. Of course we couldn't hear anything at that distance, but we could see that the trunk was open."

Rita gave a tight smile. "Crime tape keeps civilians at a distance for good reason." Then she twisted on the stoop, pointing over her shoulder. "You have a clear view of the school. Did you notice any activity this morning? Perhaps the car arriving?"

The woman shook her head. "Nope, didn't notice. I was quilting this morning. I'm trying to finish my grandbaby's blanket before the due date."

"Did you overhear traffic this morning?"

The woman thought for a moment. "This street is real quiet. I remember hearing a vehicle while I was making breakfast. That was probably Hal." She wagged a finger to the left, then the right. "Hal's on this side, Len's on the other."

"What time was that?" Rita asked.

The woman thought again. "About seven-thirty."

"And during the night?" Rita asked. "Do you recall any noises or headlights disturbing your sleep?"

"Oh, no, I sleep very soundly," the woman said. "I use an eye mask and earplugs. Have for years. Though my doctor says the foam earplugs are compacting my earwax and they'll make me hard of hearing before old age."

"Right," Rita said.

"I probably would have slept through a burglar in my kitchen," she said.

"Well, thank you for your time," Rita said. "Enjoy your evening."

Then she worked her way down the rest of the street. Residents of half the houses were home, mostly parents of young children or seniors. But no one had heard or seen anything of note. To them, it had been a typical, tranquil Wednesday night.

She returned to the cruiser and drove to Apex Hill, scanning for anything out of place or unusual. But again, she saw nothing.

When she arrived at Trevor's house, there were several cars in the driveway and along the curb. Figures moved inside the house, visible through the living room window; Trevor's family was making its own funerary preparations, as Rita was.

Only no one was filling up Otto's house. Her house. Not the way they had the night of his birthday.

A block up the road Rita pulled up to the curb. Idling, she checked her messages. Walter had left condolences for Otto, so she messaged him back, thanking him and giving him the date and time of the funeral.

I'll be there, he messaged back, then sent another one: *Thanks for signing off on my leave.*

Of course, Rita returned. Walter and Winnie had nearly lost their son, a pain too unbearable to think about. Another good reason not to have a kid, not that she was keeping track.

She typed another message: *I hope you're all doing well. Give my best to Adrian.*

Walter thumbs-upped her message.

Then she flicked through the other messages, most of them offering condolences. Next, she listened to the voice message left by an unknown number. It was Carole, stating she was in town. Rita deleted the message without replying.

When she arrived at the SCSO, she saw Cash's black GM parked out front. She felt the temptation to drive away. Maybe all the way back to New York, but instead she pulled into the parking lot behind the building.

Rita pulled the cruiser into the lot behind the building, parked beneath the cherry tree, and beside the fence. She paused. It wasn't too late to go to New York. All she had to do was call up Dale (and find another doctor).

Rita popped the door and trudged through the back door. In the bullpen, Cash was talking to Mary Lou, leaning over her desk, looking casual with his sleeves rolled up.

Something stirred in Rita's belly, and she told the butterflies to calm down.

"Hi, Cash," she said.

He looked up and smiled, then rearranged his facial expression into a sympathetic one. "How's it going?"

"Fine," Rita said.

He raised an eyebrow. "Fine?"

Rita's cheeks grew hot. "Yes, fine. What's wrong with fine?"

Cash gave her a look. "Only that your dad just died."

Mary Lou cleared her throat.

Rita glanced at her, then glared when she saw the look on Mary Lou's face.

Rita's gaze snapped back to Cash. "What's going on here?"

Then she glanced back at Mary Lou. "What are you talking two talking about?"

Then she looked back at Cash. "How can we help you?"

"Jesus, Rita," Cash said, "you sound on edge."

"Do you know what I've done today? Or yesterday, for that matter?"

Cash raised his palms in a peaceful manner. "Look, why don't we talk about this later, huh? Mary Lou's already helped me out. I needed the police file number for my insurance claim."

"Of course," Rita said, feeling the heat in her cheeks. She gave Cash a tight smile. "Glad we could help you."

Mary Lou cleared her throat again.

Rita looked at her. Then looked back at Cash. "Where are you staying?"

Cash hesitated, then moistened his lips. "With Heather."

Rita tensed. "I see."

"But he'd rather stay with you," Mary Lou said, bugging her eyes.

Rita cut her a look, then cocked her head to admire the halftone portrait of Elvis emblazoned across her t-shirt.

"That vintage?"

Mary Lou puckered her lips. "Don't change the subject."

Rita shook her head. "Look, it feels weird enough to be in Otto's house right now, okay? I don't want anyone around. Not Carole. Or you, Cash." She shrugged. "I just need some space."

"Jason's around."

"It's not personal, Cash. But you're…"

His gaze hardened. "What? I'm what?"

Rita glanced at Mary Lou's, whose gaze was equally narrowed on Rita.

"You're part of my past. Like Otto. And Carole. But Jason's part of my present."

Cash bristled. "I'd like to be part of your future."

"Jesus," Rita said, frowning. "Can we talk about this somewhere else?"

Cash's gaze softened. "Of course."

Rita sighed. "I'm sure I'll feel more settled when I've cleaned out the place."

"I'll help you," Mary Lou said, swinging around to face her computer. "I'll arrange a clean-up Sign-Up Genius." Her fingers tapped on the keyboard, navigating to the app. "A big family house like that needs an overhaul every spring. And I can tell you, your father wasn't doin' that. Shame it was just Otto in there, all by himself."

"Apparently Helen was there," Rita said.

Mary Lou clucked her tongue. "Well, either way, that place should have a baby's room in it."

Rita stared at her. "Really?"

Cash looked between them. "What?"

Rita blew out a breath.

Exhale.

And stomped into her office.

Chapter Eighteen

Rita dropped into the chair at Otto's desk.

Otto's desk.

She wondered when she was going to stop calling it his and start calling it hers. She'd occupied his office for some time now, and she ought to be comfortable laying claim to it. Especially now that he'd passed.

The paperwork on the desk, at least, she knew was all hers. And yet she felt no responsibility to take care of it.

She was rearranging the pile of unopened mail when the telephone on her desk rang. The call was coming in from Casper PD.

"Sheriff Jonas," Rita said, feeling eerie to be using her father's name even though it was her own. A chill ran up her spine.

But she didn't believe in ghosts.

"It's me," Jason said over the line. "I'm still with the Chevy in Casper. I was about to head back, but since the autopsy's taking place here tomorrow, do you want me to stay overnight and preside?"

"No," Rita said, "come on back to Still. I need to head

to Casper for personal business tomorrow morning anyways. I'll watch Bruce do his magic."

Jason gave her a level look. "I can get this one, Sheriff."

Rita read a note of annoyance in his voice. "You can get the next one," she said, her voice light. Then she hung up.

She chewed on her lip. Maybe she should have let Jason take the autopsy. It sounded like he wanted it. The only reason she wanted it was to have an excuse to stay in Casper for the day so as not to run into Carole.

And why the hell was that woman back in town anyway?

She was probably hoping Otto had left her something in the will. Or that she was legally entitled to some of his property.

Speaking of which, a copy of the will was kept in Otto's safety deposit box at the bank. That was one detail of the man's preparations that she'd known. What she didn't know was the location of the original.

Rita got back up from her desk and re-entered the bullpen.

"Hey," she said to Mary Lou, "I'm going to the bank. Then I'm going to go home to pack for Casper. Won't see you tomorrow."

Mary Lou stopped typing, though she continued to face the computer. "You joining Jason for the autopsy?"

Rita shook her head. "I'm going to handle it. He's on his way back now."

Mary Lou nodded, then dabbed at her nose with a tissue.

Rita approached. "Is something the matter, Mary Lou?"

Mary Lou looked up and stared at her, eyes red and

puffy. The screen-printed Elvis on her t-shirt stared at Rita too.

"Otto, of course," Mary Lou said. "Grief has a way of sneaking up on you, don't it?"

Rita gave a somber nod.

"I'm worried about you," Mary Lou added.

Rita frowned. "Worried? Why?"

"You don't seem to be processing your father's death very well."

"I'm doing very well. In fact, I'd say great. I'm back at work, aren't I?"

Mary Lou mirrored Rita's frown. "That's the problem."

"What's that mean?" Rita said.

"You're processing your dad's death like the way you process paperwork," Mary Lou said with a grumble. "Which is to say not at all."

Rita made a non-committal sound and headed out the back door.

Back at Otto's, she initiated the new lock by punching in her birthdate, then picked up his safety deposit key, which he kept in the top drawer of his bedside table alongside his passport and every other piece of sensitive information he'd possessed.

Rita clucked her tongue. "You'd have never made it in New York, Dad."

In the guest room, she packed her backpack with fresh clothes.

Her phone pinged: Mary Lou.

You're booked at the Best Western, the text read. *Don't forget Cash's noggin needs a pillow these days.*

Rita sent back a begrudging *Thx*. Then she headed back out to her Honda and drove to the bank.

She found a spot to park on the street in front of downtown Still branch of the Wyoming Valley State Bank, which occupied a tan, brick building with a flat roof (an earmark of its mid-century heritage). Black paint on the windowsills and trim were an obvious attempt to update the facade.

Rita went inside, her shoes echoing. She cut in line at the tellers' windows.

"Excuse me," she said to the customer at the window, then said to the teller, who was a well-endowed woman wearing a thick slick of lipstick and a nametag that read *BEV*. "I'll only be a minute." Then she turned to Bev. "I'd like to access a safe deposit box, please."

Puckering her lips, Bev looked over Rita's uniform. "Are you here on a personal matter?"

"Yes," Rita said. "The box is my deceased father's."

The customer whom Rita had cut off let out an impatient sigh.

"I'll see if Mr. Slaney is available," Bev said. "But if this isn't an investigation, I can't promise he'll be available. He is often very busy."

"Is he now?" Rita said. She crooked her fingers to make air-quotes. "I wonder if his 'busy' is as busy as my 'busy.'"

"I imagine so," Bev said. "One minute."

She bustled to the phone on the wall and punched in an extension. Her raspberry lips moved too rapidly to read, then she bustled back to Rita.

"He'll be out momentarily." Bev pointed to an empty teller's window at the end of the counter. "He'll meet you there."

Rita walked to the window. A minute later, a man approached the counter. He wore a casual summer suit, his shirt-collar unbuttoned, his hair long.

"Hello, Sheriff Jonas? I'm Aiden Slaney."

"Hi," Rita said. "I need to get into Otto Jonas's box to access my dad's will, please."

"There're some protocols to follow," Slaney said. He cleared his throat. "Which I'm sure you of all people can understand." He slid his gaze to the computer monitor and typed. "I can see some information in your father's records without accessing his account."

For a moment he read, then he licked his lips and shifted his gaze from the monitor to Rita. "You're not on his access card."

Rita leaned against the counter. "No."

"Then I'll need to see his death certificate," Slaney said, displaying he was in possession of more style than manners.

Rita moistened her lips. "It hasn't been issued yet."

Slaney folded his hands on the countertop. "Then I'm unable to help you, Sheriff."

"Is there another way to access the box?"

The manager gave her a look.

"I can assure you I'm not doing anything untoward," Rita said.

"Of course not," the manager said. He smiled with his teeth. "And I am merely conducting myself according to the protocol of my profession."

Rita lowered her brows at him. "Well, according to the protocol of my profession, my dad's dead body is over at the morgue right now. Would you like to take a look? Will that do?"

The manager frowned. "I don't find your dark sense of humor to be humorous, Sheriff Jonas. Estate law is serious business. And I require a death certificate to access your father's safe deposit box. Then, *Miss* Jonas, I'll be able to help you."

Rita bit down on her lip. "All right." Then she moistened her lips. "Could you tell me what you know about Frenchie, please?"

The manager flinched. "Who?"

"Frenchie."

"I don't know anyone by that name," Slaney said.

"That's your neighbor."

"Oh, that fellow. I hardly notice him.

"Even though he's your neighbor?"

Slaney shifted. "We have a large hedge." Then he threw Rita a look. "I like my privacy."

"I saw the hedge," Rita said. "Very large. Have you noticed any strange lights in the sky lately?"

"Is this a light pollution complaint? Because I already talked to that woman across the street about our patio lanterns shining in though her bathroom window at night."

"Hedge doesn't hide 'em?" Rita asked.

Frenchie shifted. "Not the ones on the roof balcony."

"Don't worry," Rita said. "There're no complaints about your patio lanterns." She flashed him a smile. "Thanks for your time."

Then she got back to her Honda and drove into Casper, still considering New York as an option.

In the rearview mirror, she spotted a black Toyota Camry. While maintaining an even distance, it had kept close since Still. Tracking her lane changes. Quite possibly following her.

Or was she simply paranoid, after Marcus Dwyer and his minivan? She slowed and the Camry kept pace. Her breath caught.

Inhale.

But then it passed her. Although with tinted windows, Rita couldn't identify the driver. A quarter mile ahead, it took an exit ramp and disappeared.

"Shit," Rita said on the exhale.

Chapter Nineteen

The Best Western was beginning to feel like a second home for Rita.

She requested a room change to the ground floor, on account of her legs (and her stomach) feeling like Jell-O. She hoped she didn't throw up in the hotel room.

She checked in, barely a word to the receptionist whom, at this rate, Rita should probably invite to a baby shower if things progressed that far.

She shuffled into room 112 and unpacked her bag. Her stomach growled. And yet she didn't feel hungry. She couldn't remember when she last ate. She could only recall the acidic taste of strawberry tea the second time around.

Rita returned to the lobby and walked through to the hotel's small diner, called Chauncey's Country Fare. Dark vinyl booths and bent-wood chairs lent a homespun vibe, as did the soft hum of conversation mingling with the clatter of plates. At the aroma of hearty fries, Rita's mouth watered.

"That's better," Rita said to her organs, hoping her digestive system had come back online.

The host approached with a menu and pitcher of water.

"Dining alone?" the young man asked.

Rita nodded, then he led he towards a row of tables by the window. He gestured to one of the tables with the menu. "How's this?"

Rita looked at her choice of bent wood chairs, then glanced at the cozy-looking booths on the back wall.

"I'll take one of the booths," she said.

The host displayed a toothy smile. "Couples and singles we sit here by the window." He waved the menu again. "There's a real nice view."

Rita ducked her head to peek beneath the valance. "Of the parking lot."

The host swallowed, his Adam's apple wobbling. "The booths are reserved for families, ma'am."

"I'm a family," Rita said, rubbing her belly. "I'm a duo."

The host flushed ketchup-red and led Rita to the booth in the corner.

"Thanks," she said, sinking into the cushion. "My backside's sore from the drive into town."

Then the host's neck flushed, too, and he departed without a word, leaving behind a menu and a glass of iced water.

Rita chugged the water while looking over the menu. But not even lasagna appealed to her, which was her usual because it was hard to mess up cheese and ground beef. She closed the menu and sighed. Even the fries smelled too greasy, now.

When the server arrived (a young woman with a top knot), Rita ordered a refill of ice water, a ginger ale, and a side of garlic bread.

The server printed Rita's order on a notepad. "And for the main course?"

Rita peeked inside the menu again, then shook her head. "Just the garlic bread, thanks."

The server closed her notebook. "Righto." Then she picked up the menu and scuffed away.

"Wait," Rita said.

The server paused.

"I'll take two orders of garlic bread, please."

The server diligently wrote Rita's request on her notepad, then reread it: "One ginger ale and two orders of garlic bread?"

Rita nodded. "I'm eating for two."

The server blinked at Rita. "D'you want two ginger ales?"

Rita thought for a moment. "Why not?"

The server made a notation, then scuffed away again. Rita sat back against the vinyl upholstery, scanning the restaurant. Though a popular dining spot, the crowd was a casual one, patrons arriving after putting in an honest day's work.

Movement by the door caught her eye, and she spotted a familiar figure.

A tall man wearing a gray suit stood by the host's kiosk, adjusting his silk tie as his eyes adjusted to the dim interior. When he spotted Rita, he approached the booth.

She sighed and hunched forward, resting her elbows on the table.

Alan Crenshaw looked down at her and smiled. "May I join you?"

"That seat's taken," she said.

The server returned, carrying two ginger ales. She set them both down in front of Rita.

"Thank you," Rita said, picking up one of the cups

and setting it on the far side of the table. She cut her eyes at Alan. "See?"

The server gave Rita a puzzled look, then left.

Alan laughed. "I know you're alone, Sheriff." He slid into the booth. "I'm aware of your movements."

Rita leaned back and crossed her arms. "So it's one of Tom's goons in that black Camry I've been seeing. I should have known."

Alan smirked. "What gave him away?"

"He's smart. Always stays just far enough out of sight, then passes at high speed. I haven't gotten a good enough look at his plates to look him up."

"Your friendly follower is Tom's decision, not mine."

"Of course," Rita said. "Big Daddy Thomas always makes the decisions. You're just the yes man, aren't you, Alan?"

Alan's face remained placid, as did his voice. "Thomas Gabriel would like to speak with you. That's all."

"Well, that's obvious," Rita said, as the server returned with two steaming plates of garlic bread. "That's the only reason you and I ever cross paths. I appreciate you not seeing the need to blindfold me in a minivan."

The server bugged her eyes at Rita, then Alan, and set a plate in front of each of them. Then she left without a word.

Rita dragged the plate from Alan's side of the table to hers and picked up the piece, which equaled the size of her shoe. "So what's Tommy want to talk about?"

Alan moved the glass of ginger ale in front of Rita as well. "He can tell you himself."

Rita frowned. "That's not the typical line. You're his mouthpiece."

"Not this time."

"Well, no thanks." Rita bit into the piece of garlic

bread. A flake of crust flew through the air. "Not until you return my prisoner."

Alan face reminded composed. "I don't know anything about Max Bannister."

"I don't believe you," Rita said, taking another bite. "For one, his name rolls off your tongue pretty damn easy. I'd bet he's been a hot topic of conversation lately."

"Feel free to place all the bets you'd like," Alan said with a sly smile. "But that doesn't change the facts of the matter."

Rita scowled at him and took another bite of toast. "I don't know what facts you're talking about, but I do know you're ruining my supper."

Alan chuckled, raising his hands in surrender. "All right, Sheriff, you win. We can play this game your way." He reached into his breast pocket and pulled out a brass case for business cards. "When you're ready to talk, you can reach out to me."

Rita tore off another chunk of garlic bread. "I don't need that."

Alan dropped the card on the table. "You will."

"What's that supposed to mean?"

"It means I'm Otto's estate lawyer."

Rita choked on her mouthful. She gulped some ginger ale and swallowed the wad, burning the back of her eyeballs.

She coughed. "What?"

Alan passed her the glass of water. "Mind the ice cubes."

Rita grunted and accepted the glass.

"Otto's original will is held with me," Alan said, getting up from the booth. Then he turned and walked away.

Rita flung back her head against the booth cushion. "Fuck."

Stuffing more garlic bread into her mouth, she chewed angrily. Why the hell did Otto hire Alan Crenshaw, of all people? She shoved the card in her pocket, covered in butter stains from her fingers.

She drained the first glass of ginger ale and bit into the second piece of garlic bread (now cold) as a text came in from Tilda:

Jason says you're in town. We're grabbing a bite before he leaves. Want to meet us?

Rita wiped her hands clean, then messaged back: *Already ate, thx. Going to bed. C U tomorrow after my appt. with Dr. Roseberg.*

Tilda thumbs-upped the message, then replied, *Sleep well, I remember first trimester exhaustion. BTW I e-mailed photos of the body in situ.*

Rita returned the thumbs up, then ignored the unread messages stacking up.

She finished the second piece of garlic bread (despite its now rubbery texture), then gave her room number for the tab and returned to 112.

Kicking off her shoes, she crossed to the window. The Camry was in the lot, parallel parked along the back row so that its plates were not visible. She pulled the blind, then sat and opened her laptop.

She scrolled through the photos Tilda had sent. An agonized expression distorted Trevor Bachman's face. Or what was left of it. Most of his lips and nose had been eaten away by the chemical.

Another photograph showed an empty stainless steel drinking vessel found next to Trevor's body. Tilda posited that it held the chemical (to be determined). Shuddering, Rita closed the laptop. What the hell had Trevor been involved with that he'd wound up like this?

Rita groaned, put away her laptop, and lay back on the

bed. She scrolled through her phone, ignoring the notifications. The only person she could think about messaging was Cash.

She needed to tell him. So why hadn't she?

Because she hadn't decided what to do yet.

Which seemed trickier to figure out, now that he was staying at Heather's, his ex-wife's. And her ex-husband was Rita's missing prisoner.

Rita rolled over and groaned. It was all too complicated for comfort. And yet the only thing that would bring her comfort was if Cash held her in his arms. She knew that if she asked him to come stay with her in Casper, he would. So why didn't she?

She leaned over the bedside table and plugged in her phone. Then she rolled off the bed and trudged into the bathroom to brush her teeth. Garlic and ginger still coated her tongue, and she found herself wishing for some of Otto's expired Listerine.

At the moment, the Best Western was officially the closest thing to home that Rita knew.

Chapter Twenty

Rita walked into Tilda's office. Her head was bent over her laptop as she closely studied the screen.

She looked up removed her reading glasses. "How did it go with Dr. Roseberg this morning?"

Rita shrugged. "As to be expected. I gave some pee. I asked some questions. Then she gave me a pamphlet to read."

"Which means you still haven't decided," Tilda said.

"Which means I have some reading to do," Rita said, taking a seat in front of Tilda's desk.

Tilda kept her expression neutral. "How are you feeling?"

Rita shrugged. "Hungry."

"Do you want to go down to the cafeteria?"

Rita shook her head. "Nah, nothing appeals to me."

"Nauseated, huh?" Tilda got up from her desk. "We'll skip going over the photos today and just talk."

"Sure," Rita said. "Not that I think that's going to be much better. Have you determined the substance in the stainless-steel water bottle?"

"Trevor Bachman swallowed a very concentrated solution of lye," Tilda said.

Rita's eyes widened. "Lye?"

Tilda nodded, grim. "And it's making my job damn tricky because it's hard to neutralize. Who knows what evidence it's continuing to eat through and what it already has dissolved."

"Shit," Rita said.

"In terms of physical evidence," Tilda said, "the lye was all over Bachman's hands and arms, so if he was attacked, any DNA that might have been there is probably now gone. However, I'm hoping to get a swab for the lip of a disposable coffee cup we found in the car interior."

"Was it branded with The Bighorn Bean logo?" Rita asked.

"No branding. It was a plain white waxed one, the kind we usually find in a corporate setting."

"Anything else in the car?"

"Though a bit of a beater, the Cavalier's quite clean," Tilda said, "held together with a liberal amount of duct tape. However, we did hit paydirt. I found a hair on the driver's seat headrest, which we've sent for DNA testing."

Rita raised her brow. "Not a match to Bachman's?"

"Nope. It's brown and clipped short to one inch," Tilda said. "That resemble any family members?"

"Nope," Rita said. "They're a sandy-blond crew."

"Kids, huh?" Tilda asked. She let out a breath. "Shit, I was hoping he wasn't the dad."

"What do you mean?" Rita asked.

"Kids' prints," Tilda said. "All over the back seat. And I mean all over, which makes me question the physics of children's car seats."

"Benny and Corey," Rita said. "Bachman's got two toddlers and a baby."

"Good God," Tilda said, her voice tight. She blew out a breath, then continued. "Over on the passenger side, we have unidentified adult prints."

"Probably his wife Shannon's," Rita said. "I'll get exclusion prints."

Tilda nodded. "And the rest appear to match to Bachman. We've got lots to work with. The vehicle is covered in them. Unusual for a body drop, not to be wiped clean."

"Also unusual the vehicle wasn't incinerated or submerged," Rita said. "Find anything in the sod?"

"Tire tracks indicate the vehicle slowly rolled across the field, then gently came to a stop."

"There must have been footprints around the vehicle. Half the field is dirt. And someone abandoned that car."

Tilda shook her head. "We've got a couple stuff marks on the driver's side, but no evident impressions."

"How about that water bottle?" Rita asked. "Fingerprints on that?"

"Those belong to Bachman, too."

Rita paused. "What?"

"Either the perpetrator was wearing gloves," Tilda said, "or Bachman was forced to drink the lye himself."

Rita fell silent as she considered Trevor's last moments. "Trevor Bachman seemed well loved by his family. A good father. What the hell happened to him? How will his kids deal with——?"

Her voice broke off.

"Somehow they'll know what to do with this world when they inherit it," Tilda said.

Rita looked at her. "Who? What do you mean?"

"Kids. The next generation," Tilda said. "I used to be scared to bring a kid into the world. And for a while after Bennett was born, I wondered if I'd made it a mistake: mass shootings, carjackings, home invasions."

She went quiet for a moment. "But it's okay." She nodded towards Rita's abdomen. "It's their world now. And I guess they'll know what to do with it."

Rita rubbed her belly. "I hate guessing."

Chapter Twenty-One

From the Casper PD, Rita drove to the hospital.

She rode the elevator downstairs to the morgue, where the receptionist waved her through to the autopsy room. Overhead fluorescent fixtures flooded the room in ice-cold light, bleaching away shadows. The unsettling scent of antiseptic cleaners masked the underlying odor of musty, metallic decay.

Rita swallowed her bile, gave Dylan Bruce a weak smile, and pulled on a blue disposable mask.

The medical examiner looked at her over there frame of his eyeglasses and nodded. "Afternoon, Rita." Bruce had already masked- and gloved-up. But the stainless-steel slab between them was empty.

She glanced along the bank of sinks behind her. "No body?"

"Still in the drawer," Bruce said. "Trevor Bachman's body is in a particularly sensitive state. It's severely decomposed and losing structure every day." He laid out a series of photographs on the table, each one capturing different angles of the victim's injuries. "If you fancy a review next week, you're gonna be looking at pictures of a puddle."

Rita's stomach flopped. She should have let Jason take this autopsy.

"Let's get to it," she said.

Bruce began the recording by stating today's date, then the date of the murder. He continued, "The estimated time of death is between 4 and 6 a.m. Based on the autopsy findings and toxicology reports, the cause of Trevor Bachman's death is determined to be acute poisoning due to ingestion of a caustic substance, specifically sodium hydroxide, commonly known as lye soap."

"Death by lye," Rita said, her voice hollow. "Tilda mentioned the water bottle that contained it."

"It would have been horrendously painful," Bruce said. "If I can give you any good news, it's that the victim would have passed away within minutes of ingestion, given the amount he swallowed."

"Which was?"

"Significant enough to render it impossible to discern *how* much. Let's just say, the clocksmith used a sledgehammer for the job."

"Jesus," Rita said, swallowing an acidic hiccup. "How much would be necessary?"

"Depends on the strength of concentrate," Bruce said. "But not more than a few teaspoons at domestic strength. Even less at industrial strength."

"Which is?" Rita asked.

"Fifty percent concentrate. Household lye is somewhere closer to twenty."

Rita suppressed a shudder. "Any way to tell which version he ingested?"

Bruce shook his head. "No. The only story I can work with is the path of decomposition through the body."

"Which tells what?" Rita asked.

"The pattern of corrosion indicates self-ingestion."

Rita's throat constricted. "Voluntary? Or was he forced to drink the lye?"

"Whether or not he drank it at gunpoint, I can't tell you," Bruce said. "And any bruises or defensive wounds that might have been on his arms have been eaten away. If he'd resisted drinking it, I'd expect a lateral pattern of burns to his lips and cheeks, both internally and externally. Instead, the pattern of corrosion suggests the lye entered in a stream, not a spray." He used a gloved finger to indicate a path along his own cheekbone, and down his throat. "The burns travel along the tissues this way."

"And those burn marks we see on him externally, are they internal too?" Rita asked.

"I'm afraid so," Bruce said. "Sodium hydroxide burns any tissues in contact, in this case causing immediate pain to the abdomen, particularly the chest. Which leads to spontaneous vomiting. Not to mention difficulty swallowing and breathing. In other words, he aspirated his own melting flesh. The corrosive injury to the mouth, throat, esophagus, and stomach were all extremely rapid, both narrowing and perforating the gastrointestinal tract, which lead to organ failure. Although I suspect things never progressed that far, given his heart was close to the bubbling cauldron."

Rita's voice caught. "The poor guy."

Bruce looked at her over her glasses. "There's more."

Rita swallowed. "Really?"

"He's got an open wound in his back, and I extracted something you're gonna want to see." Bruce retrieved a tray from the counter behind him and used forceps to pick up the small triangle of metal. "The tip of a blade."

Rita blinked. "You're kidding?"

"I estimate this occurred several hours before Trevor wound up in the trunk."

"And it was definitively the lye that killed him?" Rita said, for the record, "and not the stab wound or being shut in the trunk?"

Bruce nodded. "Definitely."

Rita blew out a breath, which caused her mask to inflate like a miniature parachute. "So before this guy swallowed lye as the sun comes up, someone already tried to stab him in the wee hours of the morning?"

"Yes," Bruce said. "Or possibly the late hours of the evening."

"If there's a possibility Bachman self-ingested the lye," Rita asked, "could he have self-inflicted this wound, too?"

"No," Bruce said. "The angle doesn't work. Nor the direction of the wound. The knife lodged in the spinous process of T3, directly between the shoulder blades."

"Bachman didn't take the easy road out of here," Rita said. "What about his cancer? What did the autopsy show there?"

Bruce's eyes softened. "He was extremely sick for a man so young. And would have died in the upcoming few months. If not weeks. The cancer appeared to be spreading unchecked through his lymph and lungs. I didn't find any recent signs of chemotherapy infusions."

"That surprises me," Rita said. "Bachman's wife said he'd left for a chemotherapy appointment the morning he died. She assumed he'd left as his usual time — five a.m. — but she couldn't be sure that he didn't leave even earlier."

"Thankfully those questions are your purview, Sheriff, not mine. Decomposition tells me my story, every time. Although in this case," he said, with a rare twinkle in his eye, "the lye may be covering the truth."

"Or revealing it," Rita said, mulling on the corrosion patterns. "Thanks for your work on him."

Bruce gave he a nod. "I'll write up my report ASAP."

Rita exited the morgue, walking faster out of the hospital than ever before. Once outside, she gulped in the fresh air, even if it was hot and tinged with asphalt and car fumes, as she strode out to the parking lot.

She tapped her tongue against her teeth, pondering Trevor Bachman. What the hell had he got involved in that he'd been killed in such a horrific way? And not just once, but first a stabbing and then poison — not to mention his poor body already being devoured by cancer.

Rita turned on her heel and headed back into the hospital.

Chapter Twenty-Two

At the reception desk in oncology, Rita showed her ID. "I'm here about a patient, Trevor Bachman. I'd like to speak to one of his doctors, please."

The nurse on reception pressed her lips together with concern, then looked up Trevor's records. "Yes, Dr. Farahani's on shift." The receptionist picked up the phone receiver. "I'll see if she's in her office."

"I appreciate that," Rita said.

The line was answered, and the receptionist requested the oncologist to come down to the nurses' station to meet Rita. Then she hung up and gave Rita a nod.

"Thanks," Rita said. She pointed to a small waiting area where a couple was sitting with a young child. "I'll take a seat."

The moment she sat, she breathed deep. She hadn't realized how much her back was hurting and how heavy her eyelids were. She knew there were messages on her phone waiting to be checked, probably more condolences for Otto, but she couldn't bring herself to check. Instead, she watched the child playing, a fiery delight in her eyes her parents, though smiling at her, struggled to keep aflame in theirs.

Heart constricted, Rita looked away. Hot tears pressed at the back of her eyeballs. She was going to have to ask Roseberg about these mood swings.

A young woman in medical scrubs, wearing a stethoscope and carrying a laptop, walked into the lobby. A blue cap covered her hair, except for a few wavy black strands that clung to her temples.

"Hi, Kenzie," she said, waving her fingers at the girl. "It's nice to see you." Then she glanced at the parents. "Donovan, Miho, Dr. Corman will be out soon." Then she turned to Rita. "Sheriff Jonas? I'm Dr. Farahani."

"Thanks for your time, Dr. Farahani," Rita said. "I'm here to inform you Trevor Bachman is deceased."

Farahani nodded slowly. "A little sooner than expected," she said. "But he was in stage four of an aggressive form of stomach cancer. Come with me. Let's talk someplace private."

Farahani led Rita a short distance to a nook with two chairs and small table between them, where they sat.

"So, stomach cancer," Rita said, recoiling, thinking of the sodium hydroxide hitting his cancer-ridden stomach. "Painful."

"Very," Farahani said. "Unfortunately, we found the cancer too late. He thought he was having digestive issues. His physician provided through his employer kept increasing the antacids."

"And do you recall when he was last here for chemotherapy?" Rita asked.

"No," Farahani said, "but the nurses can look that up. My last appointment with him was about six weeks ago. We had a consult about changing his treatment plan.

"Did that refer to ceasing chemotherapy?"

"Yes. And prescribing pain medications to increase his comfort."

"Do you recall the last time you saw him?" Rita asked.

Farahani's mouth twitched. "I recall. I remember the appointment because he had a lot of agency about his decision."

"Did he seem depressed?" Rita asked.

"No, not depressed," Farahani said. Then she thought for a moment. "He seemed almost giddy, actually. Fired up. He had a lot of verve about it all. I thought he might be headed for a road trip, maybe up to Yellowstone."

"Like a bucket-list adventure?" Rita asked.

Farahani nodded. "Often patients accomplish some really great feats in their final weeks. Anyway, he said he no longer saw the point, that he was simply delaying the inevitable. Sometimes patients predict their own deaths' arrival better than us. And I guess his time came sooner."

"Was there anyone else at the appointment?"

"Dr. Corman."

"Why two doctors?"

"We assess several aspects of the patient's health in stage four, including mental wellness and 'decision-making fitness', as we call it."

"And how did you assess Trevor Bachman?"

"Capable of choosing this for himself."

"Was anyone else at this appointment?"

"No. Typically one would bring their spouse. But in this case, his wife couldn't hold this emotional foundation for him; she'd often require more consolation than Trevor at appointments. She's postpartum and caring for two young kids while grieving and palliating her husband. Trevor was his own rock of resilience."

"A rock?" Rita said. "He didn't seem like the solitary

type. He had several kids, played team sports, and volunteered in his leisure time. "

"Fair enough," Farahani said.

"Are you aware his wife didn't know he'd stopped treatment?"

Farahani nodded. "Yes, he told me. It's not that uncommon for family members to withhold information about their treatment choices. When patients are ready to choose palliation, I support them to have full agency in their choice. But Shannon ... she wanted to do anything possible to save him. It didn't matter the cost to his body or mental health. I conversed on this subject several times with both Shannon and Trevor, independent of one another. Our counsellors also provided the couple services."

"Do you know if he had any other confidants? Or did he confide anything to you?"

"No."

Dr. Corman arrived, greeting Kenzie and her parents. Then he escorted them down the corridor.

"What about radiation?" Rita asked.

"Not an option for the family, because it would have put the infant at risk," Farahani said. "As well as with his wife's milk supply. I hope the family is doing well. May I ask the circumstances of Trevor's death?" Farahani asked. "I'm always concerned about their levels of pain at the end."

"Trevor died of chemical poisoning."

Farahani's eyes widened. "Chemical poisoning? As in a leak of some kind or a traffic collision?"

"Lye," Rita said.

Farahani exhaled a sharp breath and spread both hands flat on the desktop, pressing her fingers to it. "He committed suicide? Because surely this couldn't have been an accident?"

"It was definitely not an accident," Rita said. "But we're not entirely sure if he did take his own life. The circumstances of his body being discovered are unusual. Did Trevor ever indicate if he was worried about anything? Or anyone?"

For a moment, Farahani thought, then she pursed her lips and shook her head. "Only that his family would be all right after he was gone. And that's not unusual. Everyone in stage four has those thoughts."

"Understandably," Rita said. "Thank you for your time, Dr. Farahani."

∾

WHEN RITA WAS BACK in her car, she checked her messages, reading the most recent one from Jason.

I got the list of candidates from Hunter.

Rita gave a thumbs-up to his message, then composed her own:

Bachman stopped going to chemo, Dr. confirmed it. Please follow up with Shannon to find out if she knew where he was going.

Jason thumbed up her message, then texted back, *10-4.*

Rita left the Casper Hospital and drove back to the freeway. The sky arched overhead like a giant blue parachute with not one cloud, exactly the kind of sky Otto had liked.

In the rearview mirror, the black Camry stayed close. But not too close. Rita squinted to read the vanity plates.

"Fuck it," she said, pulling over onto the shoulder. She parked the Honda, got out, and gave the Camry a wave.

The Toyota slowed and pulled over, tinted windows

raised. She walked to the driver's side and rapped on the glass.

It lowered, revealing a man with a shaved and tattooed head she didn't recognize. He was at least as tall as Alan Crawford and twice as wide. Heavily tattooed arms stretched the fabric of his fitted black shirt as he clenched and unclenched his fists around the steering wheel.

"You work for Tom Gabriel," she said.

The man nodded with a grunt. Then he curled back his lip gathering his spittle before he spat a wad through the open window, narrowly missing Rita's shoulder.

She scowled at him. "I won't be intimidated, you know."

He scowled back at her. "I'm not here to do that."

"Well, what the fuck is this then?" Rita said, backing away.

He shrugged his enormous shoulders. "I'm supposed to watch over you."

"Why?" she asked.

The driver stared ahead but said nothing.

Rita snorted. "Well, I don't need watching, okay? I'm a big girl. Fully a woman, actually. And a sheriff. In fact, I wouldn't mind being a kid again." She sighed and ran a hand over her head. "Are you a parent?"

Again, he said nothing.

"Well, I guess you're gonna do what you're gonna do," Rita said. "I'd rather you don't follow me, but I recognize Tom Gabriel's pockets are a whole lot deeper than mine. So have a good night, sir. And don't tailgate, or I'll ticket you."

The man grunted and rolled up the window.

Rita walked back to her Honda and got in, glancing back at the Camry's license plates. Then she pulled back onto the freeway and punched the pedal to pick up speed.

For a few seconds, her mind chewed on the riddle:
PR0 T3X
Then she cracked it.
Protects.

Chapter Twenty-Three

"And that," Rita said, closing the daisy-patterned file folder in which Mary Lou had organized 8x10 prints of Tilda's evidence photos, "are the effects of lye poisoning."

Jason leaned back in his chair, dabbing some sweat on his brow with a tissue. "Well, if I was going to miss an autopsy, I suppose that was the one." He gave Rita a tight smile. "Thanks for taking the honors."

Rita tried for a smile. "How are things are going for you, Deputy?"

Jason cleared his throat. "Well, I was in contact with Shannon Bachman about the exclusion prints. She's coming in tomorrow. Scheduled an interview, too."

"Thanks. Did you happen to ask her about his trips to chemotherapy?"

"Yep," Jason said. "She said she stopped going with him in her late third trimester. Then the baby came, he's fussy, now teething. She says it's been months since she's gone with him. So she had no idea when he actually stopped going."

Rita tapped her fingers on the flowery file folder. "So if Trevor wasn't going to chemo, what was he up to?"

"I ran through the contacts that Shannon gave me," Jason said, consulting his computer screen. "He was well liked. He was part of a baseball team, and he volunteered at Rotary. He had a clean criminal record and had undergone multiple checks for his different volunteer positions."

"How could such a good guy come to such a bad ending?" Rita said.

Jason made a note. "I'll find out."

RITA GLANCED over at Mary Lou. "Mary Lou?"

"Yes?"

"You know everyone in town. Did you know Trevor Bachman?"

"One of the few I didn't," Mary Lou said. "I think he and his family moved here because of their employment with Apex."

"Can we get that confirmed?" Rita asked. "And the mom-in-law, too. Did she move here with them?"

"You got it," Jason said, taking out his phone.

"Thanks, Deputy," Rita said, "I'm exhausted. Gonna head out." She walked over to Mary Lou's desk and passed her the folder. "Thanks, Mary Lou, have a good night."

Mary Lou gave her a peck on the cheek. "Sleep well."

"Nice shirt, by the way. Yellow looks good on you."

Mary Lou stuck out her chest, her breasts inflating Elvis' pompadour. "Thanks. But this isn't meant to flatter me. I don't care that I look good in yellow."

Rita blinked at her. "Uh, okay."

Mary Lou clucked and shook her head in dismay. "If you knew anything about the significant dates in Elvis' life, you'd know exactly why I'm wearing his portrait every day for the next two weeks. I wear these shirts for *him*. Not me. *He* needs to look good."

Rita's eyebrows arched. "Got it. And this is why I can't be a fan. Not a true fan. I could never keep up with the celebrations."

"This year, I've incorporated a lot of Ted's participation," Mary Lou said. "And the electrician's. Which is making things easier."

Rita laughed. "The King's deceased, and he's got more traditions to celebrate than I do."

"Well, that's not my problem." Mary Lou tapped a red fingernail on her planner. "I've color-coded the major events of his life in my calendar."

Rita yawned. "Great. Good night, Mary Lou." Then she waved at Jason. "I'm out."

"Good night," Mary Lou called after her. "Remember to call Cash."

Rita stuck out her tongue and headed out the back door, practically stumbling down the three steps and across the lot to her Honda.

The moment she dropped in her seat, her stomach growled. She called Ruby Joe at The Shaft.

"How are you doing, Rita?" Ruby Joe asked.

"As to be expected."

Ruby Joe made a sound. "It's hard to believe he's not around anymore, huh? So what'll you have? The usual?"

"I'm not sure," Rita said. "I'm not feeling like myself these days."

"Well, for once I won't rib you for eating too many ribs," Ruby Joe said with a laugh. "A little comfort food is exactly what you need. Hamburger or baron of beef? Baron of beef was always Otto's favorite."

"Flip a coin and surprise me," Rita said. Then she added, "I saw you at the hospital the other night, but I didn't have a chance to talk to you."

"Right," Ruby Joe said, her voice turning thin. "I stopped in real brief."

"In the middle of the night?" Rita said.

"We'll talk more soon, Rita," Ruby Joe said, her voice suddenly distant as though she'd pulled the receiver away from her mouth. "Things are busy here and I need to catch up with the orders. Yours will be ready in twenty."

Then she hung up.

Rita dropped her cell phone into the console and buckled herself in.

Inhale.

Exhale.

Then she drove to The Shaft. But it wasn't so busy, at least not the way Ruby Joe made out.

Rita walked past a handful of customers to the back counter. She put her elbows on the bar and leaned over it, looking for Ruby Joe.

Lacey, one of the servers, approached, her hair held in a top knot by a neon green scrunchie. "I just heard your order called, Sheriff," Lacey said. "I'll go box it up for you."

"I'll eat it here tonight," Rita said. "I was actually hoping to talk to Ruby Joe. If you see her back there, could you ask her to come out, please?"

"Oh, Ruby Joe just stepped out," Lacey said. "That's why I'm watching the bar instead of working the tables."

"Do you know when she'll be back?"

Lacey shrugged. "Not before the end of my shift, I don't think. She said an urgent matter came up."

Rita chewed on her lip. "I see."

"Maybe I can answer the question," Lacey said. "I'm training to be Assistant Manager."

"It's all right," Rita said. "I'll catch her another time."

"You want to leave a message for her?" Lacey asked.

"No thanks," Rita said. "And I'll take my meal in a box, after all, please."

"You got it," Lacey said, walking away.

A moment later she reappeared through the kitchen door, carrying Rita's meal. "Have a good night, Sheriff."

Rita gave her a wave and left The Shaft, steam dampening the cardboard box and sending aromas of deep-fried food up her nostrils.

She wasn't sure if she liked the smell of things or not.

She opened the Honda and put the meal on the floor behind the driver's seat. Then she got in the driver's seat and headed to Otto's.

Throughout the drive, the food aroma intensified, and she arrived at Otto's with all four windows lowered.

As she pulled onto the gravel driveway, she inhaled a sharp breath. A shit-brown van with a teardrop window parked in the driveway.

Rita slowed, then spotted Carole sitting in one of Otto's lawn chairs. His favorite one. She slammed the Honda into park and got out of the car.

"Get out of his chair, Carole."

Startled, Carole popped out of the lawn chair. "Rita? Is that you?"

Rita marched across the gravel. "Don't play dumb, Carole."

"I've come in peace, honey."

"I'm not your 'honey,'" Rita said. "And you don't own anything here.

Carole lashed eyes widened. "I never said I did."

"Well, you're in his fucking chair like you own it," Rita said. "I know you've come to claim a share of his estate."

"Rita, you're in a rage," Carole said, her voice soft. She floated her hands in the air like two bird wings. "Let's have a moment to come to peace."

Rita scoffed. "Peace? If you don't clear out, I'm going to give you a piece of my mind."

"It'd be a good time for us to talk, honey."

"No, it'd be a good time for you to leave," Rita said. "That's how I'm restoring my peace."

Then she stomped past her mother and up the stairs to Otto's porch.

Carole followed on her heels. "Let's not be hasty, Rita."

"*We're* not hasty," Rita said, "*I'm* hasty. And you've slowly rolling into my life like a cement truck. And I'm not interested in having a conversation. In fact, I want nothing to do with you. And neither did Otto."

Carole straightened her shoulders. "That's where you're wrong, Rita."

"Ha," Rita said, without mirth.

Carole jutted her chin. "We had a functional relationship, you know, after the break-up."

"Double ha."

"It's true," Carole said. "Otto and I were in constant communication."

Rita stiffened. "You two were talking?"

"He didn't hold grudges. Like you do."

"I hold boundaries," Rita said, whirring to face the door. "And I choose to not have the woman who abused me back in town to dish out more."

She punched the key-code and the deadbolt unlocked.

"Jesus, Rita, give me a minute to apologize, would you?"

Rita stopped. "What did you say?"

"I'd like to apologize," Carole said.

Rita stayed where she was, hand on the doorknob.

"I had an unhealthy dependency on alcohol," Carole went on. "And sugar. But not anymore. The alcohol, that is, not the sugar. I'm working on that."

"Good," Rita said. "Now get the fuck off Dad's property or I'll arrest you for trespassing."

Then she slammed the door.

Chapter Twenty-Four

Rita tossed her box from The Shaft on the kitchen table. Then she crossed to the window to watch Carole.

She'd returned to Otto's lawn chair, pulling it closer to the van. In front of it was a tripod with her phone fixed to it. She seemed to be talking to someone.

Then headlights shone into the driveway. Jason's Kia rolled in, wheels crunching over the gravel, and parked beside Otto's camper van.

Jason got out of the Kia and Carole waved him over. Rita tensed as they greeted each other, then chatted.

Though she couldn't see Jason's face, she could see that he was nodding and rocking on his feet, his arms comfortably crossed. Then Carole gestured to the house, and Jason looked back at it.

Rita ducked behind the curtain. When she looked again, Jason was speaking to Carole again. But this time he didn't nod. Then he pointed back down the driveway.

Carole said something next, then gathered up her tripod and got back in the van. While she started the e, Jason moved Otto's lawn chair out of the way, folding it and leaning it against the side of the porch.

Then he stood in the driveway as she left, watching the van's taillights.

After she'd gone, he looked up at the sky, swung his arms a few times to loosen his shoulders, then went into his trailer.

Rita let the curtain fall back and went upstairs for a shower. She put on a T-shirt and sweats, then looked at the pregnancy test stick again.

She swiped open her phone. She should call Cash. Or not. It's not like there was anything to discuss or negotiate. All he could do was be her ride to the appointment, maybe a shoulder to cry on. But that would involve emotions, and that was exactly what she was planning to circumvent.

She got up, leaving her phone on the bed, and went to her old bedroom. A stack of Carole's sewing supplies were piled on the desk in the corner. She gathered up the left-over fabrics and notions and dumped them in the middle of the bed. Then she went downstairs to get a trash bag from under the kitchen sink. She returned upstairs and stuffed everything inside. Maybe Edith Mae could make use of it. Although she'd probably prefer black velveteen to the chintz prints Carole had collected.

A knock sounded on the door. Rita tensed. She looked through the upstairs window. Thankfully, Carole's van hadn't returned. Nor was the Camry around.

Exhale.

She went downstairs to let Jason in.

"I don't want to bother you," he said.

"It's okay."

He peeled off his shoes and she invited him into the kitchen. "You want a beer?"

"Sure."

Rita took two, then remembered and put one back, and passed Jason the can. "You want some supper?" She pointed to the box on the table, growing colder by the minute. "I lost my appetite."

"That'll happen, looking at photos of sodium hydroxide injection." Jason crossed to the table and used a finger to poke into to lift up the cardboard flap. "Looks like a cross between a baron and beef and a hamburger."

"Are there fries?" Rita asked.

Jason nodded. "Loads."

"I might be able to eat some fries." Rita took two dinner plates from the cupboard over to the kitchen table. "So what'd you say to Carole?"

Jason accepted a plate and dumped out half the fries on it. Then he passed it back to Rita and put the rest of the fries on the other plate. "That you'd prefer she wasn't camping out on Otto's property. I told her about the Sunny Daze Campsites. And if it's full, to get in touch and I'd find a spot for her."

"That's better than I did," Rita said. "Thanks."

"You're welcome." Jason lifted a stack of food from the to-go box. "I live here, too."

Rita nodded. "That's true." She nibbled a fry. So far so good. "And what did Carole say?"

Jason bit into the giant sandwich Ruby Joe had built. "That she's your mom."

Rita frowned. "Well, no shit. Did she say why she was back in Still?"

"Nope." A slice of pickle hung out the side of Jason's mouth, like a lolling tongue. "Just that someone 'like family' called her to let her know Otto had passed."

"Hm," Rita said, shoving the rest of a fry into her mouth so she could make air-quotes. "'Like family.' Who does she know in town like family?"

The fry went down dry. She got up, grabbed the bottle of ketchup from Otto's fridge, and brought it to the table.

Jason set down his sandwich and wiped off his fingers on a napkin. "That reminds me. I brought the list of candidates from Hunter. There's six of them."

Rita squirted a generous amount of ketchup on her plate and plunged in a fry. "So who's on the list?"

"Two are brand-new out of the Academy—"

"Well, that worked out real well last time," Rita interjected.

"And two are older than Walter."

"So they're bound for retirement and looking for an easy gig," Rita said.

"I thought I was going to make this decision?" Jason asked.

"Who are the other two?"

"Considering your opinion on the first four," he said stiffly, "I suppose one of the last two."

"I'm just trying to stack the deck in your favor, is all," Rita said, dunking another fry. The ketchup was definitely making them more palatable.

Jason shifted, adjusting his sandwich in preparation of another bite. "You just ruled out youthful enthusiasm and senior experience."

"You're right," she said. "Forget what I said. I trust whomever you choose."

"Thanks for your support, Sheriff," Jason said, chewing.

"Who's hard to trust, though?" Rita said. "Tom Gabriel."

Jason glanced at her. "What's up now?"

"He's got a car tailing me."

Jason looked at her with interest. "What's that about?"

"I don't know," Rita said, dipping a fry. "But if you see a black Camry around the SCSO, that's why."

Jason nodded. "Got it. You think you should take a leave of absence, Sheriff?"

Rita stiffened. "What makes you say that?"

"It's just there's a lot to do when someone dies. And you got no siblings to help you."

"Somehow it feels better to work," Rita said. "Maybe filling Otto's shoes brings me comfort. If that's even what I'm doing."

"Okay," he said. "But I hope you don't feel you need to ignore his death in order to do your job. I can handle whatever needs handling."

"I should have let you do that autopsy, for a start," Rita said. Then she sighed. "Maybe I'm not ignoring Otto's departure. Maybe I'm just avoiding Carole's arrival."

Chapter Twenty-Five

Rita jolted awake as her phone rang. It was dark.

She pick up her phone and squinted at the screen.

2:14 a.m.

She rubbed her face. "Mary Lou."

"Rita," Mary Lou said, with a note of impatience.

"Well, this can't be good news," Rita said, swinging her legs out of the bed. "It's the middle of the night."

"It's Frenchie, goddammit," Mary Lou said. "You gonna give that fella a call back or what?"

"I've already been out there," Rita said. "I poked around his property."

"That's right," Mary Lou said. "You've already been out there. You've talked to him. It's your case. Not mine."

"Never said it was," Rita said.

"Otto would roll over in his grave."

Rita sighed. "Give me a second to check my messages." She thumbed through her missed calls.

"Hm," she said. "Okay, so Frenchie's called a few times. Six."

"I don't care," Mary Lou said. "He's called me seven."

157

"He's called us thirteen times?" Rita rubbed her forehead. "What the hell's going on out there?"

Mary Lou grunted. "What do ya' think? It's UAPs."

"Well, I know that," Rita said, growing impatient. "But I mean, what's *really* going on?"

"Well, y'ain't goin' find out askin' me."

"I'll give him a call in the morning."

"Nope," Mary Lou said.

"Fine. I'll call him now."

"I think you'd better get your ass out there."

"Who are you now, my mother?" Rita said. "Just because Otto's not around—"

Mary Lou disconnected.

"Fuck!" Rita tossed her phone on the bed and shimmied out of the covers. She wriggled out of her pajamas, then buttoned up yesterday's uniform, hoping it didn't look too wrinkled.

As she drove the Honda out to Frenchie's, the time on the dashboard read 2:48.

Rita pulled onto his road—

And saw the lights. She braked, stopping in the middle of the lane, and turned off her headlights.

Blinking red and green LEDs cut through the darkness, leaving faint trails of color. Against the backdrop of stars, the drone admittedly looked like a miniature spaceship, its movements controlled and deliberate.

Then the lights disappeared behind a copse of cottonwoods on the other side of Frenchie's driveway.

"What the hell?"

Rita turned back on the headlights and pulled onto Frenchie's property. As before, the gate across his driveway stood closed.

She put the car in park and got out to open it. It was locked. She returned to the Honda and turned off the ignition, but left on the headlights so she could climb over the fence and walk up to the house without entangling herself in barbed wire.

But she didn't get two steps when she was greeted by a large growling beast, barely visible in the dark, except for its one-inch-long canines.

"Yikes," Rita said, catching her breath, "you weren't here last time."

The dog snarled, saliva dripping from his fang.

"I can't tell if your size is due to fluffiness or muscle," she said.

It lunged and Rita ran.

"Definitely—not—fluff—"

Rita picked up the pace. She scrambled to climb back over the gate, launching herself over it and landing in the dust. Her heart pounded. The fluffy boulder snapped at her through the wires.

Then her heart seized. Dr. Roseberg had told her to be cautious of sudden physical movement and impacts. In fact, she'd recommended desk duty. And earlier in the pregnancy than Rita had expected. But then, if Rita wasn't keeping it, what did it matter?

Something scuffed in the darkness behind her.

Rita whirled to face the dog. But instead Frenchie stood over her, the blade of a shovel raised overhead, the headlights casting sharp shadows on his face.

Rita's heart jumped. "No, Frenchie!"

"Oh, it's you, Sheriff." He lowered the shovel, flipping it around so the blade hit the dirt. The dog stood at his side, teeth bared. "Thought maybe you was one of them. I didn't recognize you in the dark."

"And I don't recognize your dog," Rita said. "New addition to the family?"

"You told me to get security. So I went to the shelter in

Beaumont."

"Good on you," Rita said, getting up to her feet. She groaned and rubbed her backside. "What's his name?"

"Fang. Although I was thinking of changing it to Lloyd."

"I think Fang's a good choice," Rita said.

"You here to see the damn lights now?"

Rita flashed him a smile. "Yep. In fact, I've seen 'em already."

Frenchie narrowed his eyes. "Well, of course you would see 'em. They've been out every goddamned night this week. Haven't you listened to a goddamned message I've left you?"

Rita took a patient breath. "What else can you tell me?"

"Nothin'."

"Can you hear anything?"

"Huh?"

"Can you hear a motor running?"

"Can barely hear you."

"I see," Rita said. "What did you do when you saw the lights?"

Frenchie grunted. "What I always do these days."

"Did you take a video?"

"Hell, no I called you," Frenchie said.

"Yes, you did," Rita said. "Anything else?"

"Couldn't tell you," he said. "They ain't from here."

"What time do they leave?"

"Dunno. When they come around, I always go indoors 'til they fly away."

"Why is that?" Rita asked.

He stared at her. "Obviously 'cause I don't want to get taken."

Rita said. "Those lights wouldn't be able to carry you away."

Frenchie bugged his eyes at her. "How the hell d'you know?"

"Because I saw them," Rita said, her voice even. "They're relatively small. Like a drone."

"A drone? That some kind of alien bug? I heard some of 'em look real waspy. Like a hornet. Or a grasshopper."

"I think hornets and grasshoppers might be quite different. In case that's any comfort."

"Well, I don't think it's any comfort that it's small. It's alien technology. Them Apple computers are real small, and they say they're real powerful. Which would mean alien technology is probably especially small. They probably shrink between dimensions. Like Gulliver. Traveling."

Rita swiped open her phone and found a picture of a DGI mini. "Here," she said, extending her phone to him. "This is a drone."

Frenchie peered at the glowing screen in the darkness. "Jesus Christ, it's just like an X-wing."

Rita put away her phone. "They're used for videography," Rita said. She peered around Frenchie's wooded property. "Though I'm not sure what it'd see at this time of night."

"Damn thing has a light on it," Frenchie said. "Or a tractor beam. It searches the ground."

"It could be some kids playing pranks," Rita said. "Are there any teenagers in the neighborhood?"

Frenchie shook his head, narrowing his eyes. "Don't know of any kids in the neighborhood. And don't go blaming teenagers for everything odd that transpires. It's aliens, more often than not, Sheriff. Don't you go thinking it's teenagers every time."

"Point taken," Rita said. "What about next door?"

"The bankers?"

"Yes, the Slaneys. They're a young couple."

"Don't think there's no kids over there. But hard to say. Those folks never leave their house and never do nothin' in that yard but water that damn laurel hedge."

"Do you not like the hedge, Frenchie?"

"It ain't natural, is it?" he grumbled. "Good soil they bought. Ma always said so. They could be growin' pumpkins or Christmas trees."

"Do you grow anything, Frenchie?" Rita asked. "Or did Ma?"

"You looked around the other day. What do you think, Sheriff?"

"I was thinking it was strange someone had dug holes, then never refilled them. Was that you?"

Frenchie frowned. "I got to turn the soil," he said. "Just the way Ma taught me. Gotta have the place fresh for planting when she comes back."

Rita gave him an understanding smile.

"Oh no, Sheriff. I know what you're thinking," Frenchie said. "You think she ain't never gonna be seen again. Well, them alien folk are here more often than you think. And I wouldn't be surprised if they just dropped her off on the roof one night." He snapped his fingers. "Crack! And just like that, she's back."

"Wouldn't that be something," Rita said.

"You'd be the first to hear from me," Frenchie said. "Or maybe that Blaze Wright fellow over at the paper."

"He'd love to hear from you," Rita said, with a yawn.

"Oh, shit, Sheriff, you're tired. You'd better come in and have a coffee."

"Sure. Why the hell not," she said. "You can tell more about Ma and your neighbors."

She followed Frenchie into his small dwelling, which

was a simple rectangular structure with a flat, metal roof. Inside, ancient wallpaper peeled off plywood walls, and the linoleum floor curled at the corners.

"That's a tripping hazard," Rita said, pointing to the floor.

"I'll deal with that soon enough, Sheriff," Frenchie said. "Right now my project is removing the wallpaper."

Rita looked around: a toaster on the countertop belched wires; a cupboard door hung off its hinges; pots and bottles filled both sink basins.

"Looks like there are a few things to deal with," she said.

"Sure been hard keeping up the place since Ma left," Frenchie said. He held up a half-empty jar of instant coffee with a red plastic lid. "Black or latté?" Then he held up a milk carton, which was wrinkled with use.

At fifteen feet away, Rita detected its pong. She smiled with her teeth. "Black."

"But like I said," Frenchie went on, "she'll be back any day now. And time runs real slow in other galaxies, so she might come back younger than she left."

"Now that you mention it," Rita said. "I noticed my ma looks younger, too. She turned up in my driveway the other night, quite unexpectedly."

Frenchie looked at her with interest. "You mean out of the blue?"

"Yep. Right out of the blue," Rita said. "Found her sitting in my late father's favorite lawn chair."

"Jesus," Frenchie said, rubbing his forehead. "Maybe that'll happen for me."

"You can always hope," Rita said.

Chapter Twenty-Six

Rita waved to Frenchie as he closed the gate behind her Honda, then she rolled back to the road. But instead of turning left to go back to Otto's, she turned right to the Slaneys.

She pulled up across the bottom of the driveway, turned off the headlights, and idled, looking at the house. All the windows were darkened, but security lights shone down from each corner of the roof and underlit the boxwood border every two feet.

But no lights in the sky. No noises, aside from the whir of an air conditioning unit. No movement.

Headlights still dimmed, she turned around the car and rolled past Irene's. It was dark too. If someone at either of these properties was operating the drone, they had already packed it away, and put themselves away to bed, as well.

Back at Otto's, she wondered if she would ever sleep again, after that cup of Frenchie's black sludge. At half past four, she popped a melatonin and fell into bed.

Rita awoke to a cascade of text notifications. Her

cheek pressed into a pile of her own drool, she peeled her face off the pillowcase and checked the time. It was seven.

She stumbled into the shower and turned it to cold, forcing herself awake. Then she dressed and walked downstairs, dragging the trash bag of sewing supplies with one hand and carting the Singer with her other.

She breezed past the kitchen, confident that nothing would appeal to her. Except perhaps ketchup.

With an iota of apprehension that Carole had returned, Rita stepped outside. But there was no shit-brown van waiting in the driveway. No Kia either. And no Camry.

She hurried down the front porch, dumped the bag and sewing machine in the back of her Honda, and hopped in. Sleep still tugged at her eyelids as she drove.

At The Bighorn Bean, Carly in place of Skyler behind the counter.

"Morning, Rita," she said brightly. Her short hair was nearly pinned back, and her flowered blouse hid her dancer's muscles. "I'm covering for Skyler."

"That's nice," Rita said. "It's good for Skyler to get a break. She likes to get out of this sleepy place from time to time."

"I like it here, all sleepy-like," Carly said. "Even Beaumont feels like a big city now compared to Still."

"Don't let Mary Lou catch you saying that," Rita said, "or she'll say you're destined to live here forever."

Carly laughed. "That wouldn't be so bad."

"Well if you're not picking up for California anytime soon," Rita said, "you can take over the lease on the apartment. I've got my dad's place now."

Carly brightened even more. "Thanks, Rita. That's fantastic. And if you want to sell any of your furniture, I'm sure I can pick up some more shifts from Skyler."

"The furniture comes with the apartment," Rita said, "and I've got a house full of Otto's things, so I don't need two toasters or kettles. Probably need my hairdryer though."

Carly laughed again. "Let me know when you want to come by for the rest of your stuff, and I'll clear out of your way."

"Sure," Rita said. "Or you can hang around while I pack, then have dinner with me. Otto's place feels damn empty these days."

"That'd be nice," Carly said. "I'll bring my Greek salad. I did it just right."

"Sounds great," Rita said.

"So what'll you have? I'm afraid I don't know your usual."

"I'll need the biggest coffee you can give me," Rita said. "And I don't mean the extra-large because that *is* my usual. I'm going to need a cup the size of a Gulpee."

Carly narrowed her eyes. "You do look really tired. Your eyelids are half closed."

"I know," Rita said. "It's because I took melatonin a few hours ago."

"Shit," Carly said. "I used to take that after dancing all night to help me sleep, especially on hot summer days. But fat chance of waking me before noon." She took a turn, surveying the supplies in the shop.

"I'm not sure about non-standard cups," Carly said. "How about I just give you two extra-large coffees?"

Rita blinked. "Good idea. You see, I'm not really thinking straight on melatonin."

"Oh, I know. Once while I was drifting in and out of sleep, Jeff wanted me to shave his back before he went to the gym," Carly said, punching in Rita's order. "I was so dopey, it looked like I'd shaved the shape of a penis and balls." She glanced up at Rita. "Anything else?"

Rita hesitated. "I'll try a muffin."

Carly picked up a pair of metal tongs. "Which flavor?"

"Not candied pecan," Rita said, pulling a face. "How about one that'll taste good with ketchup?"

Carly blinked. "Ketchup?"

Rita bent over to look through the glass cabinet at the muffins. "Yeah, sometimes Skyler's got cheese and bacon."

Carly looked closer in the cabinet too. "There's an onion and ricotta."

Rita grimaced. "Nope, don't think onion's going to work out. I'll take that pineapple one, please."

"Comin' up." Carly picked up the yellow muffin with the tongs and put it in a paper bag, then prepared Rita's two coffees.

"Thanks, Sheriff," she said as Rita tapped her credit card to pay.

Rita left, then drove to the SCSO and walked into the bullpen. She raised one of the coffee cups in greeting. "Howdy, y'all."

Mary Lou and Jason greeted her in return.

Jason said, "Thanks for the coffee, Sheriff, but I've already got one." He raised a pink coffee mug with the slogan: *Bean there, done him.*

"Good," Rita said, sitting down at Walter's desk. "Because they're both for me." She took a sip. "I'm recovering from a night up at Frenchie's."

"Did ya catch any?" Mary Lou asked. Today, her Elvis t-shirt was blue.

"Catch UFOs?" Rita said. "Is that a thing? Is it even possible?"

"I think it's possible," Jason said.

"Not these ones," Rita said. "They're little. Slip out of your grasp."

Mary Lou scratched at her stack of hair with a high-lighter pen. "Little?"

"They fly around on a mighty small aircraft. What do we know about drones?"

"Beats me," Mary Lou said, swiveling to tap on her keyboard. "But I know there are regulations."

"Drones are also known as UAVs," Jason said.

"Great," Rita said. "Now we've got UAPs *and* UAVs." She threw a look at Mary Lou. "We got a form for UAVs?"

"Ain't you the clown?" Mary Lou said, continuing to research online.

Rita turned to Jason. "You know anything about their speed and range?"

"They're remote controlled. Edith Mae's was linked to her smartphone for a real-time video feed. She brought it to our great-granny's ninety-ninth birthday party to film the celebrations."

"Did it take good footage?"

"Dunno. It crashed on the BBQ."

"Says here they typically have a range of one to five miles and can fly at speeds between twenty to sixty mph," Mary Lou said, reading from her computer screen. "With some racing models reaching up to one hundred mph."

"This one wasn't racing," Rita said. "It was definitely hovering in the area of Frenchie's property. How long can one of these things stay airborne?"

Mary Lou read aloud: "Lithium-polymer batteries provide about twenty to thirty minutes of flight time per charge. Although some advanced models can fly for up to forty minutes."

"Besides a camera, what other bells and whistles do these things have?"

"GPS," Jason said.

"And sensors to avoid obstacles," Mary Lou said, still reading.

"And what's the safety regs on these things?" Rita asked.

Mary Lou typed another request into the search engine. "Drones must be registered with the Federal Aviation Administration," she said. "They must be flown below four hundred feet and kept within sight to ensure safe and responsible operation."

"Thanks, Mary Lou," Rita said

"So why's someone's flying a drone over Frenchie's?" Jason asked.

"That's the same question I have," Rita said. "Everything at his place is old and worn out. Even his new dog, Fang."

"Those holes ain't courtesy of the dog, though," Jason said.

"Nope," Rita agreed. "Frenchie says he's gardening. But doesn't look like he's growing any food out there."

"I saw a few garbage bags filled with empty baked bean aluminum tins," Jason said.

"I'll drive by again tonight." Rita rubbed her face, coaxing her eyelids to open wider. She cut her eyes to Mary Lou. "But not so goddamn late."

"I followed up on the Bachmans," Jason said.

"Oh, right," Rita said, rubbing her eyes.

"The family moved here when Shannon was expecting their second," he said. "After Trevor was diagnosed and the baby was born, Shannon needed help, so Lynda moved out here too."

"So Apex upended all of their lives," Rita said. "First getting the job, then losing it when he contracted cancer. And they're about to do it again, by evicting them."

"No doubt," Jason said.

She blew out a breath. "You picked your new officer yet?"

He shook his head. "I'm trying to choose between two of them. But these things can't be rushed."

"You sound like me trying to choose a muffin this morning," Rita said. Then she picked up the paper bag from The Bighorn Bean and passed it to Jason. "Here. I think I've lost my appetite."

He accepted the muffin with a smile. "Thanks. You sure you don't want a bite?"

Rita picked up the second cup of coffee and headed towards her office. "I'm good."

Using her foot, she kicked the door behind her to close it. But Mary Lou's hand caught the knob and she stepped in behind Rita.

"I heard Carole was out at Otto's last night."

Rita sighed and closed the door behind them. "Jason told you, huh?"

Mary Lou nodded. "He said she was pleasant enough. But he had to make it clear that she couldn't stay there because he was renting the trailer and its environs."

Rita smiled. "Good for him."

"Jason's a good deputy," Mary Lou said. "Never makes it personal." She hovered, not making a move for the door. "You think Carole will show up at the funeral?"

Rita shrugged. "Of course. It's part of the charade of why she's here."

Mary Lou gave a slow nod. "And what about the baby? When's that due?"

Rita went cold. "What the hell? Tilda told you?"

Mary Lou looked offended. "Of course not. Tilda's a vault."

Rita wrinkled her nose, thinking back to conversations she had the past few days. "Edith Mae."

Mary Lou folded her arms with a huff. "Half this goddamned town knows, and I don't?"

"Apparently I *didn't* need to tell you, since you know anyway," Rita said. "And isn't that your way? Aren't you the town's Head Gossip?"

Mary Lou frowned. "That's not fair. I just know. Okay?"

Rita laughed. "You just know, do you?"

Mary Lou tilted her chin. "Of course I do. I knew Carole when she was pregnant, you know. And you've got the same sour expression on your face as she did for nine months."

"Great," Rita said, stalking over to her desk. She pulled out the chair and plopped into it. "Thanks for telling me how much my mother was looking forward to having me."

Mary Lou stuck out her chin. "You said it, I didn't."

"Yeah, well, I'd rather we not say anything about it at all."

"Have you said anything to Cash?"

"Not that it's any of your business," Rita said through grit teeth, "but I'm still deciding what to do about it."

Mary Lou approached the desk. Half-tone Elvis had his eye fixed on Rita, too. "That's no reason to not tell him."

"It's not his problem," Rita said. "It's not like we're committed or anything."

"Rita Carolyn Jonas, you tell that boy or I will."

Rita glared at her. "Don't call me Carolyn. And you wouldn't dare tell Cash."

Mary Lou leaned over the desk to point a fingernail at Rita. "Oh, you know I will, Rita Carolyn. That man's lost his home and one of his dearest friends in Otto. A stand-in father, of sorts. So don't you go and make him lose this opportunity to have a family."

Rita sighed and pulled out her phone. She swiped to her messages and sent one to Cash.

Dinner tonight at Otto's?

A second later, he responded with a thumbs up.

Rita shoved the phone in front of Mary Lou's nose. "Happy?"

Mary Lou gave a smug smile. "Yes."

Then she left the office.

Rita dropped her shoulders.

Exhale.

Then Mary Lou poked her head back inside the office. "Shannon Bachman is here," Mary Lou said. "It looks like she'd give anything to have Trevor back."

"I'm sure," Rita said.

"So don't be so quick to throw away Cash."

Rita sighed. "Don't worry, Mary Lou, I've got a handle on my spending habits."

"Ha, ha," Mary Lou said, "that's not punny in the least."

Chapter Twenty-Seven

"Thank you for coming in," Rita said, crossing to where Shannon Bachman sat in a plastic chair. "I know this is difficult for you."

Shannon bit down on her lip and nodded. Her nose and eyelids were swollen and pink, as though she hadn't stopped crying since Rita had notified her of Trevor's death. Beside her, Mary Lou perched in another chair.

"When you're done talking to Sheriff Jonas," Mary Lou said, "I'll take your exclusion prints."

Shannon nodded again, then followed Rita to her office.

Jason joined them, closing the door behind him. He guided Shannon to sit, then took the seat beside her. Rita sat at her desk where Mary Lou had laid out several bottles of chilled water, a package of lemon cookies, and a box of tissues.

Rita opened the desk drawer to take out her voice recorder. She set it up, then looked at Shannon with a gentle gaze. "We have the forensic reports to confirm the cause of death."

Shannon sat forward in her chair. "Yes?"

"It's difficult for me to share this information with you, Shannon," Rita said.

Shannon swallowed. Jason sat with a pencil poised over his notebook. Rita moistened her lips, then decided to crack open a bottle of water and take a long swallow. She replaced the lid and took a deep breath.

Inhale.

Exhale.

"The cause of death was determined to be acute poisoning due to ingestion of a toxic substance."

Shannon stared at Rita for a heartbeat. "Poison?"

Rita nodded. "He ingested sodium hydroxide."

Shannon made a choking sound, then spat out: "Apex!"

Rita studied her. "Apex?"

Shannon's mouth twisted into a grimace. "That place is full of toxic chemicals. He worked with them every day. They caused the cancer. Then building up in his system until—"

Breaking off in a sob, Shannon buried her face in her hands.

"Sodium hydroxide is a common chemical," Rita said. "It's lye."

Shannon looked up from her hands. "Trev died of lye soap?"

Rita nodded and Jason extended the tissue box.

Shannon wailed again. "Oh, God! Was it horrible? Did he suffer?"

Rita composed a lie. "It was over too quickly."

More sobs erupted from Shannon's throat. "I don't understand. He ingested it? Did someone make him drink it?"

"We're unsure," Rita said. "He was found in his car under suspicious circumstances."

Shannon choked again. "Everyone liked Trevor." She pulled a tissue from the box and pressed it to her nose. "Who could have done this?"

"Do you know where Trevor's been going when he said he was going to chemotherapy?" Rita asked.

Shannon shook her head, "I don't understand that either — why he stopped going. And never told me. He agreed he would do anything it took to get better. Anything for the kids to have a dad. Logan — that's the baby — he deserves some memories of his father. Trev said he'd hang on. For the kids. He said he'd hang on."

Jason passed Shannon the box of tissues.

"It must be very difficult that he withheld that from you," Rita said. "Was it possible he was spending time at a friend's house?"

Shannon hugged the tissue box like a baby. "I don't think so. Once he stopped playing ball, he didn't talk to the guys so much anymore. He never really was a guy's guy anyway. He liked to hang out with me and the kids the most. Or play gin rummy with my mom."

More tears spilled from her eyes as she pulled a tissue from the box.

"So he'd formerly played on a baseball team?" Rita asked.

Blowing her nose, Shannon nodded.

"Did he belong to any other teams?"

She shook her head. "He volunteered a lot. Rotary was more his style. He didn't drink or nothing. He was a real healthy guy, and his mom brought him up Christian. That's why it seemed so cruel that cancer was taking him. A chemical specialist dying of chemical poisoning." Her voice cracked. "Not that Apex would ever admit it."

Crying, she dropped her hands in her face again.

"Did Apex ever extend any medical leave to Trevor?" Rita asked. "Specifically, for his cancer diagnosis?"

"Of course not," Shannon said. "If they acknowledged his diagnosis, they might have to acknowledge culpability."

"Although Trevor likely presented them with proof?"

"Of course," Shannon said. "He asked for accommodations."

"Such as?"

Shannon hesitated. "I'd rather not talk about this."

"I know it's painful to review his condition," Rita said. "But the better I can understand what Trevor was going through, the better we can discover the truth."

She nodded. "Okay. It's just that ... Apex lawyers scare me."

"You're free to speak here," Rita said, softening her voice.

Shannon blew her nose, then nodded.

"Trevor worked in the chemicals department," she said. "He'd been sick for a while and was having a few things checked out before they found the cancer. Because his symptoms were similar to Steve's, he'd put in a number of OHS grievances, asking for accommodations, like time off for appointments. He also tried to negotiate shorter shifts, too, but it was never granted."

"It would be illegal for Apex to fire Trevor on those grounds."

"Technically, he was laid off," Shannon said, her voice sharp. "'Cause those goddamned liars knew that ricin gave him the fucking disease. And when Trev spoke up, they didn't want to pay anyone else's medical costs. Not after the situation with Steve Burgess. First, they accused him of failing to implement safety protocols, or something like that. Then they said the military pulled out of the contract and they shut the whole fucking department. And that's when his health really took a turn for the worse. But he had no formal diagnosis until after he was walked off the job."

"I'm sorry," Jason said.

Shannon grit her teeth. "Apex gave Trevor the same fucking treatment they gave Steve Burgess. Not that there's any proof, because Apex destroyed it when they closed the department. And now they're closing down my life, too, every which way I turn." A half-sob, half-laugh cracked in her throat. "They didn't even give us a chance to default on the mortgage, considering what a shitty severance package they gave him."

"Have you taken legal action?" Rita asked.

Shannon laughed again. "Are you kidding? Like I said, we've got no proof. And Apex lawyers eat people like us for breakfast."

"If the same thing happened with the Burgess family, why is Beth still living in Apex Hills?"

Shannon's gaze dropped to her hands in her lap, twisting the tissue. "I don't know."

"I'll email Apex," Jason said, taking out his phone.

"Do you think there's anyone at Apex who would want to harm Trevor?" Rita asked.

Shannon stilled. "Apex may have turned our lives to shit, but I can't imagine anyone personally wanting to hurt Trevor. Even at that place, he made friends with everyone he met." Shannon took a trembling breath. "That's why all this is so hard to believe."

"We can see Trevor was well-liked," Rita said. "Was there anyone else he could have been seeing? Not necessarily a friend?"

Shannon met her eye. "He wasn't having an affair, if that's what you mean."

Rita nodded. "Any old high school friends turn up recently? Any distant cousins get in touch?"

Shannon gave her nose a final dab, then shook her head.

"Did Trevor seem bothered by anything, lately?"

Shannon scoffed. "Jesus, he was bothered by everything. Apex. Cancer. Chemotherapy. Dying."

"Of course," Rita said. "Aside from the burdens of his health condition, were there any new worries? Perhaps about finances? Maybe even something seemingly insignificant, like wanting to teach the kids to ride a bike before his death?"

Shannon thought for a moment, fidgeting with her damp tissue. "A few months ago, he was spending some time with a funny old friend. Trev didn't know him real well, but there was this guy that he would go check up on every so often."

"What do you mean by 'check up'?"

"Well, this guy has a lot of junk all over his property. Trev met him when he'd bought a car off him last year — the old Cavalier — and he noticed some hazardous chemicals that were improperly stored on the property. He offered to help dispose of them. For a few Sundays in a row, he went over to help tidy up the place. And ever since then, Trev would stop by a few times a month to shoot the shit."

"Is it possible this was the friend he was visiting when you thought he went to chemo?"

Shannon thought for a moment. "It's possible."

"Have you met this man?" Rita asked.

Shannon shook her head. "No, Trev always went on his own. His friend seems real lonely out there. Trev says — said — he's always talking about his Ma." This upset her anew and she pulled another tissue. "So a couple of times I sent along home-made cookies. "

Rita caught Jason's eye. How likely was it that more than one hoarder on the outskirts of town was concerned about his Ma?

"Do you know this man's name?" Rita asked.

Shannon thought for a moment, rubbing the tissue over her nostrils. "I want to say Frankie. Or Freddy. But that's wrong."

"Was it Frenchie?"

Recognition flashed in Shannon's eyes. "That's it." She balled the tissue in her hands. "But I can't imagine Frenchie hurting Trev. It sounded like he doted on him, like a father. And he was getting frail, too." A small chuckle bubbled up her throat. "I guess Trev *did* have a recent worry. He mentioned a few times he was worried about Frenchie still using his riding mower."

"Thank you," Rita said. "Your answers have been very helpful."

Sniffling, Shannon nodded. "I'd like to think Frenchie isn't responsible. Trevor really liked him."

"We're doing everything we can to bring the right person to justice." She glanced at Jason. "Any questions?"

He shook his head and closed his notebook.

"If anything else comes to mind, Shannon, please be in touch," Rita said.

Shannon blew her nose and nodded.

"And we may be in touch with you again if we have more questions," Rita said. "When are you scheduled to move?"

"We need to be gone in ten days," Shannon said.

Rita pursed her lips. "That's not going to work. I'll talk to Apex."

"I'll walk you over to Mary Lou to take your prints,"

Jason said. He picked up the package of lemon cookies. "Here, you should take these home for the kids."

Silent, Shannon accepted the cookies and followed him into the bullpen. The back of her hair was knotted into a mat, from having slept on it but not likely tending it. Rita paused in the doorway of her office, her own heart feeling constricted in her chest.

Mary Lou settled Shannon in at her desk, then Jason stepped back to check his phone. He took a moment to read something, then returned to Rita's side.

"I heard back from Ken," he said. "He says the Burgesses and Bachmans' situations are different."

Rita sighed. "As usual, Apex isn't making much sense to me."

"Me neither," Jason said. "They always get me guessing. And you hate when I make guesses."

"You got that right."

Jason cocked his head towards the back door. "You up for heading on over there now?"

"Looking forward to it already," Rita said. "And afterwards, we'll stop by Frenchie's place. I'd like to know the last time Trevor visited."

Chapter Twenty-Eight

When they arrived at Apex, Ken stood outside, awaiting them. Rita and Jason got out of the cruiser and walked over to meet him.

Rita squinted up at the cloudless sky. "Nice day." Then she met his eye. "We're not gonna talk in your office?"

Ken made a show of unbuttoning his sports jacket and slipping his hands in his pocket. "Nope, 'cause there ain't nothing to talk about."

"You don't know what I'm here to talk about."

Ken gave her a look. "You want to know about Steve Burgess and Trevor Bachman's leases in Apex Hills."

Rita shrugged. "Not really." She jerked her head towards Jason. "But my deputy would like to know about that."

"That's right," Jason said. "I'd like to know why Beth Burgess still occupies the home she shared with Steve Burgess, while Shannon Bachman can't."

Ken bristled. "Beth Burgess is in Apex Hills because it's part of her settlement."

"She sued?" Rita asked.

Ken folded his thick arms. "Something like that. Non-disclosure agreement. I can't talk about it."

"I see," Rita said. "Well, that doesn't change the reason I'm here today."

Ken bristled. "Which is?"

"I'm here to ask you to grant an extension to Shannon Bachman."

"An extension for what?" Ken asked. "If she needs labor, Apex can cover that. We got cleaners, drivers, and muscle. Anytime she needs it."

Jason made a sound of disapproval.

"Her husband was horribly killed," Rita said, "which is reason enough. Seeing as we're both cops — sort of — you know I need the family in town until the case is closed. But beyond that basic requirement of policing, Apex might also consider the fact that Shannon Bachman is recently widowed with three little kids."

For a moment, Ken was silent. Then he grunted and said, "Two weeks."

Rita nodded. "Thanks, they'll appreciate an extra four. Thanks for letting them know about the extension today."

Ken growled but said nothing as she and Jason headed back to the cruiser.

"You drive," Rita said, tossing Jason the keys. "I don't want to fall asleep at the wheel."

Jason gave her a look. "Want me to drop you home for a nap?"

"I'm fine," Rita said. "Besides, Frenchie's driveway isn't the easiest to locate. Or navigate, for that matter. Potholes the size of the Grand Canyon."

Jason smirked. "I think I can handle potholes. But..."

Rita gave him a sidelong glance. "But what?"

Jason cleared his throat. "Don't you have a funeral to plan?"

"Otto already arranged everything with the funeral home," Rita said. "And Mary Lou wrote the obituary. Which reminds me, the service is on Saturday at two. Can you make it?"

"Sure," Jason said, "I'll be there. But…"

"But what?" Rita said. "Spit it out."

"Well, you don't really seem to be grieving," Jason said. "My mom doesn't like me very much, but I still can't imagine life without her."

"It definitely feels weird with him gone," Rita said. "But maybe he was unwell for so long, it's like death finally caught up to him. And we were already prepared."

Jason stiffened in the driver's seat. "I don't think I could ever be prepared for death."

Rita pointed ahead and told Jason to slow, showing him where to pull into Frenchie's driveway. The cruiser rolled over the ruts and up to the gate. It was closed and locked, but no sign of Fang or Frenchie.

"I'll give him a call," Rita said, "though the signal can be dodgy."

"Success," she added as the call went through. From inside one of the outbuildings, they heard the muted ring of a landline. But there was no response.

"Looks like he's out," Jason said as Rita put away her phone.

"Hm," Rita said. "I'm not sure Frenchie goes out very often."

As they turned to get back in the cruiser, they noticed Irene walking up the driveway.

"Hello there, Sheriff," Irene said with a wave. "I was just coming to check on Frenchie."

"That's neighborly," Rita said, walking to meet her. "Has he been unwell?"

"Oh, no," Irene said, bright. "But he calls me every

morning at nine. It's our way of making sure each of us makes it through the night. Of course, he thinks it's for my sake. But I do it to make sure *he's* okay. He's not got any family at all, whereas my daughter usually calls me in the afternoon."

"Did he not call this morning?" Jason asked.

"Nope," Irene said, the sunlight turning her hair a vibrant fuchsia. "That's why I'm here."

"I was here with him until 3:30 last night," Rita said. "He was fine when I left. He seems tough as nails to me, but Shannon mentioned Trevor's concerns about Frenchie growing frail."

"He's grown frailer ever since he had that hernia," Irene said.

"Is it possible he's gone out?" Jason asked Irene. "Perhaps a medical appointment?"

"Oh, no," Irene said, "I take him to all his medical appointments. And he never leaves the property unless to get groceries. Which he does every second Monday."

"Sounds like I should go up and check the house," Jason said.

Rita rattled the first gate. "Locked."

"I'll climb over the fence rails," Jason said, stepping off the driveway.

"You're injured," Rita said.

"Oh?" Irene said.

Jason paused to give Rita a look. "That was months ago."

She shrugged. "Bullet wounds take a long time to heal."

"Bullets?" Irene said.

Jason waded into the scrub. "I'm fine."

"Well, watch out for the holes," Rita said. "They're

usually about a foot wide and a foot deep. We don't need you getting another injury."

He made it to the fence line and tugged up a pantleg. "Got it." Then he climbed the rails and dropped to the other side. "All good," he said. "No barbed wire."

"Watch out for the dog," Rita said.

"That's right," Irene said. "It's new."

"And it's appropriately named Fang," Rita said.

Nodding, Jason crossed back to the driveway and made his way up the driveway.

Rita turned back to Irene. "I understand Frenchie didn't go out often. Did he have many visitors?"

"There was one young fellow that had been coming around lately," Irene said. "For the past year or so."

"Did you happen to know his name?" Rita asked.

Irene thought. "I met him a couple times, though I don't recall his name." She tapped a crooked finger on her chin. "Maybe Travis?"

"Trevor?" Rita said.

"Could be," Irene said. "He usually came around on Sundays. Though a little more often these days. In fact, I think I saw his car out here the other day, and it wasn't even Sunday."

"Do you remember the date?" Rita asked.

Irene thought for a moment. "Was it Thursday? Sorry, Sheriff, it's all a bit of a blur. It was early in the morning though, I remember that. I'm an early riser, so it must have been about five-thirty. I like to sit with my coffee in front of the window and watch the sun come up over the trees there." She swung an arm eastward, indicating a pocket of ponderosas. "That's when I spotted the young man's car leaving."

"Can you describe his car?" Rita asked.

Irene pursed her lips and tapped her double chin. "It were blue, I think. Dark blue and four doors."

"Thank you."

Footfalls sounded on gravel as Jason approached the gates. Standing behind the second one, he said, "Looks to be Frenchie's not home," Jason said, giving Irene a smile. Then he caught Rita's eye. "But there's something we should go have a look at."

Irene smiled back at him. "Well then, I'll let you two get on with your day." She looked up to the sky. "It's going to be a warm one. When you finish up around here, feel free to stop in for a strawberry iced tea."

Rita stifled a burp and smiled. "Thanks, we'll keep that in mind."

Then she and Jason watched in silence as Irene returned down the driveway and walked across the street to her property.

Rita turned to Jason. "So no sign of Frenchie?"

"Nope, didn't find Frenchie," Jason said, looking grim. "But I found his dog."

Chapter Twenty-Nine

Rita scrambled the fence, then followed Jason towards the first outbuilding. About twenty feet in front of it, Fang lay beaten to death.

Rita turned and vomited in the grass.

"It's another sign," Jason said.

Rita dabbed her lip dry. "A sign of what?"

"A sign of grieving. That you need to mourn. Bereavement can manifest as physical symptoms."

Rita straightened up inside. "That's not why I'm barfing."

"Well, it's not the worst cadaver you've seen."

Rita blew out a breath. "Compared to lye ingestion? No, it's not."

"I took a quick look around for a weapon," Jason said, "but I didn't see anything that might have been used."

"If it's here, Forensics will find it." Rita turned away from the dog's body, covering her nose. "Let's not spend any more time looking at this poor beast. Let's check inside the house." She strode towards the farthest outbuilding where Rita had had coffee with Frenchie last night.

She tried the door doorknob. It turned and shadow led the way inside. Like a shadow, Jason followed, and they cleared the building.

"That's the mug I used," she said, pointing at one on a table. "His Ma painted it. I wonder how long it will stay there. With the others."

Jason whistled as he took the time to take in his surroundings.

"Looks like someone's been having a go at the wallpaper." He pointed to a pile of torn-off panels on the floor. "Though the job's not quite done."

"I think that's the case about a lot of jobs around here," Rita said. "And this is how the place looks *with* Trevor's purported help."

Then they cleared and searched the other two outbuildings. Both which were in poorer condition and stuffed with mildewy junk.

On the way back to the gates, Rita paused. "Look." She pointed. "More freshly dug holes. They weren't this close to the buildings before. The others were out in the scrap field. Let's follow these ones. It looks like they lead to the other side of the property."

They trudged through the grass, stepping over boards of lumber and old tires and rusty pieces of machinery. They lost count of the holes, all of them roughly the same size and shape.

"What the hell are these things for?" Jason asked.

"Landing pads for miniature UAPs?" Rita said with a chuckle. "Frenchie said he was turning the soil, the way that his Ma taught him."

"No, he ain't," Jason said. "I lived here all my life, and I ain't no farmer, but two of my sisters are married to 'em, well, technically one, and the other one's just sleeping with someone else's husband who's a farmer, but either way, they both know a lot about the business, and this is no time a year to be tilling the soil like that. It only loses moisture and disrupts the good bugs and churns up all the bad seeds."

Impressed, Rita shook her head. "So many things I didn't learn on the city beat."

Jason gave a small shrug. "Yeah, well, just imagine me trying to get by in New York like you did."

Rita's eyebrows arched. "Just imagine."

Jason wiped some sweat from the back of his neck. "We must have walked every square foot of this place by now." Then he rubbed his thigh where he'd been shot.

Rita chewed on her lip. "Can you make it to the edge of the property? I want to see how well this hedge privatizes the Slaneys yard. The most common reason for a dead dog is a resentful neighbor."

They pushed through the last of the scrub on Frenchie's property and came up against the eight-foot laurel hedge.

Jason ruffled its foliage. "This is a healthy thing."

Rita pushed her hands into the leaves. "There's a fence wire here." She felt around some more, shoving the branches aside. "It's wire netting. No way Fang could have gotten onto their property."

"Maybe they don't like his barking."

"He doesn't bark," Rita said. "Or rather, he didn't. He snuck up all silent, then growled and scared the hell out of me."

"Sounds a bit like Ken," Jason said.

"Now, now," Rita said, "play nice."

The high-pitched hum of a motor caught Rita's attention. She looked up, expecting a drone. But Jason pointed through the laurel.

Rita pushed aside the beaches and caught a glimpse of

a red Tesla parking in front of the garage. A women stepped out. Her brown shoulder-length hair was brushed smooth, and she wore a forest green cardigan.

"Excuse me!" Rita called through the laurel.

The woman paused and looked around. "Is someone there?"

"Over here," Rita said. "On the other side of the hedge. It's the SCSO."

The woman approached, peering at the greenery. "The … SCSO?"

"Yes," Rita said. "Is there a gate in this fence?"

The woman shook her head, her hair bouncing. "But if you go up about forty feet behind the garage, the laurel hedge ends and we can talk across the fence line."

"Got it," Rita said, moving in that direction.

Jason fell into step and they walked to the end of the hedge. Here, the wire fence extended another twenty feet before turning at a right angle and running along the backside of the Slaneys' property.

The woman stood awaiting them in a shady alley between the back of the garage and the trees growing along the fence line on Frenchie's side.

"I'm Sheriff Jonas and this is Deputy Perry," Rita said. "We're investigating Frenchie's property, and we'd like to ask you some questions."

The woman stayed where she was, in the shade. "Who's Frenchie?"

"Your neighbor," Rita said. She indicated the ground. "He lives here. On this lot. Although, you have a French surname, so perhaps you've gone by that nickname, too? Mrs. Slaney, yes?"

Aiden Slaney's wife gave a tight style. "Yes, I'm Deborah Slaney."

"You're both new to town?

"Yes. We've recently arrived in Still to build our dream home. Land is much less expensive here compared to Boulder."

"I don't doubt it," Rita said. "Some argue it's not quite so fun out here in the country. You'd be the judge of that, though."

Deborah stiffened. "Why me?"

"Because cops don't have any fun. Ever." She looked at Jason. "Do we, Deputy?"

Jason shook his head, crinkling his nose. "Nope."

Deborah appeared to relax, though her smile remained strained. "Still suits us just fine."

"That's good. You work in town?"

Deborah's smile faded. "Aiden likes a clean house."

"That's what you do?" Rita asked. "While he's at the bank?"

"I play pickle ball, too. And I plan to volunteer at the library."

"But otherwise, you spent a lot of time here on the property?"

Deborah shifted her feet. "What is this investigation about, Sheriff?"

"How does Aiden enjoy his job?"

Deborah lifted her chin. "He's a very experienced investor. It's quite quaint for him to be managing such a tiny bank."

"So very quaint," Rita said. "Has Frenchie invited you onto his property?"

Deborah flashed a tight smile. "Of course not. Though I've only met him once."

"When was that?" Rita asked.

"Shortly after we moved in, he came and yelled at me over the fence." She paused to lick her lips. "Not unlike yourself, Sheriff."

Rita ignored the insult. "Why was he yelling?"

Deborah fluttered her eyelids. "I believe because he's going deaf. And because Aiden was using the leaf blower."

"What did Frenchie want to say," Rita asked, "when he yelled at you over the fence-line?"

"To ask my husband something." She shrugged. "I don't recall."

"I see," Rita said. "Have you noticed anything unusual lately?"

A muscle in Deborah's jaw tensed. "No."

"Nothing that could help our investigation?" Rita asked, watching her face.

Her gaze shifted between them. "Er, what are you investigating?"

"UFOs," Rita said.

"UAPs," Jason said.

"Oh, that's right," Rita said. "UAPs."

Deborah's face turned pink, then drained white, then she took a step towards the fence. "All right," she said, "I'll tell you. And I wasn't trying to impede the investigation. But I didn't think you'd believe me if I said he came over here to ask if we'd seen a UFO on our property."

"And what did you tell him?" Rita asked.

"No, of course," Deborah said.

"Did you discuss anything else?" Rita asked.

Deborah shook her head. "My answer appeared to make him angry, and he stormed off. Clearly the man's senile."

"And what did your husband say?" Rita asked. "Has he seen any UFOs?"

Jason cleared his throat. "UAPs."

Deborah scoffed. "Are you serious?" Then she said. "No, Aiden has never seen a UAP and neither have I."

"Have you heard anything unusual lately?" Rita asked.

"Yeah, an annoying dog barking at all hours. It woke me last night at two-thirty. I even heard a woman yelp. Irene, I guess."

"No need to guess," Rita said. "That was me who yelped." She smiled. "Thanks for your time, Deborah."

Looking relieved, Deborah Slaney retreated to the driveway where she disappeared around the corner of the garage. Her footsteps echoed across the patio steps, then the front door of the house closed with a click.

Rita turned to Jason. "Guess she didn't get enough sleep last night, either."

"Hey now," Jason said, wagging a finger at her, "no guessing."

Rita laughed, then sighed. "I've got an appointment in town this afternoon. Let's split up to search the last half-acre."

"Sure," Jason said.

"I'll walk the property line if you don't mind following the trajectory of the holes?"

Jason pushed into the grasses. "Ten-four."

Rita headed back towards the road, following the hedge in the other direction. She moved slowly, brittle branches breaking underfoot, and tender flowers dropping dry petals from the lack of rain. It appeared no one had recently tromped through the area.

A sharp whistle sounded from Jason.

"Coming," Rita answered.

Jason called out again. "I'm fifteen yards from the road. Next to a broken birch trunk."

Walking another ten paces, Rita emerged from a thicket of cottonwoods, into a grassy field where Jason crouched in the grass.

"I see you," she called, pushing into the fronds.

Jason looked in her direction, then waved. "I found something."

Rita waded closer. "Another hole?"

"Yup. Though Frenchie didn't finish digging this one."

"I don't think I want to know what you're about to tell me," Rita said, walking up to him.

"Then look for yourself," Jason said, stepping back.

On the ground lay a bloodied shovel. Five feet beyond it lay Frenchie.

Chapter Thirty

Frenchie lay on the ground just like Fang, beaten to death. A shovel lay next to him, the blade slick with blood and brain.

Rita whirled and kicked a plastic painter's bucket in the grass. "Fuck!"

"Looks like the shovel's the murder weapon," Jason said, his voice as hollow as the bucket Rita had splintered. "It's got blood on it."

Rita fisted her hands, seething. "No shit."

She paced back and forth. "That's the goddamn shovel Frenchie was using to turn the soil."

"It's all turned up around here," Jason said. He pointed to a pattern of holes all around Frenchie's body.

"Goddammit," Rita said. But the curse came out like a cry.

Jason glanced at her. "You okay?"

"No!" Rita said, her voice practically a shout. "This is senseless."

"Especially on the heels of Otto's death," Jason said.

Rita stiffened. "Otto has nothing to do with this. This

is … this is just evil. Pure evil. And the dog, too. I didn't even like Fang. I don't like pets. But this is wrong. Very wrong."

Jason moved closer. "If you need some space, you should take it."

Rita set her jaw. "I don't need some space. I need some fucking justice. I had coffee with this guy last night. And he's harmless. One sandwich short of a lunchbox, but he didn't deserve this. First Trevor, now Frenchie. Their deaths couldn't be a coincidence. What's the connection?"

Jason laid a hand on her shoulder. "I'm sorry you lost your dad, Rita."

Rita shrugged off his hand. "This has nothing to do with him." She turned on her heel. "I'm gonna check the house again."

Jason pulled out his phone as Rita marched in the direction of Frenchie's home. "I'll put in the call to Casper Forensics."

By the time Rita walked back to Frenchie's house, she was coated in a full-body sweat. She retreated to his dim kitchen and dropped into the same vinyl-covered chair as last night. Her focus grew soft as she scanned the room. What were these two friends into that got them both killed?

Feeling cooler and calmer, Rita got up from the chair and poked through the kitchen cabinets, then the drawers. Drifts of newsprint flyers and faded bond paper covered the countertops. She cleared the sheets off the toaster-oven, then unplugged it from the wall when she noticed the frayed cord. Other out-of-date electronics — toasters, VHS players, cassette players, radios, and bug zappers — cluttered the kitchen table. The chairs stored piles of clothing, an odd assortment of men's checked shirts and the bright floral prints on polyester.

Jason's footsteps sounded out front, and Rita returned to the front door to meet him.

"Call's made," he said.

"Thanks," Rita said. "I don't see anything out of place here. Not that anything here appears to have a place." She moved towards the door. "Let's go."

But Jason stayed where he was. "I want to apologize, Rita."

She blinked at him. "For what?"

"For what I said about Otto. That your feelings were all mixed up."

"I'm sure they are," Rita said. "I'm not getting a lot of sleep these days. And staying up late to investigate UFAOPs isn't exactly my strong suit."

"So, don't do it," Jason said. "Take bereavement leave."

Rita gave him a look. "We've already been over this."

Jason folded his arms. "Okay. I won't nag you anymore about taking time off for your dad. But I can sense when you're not telling me something."

Rita bored her gaze into him.

He stared back at her.

Rolling her eyes, she blew out of breath. "Okay, okay, you got me."

Jason smiled. "You're engaged!"

Rita snorted.

"I knew you and Cash had to be arguing about a wedding."

She laughed. "Hardly."

"You're eloping? I should have known. It's definitely your style. It's what I'd do."

Rita sighed. "I'm pregnant."

"Oh, that's gonna affect your dress options," Jason

said. "In which case, elopement is definitely the way to go."

Rita waved her hands in front of his face. "I'm not eloping. I'm not planning a wedding. And I'm definitely not engaged."

Jason scrunched up his nose. "No?"

Rita shook her head. "I'm pregnant."

"I already knew that," Jason said.

"What do you mean, you knew it?"

He shrugged. "It's kind of obvious."

Rita glared at him. Then down at her abdomen. "Obvious? What's so obvious?"

Jason flushed. "Well, maybe it isn't obvious to everyone. But I've got six sisters."

"Yeah, but as far as I know, none of them's made you an uncle yet," Rita said.

Jason tilted his chin. "I have enough familiarity with female hormones, thank you very much, to know when they're gone awry. And for several weeks now, there's something that ain't quite right about you."

Rita pouted. "Gee, thanks."

"And your boobs are at least half a cup bigger."

Rita glanced down again, this time at her chest. "Thanks? Though I'm not sure I'd trust the observational skills of a gay man."

Jason gave her another look. "Like I said, I have six sisters."

Rita sighed. "And because you live with seven women, you think you know me."

"Well, I know you've been shit to deal with lately," Jason said. "And as I suspected you were knocked up, it's nice to have it confirmed."

"How nice for you," Rita said.

Jason cracked his knuckles. "Yeah, well, you're not the

only one that can solve mysteries." He crossed to the door and opened it. "It'll take Casper some time to get here. I'm gonna go sit out in the cruiser. Too moldy in here."

"Wait," Rita said, joining him in the doorway. "Frenchie doesn't have any family, right?"

"Right," Jason said.

"But it doesn't seem right not to notify someone," Rita said. "Could you please go across the street and notify Irene?"

Jason glanced through the door, towards the secluded driveway. "You want me to go?"

Rita nodded. "I don't think I have it in me to do a NOK today."

Jason stayed where he was. "Irene's not kin."

Rita tensed her jaw. "Next thing to it."

Jason glanced around the treed property, at the scattering of outbuildings. "Plenty of places for a murderer to hide. You feel okay to pin things down here while I walk out?"

Rita studied the trees bending in the wind. "Sure."

"And you're good with bringing Casper up to speed?"

Rita frowned at him. "What kind of question is that?"

Jason shifted his feet. "You couldn't look at the dog without barfing."

"I'm not going to barf again when I show them the body," Rita said. "Besides, it's important for Irene to know."

Jason tongued his cheek. "Uh huh."

Rita cocked her head at him. "What's up, Jason? Why don't you want to notify Irene?"

Jason chewed on his cheek. "You always give me the small-town shit like knocking on doors and tracking down vehicles, while you solve crime like the big-britches city cop that you are."

Rita shook her head. "No, Jason, that's not it. I really do think it's important you let her know. Frenchie was more than a neighbor. They were friends."

Jason's shoulders dropped. "Fine, I'll go talk to Irene. You're right — she deserves to know. You got your heart in the right place, Rita."

"That's part of Elvis Presley's job description," Rita said, "not a small-town cop in Wyoming."

Jason gave her a lopsided smile. "I wouldn't be so sure about that, Sheriff."

Rita blew out a sigh. "Well, at least I've got one."

"What's that, a hometown?" Jason asked.

Rita shook her head. "No, a heart."

Chapter Thirty-One

Rita shielded her eyes from the sun as Jason walked up the dirt track to Frenchie's property.

"As to be expected," Jason said. His voice had an edge. "She's crying."

Rita sighed. "This must be a hard phase of life, huh? When all your friends start to die off." She kicked at the dirt track. "I was wondering why Mary Lou was taking Otto's death so hard. I mean, he's my family and they just worked together. But then I realized, Mary Lou's known Otto for longer than I've been alive."

Jason's eyes widened. "Wow." He paused. "Think about how many years we might work together."

"But if that were the case, you'd never make Sheriff. And even worse, I'd never leave this town again."

They both shuddered.

"They say the average adult spends more time with co-workers than in the intimate relationships of their choosing," Jason said.

"Damn," Rita said.

"That means I'll spend more time with you than my six sisters."

"There's a thought," Rita said.

Jason scratched his head. "And they said it like it's a bad thing."

"Last year this time, I didn't know I had a half-sister named Lisa," Rita said, her voice catching. "Never got to spend any time with her. I definitely appreciate having someone brotherly like you around."

Jason flushed. "You think I'm brotherly?"

Rita smiled. "Let me put it this way: if I keep this kid, they're definitely calling you uncle," Then she blew out a breath. "I'm signing this case over to you."

He raised a brow. "Oh, yeah?"

"For sure. You found the body — both bodies. It was wrong of me to insist on handing off the NOK to you. It's appropriate for you to hold things down here, to receive Casper Forensics, and handle the evidence collections."

"Thanks," Jason said. "I appreciate the experience. And at least you don't have to deal with no more UAP reports."

"I'll let Mary Lou know you're leading the case," Rita said, taking out her phone to send a message. Then she glanced at the time on her phone. "When Forensics arrives, I'm going to head over to Beth Winters' place to ask about her settlement from Apex."

"Speak of the devil," Jason said as two vehicles turned onto the property and rolled up the track to the gate. He fished the keys to the cruiser out of his pocket and handed them to Rita.

"Thanks." Rita waved to the forensics unit, then slapped Jason's shoulder. "Case is all yours, Deputy." Then she walked around to the driver's side.

Jason smiled. "Thanks, Rita. See ya back at HQ."

Rita saluted him. "You're going to make a damn fine sheriff one day."

Then she got in the cruiser and pulled out of Frenchie's property. At the foot of his drive, Irene stood near the ditch, wringing her hands. Rita pulled over and turned off the ignition.

She got out and walked over to Irene, whose eyes were red and rheumy, matching her plum-colored hair.

"The team from Casper has arrived now," Rita said.

Irene blinked at her, sending a cascade of tears down her cheeks. "Okay?"

Rita tried for a smile. "Yes. Everything will be handled now."

Irene's penciled eyebrows puckered. "Are you sure, Sheriff?"

Rita touched her shoulder. "You should feel at ease, Irene."

She shook off Rita's hand. "How can I?" She pointed a finger up Frenchie's driveway. "They've got to know," she said. "They've got to know."

"Know what?" Rita asked.

"That the aliens might be responsible."

"For the lights?" Rita said. "I saw the lights. They're harmless."

"For the murders. They might have killed Frenchie."

"More evidence points to humans than extraterrestrials," Rita said. "But we'll keep it in mind."

Irene's thin eyebrows rocketed skyward. "How in the blue blazes am I supposed to keep myself safe from human interlopers?"

Rita considered her response. "How do you keep yourself safe from the aliens?"

Irene tilted her chin. "The way Frenchie taught me. I use the dimension scrambler he gave me."

"What's a dimension scrambler?" Rita asked.

Irene gave her a look. "Just what it sounds like. That's why the ships look so tiny when they come down."

"How small?" Rita asked.

"Oh, I'd say it's roughly the size of a *DJI Phantom*."

This time, Rita's eyebrows took a leap. "That's a very specific comparison."

"I took a video of those lights and sent it to my daughter. She did some internet research and said it looked like one of the phantom drones."

Rita dug out a card and held it out to Irene. "Could you please email the video to me?"

Irene waved away the card. "Oh, I don't have it no more."

Rita's hand stayed paused, mid-air. "You've deleted it?"

"Frenchie said they'd break into my phone to destroy the evidence anyway. May as well do it myself instead of risking a security breach."

"That's logical," Rita said, chewing on her lip. "Who's they?"

Irene's shoulders tensed. "We mustn't talk about them." She leaned in towards Rita. "They're always listening."

"Would the dimension scrambler help cover our conversation?" Rita asked.

"The dimension scrambler helps with everything," Irene said, earnest. "But it's in the house."

"Geez, I should have one of these," Rita said. "Did Frenchie have a spare one for you?"

Irene nodded. "Sure did. And it's always turned on. Scramblin'."

"What's it look like?"

"Exactly like Frenchie's," Irene said.

"And what's Frenchie's look like?"

"Small, black, rectangular."

"Like a toaster oven?" Rita asked. "Or more like a VHS?"

Irene's pink eyes rolled upwards as she thought. "Yes."

Rita gave a slow nod. "I see. Well, that's very helpful information, Irene. I'm glad I stopped to talk to you."

Irene smiled, looking a little brighter. "Well, I'm glad then, too. It means Frenchie's death wasn't so senseless after all."

"Take care, Irene," Rita said, extending her card again. "Feel free to be in touch."

Irene accepted the card and Rita got back into the cruiser.

As she drove towards town, the sun sunk behind the pale trunks of the quaking aspens. Nestled amongst the trees, she approached a sign that read *Sunny Daze Campsites*.

Without signaling, she braked suddenly and made a sharp turn into the campground. Woodsmoke tinged the air with a rich, aroma of ponderosa pine.

Ashes to ashes.

She rolled past orange and green pup tents and white tear-drop trailers. Then she spotted the brown van in a picturesque site surrounded by birch. Rita slowed and parked behind the van. A ring light was set up next to a camera on a tripod.

Rita took a moment before getting out.

Inhale.

Maybe it wasn't such a good idea to visit her mother while carrying a weapon.

Exhale.

But it was too late. Carole had spotted the cruiser and was headed over.

Rita popped the door and got out.

"Hello, Rita," Carole said. Despite wearing a buffalo

check shirt and baseball cap, Carols' makeup was perfectly applied. "I knew you'd come around, if I left you alone long enough."

"What, like fifteen fucking years?"

Carole's mouth formed an O. "Has it been that long, honey?"

"It's been more. But I stopped counting."

Carole forced a chuckle.

"What the hell are you doing back in town?" Rita added.

Carole stopped, her jaw hanging open. "Goodness, Rita, is that any way to greet your mother?"

Rita scowled at her. "I'm grieving."

Carole dropped her shoulder. "Well, I am too. And Otto's passing is obviously the reason I've come."

Rita wagged a finger at the AV equipment. "What's all of this?"

Carole glanced at her set-up. "I have a YouTube channel. It's called SilverNomad."

Rita chewed on her lip for a moment, then said, "Okay. Well, you have fun with that. Just don't come around Otto's again."

"Then I'll see you at the memorial service," Carole said.

"No, you won't," Rita said. "Because I didn't invite you to the funeral."

"You didn't invite anyone," Carole said. "Otto planned his own funeral."

"How do you know that?" Rita asked.

Carole threw up her hands. "I told you, we were in more frequent communication than you and I."

"If you show up at his funeral, you'll be escorted out."

"Oh goodness, Rita, listen to you," Carole said. "You're acting like a child."

"A child?" Rita supplied. "Yes, because I'm *your* child. Except you didn't exactly act like a mother, did you?"

"And you're not exactly behaving like a daughter. Or at least, not any daughter that I'd be proud of."

Her words seared though Rita's chest. "I've forgotten what it's like to be someone's daughter, seeing as it's been so many years since anyone treated me like one. Or at least, since you did."

"You've turned out so much like him," Carole said, a dreamy look on her face.

"That's right," Rita said. "I'm sheriff of this town now. And I'll move you along if I need to."

Then she returned to the cruiser and spun gravel as she peeled out of the campsite.

Chapter Thirty-Two

Before driving to Apex Hills, Mary Lou swung past Lisa's place, scanning the sidewalk for Arbuckle. She spotted him pacing the pavement and pulled over.

She lowered the window. "Arbuckle!"

He waved and ran over. "Howdy, Sheriff."

"How's the job going?" Rita asked.

Arbuckle grinned. "Great."

"Good to hear," Rita said. "Listen, I've got a question I was hoping you could answer."

Arbuckle's grin expanded. "Hit me up, Sheriff."

"Do you know Frenchie?" she asked.

Arbuckle nodded. "Sure do, is he all right?"

"No," Rita said. "That's why I'm here. I can't tell you the details, but I need to know if Frenchie was in any danger. Do you know how he made his living, what sort of business he did?"

"He was buying and selling scrap," Arbuckle said, "but he wasn't hurting for cash, that's for sure. He gives me all his empties, provided I got a working bicycle to pick 'em up. Mind you, he didn't drink no beer, only Sprite."

"Do you know where he got his money?"

Arbuckle pulled on his chin. "It's funny you should ask, Sheriff. Always was rumors circulating about him."

"Like what?" Rita asked.

"Different things, like maybe Frenchie was a gangster living under witness protection. Or a trust fund kid running away from the family business."

"Thanks," Rita said. "I hadn't heard those theories yet. What about his Ma? Do you know what happened to her?"

Arbuckle cocked his head. "Oh, she ain't been around for years. Poor Frenchie still longs for her, though."

"Do you know where she went?" Rita asked

Arbuckle nodded. "Ran off with a motorcycle gang one night. And she never came back."

"Well, shit," Rita said, "ain't that what happens to all of us? In a manner of speaking."

Arbuckle blew out of breath as he rocked on his heel. "Pretty much. Frenchie was only a young'un when she left. No more'n twenty. Hell, I was a young'un then. Must be goin' on forty years now since she left. Maybe fifty."

"Thanks for clearing up that mystery," Rita said. "Though it still doesn't explain how he paid his property taxes."

"Good luck, Sheriff," Arbuckle said. "Only treasure I ever saw out at his place were those piles of Sprite cans."

Rita paused. *Treasure.*

"Thanks, Arbuckle," she said, "I can always count on you to tell it like it is."

Arbuckle grinned. "Anytime, Sheriff." Then he waved and headed back up the street.

Rita swiped open her phone to text Jason:

While you're at Frenchie's can you take another look at the holes pls? They may have not been dug to deposit something, but rather to unearth something.

Jason gave her message a thumbs up.

Then she turned around the cruiser and drove to Apex Hills. The moving pod still stood in Shannon Bachman's driveway, surrounded by several vehicle bearing bumper stickers with Christian slogans or kids' sports leagues. The convoy of cars reminded her of the night Lisa had died, and how busy the Myers' house had been.

Rita drove past the Bachmans to Beth Winters' address. Her house was a copy of Shannon's, except that the porch pillars were painted burgundy.

Rita walked up to the door. Before her knuckles hit the door, she heard a baby shriek. She Waited a moment, till the wails subsided, then knocked.

A minute later the door flung open. Beth Winters wore a pair of striped pajamas, holding a red-faced baby. With one look at Rita, its mouth twisted into a grimace.

"Sheriff Jonas?" Beth said.

"Hi, Beth," Rita said. "Can I come in for a brief chat?"

Beth nodded and stepped back, still bouncing the baby. "She'll last for about fifteen minutes before I need to feed her. She's just woken up, and she's as mad as an old bee."

"I'm sure I won't need any more of your time than that," Rita said, stepping inside the small foyer and closing the door behind her. The house smelled like sour milk and soiled diapers. Stomach acid bubbled in the back of her throat.

She swallowed and gave the baby a broad smile. "Who's this?"

The baby whimpered and buried its face between Beth's breasts.

Beth kissed the baby's furry crown. "This is Stephanie."

The baby grizzled.

"You named her after Steve," Rita said.

Beth buried her nose in Stephanie's neck, which looked like a stack of donuts. "Turns out Stephanie looks more like him than me." She gave Rita a wobbly smile. "Now I'll never have to forget her dad's eyes."

Then she turned and motioned for Rita to follow her to the back of the house. "We'll talk in the sunroom. It gets the afternoon sun."

Rita followed her down a narrow hallway. Several photos of Beth and her deceased husband hung on the wall. She paused to study one of Beth and Steve drinking colorful cocktails in a tropical location. Next to it, a group shot included Trevor and Shannon among other young couples at a backyard BBQ. She couldn't tell if they were at the Bachmans' or the Winters', given the common architectural features between the two houses. In another photograph, Rita peered closer to recognize Shannon and Trevor wearing Scooby Doo and Shaggy costumes in a shot taken at a Halloween party.

Rita turned and caught up to Beth in the sunroom, where she lay Stephanie on a playmat spread over a sheepskin. Stephanie giggled with glee.

A giggle Steve would never hear.

Rita's heart skipped a beat. "She's precious," she said, her voice as tight as her chest. "I'm sorry for your loss."

Beth nodded and turned away, then moved to shut the nearest window. "If it gets too hot in here, let me know. But the neighbors don't like to hear Stephanie cry."

"She's not crying now," Rita said, her eyes fixed to the laughing baby.

Shannon laughed. "Oh, she will, the minute she decides it's num-nums."

The baby looked up and Shannon laughed again. "See? She just heard me say the word."

Rita smiled. She wondered if she'd ever say something like 'num-nums.' "Well, I'm sure everyone understands," she said, taking a seat in a wicker chair.

Beth closed the next window. "Sometimes it's me that's crying."

"Like I said," Rita said, "I'm sure everyone understands. You all live close to one another."

"We sure do," Beth said, where tone cryptic.

"Given your loss," Rita said, "I'm glad you've been able to remain in the house here."

"Mm," Beth said, non-committal. Then she shrugged. "This is my favorite room by far. Not all the floorplans in the subdivision have one of these. Only the lots that face east or west." She pumped her thumb towards the bank of windows. "The south-facing lots have decks and gardens."

"That sounds nice, too," Rita said.

Beth nodded and took a seat in the other wicker chair. "You got to make the best of what you get in life, huh? The sunrooms hold more property value."

"I've actually come by to ask you about your home here in Apex Hills," Rita said. "About your settlement."

Beth stiffened. "I thought you came by to talk about Trevor."

"What have you heard about Trevor?" Rita asked.

Her gaze shifted away. "That he died of suspicious circumstances." She leaned out of the wicker chair to tickle Stephanie on the playmat. "And that the police are investigating."

"That we are," Rita said. "Would you please tell me about the settlement?"

Beth picked up Stephanie and hugged her. "I sued Apex."

"For the house?"

"For money. They gave me the house as a payout instead."

"You did this following Steve's death?"

She laughed, bitter. "Yeah. It was the last thing I wanted to do when I was bereaved. But I knew I had to. For Stephanie's sake."

"You did right by your child."

Beth paused, tears slipping down her cheeks. "I felt like I'd let Steve down. He gave his life for that fucking company. And I should have fought for more. Demanded more for his daughter. But I just wanted the nightmare to end. And to grieve my husband instead of talking legalese." Beth rocked Stephanie. "The whole process was exhausting and overwhelming."

"It must have been very difficult," Rita said.

"What's more difficult is staying here, being reminded of Apex every day," Beth asked. "I plan to resell. When the rest of the construction is done in this shit-ass little town, the prices will go up. Rumor has it Apex is bringing in new industry. So when the market is hot, I'll sell. Then take the proceeds and find myself a smaller place over in Beaumont."

"You've given this all a lot of thought," Rita said.

Beth scoffed, a tear running down her cheek. "Lots of time to think. No one to talk to but Stephanie." Then she kissed the baby's head.

"There must be other mothers at home in Apex Hills," Rita said. "Like Shannon Bachman."

Beth stiffened. "I mostly keep to myself."

"I saw photos of the Bachmans on your wall. Are you still friendly with Shannon? She mentioned you were."

Beth averted her gaze. "She distanced herself with me when they received notice to move. She's envious I'm still here, in a house as big as hers, with only one kid." Beth's voice hardened. "But she doesn't know the hell that I went through to get this place after losing Steve."

"I have a feeling she's experiencing a very personal hell right now," Rita said. "It's good to see a lot of folks calling in on her. And Apex has given them an extension, which will help matters." She leaned towards Beth, trying to make eye contact. "Is there anything you need, Beth?"

Beth scoffed. "Uninterrupted sleep."

Rita smiled. "Okay, I'll give that some thought. And thank you for explaining the terms of your settlement, since no one at Apex seems to be willing — or able — to read an employee's records. They're always leaving out whole words and paragraphs. Sometimes pages."

"The PD's met their administrative magicians, then, too, huh?" Beth said. "My lawyers had all sorts of fun with that bullshit."

They shared a laugh.

"Since I'm here," Rita said, "let's talk about Trevor. Maybe you can shed some light into his circle of contacts. Did you know him well?"

Shannon returned Stephanie to the playmat and showed her a rattle. "They met on the job and we hung out as couples."

"Often?"

Beth nodded. "Yeah. We saw each other at Apex events and neighborhood events and stuff around town, like the Christmas Light-Up."

"In the photos in the hallway," Rita said, "it looks like you've had them over as guests here."

"For sure. We've had dinner parties together, and I hosted Logan's baby shower, and we've been over their to the boys' birthday parties."

"You sound very close," Rita said.

Beth shifted.

Rita read her silence. "But not now?"

Beth shook her head.

"What happened?" Rita asked.

Beth shrugged. "Life happened." She scoffed. "Widow-hood, I suppose."

"That is now common ground for the two of you."

A shudder shook Beth. "Jesus, you're right."

"Can you think of anyone who may have wished Trevor harm?" Rita asked.

Beth's sighed. "Trevor was a real sweet guy, you know. Like a lamb. It's Shannon who's the lion in that duo. If you know what I'm saying."

Rita gave an obliging shrug. "Sure. So you're not aware of any disputes that Trevor may have been involved with?"

Beth paused. "Disputes? Sure, he had some disputes. Not exactly enemies. But he was mad as hell about that asshole from Apex."

Rita sat straighter.

"Asshole from Apex?"

"Yeah, Boyd's gremlin."

"Ken Saunders?"

Beth nodded.

"What do you know about their dispute?"

"Las week I had to go to Apex to get some paper documents — legal stuff takes forever — and I saw the two of them having an argument at the gate. Looked pretty intense. So I slowed down, wondering if I should intervene."

"Did you?" Rita asked.

Beth shook her head, then gestured to Stephanie. "She was due for a feed and a nap and. What was I supposed to do?"

"If you were to speculate what they were arguing about," Rita said, "what would that be?"

Again, Beth laughed bitterly. "That Apex killed Trev, just like it killed Steve."

Rita gave her a grave nod. "Thank you for answering my questions. I know these are difficult things to talk about. But everything you've shared will help the Bachman family."

Beth nodded, tears now spilling down her cheeks. "You're welcome, Sheriff Jonas."

"And if *you* need anything, Beth, please call the SCSO." Rita stood. "Thanks for your time."

Then she showed herself out of the house and returned to the cruiser.

And headed to Apex, flying past the guard at the gate and pulling into the space next to Ken's designated parking spot. But his Audi wasn't there.

Rita got out, took out her phone, and called Ginny on reception.

"Sorry, Rita. He's not in right now."

"Do you know what time he'll be back?"

"I'm not sure. He might not come in again this afternoon. He's in Casper."

"Okay, thanks," Rita said, then hung up. She pulled out of the parking stall and headed back to town, grumbling as she drove.

The only thing she hated more than guessing was being lied to.

Chapter Thirty-Three

Rita drove back to the SCSO, slowing as she pulled into the parking lot. A charcoal Prius parked out front. Whoever that was, they weren't from Still.

She turned off the ignition and went into the office through the back door. Crossing the bullpen, she headed for her office.

"I wouldn't do that if I were you," Mary Lou said.

Rita turned to her. "What do you mean?"

"Hunter Green's in there," Mary Lou said. "Thought you might want a minute to prepare."

"You're right," Rita said. "Although I think I'd rather use that minute to vacate than prepare."

"He's brought flowers," Mary Lou said.

Rita stared at her. "Flowers?"

Mary Lou nodded, nearly toppling her beehive. "For Otto."

Rita blinked. "But he's dead."

Mary Lou slapped her hand. "Shush, child. In his memory."

"Well, then he should take them to the funeral home," Rita said.

Mary Lou threw up her hands, rippling the Warholesque portrait of Elvis on her t-shirt. "Are you always this impossible to support?"

Rita glared at her. "I've brought something, too."

Mary Lou took the bait. "Oh, yeah?"

"A trunkful of sewing supplies. They used to be Carole's."

Mary Lou curled a plum pink lip. "You want me to swing by the dump? Or truss her up in 'em when she next comes?"

"Appealing as that sounds," Rita said, "I was hoping to stash them at the station and invite Edith Mae down to take whatever she wants. She was pondering what to wear to the funeral. Maybe she can make use of the machine."

"Sure," Mary Lou said.

Rita gave her the key to her Honda. "Thanks, I appreciate it."

Then Rita turned and entered her office.

Hunter greeted her with a smile as she entered. Then he said, "Chair's broken."

"Not as bad as the other one," Rita said, taking her own seat at her desk. "What can I do for you, Hunter?"

"I'd love a cup of coffee," he said. "Heavy traffic on the freeway today. Some sort of festival down in the one of the state parks."

"That explains where my barista got to," Rita said. She curled her fingers to make air quotes. "Even in my day, 'going hiking' was a code word for bush party."

"So how about it?" Hunter asked.

Rita gave him a small smile. "How about what?"

"That coffee?"

"There's a machine in the foyer," Rita said.

Hunter stared at her.

Rita stared back at him. "You're kidding me."

But Hunter said nothing.

Rita sighed again and made a show of getting up from her desk and stalking out of the room. If this was small-town sheriffing, maybe Jason should take the job.

In the staff kitchen, she selected one of the last two clean mugs (both Jason's), choosing the slogan *Love U like my brew* over *Let's grind together.* She filled it with coffee, grabbed the small bowl filled with creamers, sugar packets, and stir sticks, then stalked back to her office.

She set the mug and the bowl on her desk next to an official looking file folder.

Rita looked up at him. "What's this? Am I being fired?"

"Hell, no," Hunter said, pulling in his chin. "What makes you say that?"

"The fact that you drove out here in person," Rita said, "and have your file folder laying on my desk."

"These are photographs," he said. "A torso was pulled out of Lake De Smet."

That surprised Rita. She took her seat again. "Oh, yeah?"

Hunter opened the folder. "The victim was first tortured. As you can see here."

Rita glanced at the photos, then swallowed, her stomach acid bubbling. "Oh, shit."

Hunter closed the folder. "Based on tattoos, we're almost certain the torso belongs to Max Bannister."

"Any sign of the other body parts?" Rita asked.

Hunter shook his head. "Not yet."

"And what about Vee?" Rita asked.

Hunter's shoulders shifted. "We've had no sign of

Officer Logan. It's like she disappeared off the face of the earth."

"Maybe she did," Rita said. "I've got a murder victim who was talking to me about aliens just yesterday. And he'd be inclined to agree with you."

"Well, the moment she materializes, I'll let you know."

"Speaking of Tom Gabriel's goons," Rita said, "he's put a man on me."

"Oh yeah?" Hunter said. "What's that about?"

"I thought you might have a hunch," Rita said. "If you hear anything, let me know. Before I'm a bobbing torso in De Smet."

Hunter adjusted his sports jacket. "Keep in touch about it. And keep perspective. Officer Logan was an anomaly."

"So are UFOs," Rita said. "And yet everyone's seeing them these days."

"I also came for personal reasons," Hunter said, standing. He leaned over the chair beside his and picked up a ceramic bowl of lilies he had place on the seat, below Rita's field of vision from the desk. "Please accept my condolences, Rita." He extended the bowl of flowers. "Your father was a good man."

She accepted the flowers. "Thank you, Hunter."

"Take care, Rita," he said. Then he let himself out of her office, quietly closing the door behind him.

Chapter Thirty-Four

Rita called The Shaft. But instead of Ruby Joe, Lacey answered.

"I'll have the classic burger to go, please," Rita said. Then she remembered Cash. "Double that order, please."

After she'd hung up, she texted Jason to check in on the crime scene.

Still at Frenchie's, Jason texted back. *Casper's joined in the search.*

Good luck, Rita texted back, knowing how slow going it was to pick through Frenchie's property. *Headed home, if you need me lmk.*

Rita put away her phone and drove to The Shaft. Her order awaited at the bar, but there was no sign of Ruby Joe.

Rita waved down Lacey, who moved around the back of the bar to the till. Tonight her scrunchie was leopard print.

"Where's Ruby Joe tonight?" Rita asked

"Oh, she's not in tonight," Lacey said, pushing in Rita's order.

Rita tapped her bank card on the payment terminal. "Where is she?"

Lacey ripped off the receipt. "Something about a family emergency. Needs some time to herself."

"Hm," Rita said, unable to imagine Ruby Joe needing some time to herself, no matter the circumstances. Ruby Joe was The Shaft, and The Shaft was Ruby Joe.

Rita dropped some bills in the tip jar, then scooped up the two burger boxes. "Thanks, Lacey. Have a good shift."

Lacey smiled and wished Rita the same, then waded back into the tables. Rita headed out to the parking lot, making a mental note to check in on Ruby Joe in a few days.

Back at Otto's, Cash sat waiting for her on the porch, in Otto's favorite lawn chair. The one Carole had sat in. It suited him.

She got out of the Honda and walked towards him. A bag from Ruby Joe sat at his feet. She laughed and held up hers.

"Looks like we've got supper for tomorrow night as well," Cash said, standing. "I would have taken it inside to heat up, but I noticed you've changed the locks."

"I didn't," Rita said "Marnie did."

"Don't be an ass," Cash said.

"I had to," Rita said, entering the code. "Carole's back."

"That's surprising," Cash said.

"I'll say." Rita said, pushing open the front door. "The keycode's my birthday." Then she thrust the boxes from The Shaft at Cash. "Take these into the kitchen while I go change out of my uniform?"

"Sure," he said, taking the armload of soggy boxes through to the kitchen while Rita headed upstairs.

She paused on the second tread, her eye catching on

the tower of Otto's unopened birthday gifts, as though the occasion had been frozen in time.

She ran up the rest of the treads, stripped off her uniform, and shrugged on some sweatpants and a T-shirt.

Downstairs in the kitchen, Cash had laid out two plates and cutlery.

He looked up when she entered. He gave her a smile. "You can choose from burgers or burgers."

"Good pick," she said. "I'll take a burger."

She took a seat while Cash crossed to the fridge and pulled out a couple beers. But she waved away the offer and he returned with a single can for himself.

"Those are Otto's preference," Rita said, as Cash cracked a can. "Once they're gone, they'll be gone. I don't expect I'll ever buy Coors again. Only ever drank them because that's what he had in his fridge."

Cash gave a shrug. "Maybe I'll raise a Coors on Father's Day. In Otto's honor."

Rita matched his shrug. Then took a tentative bite of her burger. She chewed in silence. Father's Day would never be the same. For one, Otto was gone. And whatever decision she made about the situation in her uterus would forever come to mind on that day. Because how could it not?

"A penny for your thoughts?" Cash said, taking a sip of beer to clear his mouth.

Rita glanced up at him, then took another bite, stalling. She swallowed. "Cash…"

He looked at her expectant. "Yeah?"

"Just a minute," she said, pushing back from the table. She got up to fetch herself a glass of water, then returned to the table. She took a long swallow, then dabbed her lips on a paper napkin. "I'm not sure how to say this."

Cash's gaze softened. "You don't need to say anything

if you don't want to. Your dad just died. That's a head trip. Take all the time you need. You don't got to give me a set of keys anytime soon if you don't want. Uh, proverbially speaking, since I already know your birthdate."

Rita gave a slight nod, her throat feeling tight. "Um, how are things at Heather's?"

Cash sipped his beer. "It's okay." He met her eye. "But I'd rather be here."

Avoiding his gaze, Rita took another bite of her burger.

"Is there something wrong?" Cash said. "I mean, aside from Otto's death. Is there something wrong with us?"

Rita stiffened, then swallowed. "I'm trying to work out something. But it's not so straightforward."

She paused.

Cash stayed silent, watching her. Patient.

"When I know what I'm going to do, I'll tell you," she said.

Again, Cash stayed silent, watching her. Chewing. After a minute, he said, "You're leaving town, aren't you?"

Rita looked at him. "Huh?"

"You put in for a transfer."

"No, not that."

"But you're gonna, aren't you? It's never been a mystery what you think of this town," Cash said. Then added, "And everyone in it."

"That's not fair," Rita said. "I might have come back for Otto's sake. But he's not the only reason I stayed."

"Oh, no?" Cash folded his arms. "Because it certainly doesn't seem like you've stuck around for my sake."

Rita's mouth went dry. "Quit telling me what I'm supposed to feel about my dad's death," she said. "You don't know what it's like."

Startling her, Cash pushed up from the table. "Don't know what it's like?"

Rita blinked up at him. "Your dad's still alive."

"Fuck it, Rita," Cash said. "Haven't we talked about this before? I've barely had contact with my dad in over the past decade. It's been years since I've actually talked to him. He may as well be dead — except he still messes in my life. In fact, I haven't got a fucking house now, thanks to him."

"You're right," Rita said, carefully forming the words.

"Yeah, I'm fucking right," Cash said. "It hasn't been easy, and you've never even bothered to ask what it's been like."

"I'm sorry," she said.

"Maybe you find it real easy cutting people out of your life, Rita. But I don't work like that."

Rita's cheeks burned. "Who have I cut out of my life?"

Cash let out a bitter bark of laughter. "Oh, how about Otto? Carole. Me."

Rita shook her head. "It's not like that. I didn't leave all of you. I left this town."

"And what's a town if not it's people?" Cash said. "You're only running away from relationships. And I try to make things work, when it comes to people. I fucking miss having a dad. So why do you think I spent so much time with Otto? I want a family too, you know. And I'm willing to put in the work. To build it. To create it out of nothing, if I have to. Unlike you."

Rita wanted to say something, wanted to touch his arm, but she sat frozen in front of her half-eaten burger.

"Oh, fuck it," Cash said, turning away from the table. "Why do I keep picking up with women who don't plan on staying?"

Popping out of her chair, Rita at last found her voice. "Cash, please—"

"Please what?" he asked. "I'm done, Rita. I've made myself available to you, done everything I can to show you I still care. But whatever we had going, it's over. I need to find someone who actually cares about me."

And he stormed out of the kitchen.

For a moment, Rita was frozen. Then she took a swallow of water and went into the foyer where he was putting on his shoes.

"Where are you going?" Rita asked.

"Where the hell do you think? To Heather's. And thankfully, I didn't cut her out of my life, because then who the hell would help me when I'm homeless? Hers is the only home I got these days, since you've locked me out of this one." He flung open the door and pounded down the porch steps. At the bottom he looked back at her. "Do you know how much time I used to spend here, with your dad?"

Rita walked out onto the porch. "I'm sure he always enjoyed your company."

"Who the hell do you think mowed his lawn the last five years?" Cash shouted. Then he slammed into his pickup truck and peeled out of Otto's drive, spraying gravel.

Rita watched until the taillights disappeared, then stepped back inside the house and softly closed the door. She drove home the new bolt and stood in the foyer, shaking. She couldn't bring herself to return to the kitchen to clean up their uneaten dinner.

Instead, she walked into the living room and sunk onto the sofa. The array of Otto's birthday gifts glistened on the coffee table, each one neatly wrapped in shiny, metallic patterns.

Rita ripped them open.

Chapter Thirty-Five

A knock sounded at the front door.

But Rita stayed where she was on the sofa, staring at the spread of Otto's birthday gifts on the coffee table. A moat of crumpled gift wrap floated around the table.

The door opened and someone stepped into the foyer. "Cash?"

But it was Jason, wearing navy sweats and a heather-gray T-Shirt. "I saw the light on. Okay to come in?"

Instead of answering, Rita held up one of Otto's birthday gifts: an ashtray in the shape of a bison. "Perfect for a guy with terminal lung cancer, huh?"

He made no comment, opting for a sympathetic smile, and sat on the sofa next to her.

"These are some nice shirts," Rita said, running a hand over a set of three cotton button-downs. Then she showed him a packet of Merino socks. "And he got more socks than I can shake a stick at."

Jason picked up a beat-up copy of Gary Larsen's *The Far Side*, laughed at the cover, then selected a brand-new leather wallet in a box. He put it to his nose. "This is nice."

"Yeah," Rita said with a sigh. She picked up a jigsaw puzzle of flamingos. "I didn't even know he liked puzzles. Or maybe it's flamingos he liked."

Jason picked up a t-shirt with a screenprint of ABBA. "I didn't know he liked ABBA."

Rita blew out a breath. "The world is full of mysteries." She waved a small, green hand-tool in front of Jason's nose. "Like this. What is this?"

"Maybe for the garden.?"

"Hm," Rita said, dropping it back on the coffee table. "Maybe Cash'll know." She sighed. "It seems like his friends knew him better than me." She picked up a set of golf tees and a pocket guide to bird identification. "How did all these people know about his hobbies? And since when did he *have* hobbies?"

Jason shrugged. "Maybe he picked them up when he retired."

Rita grunted. "What the hell am I supposed to do with all this stuff?" She looked at Jason. "You want it?"

Jason gave her another small smile. "You don't need to decide today, Rita. Let it be for now."

She nodded and echoed his words. "Let it be."

"So did you tell Cash?" Jason asked.

Rita shook her head.

Jason gave her a questioning look.

"I'm not going to." She cleared her throat. "I'm not keeping the baby."

Jason's gaze remained on her, but he said nothing.

"Don't look at me like that, Jason. I've thought about this. I'd make a terrible mother."

He laughed. "Haven't we been already over this?"

Rita sighed. "Well, he'd make a terrible father."

This time Jason's eyebrows shot up. "I don't think that's fair."

Rita lowered hers at him. "What d'you mean?"

"I think you're mistaken about that one," Jason said, "because he's caring. He looked after Otto while you were away in New York. He takes care of you. *My* dad sure isn't interested in taking care of no one else."

Rita gave a slow nod. "He did a lot for Otto, that's for sure."

Jason mirrored her nod. "He's a caring guy. Doesn't hold grudges. Doesn't get hot under the collar."

Rita scoffed. "You should have been here earlier."

He reached across the couch cushions and squeezed her hands. "I was here earlier. I heard his truck leave."

She nodded, then changed the subject. "How'd the search go at Frenchie's?"

Jason leaned back against the cushions, relaxing. "We found some pieces of a drone at the base of a tree. Aside from being broken, it didn't show a lot of wear. Probably came down within recent weeks. Casper will ID the brand and model."

"Confirmation that someone's diligently watching the place," Rita said.

Jason nodded. "We dug up several areas near where Frenchie had already made holes, though we didn't find anything considered treasure, Some old magazines, some ammunition, a half-empty bottle of rum. Casper has continuity overnight. I'll continue the search in the morning."

"Thanks," Rita said.

"How'd your day go?" Jason asked.

"Well, I learned that Trevor Bachman and Ken Saunders had an argument the other day," she said. "I'll bring in Ken tomorrow and ask him why he lied about not seeing Trevor recently. Which means he probably also lied about the scratch on his face."

"I wonder why Shannon Bachman didn't mention the fight."

"That's a good question," Rita said. "I'll talk to her in the morning, too."

"Sounds good," Jason said, getting up from the sofa. He kicked a crumpled piece of gift wrap on the floor. "You want some help cleaning up?"

Rita stood as well. "I'll deal with it in the morning. I'm exhausted right now."

Jason nodded and Rita walked him to the foyer.

He knocked a knuckle against the door. "I see Marnie was here."

Rita gave him the code, then she wished him goodnight and locked the latch behind him.

Silence settled over the house.

She walked back towards the living room and stared at the mess. Agnetha, Björn, Benny, and Anni-Frid stared back her from the ABBA t-shirt.

"Oh, forget it," she said, turning her back on the coffee table and mounting the staircase.

Upstairs, instead of going to the guest room, she went into the master suite. For a moment, she stood scanning the room around her, feeling like an intruder in her own father's room, even though he was no longer here.

In a way, she felt like an intruder in his life. Flamingos? ABBA? Who had Otto been, really? She'd only learned about Lisa a few months ago. And she might have easily never found out. What other secrets did Otto take to the grave?

She moved to the window and looked out over the neighboring rooftops, the rolling flatlands beyond, and the Laramie mountains rising up in the distance.

Then she lowered the blinds, as though Otto planned to bed down for the night. On the side table, a half-empty cup of coffee grew a thick layer of white and green mold. She picked up the mug and emptied it in the toilet. Then she rinsed the mug in the sink and set it on the counter to dry.

Returning to the bedroom, she crossed to his dresser and pulled open the top drawer. Underwear and socks. The man already had enough, some of them still in their packages.

Detecting the faint smell of tobacco, she found an open pack of cigarettes at the back of the drawer. Her fingers closed around it. Like Otto, there were moments in life when she found it difficult to not indulge in the old habit. To ease the worry.

Shoved the partially used pack to the back of the drawer, she noticed a corner of paper. She shoved aside the socks to find a yellow greeting card envelope from Hallmark full of photographs.

Rita sat on the edge of the bed to look through them. Aside from a couple shots of Helen, none were recent. The collection held Polaroids, faded 4x6 color prints, and a handful of black and white ones.

Some photographs featured a young Carole. She wore her hair loose, which flowed like a waterfall to her waist, unlike the short style Rita had always known her to have. Her smile looked relaxed, also unfamiliar to Rita. She could see why Otto had been attracted to her.

The stack included a few shots of other women, too — women Rita didn't recognize.

In one, he kissed a red-headed woman beneath the mistletoe. In another, he wore a tropical shirt and had his arm around the shoulders of a Black woman, the iconic Hollywood sign in the distant background. How many lovers had Otto wooed over the years?

She sighed and flipped to the photographs at the

bottom of the pile, all of which were black and white. They showed a much younger version of Otto in various settings (next to a picket-fence; beside a Christmas tree; leaning against a Buick), accompanied by a woman with the same dark eyes and hair.

She looked familiar. Yet Rita couldn't place her. She flipped over the prints, but only the date was recorded. All of the photos having been taken in the 1960s. There was no indication of the woman's identity.

She took out the photograph of the young pair beside the Buick and put it in the breast pocket of her uniform. Then she replaced the enveloped of photographs to the drawer, as though it would matter to Otto.

Leaving his room, she crossed the hall to the main bathroom where she washed and brushed her teeth. In the guest room, she undressed and got into bed, every fiber of muscle unwinding with relief. She swiped open her phone and navigated to YouTube, where she looked up the SilverNomad.

And there was Carole's life journey, recorded as testimonies and photographed in detail: sobriety, meditation, and ultimate freedom. And she had nearly a hundred thousand followers.

Rita scrolled through her posts, then read a smattering of comments. Most of them were positive, praising Carole for making the best from a difficult life and declaring her an exceptional mother.

An exceptional mother? She was exceptional all right. Rita closed the app and turned out the light.

Chapter Thirty-Six

The next morning, Rita overslept. And she hadn't even taken a melatonin.

She dragged herself out of bed and opened the blind. Jason's Kia was already gone. And there was no sign of the shit-brown van.

Exhale.

Rita rubbed her face, then shuffled into the shower, practically falling back asleep despite the streams of water pounding her scalp.

Five minutes later, she stumbled out of the shower and toweled off. Then she braided her hair, dressed in yesterday's uniform, and headed downstairs, debating whether to attempt eating last night's leftovers. Or skip breakfast altogether.

But as she went downstairs, the scent of cinnamon met her nose.

She entered the kitchen and stopped in her tracks. The table was laid with cinnamon-raisin bagels, cream cheese, and sliced apples. If this was the kind of breakfast Jason served, no wonder Blaze Wright didn't mind the discomfort of sleeping over in Otto's old trailer.

Feeling her hunger for the first time in days, Rita toasted a bagel and tucked in. Then, licking cream cheese from her fingers, she headed to the foyer. As she passed the living room, she noticed it had been tidied. The wrappings and ribbons strewn on the floor were now gone, and the presents were neatly stacked on the coffee table.

Smiling to herself, Rita crossed to the coffee table. She selected a large paper gift bag and packed it with the button-down shirts and socks, along with the wallet, a pair of gloves, a bottle of aftershave, and some other personal items.

Then she walked to the foyer closet and added Otto's collection of old ball caps to the bag. Outside, she put the bag in the backseat of her Honda, behind the passenger seat. The trashcan next to the carport overflowed with wrapping paper and party decorations.

"Thanks, Jason," she said to the wind blowing through the aspens.

Rita got into the car and drove to town, first stopping outside of Lisa's Place. She scanned the sidewalk, then tapped the horn twice when she spotted Arbuckle. He looked, then jogged over to the driver's window.

"Hi there, Sheriff."

"Hey," Rita said, "I have something for you." She passed him the flamingo bag through the window.

Arbuckle poked through the bag. "Nice socks. Shirts. Gloves."

"Among other things," Rita said. "They're Otto's birthday gifts. I was hoping you can take them off my hands. I think you're about the same size as him."

Arbuckle gave her a stoic nod. "Sure, Rita, I'd be

happy to take these things." He pulled out a bottle of Old Spice. "Aftershave? But Otto had a beard."

"That's what I said," Rita said. "Someone also gave him an ABBA t-shirt. And I didn't know he liked flamingos."

Arbuckle poked through the bag some more. "Thanks for thinking of me, Rita."

"Of course," Rita said. "I put his favorite ball caps in there, too. I'm sure he'd like for you to have them."

Arbuckle pulled out a cap with an outdated SCSO logo and put it on his head.

"Suits you," Rita said.

Arbuckle grinned. "I get more and more official lookin' every day." He smoothed his navy Apex-issue shirt. "Though it don't match the blue so good."

Rita laughed. "You look like you're playing for both teams."

Arbuckle laughed, too.

"Can you come to Otto's memorial service on the weekend?" Rita asked. She gave him the details. "Otto would want you to be there."

"I'm usually sleepin' on Saturday," Arbuckle said, "so I'll trade my Friday night shift with Terry. He's auxiliary, too, and real easy goin'."

"Great," Rita said. "If you need a ride to the funeral home, call the station, okay?"

"That'd be real nice, Sheriff." He ran a hand over his stubbled chin. "And if you don't mind, can I stop by the cells for a shower and a shave?"

"Of course." She started the ignition. "Anytime. See you at the service, Arbuckle."

"See ya', kid," he said. "Er, I mean, Sheriff. No offense taken, I hope. Couldn't help myself. Now that your dad's gone, you're gonna need a father figure."

Rita forced a laugh. "Call me 'kid' all you like, Arbuckle. But I think Otto was all the dad I can handle in this lifetime."

Giving him a wave, she pulled away from the curb and drove back to HQ. Rita parked, then jogged up the back steps and strode into the bullpen.

She walked up to Mary Lou, who sat typing at her desk. "What do you know about SilverNomad?"

Mary Lou, wearing a denim Western shirt with white fringe, blinked at Rita. "What in blue blazes are you talking about?"

Rita blinked back at her. "Where the hell's Elvis?"

Mary Lou shot her a look, the fringe on her shoulder seams swaying. "You makin' cracks about the King's ghost?"

Rita waved a finger at her Western outfit. "I only wondered, why the interruption in your streak of Elvis T's?"

Mary Lou patted her shoulder. "It's all right. Pregnancy makes a girl forgetful."

"I'm not forgetful," Rita said, "I'm genuinely confused why you aren't wearing an Elvis T-shirt today."

Mary Lou frowned at her. "Do you not have *any* idea what the date is?"

"Fine, I'm forgetful," Rita said. "So what do you know about SilverNomad?"

Mary Lou folded her arms. "I have no idea what in the hell you are talking about."

Rita sighed. "That makes two of us."

Mary Lou's eyebrows darted together. "Is this another of your keen interrogation skills, Sheriff? To thoroughly confuse the interviewee?"

"Look it up," Rita said, indicating Mary Lou's keyboard. "On YouTube."

237

Mary Lou turned to her keyboard. "SilverNomad?"

"That's it," Rita said, leaning over her. "It's Carol's channel."

Mary Lou snorted. "What's a nomad anyway? Isn't it someone who sleeps in a yurt?"

"It's someone who roams around," Rita said. "You can't roam around with a yurt."

"So where's Carole roaming?" Mary Lou asked, bringing up the page.

"She drives all over the fucking place. She's got a roster of her favorite states."

"You seem to know a lot about your estranged relative."

Rita grumbled. "So help me, God, I went down the rabbit hole of her channel last night." She indicated the column of SilverNomad videos, each one published daily. "You can find out as much for yourself, too, if you like."

Mary Lou gave her a look. "Not interested."

Rita blew out a breath. "You have more willpower than me." Then she pulled out the photograph of Otto and the young woman from her chest pocket. She passed it to Mary Lou. "Do you know who this is with Otto?"

Mary Lou studied the photograph, then she handed it back. "Nope."

But her eyes betrayed the lie.

Rita studied her. "If you remember anything about this photo, or hear any gossip about Carole, please tell me."

Mary Lou's gaze darted away. "Ten-four, Sheriff." Then she folded her arms. "How did it go telling Cash?"

"I didn't," Rita said.

"What?" Mary Lou's voice matched the pitch of a kestrel's call.

Rita shrugged. "We had a fight."

Mary Lou glowered. "So?"

Rita sighed. "Well, now he doesn't want to see me anymore."

Mary Lou huffed and threw up her arms. "For the love of Elvis!" Then she pointed one of her long fingernails at Rita. "You've got to fix this. Now."

Rita drew herself up. "I don't solve relationship problems, I solve crimes."

"Not with that interview process you won't. Bloody nomads and slurs against Elvis…"

"Slurs against—? Look, I did my best, okay?" Rita said. "I've never told anyone I was pregnant before. And how the hell was I supposed to know Cash was gonna shack up with his ex-wife?"

"Oh, come on," Mary Lou said. "Grow up, for the sake of the baby."

Rita bristled. "I'm not planning to keep it."

Mary Lou fell silent.

Rita squared her shoulders. "I've already talked to a doctor in Casper about it."

Mary Lou scowled. "I don't believe you."

"Well, I'm going back to work now," Rita said, turning on her heel. She slammed into her office and dropped into the chair at her desk.

Inhale.

Exhale.

Then she picked up the receiver and called Shannon Bachman.

"Hello?"

"Hi, Shannon," Rita said, "it's Sheriff Jonas. How are you doing today?"

"I'm all right, Sheriff. I want to thank you for requesting an extension on our move-out date."

"You're welcome," Rita said. "I'm calling to find out if

you're available at home in the next half-hour? I'd like to stop by for a chat."

Something crashed in the background, and Shannon hesitated. "Can we talk on the phone? The boys are a bit troublesome today."

"I prefer to talk in person," Rita said.

There was a beat of silence. Then, "Okay."

Rita drove out to Apex Hills, replaying in her mind the conversation she had with Mary Lou. She pulled into Shannon's driveway and parked behind the moving pod. The lawn now lay clear of the toys which had been left out for free, the faded plastics most likely now re-homed to different yet identical backyards.

This time, when Shannon opened the door, there were no children in sight. A raucous cartoon played in the background, its characters' voices high-pitched and squeaky.

"I put them in front of a screen," Shannon said, "so we can talk undisturbed."

"Have you had support from your mom these days?" Rita asked, following Shannon into the kitchen.

Nodding, Shannon crossed to the cupboard and took out two glasses. "She stops by every day. Sometimes, if I've been crying a lot, she doesn't bother trying to talk to me. She just tidies up the dishes and then puts the kids to bed so I can have a bath."

She moved to the faucet to fill the glasses. "Or if the day's been a bit easier, we'll take a break from packing to go for a walk. Try to make life feel a little bit normal, y'know?"

Rita made an affirmative sound as she scanned the kitchen. Children's artwork hung by magnets on the refrigerator. Apples, bananas, and avocados ripened in a bowl on the counter. A bouquet of wildflowers and weeds in a mayonnaise jar sat in the center of the table.

"There are a lot of memories here," Rita said.

Shannon nodded. "It's going to be difficult to leave. Thanks again for talking to Apex on our behalf."

"Of course. Actually, one of the things I've come to ask about is Apex." Shannon stiffened. "I'm trying to find out more about a conversation Trevor had with Ken Saunders last week."

Shannon's eyes flashed with surprise. "I didn't know Trevor had been up to Apex."

"He was seen having an argument with Ken Saunders out front of Apex."

Shannon watched Rita, intent. "Really?"

"A witness reports that the altercation turned physical."

Shannon put a hand to her mouth. "That's terrible."

Rita studied her. "You didn't know?"

Tears moistened Shannon's eyes. "He didn't tell me. I — whatever was on his mind — I wish I knew."

Rita nodded, then licked her lips and took a breath. "I'm also here to inform you that Frenchie is deceased."

"Oh, no," Shannon said, her eyebrows drooping even more. "Trevor would be so sad to know. Though I suppose Frenchie was on in years. Was he mowing the lawn?"

"No," Rita said. "If you think of anything at all about Frenchie's affairs — his circle of acquaintances, anything at all — please let me know. It's possible that the two deaths are connected."

Shannon's eyes widened. "Frenchie and Trev?" She put her hands to her mouth. "Do you think we should move after all, Sheriff?"

Rita met Shannon's eyes. "I suspect whatever's going on is related to Frenchie's property. And not Apex Hills."

Shannon gave a stiff nod, still looking unsure. "But ... do you think the killer will come after me and the kids?"

Rita leaned in. "If I ever suspect you're in danger, I'll

take actions to protect you and the family." She handed Shannon another of her cards. "And if you want to me to drive by or check out anything odd, call, okay? Anytime."

Shannon took Rita's card as she had the other times and held it close. "I will, Sheriff, thank you." Then she stood and followed Rita to the foyer.

"Have you ever considered suing Apex?" Rita said, pausing in the doorway. She looked around the foyer where a picture on the wall read *Home Sweet Home*. "So that you can stay?"

"You mean suing them to gain ownership of the house?"

"Yes," Rita said. "Like Beth Winters."

Shannon stiffened. "Yes, well, Beth always gets what she wants."

Rita studied her. "What do you mean by that? That she's always getting what she wants?"

Shannon snorted. "After Steve died, she and Trev had an affair."

Chapter Thirty-Seven

Rita pulled into the driveway at Beth Winters' house and parked. Beth answered, this time without Stephanie.

"Hi, Sheriff," she said, her voice phrasing the salutation as though it were a question.

"I'd like to talk a bit more about Trevor Bachman," Rita said. "Is this a good time?"

Beth pulled back the door, "Sure, okay, but I don't know if I can help you." She cleared her throat. "Steve knew him better."

"That's interesting," Rita said, stepping inside. "Because I heard that you and Steve were quite close."

Beth's spine stiffened as she turned to lead Rita into the kitchen. "If we talk in the living room, our voices will carry up the stairs, and Stephanie just went down for a nap."

"Thanks for meeting me when I'm sure you could do with some shuteye," Rita said. "I've been feeling the need for some catnaps lately myself." She shrugged. "And I'm not even a cat person."

Leaning against the counter, Beth gave her a wan small. "What would you like to discuss about Trevor?"

Rita took a seat on the banquette. "Your affair."

Beth frozen, except for her fingers which picked at a tea towel. "An affair?"

"Shannon Bachman told me," Rita said.

A tear leaked down Beth's cheek. "It's just that — well, Steve and Trev were good friends. And town's small, and so's this neighborhood, so we were all hanging out a lot." She shrugged with one shoulder. "Me and Trev became friends, too." Two pink spots bloomed in her pale cheeks. "He was so damn nice, you know? You ever meet anyone like that? Doesn't say a mean word about anyone. Always got a joke up his sleeve." She dropped her head. "Notices the small things that matter to you."

"What happened?" Rita asked.

Beth took a steadying breath, bunching the tea towel into a ball. "After Steve died, Trev was coming over to help out with stuff around the house. I was pregnant and couldn't afford a handyman for everything. He built the crib and hung the mobile. Stuff like that. I didn't think it would lead to anything. I never thought he was doing it for me. I thought he wanted to do these things for his friend's kid. 'Cause he'd been by Steve's side, all the way to the end." She glanced at Rita. "Trev is both the gentlest guy I ever met, and the strongest."

"Then what?"

"He started stopping by even if there were no odd jobs. I think he sensed I needed to talk about Steve. Or maybe he needed to talk about his feelings. Either way, our sadness brought us closer. And we had a connection. One afternoon … it got out of hand."

"Did it happen again?" Rita asked.

She let out a bitter laugh. "Once more. When we met to talk about it never happening again. After that, we promised to just not ever meet up again without his wife around. He said if I needed help around the place, to invite over Shannon and the kids and he'd come along and do it." She shook her head. "That would have been torture, seeing him with his wife and kids like that. And me missing Steve. And knowing I could never be with Trevor. Not without hating myself." She bit back a sob. "It wasn't like we were carrying on an affair. It was just ... a whole bunch of feelings tangled up."

"So Trevor did have secrets," Rita said. "Do you know how Shannon found out?"

Beth's shoulders dropped. "When he started having stomach troubles, he thought our secret was eating him up. So he told her, to be rid of the secret and stop the lies. To get the guilt out of him. He found a marriage counsellor for them in Casper and everything. He asked his mother-in-law to watch the kids for a weekend and he took her to Thermopolis." Her mouth twisted into a grimace. "But his stomach aches didn't go away. And neither did my heartache. Everything just became worse." Fresh tears spilled down her cheeks. "At times, I thought God was punishing us." Her bottom lip trembled. "Punishing me, for something I've done."

"You have to throw out those thoughts," Rita said. "It's Apex who's at fault. Not you. Not God. Not Trevor or Steve. Only Apex."

"Shannon punished me. Still does."

"How so?" Rita asked.

Beth sighed. "She was angry when she found out, despite the couple's therapy and romantic getaway."

"Did the two of you have a conversation about what happened?"

"She came over and threw a bunch of trash all over my front yard, screamed at me that I had defamed Steve's memory, and then kicked over my planter. Ever since, we've kept our distance." She gave a hollow laugh. "Even though we walk to the same community mailbox and our houses are almost exactly the same."

"Did you love Trevor?" Rita asked.

Beth shook her head. "No. Yes. I don't know. I just know things hurt less when he was around, and I hurt all over again when things ended with him."

"During the times you met," Rita asked, "did he ever talk about a friend called Frenchie?"

Beth shook her head again, "No, we only ever talked about planning for the baby or what happened to Steve. Trev didn't like to talk about Apex. At least not with me."

Upstairs, the baby cried.

Beth turned, "I should go get her."

Rita slid out of the banquette. "Thanks for your time. Before you go, did Trevor ever mention having any other troubles aside from Apex? Anything that might make someone want to hurt him?"

Beth shook her head. "Everyone liked Trev." She blushed again. "Some of us too much."

Beth's eyes darted to the ceiling as Stephanie increased her volume.

"Thanks," Rita said. "If you think of anything else, I would appreciate you contacting me. I'm sure you want answers to Trevor's death as much as anyone."

Nodding, Beth choked back a sob and hurried from the kitchen.

Rita let herself out the front door. Before leaving Apex Hills, she passed Boyd Farmer's old house address, a familiar Audi parked in the driveway. She paused. It couldn't possibly be, right?

She pulled over the cruiser, turned off the ignition, and walked up to the door.

A woman in her twenties answered. Snug yoga clothes

accentuated her toned muscles, and a wide smile paired with bright eyes gave her an approachable presence.

Rita smiled. "Hi, I'm Sheriff Jonas. I'm looking for Ken Saunders." She jabbed a thumb over her shoulder. "I recognized his vehicle in the driveway."

The woman turned, flipping her ponytail, and hollered for Ken. Then she disappeared into the back of the house.

A moment later, Ken emerged from the shadows, his large body filling the open doorway. Standing in the dim interior, he blinked into the sunlight. Rita wasn't used to seeing Ken without his shades.

"Afternoon, Sheriff."

She smiled. "I didn't know you lived in Boyd's old home. You already have his office at Genius HQ. And now this place."

Ken scowled. "Genius—? Oh, you mean Head Office?"

Rita smiled. "I don't mean Feet Office. Though I'm sure there're a lot of heels who work there."

Ken glared at her. "I don't find that funny."

Rita cleared her throat. "And I don't find it funny that you had a fight with Trevor Bachman last week and didn't tell me." She set her lower jaw. "In fact, you lied about it."

Chapter Thirty-Eight

Rita followed Ken into the kitchen. Like the other houses in Apex Hills, this one was small and compact. But instead of the builder-basic finishings, Boyd had replaced the countertops with granite and the laminate flooring with pine boards. But Ken's kitchen boasted none of Boyd's touches, like his collection of olive oils or hanging ropes of garlic.

"Must be nice to stretch out, huh?" Rita asked.

Ken's gaze circled the bare room. "It's nice enough."

Rita crossed to the window and looked into the backyard. A greenhouse stood at the far end, the louvers closed and the poly walls pocked with condensation. Behind the misty panes hung limp gray strands, like forest lichen.

She turned to face Ken. "You're not much of a gardener, huh?"

He got out two Cokes. "Dunno. Moved in not too long ago." He set the drinks on the table, then took a seat, motioning for Rita to do the same.

Rita crossed to the table and pulled out a chair. "Those tomato plants in there are a bit like Boyd."

Ken blinked at her, his eyes without sunglasses appearing small in his large cranium. "Huh?"

"Once full of life," Rita said, sitting, "now turned to dust."

Ken's tiny eyes widened. "Jesus Christ, Rita, what a thing to say."

"Sorry," she said. She shrugged. "My dad just died."

Nodding, Ken passed her the can of Coke. "Right."

Rita waved it away, remembering Dr. Roseberg's recommendations. "I'm actually cutting back on caffeine," she said. "I'd love a water."

"Sure," Ken said, getting up and going to the sink.

Rita pointed a finger towards the front door. "The woman who answered the door — she come with the house?"

Scowling, Ken cranked the faucet, sending a powerful jet of water into the glass. "What kind of remark is that?"

Rita shrugged. "I just wondered if she knew Boyd as well."

Ken set the frothing glass of water in front of her. "Haleigh?"

Rita counted off on her fingers. "Boyd's office. Boyd's house. Boyd's woman."

"That's crass," Ken said, cracking his can of Coke. "You're in a dead man's boots, too."

Rita sighed and dropped her hands. "You're right." She took a sip of water, then met his eye. "I live in Otto's house, too."

For a moment, they sat in silence, sipping their drinks.

Inhale.

Exhale.

Then Rita set down her glass and cleared her throat. "There's only one thing I like less that guessing, Ken. And that's—"

"Hi, there," said the woman who had opened as she breezed into the kitchen. She flung open the refrigerator door and grabbed a chilled sports drink with a pink label. She flashed a smile Rita's way. "I'm Haleigh. Like the comet."

"Hi," Rita said. "I'm the sheriff. Like the only one in town."

Haleigh laughed, then dropped into Ken's lap.

"Are congratulations in order?" Rita asked.

Ken blinked at her. "What does that mean?"

Rita shrugged. "You two look ready to be engaged."

Haleigh burst into laughter, like a balloon that had been burst.

"Go on now," Ken said, patting her arm, "give me and the sheriff some space to talk."

Haleigh giggled and kissed Ken on the cheek. "Sure thing, baby." Then she winked at Rita. "It's hard to get used to being with a man who has such an important job."

Rita raised a brow. "Is that right?"

Haleigh giggled some more. "Sure. Ken's gone all sorts of odd hours." She waggled her eyebrows. "Out doing dangerous things."

Rita met Ken's eye. "He sure does. Especially out at the reservoir."

Haleigh's eyes widened. "The reservoir? Oh, I can only imagine!" Her gaze swung to Rita. "I bet you do dangerous stuff, too."

"Sure do," Rita said. "The other night I was out scouting for a UFO."

Haleigh's mouth formed an O. "Oh my God, are you okay?"

Rita smiled and spread her hands. "I'm here to tell the tale."

"This is so quantum," Haleigh said. She tapped her

chest with a blue-painted fingernail. "I'm named after a comet"—she swung the blue-tipped finger at Rita—"and you know about space invaders."

Haleigh turned to Ken, her eyes sparkling. "Do you know about UFOs, too, baby?"

"Goodbye, Haleigh," Ken said, attempting to shift her from his lap. "The sheriff and I have some important work to do."

"Are you discussing the UFO?"

Ken puckered his brows. "We'll talk later, okay?"

Giggling, Haleigh tweaked his nose. "But not about anything official."

He forced a smile. "Nothing official."

Haleigh glanced at Rita. "We can never talk about anything official. So don't worry if I overhear you talking about the aliens. I've learned so much, dating a cop."

Rita raised an eyebrow. "You don't say?"

"Like, everything is confidential," Haleigh said. "And I mean everything. Kind of like *my* business. I have to maintain client confidentiality, too."

Rita nodded. "Don't we all?"

Haleigh detangled her thin limbs from Ken's lap. "Okay, baby, I'll see you later." And she bounded towards the kitchen door. She twiddled her fingers. "Nice to meet you, Sheriff."

When she had gone, Rita turned to Ken. "Maybe she won't return till 2061."

"Huh?" Ken said.

"Like the comet," Rita said.

Ken glared at her. "Be nice."

"Sorry," Rita said, "I'm sure she's very nice to have around. A bit like a Pomeranian."

Ken frowned. "A what?"

"Or maybe a Maltese."

Ken stiffened. "What's that supposed to mean?"

Rita shrugged. "She's peppy. Perky. Has good hair."

Ken grumbled in his throat. "Nothing wrong with perky."

"Nope," Rita said. "Though I'm more of a cat person, myself. If I liked pets."

Ken blew out a breath. "Can we get on with talking about Trevor Bachman?"

"Please," Rita said, leaning back in her chair. "So why'd you hold out on me?"

Ken sighed. "Because it got physical." He threw her a look. "And you state troopers don't like that shit."

"Bingo."

Ken straightened his shoulders. "Not that I beat the crap outta him or nothin'."

Rita gave him a look.

"I didn't even touch him. Really." Ken spread his thick hands. "Except to defend myself."

Rita laughed. "You? Defending yourself against a man dying of cancer?"

Ken put his elbows the table. "I was telling the truth when I said I hadn't seen or spoken to Trevor Bachman in months."

Rita took another sip of coffee. "Until last week."

Ken nodded "For some reason, he showed up that day and picked a fight."

"About what?"

"His termination. And it wasn't even me that fired him."

"Who did?"

"It was Angela's directive."

"So why do you think Trevor confronted you?"

Ken fiddled with the tab on his Coke can. "Probably 'cause I'm the one that escorted him off the premises."

"Right," Rita said, her voice dry. "The Personnel Optimization. So what happened with Trevor the other day?"

Ken shrugged his massive shoulders. "He threw some punches and left."

"He threw some punches and left?" Rita repeated.

Ken nodded. Yep."

Rita chewed on her lip, studying him. "You threw some punches too?"

Fire flashed in Ken's eyes. "No."

"Why not?" Rita asked.

Ken looked offended. "I was on the job."

Rita narrowed her eyes at him. "Hasn't stopped you before."

Ken grit his teeth. "I didn't hit him."

Rita leaned in to look at his cheek. "But you got scratched."

"Yes." Ken grit his teeth. "I also got clawed, kicked, and bit. But I didn't hit back. So I picked him up — with as much goddamned dignity I could give him — and carried him to his car in the parking lot."

"And then what?"

"He left."

"And?"

Ken folded his arms. "Never saw him again."

Rita studied him. "No other interactions?"

He shook his head. "Nope."

"Is there anyone else at Apex that Trevor had issues with?" Rita asked.

Ken obliged her, taking a moment to think while he sipped his soda. "I don't think so."

"And you didn't have any other issues with Trevor Bachman?"

"No."

"Just the one dust-up?"

"That's right."

"And what about other Apex employees? Anyone else have altercations with Trevor?"

Ken thought for a moment. "Not that I'm aware of. Nothing in his employment records."

"Those records were what you might call bare bones."

Ken shrugged. "Bachman was a good employee. Nothing to report."

"What about all his grievances and accommodation requests?"

Ken blinked at her. "Look, I ain't in Human Resources. I just walked the guy out his last day and carried him out to the lot last week. That's it."

"Thanks," Rita said, "I appreciate you answering my questions. I'll let you get back to your day now."

She got up and Ken followed her to the front door.

"Thanks for your time," Rita said, as he pulled open the door. "And say goodbye to Haleigh for me. Unless her bedtime's already passed."

Ken cut her a look. "Knock it off, Rita."

"I can't help it, I'm the Sheriff," Rita said. "How old is she?"

"She's legal," Ken said.

"Are you sure?" Rita said. "Because I'm sure she wasn't alive the last time the comet came by."

"Appearances aren't everything," Ken said.

Rita paused. Then she sighed. "We cops can get used to looking for the mystery. The anomaly. But mysteries get solved by looking for what isn't evident. What's hidden."

"Bye, Rita."

She gave him a salute, then walked down the steps to the cruiser.

Next, Rita drove downtown to Wyoming Valley State

Bank. Inside, she walked to the front of the line, which was only two people, and cut in front to pull aside Bev.

She wore a checked pantsuit and large hooped earrings. "Can I help you, Sheriff?"

"I'd like to speak to Aiden Slaney, please," Rita said.

Bev smiled, two dimples appearing in her rosy cheeks. "He asked me to hold his calls. Can I take a message?"

"Please ask him to call me when he's done."

"Will do," Bev said, puckered her lips and accepting Rita's card.

Rita returned to the cruiser and drove to HQ. When she arrived at the station, Mary Lou pushed back from her desk.

She waved a pink Post-It. "Phone message for you."

"Any chance it's the Aiden Slaney?" Rita asked.

"Shannon Bachman," Mary Lou said.

Rita swiped the Post-It. "Has she remembered something important?"

"No," Mary Lou said. "She says their insurance company needs a copy of Trevor's death certificate before they can start the process."

"We're going as fast as we can," Rita said.

"I explained that it's gonna take some time," Mary Lou said. A red light lit up on her phone. She leaned over to read the number. "Tilda's calling."

"I'll take it in my office," Rita said, crossing the bullpen. She closed the door behind her and dropped into the chair at her desk.

She picked up the receiver and hit the first line. "Hi, Tilda, what've you got?"

"Two juicy bits," Tilda said. "First, I've got the chemical breakdown for the lye. It's an industrial variety of sodium hydroxide. Apex is the likeliest culprit to have it on-site, so I'm gonna send a request to secure a sample for comparison."

"Do it," Rita said. "What else?"

"We ran the hair that was found in the car," Tilda said, "Same DNA as the saliva on the disposable coffee cup."

"This sounds too good to be true," Rita said. "Is it too much to hope that you got a match?"

"Yup, we got a match," Tilda said, the tone of her voice shifting. "You sitting down?"

"Sure am," Rita said, swiveling in her the chair to look out through the window. "Hit me."

Tilda's tone was measured. "The DNA matches one of the men that attacked you a few months ago."

Rita sat up straighter. "What, at the reservoir?"

Tilda made an affirmative sound.

"Fuck me," Rita said. "I'd hoped I'd seen the last of Clyde. But here he is, back in Still."

Tilda was silent for a beat. Then she said, "Clyde's not the match, Rita. It's Ken."

Chapter Thirty-Nine

Rita gripped the receiver to her ear. "Hang on, Tilda, I've got to get this clear."

"Can't get much clearer," Tilda said.

Rita sat forward, resting her elbows on the desk. "So you're saying the hair and saliva are a match to Ken Saunders?"

"Uh-huh," Tilda said. "And it's about to get a whole lot clearer."

"You're kidding."

"Nope. We found a tissue wedged in the trunk. Microscopic traces of blood on it. Also a match to Ken."

Rita blew out a breath. "Well, thanks. I guess. I wasn't expecting that."

"Sorry for the shocker," Tilda said. "It happens every once in a while. That's small-town living."

"You're right. Cases in New York rarely hit this close to home."

She thanked Tilda and hung up, then called Jason.

But only his voicemail picked up. She disconnected and

opened her desk drawer. She pulled out a business card, read it over, then dialed the number on the landline.

"Angela Ruiz," a professional voice answered.

Rita flicked the card with her fingernail. "Angela, it's Sheriff Jonas."

"It's good to hear from you, Rita. Are you calling to accept my job offer?"

Rita ignored the bait. "Not today. I'm calling to let you know I've got evidence that Ken Saunders may be involved in an Apex ex-employee's death."

There was a beat of silence. Then Angela said, "Why are you calling me?"

Rita tried to keep the edge from her voice. "Oh, I don't know. I thought you might be interested in the possibility of an employee's participation in murder. And a grisly one, at that. And a security employee, of all things."

"I trust you'll do what you have to do," Angela said. "Like you always do, Rita. Now, please excuse me, I have a meeting to attend."

Rita muttered a goodbye, but Angela had already hung up.

Then Rita called Ken.

"I need you to come into the station and answer some more questions."

Ken said something unintelligible. "Is this about Trevor Bachman again?"

"Yes. And this is an official interview," Rita said.

Then she hung up, got up from her desk, and walked into the bullpen. "Mary Lou, could you please request a warrant for Ken Saunders' Apex office, home address, and his Audi?

"Pulling out the big guns, huh?" Mary Lou said.

"We've got DNA evidence that Ken was at the crime scene," Rita said.

Mary Lou paused, pressing her lips together. "Consider it done."

"Thanks," Rita said. "Because I've got a headache coming on the size of Yellowstone."

"Then you might want to steer clear of SilverNomad if you don't want a bigger one," Mary Lou said.

Without a word, Rita spun on her heel and walked back into her office. She closed the door behind her and sat back at her desk. She woke up her desktop and navigated to Carole's page.

There was a fresh upload.

Her finger itched to hit play. But Mary Lou was right. She shouldn't watch it. Mary Lou was always right.

Except about some things.

Rita rubbed her belly, willing herself not to look. But if she was going to be a mother, shouldn't she have the resilience to face her own?

Rita pressed play.

Carole's made-up face launched into the sad tale of her returning to her hometown following her late ex-husband's death, only to discover her daughter had changed the keys, locking her out of the house for perpetuity.

Rita didn't even know that Carole knew the word "perpetuity." Then Rita did the worst. She looked at the comments. Dozens upon dozens of emojis — smiley faces and floating hearts and yellow bicep-pumping arms — taunted her. Rita's stomach lurched.

Fearing more vomit, she closed the browser window and walked away from her desk.

And straight into the bullpen. "I'm leaving for the day," Rita said, walking past Mary Lou's desk.

"I warned you," Mary Lou said.

Rita turned and glared at her, hands fisted. "I'm entitled to my anger."

"Think of the baby."

Rita grunted and stormed out the back door. Tapping her teeth together, she got in her Honda and headed to the Sunny Daze Campsites.

She drove through the sites until she found Carole's van. And Carole, seated by a campfire, talking into a camera on a tripod.

Rita strode across the campsite. "Carole."

Carole looked up, startled. "Rita." Then she stood and looked at the camera with a broad smile. "We're live, everyone, and my daughter's here."

"Fuck that," Rita said, knocking aside the camera. "What the hell is this video about?"

"My gear!" Carole shouted, shoving Rita aside.

Riga snagged her arm, pulling her back. "Leave it."

"It's a livestream," Carole said, yanking her arm free and pushing Rita away. "Called *Campfire Confessions with Carole*."

Rita stumbled back into a tree trunk. "Well, go find a campfire somewhere else." She dusted the crumbles of bark off her uniform. "Outside of Still County."

"Look, Rita," Carole, spreading her palms, "I know you're upset about me expressing my feelings about your unwelcoming attitude. But if you look at things from my perspective—"

"Cut the bullshit," Rita said. "Why are you really back?"

"I already told you," Carole said, "I'm here for closure with your father."

"I don't believe it," Rita said. "I think you came for the estate."

Carole threw up her hands. "Well, why wouldn't I? I lived in that house for fifteen years. That's where I raised you up."

Rita let out a bitter bark of a laugh. "Oh, you raised me up, huh? Well, every dark corner of that goddamned house holds bad memories for me. So if you think you're getting a single floorboard out of that place, you've got another thing coming."

"I'm glad this is livestreamed," Carole said. "So you can hear yourself later, you entitled brat. Do you know what it takes to raise a kid?"

"It doesn't take bourbon," Rita said.

"Oh, here we go again! Otto's so perfect, isn't he? Well, he wasn't, you know. The whole time we were married, he fucked around on us."

"On *us*?" Rita said. "He was always there for me, in his way. It's you he fucked around on, and I'm not surprised."

Carole let out a wail. "How dare you?"

"Well, it's true," Rita said. "And no, he shouldn't have slept around on you. You two should have split. You should have left sooner."

Tears streamed down Carole's cheeks. "Is that what you really think? That I should have left sooner? Is that what you wanted?"

Rita scoffed. "Jesus, if only you knew. But you've never known what I've wanted."

"How could I?" Carole said. "You've barely talked to either of your parents in years, moving out of state. If you go back and watch my reels, you'd actually find out about the people you come from."

Rita stilled, as a memory of Lisa's battered body flashed through her mind. "You should leave town," she said, her voice returned to calm. "There's nothing here for you."

Carole looked frightened. She glanced at the tripod lying on the ground, the camera still showing a green light for 'record.'

"I have nowhere else to go," she said.

Rita backed away. "That's not my problem."

Then she turned and got back into the Honda. As she pulled out of the site, Carole picked up her tripod and repositioned the camera. Then she moved back in front of the fire and started talking again.

Rita drove away, unable to help wondering why it was that Otto got cancer and not Carole.

Even though she knew she probably shouldn't be having thoughts like that.

Chapter Forty

Rita threw the Honda into park and slammed into the SCSO.

"That woman is dead to me," she said the moment she saw Mary Lou.

Mary Lou spun around at her desk, then ogled Rita head to toe. "It's one hell of a live stream," she said. Then she tapped a red fingernail on the computer screen. "You should read the comments."

Rita retied her bun. "I definitely should not."

"On second thought, you're right," Mary Lou said. "Although some of these are really good. You should see how many suggest Carole should call the police on her lunatic daughter." Then she swung back to face Rita and gestured toward her uniform. "Didn't they notice you already are the police?"

Rita grunted and stalked to the bathroom. She locked herself inside and checked out her reflection. No scratches, but some dirt smudges. She tidied as best she could. Then leaned over the sink and threw up.

"Fuck." She washed out her mouth and dried her lips.

A knock sounded on the door.

"Who is it?" Rita asked.

There was a moment of silence. "Well, who the hell do you think it is?" Mary Lou answered. "It's the King."

Rita threw open the door. "What do you want?"

Mary Lou gave her a look. "To go 'mama' on your ass." She grabbed Rita for a hug. Then pushed her back, gripping her shoulders to look at her. "You just had a fist-fight with your mother. And your father's dead. And you got a baby in that belly."

Rita sighed. "Don't remind me. I can't keep anything down."

"That's going to be a problem," Mary Lou said. "Bananas. Rice cakes. Soda crackers."

Rita grimaced. "Sounding better by the minute."

"I'm also here to tell you Ken's arrived."

Rita peered over her shoulder into the bullpen. "Oh, yeah?"

"I left him in the foyer," Mary Lou said. "He looks worse than you do. If that's any consolation."

Rita stepped out of the bathroom and smoothed her uniform. "Thanks, Mary Lou. Wish me luck."

She walked to the front of the SCSO and poked her head into the foyer. Ken sat hunched in the plastic chair, pale as a snowman, his eyes hidden behind reflective shades and his lips pressed into a hard line.

"Thanks for coming down, Ken," Rita said. "Let's go talk in my office."

He stood and followed her, his hands shaking slightly.

After Rita had closed the door, he took a seat and said, "What's this all about? I already told you everything I know about Trevor Bachman."

"I disagree," Rita said, taking a seat at her desk. Then

she turned on her voice recorder. "How come your DNA was found at the crime scene?"

Ken laughed. "Nice joke. Now what are we here to talk about?"

Rita said nothing, continuing to watch him.

Ken removed his sunglasses and leaned forward. "You're serious, aren't you?"

"Dead serious," Rita said. "I told you this is official."

Ken blinked at her. "Well, I don't know. What the hell was found?"

Rita folded her hands. "A hair on the driver's seat. Blood on a tissue. Saliva on a coffee cup."

What little blood remained in Ken's complexion drained from his face. "I'm being set up."

Rita didn't expect that. "Set up?"

Ken thumped his chest. "I wasn't there. And I don't know how any of that shit got there."

Again, Rita said nothing, watching him.

"You gotta believe me, Rita. I mean Sheriff Jonas."

"I could understand the coffee cup being circumstantial," Rita said. "Maybe Trevor Bachman was a dutiful anti-litterbug, gleaning junk from the Apex parking lot. But two other instances of DNA in the vehicle?" Rita spread her hands on the desk. "I'm sorry, Ken, but the evidence suggests you're involved in some capacity."

Ken fell silent. After a moment, he said, "I'm not saying another damn thing."

Rita nodded. "I think that's a good idea."

"So what next?" Ken asked.

"You won't be allowed back in your office at Apex. Or your house at Apex Hills. Or in your Audi. Until the SCSO have searched each."

Ken's blood came back to his face. "Wait until Angela hears about this."

"I've already called Angela," Rita said.

Ken blinked at her. "How'd she take it?"

"All right."

"All right? Well, what is she doing?"

"Going to a meeting, apparently," Rita said.

Ken bristled. "I mean about this situation? What is she doing about me? To help me? Apex is lawyered up. What did Angela have to say?"

"She told me to go ahead and investigate," Rita said.

"Jesus Christ," Ken said. "Give me a break here, Rita. I didn't do anything. I'm not a violent guy."

Rita gave him a look. "You, me, and Hunter Green know that's not true."

"Oh, come on," Ken said. "Don't bring up the past."

"You know I'm just doing my job, Ken." She gave him an encouraging smile. "The easier you cooperate, the quicker I can search. And the quicker we can clear your name." She softened her smile. "May I have your keys, please?"

Grumbling, Ken pulled a ring of keys from his pocket and turned them over. He pointed out his house key and gave her the number to his security system.

"Thanks. Can Mary Lou call Haleigh to come pick you up?" Rita asked.

Ken chewed on his lip. "She's at work. Besides, where the hell would I go?"

"That's a good question," Rita said, "considering the Still Haven Inn went up in a blaze of an arsonist's glory. I'd suggest asking Mary Lou about a local B&B."

Ken's eyebrows shot up. "A B&B? You think Haleigh's going to be happy about that?"

"Then maybe she has a suggestion," Rita said, cheery.

Ken sighed. "Yeah, like her grandmother's house."

Rita cocked her head. "Sounds like an option."

Ken grumbled in his throat. "It's not an option."

Rita squeezed his arm. "I'm sorry you're feeling out of options, Ken."

He shook off her hand. "Think I'll walk into town and meet her when she gets off work."

"Take some water with you," Rita said. "It's hot out there."

Ken cut his eyes at her. "Okay, Mom."

"I nearly passed out walking into town the other day. I met a bison who looked about as parched as I was."

Ken crinkled his nose. "There are no bison out this way."

Rita nodded. "That's what I thought. Oh, and don't leave town without letting me know where you're going."

"Fine," Ken said, getting up. The chair creaked. "You can text me when you're done searching." Then he walked out of her office and out through the bullpen. As he left the SCSO, he slammed the front door.

Rita exchanged a look with Mary Lou. "Well, that's done," she said.

Mary Lou let out a sigh. "The warrants have come through."

"Great." Rita took the fob from the key ring and passed it to Mary Lou. "And can you call Casper to come get Ken's Audi for a forensic sweep?"

"Ten-four."

"And in the meantime, I'll start with his office at Genius HQ."

Chapter Forty-One

Rita surveyed the office.

A thin layer of dust coated the furnishings which had once been used by Boyd Farmer. It seemed Ken had barely touched anything since taking over the office. Admittedly, the room felt haunted by Boyd; even in death, the man had an immense presence.

Rita searched the perimeter of the room, but as most of the shelves were empty, she found nothing. Then she looked through Ken's desk. The top drawer held a small variety of nondescript stationery supplies. The second drawer contained Apex files.

On the desktop lay another file, this one labeled "Trevor Bachman."

Rita flipped open the cover. Trevor's employment record. Rita scanned the pages. Nothing mentioned his health condition. And nothing suggested Trevor was anything other than an exemplary employee.

She closed the file folder and picked up the receiver to call down to reception.

"Hi, Ginny. I finished searching Ken's office," she said.

"Could you tell me if Ken had access to other areas of the building?"

"Sure, Sheriff Jonas," Ginny said. A keyboard clattered. "Being in security, he had clearance to all areas of the building."

"Nothing was off access to him?"

"That's right."

"Thanks," Rita said. "And Ginny — I know it's awkward that I'm investigating an Apex employee. Getting through this will helpfully clear everything up as soon as possible."

A moment of silence suggested that Ginny might have been nodding. Then, "I understand, Sheriff."

"Do you happen to have any lye on the premises?" Rita asked.

"Lye?" Ginny repeated.

"Sodium hydroxide," Rita said. "The chemical formula is NaOH."

"I'll search it in our database," Ginny said. "Just a sec." The sound of keys tapping echoed over the line. "Yes, it's on the premises," Ginny said. "Do you want to talk to the safety manager about it?"

"Yes, please," Rita said.

"I'll call the safety manager to come down to reception."

Rita thanked her and hung up, then headed down the curved staircase to the glass-encased foyer. Ginny sat at the front desk, wearing a headset, large-framed glasses, and a worried expression.

She looked up as Rita approached, looking no more encouraged than when Rita had given her a copy of the search warrant.

"It's odd, you asking all these questions about Ken," Ginny said. She shivered. 'First Boyd. Now, well…" Her gaze flickered away from Rita's. "Everyone's innocent until proven otherwise, right?"

"Right," Rita said. "I'm only doing my due diligence."

Ginny nodded, her eyes moist with tears.

Rita let out a breath. "The hardest part of living in a small town is maintaining professional distance." Then she smiled. "Ken'll bear it up. He's a strong guy, and I don't just mean his lats."

Nodding, Ginny removed her glasses to dab at her eyes with a tissue. Then she returned them to her nose and pointed over Rita's shoulder.

"There's Bill."

Rita turned to see a tall man with short gray hair and sharp brown eyes. He wore khaki cargo pants, steel-toed boots, and a reflective vest with an Apex logo.

"I'm Sheriff Jonas," Rita said, extending a hand.

The man shook it. "Hello, Sheriff, I'm Bill Lapinski. I'm the safety manager on shift today."

"I appreciate you showing me the chemical stores," Rita said. "I have some questions about the sodium hydroxide on site."

"You bet, Sheriff," Lapinski said. "Casper Forensics already called for a sample, which I've sent." Lapinski gestured down a corridor which terminated at an exterior door. "We need to go this way to see the chemical lockers. They're in the next building."

Rita fell into step with Lapinski They passed through the door to a shaded breezeway which led to a smaller steel and concrete building devoid of windows. Red signs warning danger and yellow triangles with exclamation points alerted people to the hazardous chemicals inside. A half-dozen "No Smoking" symbols peppered the wall.

Lapinski swiped his security pass across the pad beside the steel door, then led the way inside the warehouse.

Two sets of firesafe double-doors branched off an epoxy-coated concrete foyer.

"The flammable stores are in warehouse A," Lapinski said, waving a finger at the door on the left bearing additional warning signs. "The corrosive chemicals are stored in warehouse B."

On this door, a sign showed a test tube spilling droplets onto a hand (corroding the flesh) as well as what Rita presumed was an iron bar, but which made her think of chocolate. Her stomach growled. There weren't many things she'd wanted to eat lately. And here was a solution.

She willed her guts to be quiet and glanced around the foyer. The walls housed multiple fire extinguishers, an eyewash station, a defibrillator, and more signage. Overhead, a sprinkler system snaked between the silver ducting of the ventilation system.

Lapinski pulled open the door and they entered warehouse B. Inside, despite the whir of the ducting system, the air had an acrid odor. Here, there were more eyewash stations. He passed her a pair of protective glasses from a shelf of PPE, then slipped on a pair of his own, which he'd carried in his cargo pocket.

He led her to a bank of yellow chemical lockers and stopped in front of the fourth cabinet. With a quiet clang, Lapinski unlocked and opened the metal door. Inside stood a 55-gallon drum labeled NaOH.

"Fifty percent concentrate?" Rita asked.

"That's right," Lapinski said.

"What's it used for here?"

Lapinski shifted his feet. "Disposing of animal carcasses."

Rita's eyebrows arched. "Animal carcasses? At Apex?"

"From the animal-testing department."

Rita's stomach flipped. She hid a grimace. "Is all the lye accounted for?"

"Our sign-out procedures indicate yes."

Rita's brow puckered. "In the case of theft, one would presumably bypass the procedures."

A slight flush touched Lapinski's cheeks. "Right."

"How many people have access to these lockers?"

"Not many," Lapinski said. "Even those with access to the warehouse need to request specific access to each locker."

"I'll need to know everyone who has access to all the lye lockers," Rita said.

Lapinski nodded. "Sure thing."

"Do you have access to all the lockers, Bill?"

"Yes. I perform the audits."

"What's involved in an audit?"

"It's a compliance check to ensure that the storage conditions still meet safety regulations."

"Anything suspicious on your last audit?"

He shook his head. "No."

"And when was that?"

"Three months ago. This quarter's audit is coming up in a couple weeks."

"So it's been months since you've opened this locker?"

"Yeah, until earlier, when I sent that sample to the folks at Caper Forensics."

"Has lye ever been stolen from the premises before?" Rita asked.

"No."

"How about other dangerous chemicals?"

"Not that I'm aware of."

"Thanks," Rita said. "I appreciate your time today." She passed him her card. "Please get back to me as soon as possible with that list of employees who have access."

"You bet, Sheriff Jonas," Lapinski said, pocketing her card in his cargo pants. Then he relocked the cabinet and led Rita to the door, where they removed their glasses before leaving.

From the warehouse, Rita walked directly to the parking lot and drove to Ken's house in Apex Hills.

She rolled into the driveway and parked. Why had Trevor picked a fight with Ken out front of Apex HQ, when he lived only a few blocks away from him? Had he intended to create a scene? Garner witnesses? Or backup? Because the fight was doomed from the get-go. Trevor Bachman knew that Ken outweighed him.

Rita took a pair of nitrile gloves from the glovebox and got out of the cruiser. From the trunk, she retrieved the latent prints kit and the Nikon D3500. She powered it on and snapped a photo of the front of Boyd Farmer's former house. She had last been here to interview Boyd.

And this was the property where he'd taken his own life — as Apex claimed was the case.

She walked up the front path, dried stalks whipping her shins. Without Boyd's tending, the flowers had given way to deadheads, and the shrubs had outgrown their tidy silhouettes.

The building, however, remained in good repair, clad in the same vinyl siding as the other houses in Apex Hills.

She walked up the front steps to the porch, which was well-swept and bore a plain door mat which refrained from welcoming anyone. Compared to the Bachmans' front porch, littered with children's shoes and decorated with Trevor's planter, Ken's entrance suggested that the house was being prepared for resale.

Rita unlocked the front door and stepped inside. The security alarm announced her arrival with a series of pings. She punched Ken's code to disarm the security system into the panel on the wall.

The tiled foyer offered no furnishings or decorative items, only a coat closet containing a variety of sporting equipment, three men's jackets, and a pink running jacket in Haleigh's size.

Rita took photos, shut the closet door again, and walked through to the kitchen. The room smelled like Mr. Clean products instead of last night's dinner. She peeked under the sink.

No lye.

She deposited the copy of the warrant on the granite countertop, which held a blender, an electric kettle, and a toaster oven, though no canisters, salt and pepper shakers, or houseplants.

Inside the refrigerator, Rita found a variety of flavored protein powders, all branded with a pink Vita-Boost logo, two cartons of eggs, and three gallons of milk.

Closing the refrigerator, she turned to the cabinetry. Half the drawers were empty, and she quickly moved onto the cupboards, first searching the uppers, then the lowers, taking photographs as she worked. The only cupboard that was full contained multiple plastic bottles of vitamins, greens powders, and more whey. All were branded Vita-Boost.

Aside from the vast Vita-Boost collection, she found nothing out of the ordinary, unless it was out of the ordinary to have everything perfectly aligned: the cutlery in its tray; the nested measuring cups; the mug-handles oriented towards the Laramie Mountains.

She closed the last cupboard door, confident that neither Ken nor Haleigh were baking a pie anytime soon.

Nor was there any indication that Ken (or Haleigh) owned a pet of any kind.

Off the kitchen, Rita searched the small laundry room, deciding that Ken's modern washer and dryer were like Tonka toys compared to the growling beasts in Otto's basement.

There was no lye.

The dining room had been turned into a home gym, containing a large rebounder, a giant silver exercise ball, and a collection of medicine balls. On the back wall, a mirror hung above a shelf of free-weights and kettlebells. Beside the bench, a basket held fresh, rolled-up towels.

Rita snapped some more pictures, then walked through to the living room.

A gray three-seater sofa and an armchair faced a flat screen TV mounted over the black tiled fireplace. A glass coffee table held nothing but two vacant cork coasters.

On the walls, instead of family photos, watercolor paintings showed generic scenes of the Wyoming country-side. In one, a series of brown droplets represented bison grazing in a vale. Considering his mass and might, Ken was actually quite like one.

What had Edith Mae said bison represented? *Strength and resilience.*

Rita's hand drifted to her belly. Though not to her stomach this time. Lower.

Something flopped.

Then flipped, like a miniature minnow. She felt the urge to sink onto the sofa and rest.

The oatmeal throw cushions were arranged in an upright row, overstuffed and stiff. At least she thought the color was called oatmeal. She remembered Carole making her an oatmeal play suit as a child. Made out of corduroy, it had been scratchy and squeaky and caused Rita to shiver.

But Carole had insisted she wear it because of how

much she'd labored on it. To which Rita had replied, "I don't like oatmeal."

Which had not been the correct answer.

Overcoming the urge to lay on the sofa, Rita took a photograph of it. Then she turned around to take one of the fireplace. A pile of ash in the grate suggested something had been recently burned.

She crouched to take a closer photograph, then opened up the prints kit and dusted the black tile surround with a layer of black powder.

But the fireplace had been wiped clean.

She moved the brush to the fire irons — a poker, tongs, a brush, and pan — and repeated the process, inspecting each tool. These, too, were wiped clean. In fact, there wasn't an errant hair in Ken's house (either his or Haleigh's two-foot-long strands). Yet his DNA was everywhere in Trevor's car.

Rita put on a fresh pair of nitrile gloves and used the brass poker to stir the ashes. A white scrap bearing part of Apex's unmistakable logo flipped out, its edges singed. She bagged it for evidence, then stirred the ash again. But it yielded no further scraps.

What was it that Ken had wanted to burn? And were there any other telling documents on the premises that he hadn't yet burned?

Rita packed up the prints kit and headed upstairs. But she found no office — only the master bedroom with en suite, a full bath, and a guest bedroom (which housed nothing more than a folded-up futon, a simple side table with a lamp, and an empty closet).

Rita chewed on her cheek. Ken must keep all his paperwork electronically, or at Genius HQ, even though she'd seen nothing of note. Or might he keep a letter in his drawer, like Otto kept a photograph of a mysterious woman in his sock drawer?

She entered the master suite, which featured more gray and oatmeal things (headboard, bedding, and blinds) and very few personal affects. Although she hadn't searched the side tables yet. And that was the least favorite place she liked to look in anyone's house.

She crossed to the dresser and pulled open the top drawer, feeling as awkward as she had in Otto's room. When she'd worked the beat in New Work, she'd certainly never searched the apartment, least of all underwear drawers, of anyone she knew.

Ken's drawer held eleven pairs of briefs, all of them black, and eleven pairs of socks, also all black. But there was no Apex letterhead. Or photographs of a slightly recognizable (albeit unidentifiable) woman. Or of Haleigh, for that matter.

She took a photo, then opened the next drawer.

Finally, here was Haleigh's presence, represented in a jumble of colorful G-strings, brassieres, scrunchies, ankle socks, and yoga headbands. Plus another elastic accessory with a mysterious function. Failing to deduce its purpose, she dropped it back into the mix and photographed the drawer.

The bottom two drawers held folded t-shirts and sweatpants, all of them heather gray. She found nothing of Haleigh's here. She took pictures of both drawers, then moved to the walk-in closet.

Which housed nothing more than a couple of suits and some extra pairs of reflective sunglasses. Again, Rita found nothing of Haleigh's. Rita presumed her wardrobe was at her place of work. Or her grandmother's house.

Steeling herself, Rita moved to the first of the two side tables. She took a breath and pulled open the drawer.

A few objects rattled inside: some pens, a flashlight, some expired ID cards, a passport, a pack of tissues, and a tube of personal lubricant. No medications, no pocket-book, no journal, no Apex letterhead.

She moved around to the other side.

No tube of lube in this drawer, but a few jars of nail polish, some nail files, and more scrunchies. Some celebrity gossip magazines were crammed in the bottom drawer, along with some empty pink wrappers for what looked like some kind of healthy candy.

She took some more photographs, then returned downstairs and went into the double-door garage. Half the garage sat empty, awaiting Ken's Audi. On the other half stood a treadmill, an elliptical trainer, a lat pull-down machine, and a stationary bike.

Rita crossed to a bank of upper cabinets on the back wall and looked inside. Garden products packed one shelf, likely left over from Boyd's tenancy. The other shelves held a scant number of tools and automobile fluids.

But no lye.

Rita returned to the kitchen and took a final scan of the room. She was about to leave when her eye caught something out of place which, after searching Ken's house, now appeared obvious.

She took a step across the kitchen and peered closer at the overhead ceiling vent. One of its screws hung loose by several threads. She returned to the garage to fetch a screwdriver, then returned to the kitchen and placed a chair beneath the vent.

Climbing up onto the chair, she removed the other three screws, then the vent plate. These she placed on the countertop, next to the warrant.

At first, she saw nothing behind the vent cover. But as

she reached inside the duct, her fingers brushed a piece of
paper.

Chapter Forty-Two

Rita withdrew a manila envelope from the vent. She opened it with ease, as the paper strip had not been peeled from the adhesive strip, and removed a letter. It read:

ATTN: *Ken Saunders,*

I am writing in regards to the matter of my hazardous exposure to dangerous chemicals at Apex. Enclosed with this letter is documentation that clearly outlines the serious nature of my health condition.

If you do not take immediate action to address my concerns, I will forward all this evidence to the Still County Sheriff's Office for an official investigation. Your prompt response to this matter will determine whether this issue is resolved quietly or escalated to the authorities.

Consider this your final notice. I expect a swift resolution.

Trevor Bachman

RITA PUT the note in an evidence bag, then brushed the

envelope for prints. It was clean. Lastly, she took photos of the duct and vent cover.

Then she let herself out, setting the security system and re-locking the front door behind her.

As she was peeling off her nitrile gloves, a black Jeep pulled into the drive. The engine cut and the door popped open, ejecting Haleigh.

"Oh, hi, Sheriff," she said, bouncing up the steps. "Are you here to talk shop with Ken again?"

"Not exactly," Rita said.

She glanced over Rita's shoulder at the closed door. "He's not here?"

"No," Rita said. "He mentioned he planned to meet you in town, after your shift."

Haleigh's smile faded. "Oh, but I didn't finish my shift."

"No?"

"No, I quit at noon."

"Oh?" Rita said.

Haleigh snapped a bubble in her gum. "Yeah, a creepy guy wanted me to put oil on his back."

Rita cringed. "Where do you work?"

"Glow with the Flow Tanning Studio," Haleigh said. Then she shrugged. "It's a play on words."

"Where have you been since you left the salon at noon?"

Haleigh displayed her left hand, the nails a glowing yellow. "When I walked off the job, I went over to Kimmy's and got my nails done. This color is Tropical Banana."

"Isn't that redundant?" Rita asked.

Haleigh blinked. "Redundant? Like getting fired?"

"Like repeating what isn't necessary," Rita said. "Presumably bananas only are in the tropics. There isn't a non-tropical version."

Haleigh blinked again, her eyelids framed with an abundance of false lashes. "I don't know about redundant bananas, but I thought of another play on words: shop talk."

Rita blinked back, her eyelids feeling gloriously unburdened. "How's that a play on words?"

Haleigh giggled. "'Cause you like to work *and* you like to shop."

"Not really," Rita said, shifting her weight.

Haleigh laughed. "Well, you're both cops, and Ken likes to work and shop."

"Oh, yeah? What does Ken like to buy?"

"Fitness equipment mostly," Haleigh said. "And supplements. I sell supplements, actually. Ken's one of my customers. Which is why it's not a big deal I flipped off Glow with the Flow."

"Vita-Boost," Rita said to herself, recalling the contents of Ken's refrigerator.

Haleigh smiled, wide. "You know it?"

"Only just," Rita said.

Haleigh's tone took on a *gravitas*. "It's a great brand."

"Is that how you and Ken met?" Rita asked. "By selling him Vita-Boost?"

Haleigh shook her head. "No, but it's a big part of what makes as a good couple. Of course when I met him, his whole dietary regime was a mess. But a man can change, right? I pointed out the deficits in his nutritional profile, and he started buying products through me."

"What supplements are you selling him?" Rita asked.

"That's private personal health information, Sheriff," Haleigh said, offering a one-shouldered shrug. "I'm sure you can understand that I can't tell you, since it's not pertinent to the case."

Rita shrugged back. "You're probably right about that."

Haleigh nodded. "Do you take supplements, Sheriff?"

"Sure," Rita said. "Caffeine."

Haleigh wrinkled her nose. "Hm." She whipped a pink card from her shoulder bag. "Here's my number in case you change your mind."

"Thanks," Rita said, taking her card. She tapped the fuchsia square. "It won't be easy to misplace."

"I love pink," Haleigh said with conviction. "Everyone always says green means health. But at Vita-Boost, we know pink is the greatest indicator of health. Bright, flush, moist magenta. Like our bodies. Well, at least like *one* body part in particular."

Rita hoped Haleigh wasn't talking about what she thought she was. The minnow swam faster.

"My tongue?" Rita said, hopeful.

"Nuh-uh." Haleigh used a tropical fingernail to pull down her lower left eyelid. "The inside of your eyelid indicates your overall health." She used her other hand to point to the inside of her lid. "Mine are very pink. But many people will have variations in hue, which indicated underlying medical conditions."

"Oh yeah?" Rita said, taking a step backwards to keep her eyelid out of the reach of Haleigh's fingernail. "I've never met a doctor who pulled down my eyelid. Except the optometrist."

Haleigh snapped another bubble. "You're gonna start thinking about pink in a whole new way, Sheriff. Like this Bubble Yum gum — it's not what you think."

"It's not?"

Haleigh shook her head, ponytail dancing. "It's healthy."

"I'd noticed it's very pink," Rita said.

Haleigh nodded. "It's homeopathic. Part of the Vita-Boost line."

The minnow flipped in Rita's lower belly. "Maybe I should start taking some vitamins."

Haleigh reached under Rita's nose to tap the card. "You can order on my website and get it shipped to your door. Or if you don't mind waiting, you can skip the shipping charge. Your order will come to my grandma's house in Casper, and I'll give it to Ken to drive over to the station."

"Sounds like exceptional service," Rita said. "And I'm sure Ken'll love that arrangement. Speaking of Ken, you may wish to go pick him up now. He said he was headed to The Bighorn Bean to wait until you were done work. Maybe he's still there."

"Oh," Haleigh said, "I don't eat muffins. I was thinking of driving into Casper to the Lettuce Eat Café."

"Have you got somewhere to stay in town?" Rita said.

Haleigh blinked at her. "In Casper?"

"Yes."

"Why?"

"You can't stay here at the moment."

"Why not?"

"Search warrant."

Haleigh's eyes bugged. "Does Ken know?"

Rita resisted a sigh. "Yes. That's why he's not at work. And why he's biding his time at The Bighorn Bean, till he meets you after your shift."

"Oh, I already told you, I'm didn't finish my shift."

"Of course," Rita said. "That's why could two should meet up to make plans for tonight."

"Where's he planning to stay?" Haleigh asked.

Rita let loose the sigh. "It's best if you ask him these questions for yourself."

"Okay," Haleigh said, turning to walk back to her Jeep. "I'm gonna go head to my grandma's for the night. She doesn't mind vegan takeout. If you see Ken, can you let him know?"

Rita sighed. "Sure. Oh, and Haleigh — I have a personal question, if you don't mind?"

Haleigh stopped and turned. "Yeah?"

"How did you and Ken meet?"

Her bright smile reappeared. "We met on a dating website. *Fish in the Sea.* As in, everyone on there's a catch."

Rita offered a smile. "Or as in, there's plenty of others to choose if this one's a dud?"

Haleigh paused to consider. "Gosh, I guess so. The ones that don't work out I call carps. So do all my girl-friends."

"How long have you and Ken been dating?"

"Hmm." Haleigh tapped her lips. "This is the third month he's been on my Vita-Boost order form. So I'd say between twelve and sixteen weeks."

"Thanks," Rita said. "One last thing before you go?"

Haleigh nodded. "Okay."

"Did you ever hear Ken mention someone by the name of Trevor Bachman?"

Haleigh snapped another bubble. "Oh, yeah, that was that asshole who picked a fight with him last week at the Apex headquarters. Scratched up his face. But Ken put him in his place. He's head of the security there, you know."

"And how about Frenchie?" Rita asked.

Haleigh frowned. "What's that?"

285

"That someone else's name," Rita said. "Frenchie, like fries. The same way you're like a comet."

Haleigh's smile returned. "Oh, I get it, yeah. No, I dunno anyone called Frenchie. Does he tan?"

"Not in town," Rita said. "He's an old-fashioned guy. Thanks for your time, Haleigh. Have a good night at your grandmother's. And thanks for your number. I may need more answers."

"And supplements," Haleigh said.

"And if you think of anything else, here's my card," Rita said.

Haleigh took her card. "You mean, related to Frenchie and the Bookman?"

"Yep," Rita said. "Like Frenchie and Trevor Bachman. Feel free to give me a call anytime."

Haleigh smiled. "Sure, I could give you a call." Then she rummaged in her shoulder bag. "I could also give you this." She passed Rita a small paper packet, also pink. "It's a sample of the gum."

Rita read the package. "Vita-Boost Bubble Yum."

Haleigh grinned. "Yeah, it'll perk you right up. You look really tired."

"That's a fair assessment," Rita said, pocketing the packet. "Thanks."

Chapter Forty-Three

"Well, I'm back," Rita said, walking into the bullpen. "And I got evidence, photos, and a headache. But no prints."

Mary Lou swiveled around in her chair. "His place was wiped clean?"

"By my estimate," Rita said, headed for her office. "But can you arrange Casper forensics to go do another sweep of his place?"

"Ten-four," Mary Lou said, returning to her keyboard.

Rita closed the office door and sat at her desk. A light on the telephone flashed, indicating voicemail. She picked up the receiver and dialed to listen:

"Good afternoon, Sheriff Jonas, this is Aiden Slaney returning your call. May I remind you that there's no access to your father's box without the death certificate. I'm sure we've been over this before. Also, you and your officer startled my wife quite terribly, watching her through the hedge like that. I'm sure you can understand me when I request any further communication be done so in a professional manner."

Rita rolled her eyes, deleted the message, and hung up the phone. Then she walked back into the bullpen.

"I'm headed over to The Bighorn Bean," she said. "Ken's waiting there for me."

"Have fun," Mary Lou said, tapping on the keys on her keyboard.

Across the street, Rita found Ken seated alone at a table by the window, reading the newspaper. Three empty coffee mugs cluttered the table.

She pulled out a chair and sat down opposite him.

Ken looked up at her and folded his arms. "I told you, you wouldn't find anything."

Rita met his eye. "But I did."

Ken's brow furrowed. "Bullshit."

"I found a letter addressed to you from Trevor Bachman."

"Bullshit."

Rita fired back at him. "I held the thing in my hand, Ken."

"This is a setup."

Rita knit her brow. "A setup?"

"Yeah," Ken said, turning purple. "You're setting me up."

Rita frowned at him. "Why?"

"All you got is revenge on your mind."

"Because of the reservoir?" Rita took a breath. "Look, I found evidence that suggests sensitive documents were burned in the fireplace."

Ken's purple face blanched. "My house was broken into a few days ago."

"With that security system?"

The pink flush returned to his face. "Haleigh never remembers to set it." He cleared his throat. "We've had words about it before."

Rita crinkled her nose at him. "Did you report it?"

"To myself?" Ken sputtered. "That would be stupid."

"To me."

Ken avoided her eye. "I figured it was kids."

"What made you think that?"

He shrugged. "Only thing touched was the fireplace. I figured they were up to some stupid ritual or something. Maybe having a *Kumbaya* moment. I was just happy there were no used condoms left behind. Only some ashes."

"Where were you Thursday morning?" Rita asked.

Ken let out a slow breath. "I was in bed with Haleigh. Ask her."

Rita gave a slight nod. "I will. In the meantime, Ken Saunders, I'm going to put you under arrest for the murder of Trevor Bachman."

"Jesus, Rita," Ken said, folding his hands on the table as though clasping a prayer. "Can't you see I'm being set up?" His knuckles shook, and he knocked over one of the mugs.

Rita set it upright. "You know I'll do my due diligence, Ken. Look, you understand. We're both cops. Of a sort. If you're innocent, I'm gonna find out. So right now, you've got to trust me to do that, okay?"

He swallowed and nodded.

"Great," she said. "Hold your faith in me, and we'll be on the same side." Then she reached across the table and slapped his shoulder. "Smile, huh? That way we look like we're just talking shop."

Ken nodded, moisture gathering in his eyes.

"Come on," Rita said, cocking her head towards the door. "I'm not gonna cuff you in public. Let's head out in public."

Ken nodded again and put on his shades.

Rita stood. "Okay, let's head out."

Ken followed as she pushed open the door. They stepped outside. The hot, late summer air hit them like a furnace. For a moment, Ken tensed beside her, fisted his hands as though preparing to bolt.

"Ken, if you run…"

"You'll shoot me?"

Rita snorted. "Hell no, of course not. But it wouldn't be a good look for you. And then I'd have to reevaluate all the evidence. I'm supposed to be doing the thing where I find out you're innocent, right?"

He loosened his shoulders and fell into pace with her, as if they'd just shared a casual coffee. They walked across the street to the SCSO.

Inside, Rita led him to Mary Lou's desk. "Have a seat, Ken."

Ken nodded and lowered himself into Walter's chair.

Mary Lou took off her reading glasses, set them beside her keyboard, and turned around in her chair.

"Hi there, Ken."

"I'm gonna read you your rights now," Rita said, before doing so. Then she asked, "Do you want your lawyer?"

Ken shook his head. "No, because it'll be an Apex lawyer, and I'm not sure I'm ready for them to find out I've been arrested."

"Are you worried they'll dispose of you like they did Boyd?" Rita asked.

Ken chuckled, but his eyes gave away his reservations. "That's only rumors."

Rita got up from sitting on the edge of Mary Lou's desk. "Come on, Ken, I'll take you down to the cells."

Rita led him downstairs to the holding cells, the walls painted a slightly lighter shade of beige than upstairs, in an attempt to brighten the basement.

Without a word, Ken stepped through the door to the cell, surveyed it, and turned back around to face Rita. "When you find out who's setting me up, Jonas," Ken said, his jaw set, "you promise to tell me, huh?"

"You bet," Ria said, as she locked him in. "Good night, Ken."

"Wait," Ken said.

Rita paused. "Yes?"

"I read about your dad in the paper. His obituary … it was good."

Rita nodded. "I'm sure it was good," she said. "He wrote it for himself."

"You didn't read it?" Ken asked.

Rita stiffened, then gave him an encouraging smile. "Sleep well, Ken. See you tomorrow."

Chapter Forty-Four

"I'm headed for Casper," Rita said, marching for the back door.

"Hold up," Mary Lou said, getting up from her desk. "What about Ken?"

Rita paused. "What about Ken?"

"You want me to leave Ken alone overnight? I let Beaumont know we're still down a man, but I ain't stickin' around. I got a date with the sparky."

Rita pursed her lips. "Hm. Jason's still selecting the new officer. See if Arbuckle is interested in a guarding gig?"

Mary Lou tongued her cheek. "What am I gonna do, call him on a bullhorn? He don't have a cell phone."

"If you call Apex security, someone can dispatch a radio message to him. He's legit now up at Lisa's Place."

Mary Lou cocked her head. "Well, then, I might stay after all, just for the entertainment value."

Rita laughed. "Use petty cash to pay him, all right?"

"Ten-four."

She walked out the back door and headed across the

street to The Bighorn Bean, the late afternoon sun giving its brick facade a golden glow.

"Hi again, Rita," Carly said, wiping the countertop. "I've seen you more than once here today."

"Yeah, now I'm looking for the newspaper my colleague was reading," she said. She crossed to the recycling bin and rummaged inside, pulling out the top newspaper.

She opened to the Lifestyle section and found the photo of Otto. She folded the page into eighths and pocketed it.

Then she waved to Carly on her way out. "Have a good night. Any plans?"

Carly grinned. "Aside from having a bath and painting my toenails? 'Course not. After all those years at The Revue, I'll take all the peace and quiet that I can get."

"Have you taken up jigsaw puzzles yet?" Rita asked.

Carly laughed. "I wouldn't put it past me."

"Sometime I'll drop off a flock of flamingos in a thousand pieces."

On her way back to the parking lot behind the station, Rita called Haleigh.

"I have a few more questions I'd like to ask you in person," Rita said after Haleigh had picked up. "Are you in Casper?"

"Yeah, I just got to my grandma's," Haleigh said, then gave Rita the address.

Rita got in the cruiser, pulled out of the parking lot, this time waiting for the black Camry to follow her. Like the consistent shadow it was, it followed her onto the freeway towards Casper.

The Camry kept the same speed behind Rita, maintaining a distance of a quarter mile between them. She watched for the blue and white sign that announced a roadside Rest Area, then signaled, slowed, and pulled over. The Camry pulled off too, but didn't turn off its ignition.

Rita got out and walked back to the driver's side window. It was already lowered and the driver rested his arm on the top of the door, displaying intricate tattoos.

"Okay, I'll see Tom Gabriel," Rita said to the man. "But first, I want a meeting with his lawyer, Alan Crawford."

The man inclined his head. "You got it."

Rita gave him a pert nod. "Thanks." Then she returned to the cruiser and drove without stopping again to the Best Western in Casper.

At the reception desk, she asked if Jason had already checked in.

"No, Officer Perry hasn't arrived yet," the desk clerk said, reading the computer screen. "When he does, I can let him know your room number, Sheriff."

"Thanks," Rita said, then she walked down the hall to 112, where she freshened up in the bathroom and unpacked her belongings. Then she looked out of the window, watching for the Camry.

The moment she pulled back the curtain, its headlights illuminated and it pulled out of its stall, rolling into the portico.

Rita dropped the curtains and went outside. The Camry idled in front of the glass doors of the lobby, its back door already open for her.

She slid into the back seat and buckled in. Thankfully, there was no equivalent to Marcus Dwyer along for the ride, insisting she wear a blindfold.

Nor did they arrive at a warehouse. This time, the Camry rolled up to a glass facade office building.

"Nice place," Rita said. "I'm not used to this level of luxury from Tom Gabriel."

The driver grunted and got out, standing a foot shorter than Rita had anticipated. He swiped a security card to enter the building and led her upstairs to a corner office with two glass walls. Bookshelves lined the other two walls.

"Rita Jonas," Alan Crawford said, spreading his hands. On his desk lay a fan of paperwork, clearly arranged for her arrival.

"Hi, Alan," Rita said, taking a seat in front of his desk. The chair's upholstery was plush and soft. She rubbed the suede armrests. "I need to get one of these in my office."

Alan gave her a bland smile. "I'm not sure your budget would cover it, Sheriff."

She picked up a blown-glass paperweight containing suspended antique coins and studied it. "So how is it you became my dad's lawyer?" The shiny discs flashed in the light as she turned it. "He was a real blue-collar guy."

Steepling his fingers, Alan rested his elbows on the desk. "This is what you wanted to ask me?"

Rita returned the paperweight to Alan's desk. "Please answer the question."

"Through Tom, of course."

Rita laughed. "You're saying it was a personal recommendation? Some of Tom's friendly advice to help a guy get along?"

Alan's smile tightened. "Why not?"

Rita twiddled her thumbs. "I've gotten advice from Tom before. Though it often sounds more like a threat."

Smiling, Alan leaned back in his chair. "They may not have been friends, but they respected one another."

Rita raised a brow. "Respected?"

Alan shrugged. "Professionally."

She laughed. "Professionally?"

"Let's get to business, shall we?" Alan said. "And

discuss your father's will?" He slid the fan of papers, across the desk towards her.

Rita read the first page:

I, *Otto Nolan Jonas, of Still, Wyoming, being of sound mind and memory, do hereby declare this to be my Last Will and Testament. I revoke all previous wills and codicils made by me. This document reflects my wishes regarding the distribution of my estate upon my death and the appointment of individuals to manage my affairs.*

I appoint Alan Crawford, of Casper, Wyoming, to be the Executor of this, my Last Will and Testament. If Alan Crawford is unable or unwilling to serve, I appoint Ruby Joe, of Still, Wyoming, as alternate Executor.

RITA DROPPED her hands to her lap. "Ruby Joe?"

Alan raised an eyebrow. "That surprises you?"

"It's only that … well, Dad never hung out much at The Shaft, and it's not they were especially friendly with each other."

She read on:

I GIVE *and divide my real property to Marguerite (Rita) Carolyn Jonas. If Rita Jonas predeceases me, the property shall pass to the city of Still, Wyoming for the intention and sole purpose of serving as a cold weather shelter for those unhoused.*

I give all the rest, residue, and remainder of my estate, excepting the Singer sewing machine, to Rita Jonas, of New York, New York. If Rita Jonas predeceases me, I give the residue of my estate to the city of Still, Wyoming, to fund the operations of a cold weather shelter for those unhoused.

The Singer sewing machine I give to Carolyn Grace Hyatt.

. . .

"SHIT," Rita said, glancing up at Alan. "I just gave that away."

"You may substitute a similar item of equal value or provide monetary compensation to the intended beneficiary," Alan said. "Unless the specific item was of sentimental value, in which case this should be discussed with the beneficiary."

"I'd prefer not to discuss it," Rita said.

Alan leaned forward, folding his hands on his desk. "The goal is to ensure that the distribution of belongings aligns with Otto's wishes as closely as possible."

"Carole's never asked for it in all these years. And she never took her with it in the first place. I can't imagine it's sentimental."

Alan flashed a brief smile. "It would be prudent to find out."

"Then I'd have to talk to her."

Alan's smile returns. "As executor, I'd be happy to reach out to her and ask."

Rita blew out a breath. "No, it's all right, I'll do it."

She returned her gaze to the will. At the bottom of the third page, Mary Lou and Walter had signed as witnesses. She returned the papers to Alan's desk.

"That's that, then," Rita said.

"Yes," Alan said, "a fairly simple estate to settle, given Otto had only one beneficiary. Er, besides the Singer."

Rita paused, her chest tightening. One beneficiary. But not one child.

"When did Otto draft the will?" she asked.

Alan checked over the first page. "Twelve years ago."

She gave a slow nod. "He's kept the Singer all this time, intending to give it back to her." Then she met Alan's eye. "Thank you. What's next? Seen my share of cadavers, but haven't seen a will before."

"Then I recommend you create one," Alan said. "Next, we file for probate. Once I settle any debts, taxes, and administrative expenses, I'll distribute the remaining assets — namely to you."

Rita nodded again. "Thank you."

Alan stood as well and moved to open the door for her. "Are you feeling better these days?"

She glanced at him, inquiring.

"Your driver mentioned it." The corner of Alan's mouth turned up. "Touch of food poisoning?"

"I'm doing just fine," Rita said, "and yes, my stomach bug seems to be clearing up."

Alan smiled with his teeth. "I seem to recall you double-fisting the ginger ales when we last met." He stepped back. "Have a good afternoon, Sheriff Jonas."

"Before I go," Rita said, pausing in the doorway, "are you the one who called Carole to let her know about Otto's death?"

Alan's face remained composed. "Not at all."

"Good to know," Rita said, walking out.

Downstairs, she took the passenger seat of the Camry instead climbing into the back.

"I need to make a stop before we meet with Tom," Rita said, buckling her seatbelt. Then she gave him the address of Haleigh's grandmother's house.

Without a word, the driver pulled away from the curb.

Ten minutes later they drove through an established neighborhood, a boulevard of elms and aspens dividing the street and towering above the modest bungalows. As the Camry rolled past chain-link fences and children's bikes discarded on sunburnt brown lawns, Rita scanned the house numbers.

"That's the one." She pointed. "Blue one on the left."

The driver pulled into the drive, yellow blades of grass growing through the cracks in the pavement.

"I can't imagine I'll be longer than half an hour," Rita said.

Then she got out and walked up to the house. Despite the faded blue siding and creaky wooden porch boards, the home emitted a solid sense of security.

She knocked on the front door.

Haleigh, instead of her grandmother, answered.

"Sheriff," she said. "Come on into the living room. Gramma's gone over to the neighbor's, so we can chat. And I think I found somewhere for Ken to stay, too. My Uncle Darren heads up to Medicine Bow this time of year to open up his hunting cabin. Of course I can't ship any Vita-Boost out that way, but if he swings by here first, he can stock up. I keep a bunch of inventory in my room here."

Rita followed Haleigh into living room, its cream-colored walls adorned with mismatched framed photos of Haleigh throughout childhood. A pink sofa with a cherry-blossom pattern, slightly worn at the edges, anchored the room.

"I'm here because I've placed Ken under arrest," Rita said.

First Haleigh's jaw dropped open, then she dropped in the armchair beside the fireplace. She stared at Rita, silent, while a clock ticked on the mantelpiece.

"Arrested?"

"Yes," Rita said, taking a seat on the sofa. "I'm sure the news is shocking."

"Then he can't go stay with Uncle Darren?"

"No," Rita said.

Haleigh chewed on a banana-yellow fingernail. "Does that mean ... is he in jail?"

"He'll spend the night at the SCSO," Rita said. "And so it's important I ask you some questions."

Haleigh nodded, biting down on her thumbnail.

"Where were you last Thursday morning between four and seven a.m.?" Rita asked.

"Definitely in bed," Haleigh said, recovering her voice. "I'm not an early riser."

"And Ken?" Rita asked.

She hesitated. "In bed, too?"

Rita narrowed her eyes. "You sound uncertain."

Haleigh chewed on her fingernail. "It's just ... well, when I told him you were coming over to ask me some questions, he said I should tell you he was in bed, too."

"But he wasn't?"

Haleigh pressed her lips together. "No."

"Thanks for being honest," Rita said. "It's best for Ken."

"Okay."

"Can you tell me where he was?"

She shook her head, ponytail waving. "No. He left real early."

"How early?"

The fingernail escaped her teeth to tap on her lip. "Um, I think it was about four."

"Was it unusual for him to go out at that time?"

"Yeah," Haleigh said. "But also, not really."

"What do you mean by that?" Rita asked.

"From time to time, he'd get up real early and shower and shave and go out. Policing is like that. Like, 'round the clock." She shrugged. "Ken always says important work knows no bounds."

"Did you have any suspicions of where he might have gone?"

"I figured it was an important investigation. He was dressed real nice."

"Did you ask about the investigation?"

She shook her head, ponytail waving.

"Why not?"

Haleigh snapped her gum. "He gets real jumpy when I ask about police business. He tells me to mind my own."

"Then I appreciate your honesty today, Haleigh. As I said, finding out the truth is what will help Ken the most right now."

Earnest, Haleigh nodded. "Okay, Sheriff. And honestly, what I think would help you right now would be getting some fresh air. You don't look so rosy."

Chapter Forty-Five

Rita's guts rocked with each step as she returned to the Camry. She popped open the passenger door and got in, burping as she sat.

The driver have her a look, then eased the car away from the curb. Rita pulled the sample of homeopathic gum out of her pocket, then buckled her seatbelt. Maybe some Vita-Boost Bubble Yum would quell the churn in her stomach.

She turned over the packet to read the ingredients. Some were recognizable, some were not.

"Seaweed?" she said aloud. Her stomach pitched and she burped.

"Don't throw up on the upholstery, huh?" the driver said. He ran his tattooed hand over the dashboard. "I just had it detailed."

She put the gum back in her pocket, then lowered the window, stifling another belch and lifting her nose to the wind.

Inhale.

Haleigh was right. Fresh air was exactly what she needed.

They arrived at the Natrona County Jail and Rita swiftly signed in, greeting everyone on staff by first name.

"Gabriel's on his way down to see you," Sabrina said as Rita walk up to the counter and signed in.

"Hm," Rita said, "he usually keeps me waiting. Ready to hold court, is he?"

Sabrina smirked. "Somehow I don't think you're one of his loyal subjects." She cocked her head, indicating the glassed-in visitation room behind Rita's shoulder.

Rita glanced back to see Thomas Gabriel, wearing an orange jumpsuit, being escorted into a booth.

Rita gave Sabrina a fist pump, then crossed to the booth where he awaited her on the other side of a glass partition, scowling with the receiver in his grip.

Rita picked up the receiver on her side. "Where's Max Bannister?"

"Who knows?" Thomas Gabriel leaned back in his chair, stretching one arm and resting his hand behind his head. "Rumors say parts of him were found."

"Rumors, huh?" Rita said, eyeing him up.

"Well, damn, Sheriff," Gabriel said, rolling his eyes around in their sockets, "look at where I live." He leaned forward, putting his elbows on the ledge in front of the partition. "Word travels fast among the likes of us."

"What about Logan?" Rita asked.

Gabriel puckered his mouth. "Who?"

"Vee."

"Don't know nobody called Vee," Gabriel said, his gaze hard.

Rita stifled a burp. "Yeah, I bet you don't."

He sat forward. "I'd never hurt anyone loyal to the Gabriels."

Rita narrowed her eyes at him. "What are you inferring?"

Thomas Gabriel held her gaze. "I never infer anything. I'm always direct."

Rita maintained eye contact. "Got it."

"I heard about Otto," Gabriel said.

"You're changing the subject," Rita said.

"You're the one who barged in with questions about Max Bannister," Gabriel said, his lips peeled back from his teeth. "That was changing the subject. I'm only turning the topic back around to the purpose of this meeting."

Rita sighed. "And what purpose is that?"

"To discuss family."

"Well, thanks for the condolences," Rita said. "Presumably you heard through Alan Crawford?"

Gabriel chuckled. "Don't matter who I heard it from." He spread his hands again, smiling wider this time. "Have you met my neighbors?" Then he leaned even father forward, an inch or two away from the glass partition, his smile disappearing. "So why the hell haven't you told Cash you're knocked up?"

Rita's stomach dropped. "What did you say?"

Gabriel laughed again. "You heard me."

"Are you telling me that rumors in the big house are going around about *my* baby?"

Gabriel's lips curled into a sneer. "That's *my* grandson you're carrying, Rita. And now that your own daddy's gone, that kid's gonna need a father figure. And as I'm looked up in here, that baby's gonna need his biological daddy, whether you're fucking him these days or not."

Bristling, Rita stood. "I'm done."

"And as long as you're continuing on as Sheriff of Still," Gabriel continued, "I'll have someone watching over you, making sure you stay in line and everyone else keeps their hands off you. No one's gonna hurt my grandkid."

Rita laughed. "That's why 'Protects' is tailing me? To

babysit me?"

"Think of him as a bodyguard. And he prefers 'Protex,'" Gabriel said, sounding serpentine.

Rita rolled her eyes. "That sounds like a condom brand. Something I should have thought about a couple months ago."

She hung up the receiver and turned to go.

Gabriel banged his receiver on the glass.

Rita snatched up the receiver again. "I'm pretty sure behavior like that'll get you a lot of demerit points."

"I'm serious, Jonas."

"So am I," Rita said. "I know how to do my job. I don't take foolish risks. And other than your goons, I don't have anyone hot on my tail."

Then she returned the receiver to its cradle for a second time and turned to go.

And stubbed her toe on the chair.

"Fuck!"

She belched, then threw up, spraying a thin skiff of vomit across the glass partition and other hard surfaces of the booth. It looked like an uncooked omelet had exploded.

"Jesus Christ," Gabriel said, his voice muffled by the partition as he stared at her through the splatter. "Protex said you'd been losing your biscuits."

Rita snatched up her own receiver. "What the hell do you expect? I'm in my first trimester." Then she slammed it down in the cradle.

Gabriel dropped his own receiver and cupped a hand to shield his ear. "Fuck!"

Rita stepped over the puddle of vomit on the floor and marched back to the front desk.

"I'm sorry, Sabrina, but you're gonna have to call custodial. If I clean up that booth myself, I'm only gonna puke some more."

Then she stalked back to the Camry and slammed into the passenger seat.

She chewed on her lip, then stopped when she tasted bile. "How the hell did he know?"

Protex looked at her. "Huh?"

"Who told Gabriel? Mary Lou? No. Tilda? Unlikely. Jason? Come on. Those are the most trusted people in my life. And you weren't following me until only a few days ago. After the news broke."

Protex blinked at her a couple times. "Can I start the ignition now?"

Rita flapped her hand. "Yeah, let's go." She tapped her fingers on the door-rest. "Oh, shit," she said, with a sudden realization. "It was Edith Mae, wasn't it?"

"I don't know what you're talking about," Protex said.

"I should have never asked Edith Mae to get me that pregnancy kit on the same day she was picking up fifteen milligrams of lidocaine. The entire piercing studio probably knew by lunch break."

"But Tom gets his tattoos in prison," Protex said.

"Or she might have told to Stu and Vic," Rita said. "And as dumb as they are, they're in deep with Tom Gabriel."

Protex glanced at her. "Who?"

"Stu and Vic."

"Don't know 'em."

"Vic? And Stu?"

Protex slowed and flicked the turn signal. "Dunno."

"It's all right," Rita said with a sigh. "I'm an idiot."

"Dunno about that, neither." Protex turned left. "Where do you want to go?"

"Back to The Best Western, please."

Rita settled back into the seat for the drive, then her phone rang.

She picked up. "Jason."

"Hey," he said. "I just arrived in Casper. Do you want to meet up to review any evidence?"

"No, thanks. I'm actually headed out now. Back to Still."

"You all right?" Jason asked.

"Yeah. I need to take care of some stuff there," she said. "And I don't think it can wait till the morning."

"Ten four," Jason said. "I'll see you tomorrow."

Rita hung up as they arrived at the hotel. "I'm checking out," she said to Protex. "Give me twenty minutes."

She returned to room 112 and took a moment to breathe, leaning against the back of the door.

Inhale.

Exhale.

Damn Thomas Gabriel and his long reach. But the law's reach was longer.

She stripped off her uniform and took a hot shower, washing away the day, gulping and gargling the hot streams, scrubbing out the acidity in the back of her throat.

After toweling off, she blow-dried her hair and brushed her teeth. Twice. Then she put on her cleanest smelling T-shirt, comfiest yoga leggings, and packed up the rest of her items.

At reception, she closed out her bill and left her

keycard. Then she walked into the parking lot towards her Honda, giving Protex a wave as she passed.

The Camry started its ignition and the headlights came on.

Then she drove into the night, the stars studding the sky like rhinestones, and the headlights behind her like two eyes in the darkness, watching. Following. Protecting.

Strong and resilient.

Rita found herself relaxing. Sleep tugged at her eyelids.

Fighting off her fatigue, she took the exit into Still, the black Camry still trailing her. But instead of driving to Otto's, she headed into town and drove to Lisa's house. Or rather, where Lisa used to live.

It was Heather's house now.

Rita pulled up to the curb and parked. Cash's black pickup was parked in the driveway, like a giant sleeping beast, strong and resilient.

"What are you doing?" Rita said to herself. "Go home. It's late. You don't have to do anything Thomas Gabriel says."

But maybe it wasn't Gabriel who had bullied her into coming here, at this hour. Perhaps Mary Lou had succeeded in persuading her. Or perhaps Rita had finally listened to her own conscience.

Whatever the reason, she dragged herself out of the driver's seat and trudged up to the front door. The house was fully dark.

"They're sleeping, Rita," she said. "You should go."

But she didn't go.

Exhale.

Hesitant, she knocked. No one came. She rang the doorbell, then cringed. In the solitude of the cul-de-sac, it seemed the chime would wake the dead.

A fixture turned on inside the house, then on the porch. Rita squinted in the sudden flood of light.

Cash opened the door, wearing a pair of sweat shorts hastily pulled up to his hip bones.

"Rita?"

"I'm pregnant."

Chapter Forty-Six

Cash stared back at Rita, blinking.

And Rita stared at Heather, whom she'd not noticed standing behind Cash's shoulder.

"Oh, shit," Heather said, glancing between Rita and Cash. "I'll leave you two alone." Then she turned and disappeared inside the house.

Cash stared at Rita for another heartbeat, then swept her up into a hug.

She hugged him back, tears pushing against the back of her eyes. Willing them away, she took a deep breath—

Inhale.

"Let's go inside," she said.

From upstairs, Heather called down. "I've put the kettle on and I'm going back to bed."

"Thanks," Cash called up. Then they went inside and he led Rita to the kitchen, the only source of light coming from the vent over the oven. On the countertop an electric kettle streamed, nearing it boiling point.

He picked up a half-cut lemon on the cutting board.

"You want some hot lemon? I made some earlier for Heather's youngest."

Rita nodded. "Sure."

Cash poured the steaming water into a mug, then squeezed the lemon, the muscles in his forearm extracting every last drop. Then he added a spoonful of honey from a jar and stirred it.

"I feel so much better to have finally told you," Rita said, accepting the warm mug.

"I don't doubt it," Cash said. "I knew you were holding back on me about something."

Rita gave a nervous laugh. "I'm sorry. To be honest, I'm scared."

His brow creased a little. "Oh, yeah? Why is that?"

She shrugged. "It's not part of the plan. I don't know what to do."

At that, Cash laughed. "And coming back to Still was part of the grand plan?"

Rita sighed. "I guess you're right."

"So if you're scared, what do you want to do?"

She gripped the handle of the mug tighter. "I've been thinking about it a lot. And lately I've been wondering what you would want to do?"

For a moment, he was silent, nodding his head. Then he spoke carefully, composing his words. "I'm pretty sure the choice is up to you."

She reached out and squeezed his hand. "Thanks. But I'd really like to know what you think."

He relaxed again. "It'd be fun to meet a mini version of me."

Rita smiled. "But what if it's a mini version of me?"

Cash pulled a face. "Good God, then we'll have to see what Mary Lou or Jason are doing for the next eighteen years."

"You seem pretty happy about all this," Rita said, studying him.

"Hell, yeah," Cash said. "I always wanted a kid. Your kid."

That caused Rita's breath to catch. "You did?"

Cash frowned. "Why the hell do you think I wanted to marry you? Or at least tried to marry you?"

Rita managed a wobbly smile. "That's very sweet. But in all seriousness, I'd probably make a shit mom."

"A shit mom? Don't be ridiculous."

"How do you know? I have Carole for a mom."

"We don't follow in our parents' footsteps. Look at me. I'm not like my dad."

"I'm like mine," Rita said.

Cash laughed. "Maybe, in some ways. At any rate, you're not gonna turn out like Carole."

"Are you sure?" Rita said. "Carole ran away from me, and I ran away from you. What if I run away like Carole did?"

"I always thought you were running away from Still, not me. Or at least that's what I liked to tell myself."

She smiled.

Cash met her eye. "You came back to Still. Carole didn't. Or at least not for a really long time."

Rita shrugged. "Yeah, I suppose. Because Otto was dying."

Cash's face remained bright. "Sure, but you came back to take care of someone, not because there was anything in it for you. And if you had wanted to take off, wouldn't you have done it by now? It's not like the last few months have been a walk in the park."

Rita laughed. "You're not wrong." Then fell silent. "But what if I'm a shitty mother?"

Cash laughed. "I'm pretty sure those are the hormones talking."

"But I'm a shitty daughter," Rita said.

"Now your hormones are *really* talking. Why do you think you're a shitty daughter?"

Rita took a sip of her hot lemon drink. "If you were a follower of SilverNomad, you'd know."

Cash raised a brow. "Should I start following?"

"Definitely not." Rita hugged her mug tighter. "I scrapped with Carole."

At that, Cash laughed again. "I don't think Carole's opinion of you should inform your self-confidence."

"But that's just it," Rita said. "I dunno *how* to be a mom."

Cash shrugged. "I don't know how to be a dad."

Rita ran her hands over her head. "See? We're doomed."

"I was trying to encourage you," Cash said. "We're not meant to know *how* to do this. We'll learn."

Rita nodded.

Cash reached out and took her hand. "And we'll have help. People here are good, Rita."

"That's true. Already, several people have been so supportive."

Cash lowered his brows. "Who else knows? I have a feeling I'm not the first."

Tom Gabriel's name flashed through her mind. Instead, Rita said: "Jason, obviously. And Mary Lou."

Cash gave her a look. "You told everyone at work before me?"

She narrowed her eyes back at him. "They guessed."

Cash grunted.

Rita hid behind her mug. "And Edith Mae."

"Well, shit," Cash said, "the whole town's gonna know

now. If Jason told one of his sisters, it won't be long until the others—"

"Jason's a vault," Rita said. "Edith Mae only knows because I asked her to pick me up a pregnancy kit."

"A what?" a squeaky voice asked.

In unison, Rita and Cash turned to look over their shoulders. A bleary-eyed boy wearing dinosaur-print pajamas stood in the doorway, hugging a plush T-Rex.

Cash chuckled. "Do you need something, Devon?"

"I forget," the boy said, rubbing his eyes. Then he blinked at Rita. "I heard voices."

"Do you want some water?" Cash asked, getting up from the table. "Or do you have to pee?"

Devon nodded. "Yeah."

Cash approached and touched the boy's shoulder. "Which one?"

Devon thought for a moment. "Pee."

"Yeah," Cash said. "You okay to go do that on your own?"

Devon nodded, then shuffled out of the room with his dinosaur.

"Atta boy," Cash said. For a moment, he watched after him, down the darkened hallway until the bathroom door closed. Then he returned to the table.

"Cute kid," Rita said.

Cash shrugged. "Six is a hell of an awesome age."

Rita smiled. "You'll be a good dad."

Cash scoffed. "It's not rocket science, Rita."

"Carole would have barked at me to go back to bed."

Cash made a sound in his throat. Then he took her hand again and kissed the back of it. For several minutes they sat in silence.

Rita broke it, clearing her throat. "You know, when you mentioned moving into Otto's…"

Cash looked at her. "Yeah?"

Rita took another sip of honeyed lemon. "Did you mean like roommates, or…"

"I meant official grown-up stuff."

Rita was silent again, sipping her drink. Then she looked at him. "I'd like that."

He pointed to her belly. "But if we do this?"

"Yeah?"

"I'd like to raise the baby on our own." He rolled his shoulders. "Like, in our own place." And he pulled her hand closer to his chest. "Somewhere without history." He cast up his eyes to the ceiling. "'Cause I ain't so sure I can ravage you in all the ways I've imagined under the same roof where your dad raised you."

Rita laughed, her cheeks hot. "You've given this topic some thought."

Cash grinned. "I've spent years considering the options."

"Well, since your place is in ashes, carrying out plans for ravaging would require selling Otto's property."

"I know," he sighed. "It's too soon."

"More like I should probably list before winter," Rita said. She matched his grin. "It might take me some time, but I'll do it."

Chapter Forty-Seven

Rita awoke to the scent of fabric softener she didn't recognize.

She blinked her eyes open. Why was the window on the other side of the room? A giant stuffed T-rex stared back at her, surrounded by a collection of smaller dinosaur stuffies. Trains and cars littered the floor, and the shelves boasted an exhaustive collection of Mo Willems books.

This was Heather's kid's room.

Max Bannister's kid's room. Whose father was now diminished to a torso fished out of Lake De Smet, something his own kin didn't know about, and yet Rita had seen the full-color photos. And judging by the aroma of waffles wafting under the door, she was about to eat breakfast with children.

Rita groaned and rubbed her face.

Cash's voice echoed downstairs. He'd lain with her to go to sleep. But she had no idea when he'd gotten up and left her in Devon's room, while Devon bunked in with his mom for the night, and Cash took the sofa like usual.

She shuffled down the hall into the bathroom and peed

what felt like three times more than she ever had in her life. Then she washed her hands and face and swished some water through her mouth.

"Well, Rita," she said to her reflection, "I guess we're doing this thing." Then she took several deep breaths and went downstairs.

She almost collided with Cash, who ran out of the kitchen carrying a four-year-old girl on his shoulders. She perched with arms spread like wings, shrieking with laughter.

Cash stopped. "Morning. You sleep okay?"

Rita rubbed her head. "Pretty good, considering the bed's the size of a sardine tin."

"Well, we can spend twice as long in bed tonight to make up for it.". Then he ran off with Devon into the kitchen, shouting, "Who wants waffles?"

Rita followed and poked her head into the kitchen. Batter splatters covering the counter and cupboards. "I gotta go to work."

"Heather's getting ready for work, too," Cash said. "So I made waffles. Kids helped, didn't ya, kids?"

Devon and his sister cheered.

"I see that," Rita said. "They smell great." She jabbed a thumb over her shoulder. "But I got some sheriffing to do. I'll see you tonight."

A shadow fell across Cash's face. "What are you gonna do about that?"

Rita blinked. "About what?"

"Work."

"I don't understand."

Cash dodged a nerf dart while pouring more batter into the waffle iron. "How long are you planning to work?"

"I'll be back at Otto's around six. Feel free to head on

over with your stuff. And if I'm late, you can eat without me."

"That's not what I meant. I mean, what are you going to do about work now that we're expecting?"

She shrugged. "Same thing as last week. I was expecting then, too."

Cash gave her a look. "You know what I mean. It's a dangerous job. A physical job. And you're about to get bigger. Because your boobs are already bigger."

"That's enough," Rita said, raising a hand. She sneered at Devon, who'd stopped launching nerf-darts to stare at her chest. "I've got enough to think about at work today. We can discuss this tonight, okay?"

Cash nodded, his jaw tense. "Okay."

"Have a good day, everyone," she said.

"What about the waffles?" Cash said.

"No thanks," Rita said. "But they smell great."

"Yeah, you already said," Cash said. "You can take some to go, if you like. Breakfast is the most important meal."

She nodded. "I know. But I think this is why it's called morning sickness." She covered her mouth to dampen a burp. "I can't help it. I wake up like this."

Then she crossed to the stove to peck his cheek, said goodbye to the kids, and let herself out of the house.

Rita drove back to Otto's, where she showered and put on a fresh uniform. Then she arrived at the SCSO, her mouth watering at the scent of Mary Lou's coffee. She headed straight for the kitchen and filled one of Jason's mugs, which said, *Let Me Wake You Up.*

Then she returned to the bullpen and dropped into Walter's vacant chair.

"Didn't go to the Bean today?" Mary Lou asked.

"Slept in," Rita said, raising the mug to her lips. "What's the news from Casper?"

"Well, they have confirmation of a break-in at Ken's place," Mary Lou said. "A broken window latch suggests forced entry, although the window dimensions are small and rules out a lot of potential suspects based on size alone."

"Ken mentioned he suspected teenagers. How about Stu or Vic? Could either of them fit through the window? They're slender."

"Sure," Mary Lou, "they'd be the right body type."

"Anything else?"

"Like you said, no latent prints on the doorknobs."

"So there might be some substance to Ken's story," Rita said. "That someone planted evidence."

"That'll bring him hope," Mary Lou said. "Speaking of hope, have you told Cash?"

"For God's sake, I came back late last night from Casper and spilled the beans. Are you happy?"

"Barely," Mary Lou said. "You took your good goddamned time to get around to it and that caused me a lot of stress. That baby practically has a mustache by now. And half the town knows before the poor father."

Rita narrowed her eyes at her. "Half the town?"

Mary Lou straightened her shoulders. "I haven't told a soul."

"Good," Rita said. "And it better stay that way."

"Only Lucky," Mary Lou said, her gaze sliding away.

"Is that one of Ted's friends?" Rita asked.

"No, it's one my friends," Mary Lou said. "Lucky's the sparky."

"Point in case," Rita said. "Don't tell me that doesn't sound like a puppy."

Mary Lou's eye glazed over. "Oh, Lucky's a real pup all

right. Got the fuzziest belly fur. And for an electrician, he's surprisingly—"

"I'm pretty sure I don't want to hear the rest of that sentence," Rita interrupted. She covered a burp. "I'm not feeling my best at the moment."

"Fine," Mary Lou said. "Then I'll let you know a security manager from Apex called." She adjusted her reading glasses and consulted a rainbow-striped notepad.

"Bill Lapinski," Rita supplied.

"That's the one." Mary Lou tore an orange page from her notebook and passed it to Rita. "Here's his number."

"Thanks," Rita said, taking the paper. She headed into her office and dialed the manager.

"Hi, Sheriff Jonas," he said. "Thanks for returning my call. I've done a thorough inventory in the supplies warehouse. And yeah, we're short on lye."

"How much?" Rita asked.

"Three hundred milliliters."

Rita cringed. "That's a hell of a lot more than a few teaspoons."

"Sheriff?"

"But easily obscured in a stainless-steel water bottle," Rita said. "Do you know when it was taken?"

"No," Lapinski said.

"Have you become aware of anyone else that may have had access? Or come across any other significant details?"

"No," Lapinski said again. "But if I find out anything further, I'll let you know."

"Thanks," Rita said.

After she hung up, she left her office and went down to the cells. Arbuckle lay asleep on a cot in an empty one. She walked past him to Ken's holding cell.

She unlocked the door and entered. Ken sat on the cot,

his shoulders hunched. His pallor was as gray as the steel bars.

Rita sat on the cot next to him. "I spoke to Haleigh."

He grunted.

"Why did you ask her to lie?" Rita asked. "About you being home with her?"

Ken shifted. "Because I knew I didn't have an alibi. But..."

"Yes?"

"You know, I've had a lot of time to think, sitting here. And in the coffee shop yesterday. And I've been thinking ... like *a cop*."

Rita nodded. "Of course you have."

"And from one cop to another, Rita, you gotta clear my alibi." His eyes searched hers. "That's my way out of this."

Rita squeezed his arm. "I know it, Ken." She studied his eyes. "Where were you Thursday morning?"

Ken tensed his jaw. "Do you have my phone?"

"I'll get it," Rita said. She left the cells to retrieve Ken's phone from the evidence room, then returned.

She passed it to him to power up and unlock. Then he navigated through some screens and passed it back, open to a message. It was from someone with the initials J.H. She read the content of their exchange, then looked at Ken.

"You planned to meet this J.H. at four in the morning at the reservoir?"

He nodded.

Rita rolled her shoulders, recalling her own meeting with Ken in the dark at the reservoir. "For an altercation?"

Ken looked offended. "No. For ... you know..."

Rita raised a brow. "A tryst?"

Ken's neck turned the same shade as a Vita-Boost label. "Yes."

"Have you contacted J.H. to come forward to confirm your alibi?" Rita asked.

Ken shook his head.

"Because you're unfaithful to Haleigh?"

He scoffed. "Well, yeah, but that's not the reason." Ken took back the phone, swiped through some screens, and returned it to Rita. Now, the screen showed J.H.'s profile.

Jacked Hammer: I always nail it. If you're looking for a no-strings-attached experience with a built, bold, handyman, I'm your guy. Into BDSM, keeping it real, and making sure we both leave satisfied. Hit me up if you can handle power tools.

Rita passed back Ken's phone. "How long had you been seeing Jacked Hammer?"

"We've been talking for a couple of weeks," Ken said. "But that was out first meet-up. Except he didn't show."

"Oh, no?" Rita said.

"At first I thought I'd been stood up," Ken said. "But now I know it was a setup. I went back to the dating site. Jacked Hammer's profile is still there, but the account has had no activity since last Thursday."

"What time did you leave the reservoir?" Rita asked.

"I waited an hour. Like the stupid idiot I am." He dropped his large head in his hands. "Jesus Christ, why is someone doing this to me?"

Rita touched his shoulder. "I'll figure it out."

A shudder shook Ken's shoulders, and he nodded.

Rita rubbed his shoulder. "Stay strong. You're resilient."

Ken choked back a sob. "Doin' my best."

"And you're very good at it, so keep going."

Ken inhaled a sob. "Thanks."

Rita got up from the cot and relocked the cell, then turned to find Arbuckle now standing at attention. He wore the Apex branded security guard uniform she'd seen him wearing the other night.

She looked him up and down. "Hey, Arbuckle. We sure appreciate you being able to stay the night."

"Ain't no trouble for me, Sheriff. I'm gettin' used to bein' up all night."

She cocked her head towards the cell he had occupied a few minutes earlier. "Feel free to grab a few more winks before leaving if you'd like."

His shoulders relaxed. "Think I might, if you don't mind."

Rita smiled. "You can claim one of the lockers, too. Hang up anything you want to leave here for next time."

"Oh, I was just doing y'all a favor, Sheriff. I appreciate having a warm, dry place for the night."

Rita gave him a level look. "Look, you're gonna be compensated, all right? What do you think you're doing here? You just worked twelve hours for me."

"Well, sure, but I'll just head on up to the kitchen and clean out all your empties. Maybe borrow one of them unclaimed bicycles in your locker to get on over to the depot."

"Feel free to have one of the bikes," Rita said. "Mary Lou can open up the locker. And pay you out of petty cash."

Arbuckle cleared his throat. "Oh, I—"

"And no arguments," Rita said. "That is, if you're interested in being a jail guard?"

Arbuckle stilled. "Geez, I never thought of anything like that."

"Well, please consider it seriously," Rita said. "We're down a man and could really use someone here in the cells. We don't often have prisoners, so I can't employ you full-time. It'd be an on-call position." She paused, looking him up and down. "Of course, as jail guard at the SCSO, we'd have to kit you out, instead of wearing that Apex security uniform."

Arbuckle looked down at his navy blue logo'ed Apex wear.

"You work Friday and Saturday nights, right?" Rita asked.

Arbuckle looked up at her again. "Yep."

"Hm," Rita said. "Since those are the mostly likely nights I'll have someone in the holding cells, I'm gonna need to chat to Apex about putting you on some different shifts."

Then she pushed through the door to head upstairs.

Chapter Forty-Eight

Rita pulled into the parking lot at the reservoir and turned off the ignition. The Camry followed, as comforting as a shadow.

For a moment, she sat with the windows lowered, listening to the hum of grasshoppers and the wind in the grass growing along the rocky shoreline. Sun glinted on the surface of the reservoir, and a row of sparse pine trees stood like sentries, silent witnesses to past events.

The memory of the night Arnold was shot flooded her mind. Swallowing bile, she squeezed her eyes shut. And saw the night Ken and Clyde attacked her. On instinct, her hand moved to her belly, protecting the minnow from their fists now pummeling her imagination.

Inhale.

Exhale.

Rita unbuckled and bolted out of the car, shaking her head clear. She had to get moving to override the past. And to prevent herself from puking.

A car had recently parked in the lot, leaving dusty tracks. The tire treads weren't very discernible, but the footsteps around the driver's side were. She got the Nikon from the trunk and took photos of both.

Then she returned to the office to upload the photographs to her desktop. She sent them to the printer queue, studying each one at actual size as she did so. The shoes were a size thirteen, branded *Timberland*.

While the photos were printing, she went downstairs to the cells.

"Ken," Rita said, opening the door. "I went out to the reservoir."

He opened his eyes and lifted his head from where it rested against the wall. "And?"

"Let me see your shoe treads."

Ken wiggled his right foot out of an ankle-boot and passed it to her.

She flipped it over and had a look at the tread. *Timberland* size thirteen. She took a photograph with her phone, then passed him his boot.

"Thanks, Ken."

"I should probably be thanking you," he said.

"Wait till I tie up all the loose ends," Rita said.

Then she returned upstairs and printed the photos of Ken's boots. The printer spat out the last one and she delivered the stack to Mary Lou's desk.

She pulled up Jason's chair and sat across from her. "Check this out."

Mary Lou pulled a face. "I'm not sure I can take any more news about Carole."

"This doesn't pertain to the SilverNomad," Rita said. "Just doing my job this time."

Mary Lou sat forward, leaning her elbows on the desktop. "What is it?"

"I don't think Ken did kill Trevor," Rita said. "I think I cleared his alibi."

Mary Lou raised an eyebrow. "Oh, yeah?"

Rita showed her the photos. "I just placed him at the reservoir at the time of the murder. Besides the evidence, is all too convenient. Even Ken isn't stupid enough to kill someone and dump his coffee cup at the crime scene. And none of his prints were found in the car, but a single hair was? It's all circumstantial."

Mary Lou gave a slow nod. "We also ain't got nothing that links Ken to Frenchie."

"Right," Rita said, getting up from Jason's chair and returning it to his desk. "I'm going to go chat with Mr. Slaney at the bank," she said. "I'm tired of playing telephone tag."

"Roger," Mary Lou said.

Rita headed out the front door of the station and walked the four blocks to the bank. By the time she arrived, she'd broken out in a light sheen of sweat. She patted her brow dry, then entered the building.

Inside it was deliciously air conditioned. She approached Bev, cutting in line like before.

"Could you please tell Mr. Slaney I'm here to see him today, now?" Rita said.

Bev pursed her lips and gave Rita a pert nod, then she bustled off to the phone mounted on the wall. A second later, she hung up and returned to Rita, giving her a tight smile. "Mr. Slaney will see you now." She indicated a series of doors opposite the tellers' counter. "Second door from the end."

Rita thanked her and walked to his office. The door stood open, and she entered.

Aiden Slaney sat at a black particle-board desk. Behind the desk stood a series of roll-up banners advertising investment products and mortgage rates. Rita sat in a vinyl-upholstered chair in the same vibrant shade of cranberry as the bank's logo.

He looked up from his keyboard, flashing her a smile. "Good afternoon, Sheriff Jonas. Did you bring your father's paperwork?"

Rita sat in a vinyl-upholstered chair in a shade of cranberry that matched the bank's logo. "Nope, I'm here to talk about Frenchie."

Slaney scoffed. "What could we have to possibly discuss about Frenchie?"

"Plenty of things, I should think," Rita said, matching his smile. "Being neighbors."

"Doesn't mean we're friends."

"Of course not," Rita said, with a smile. "No reason to be unnecessarily friendly. One question I have, though, considering you're within earshot, is whether you've heard — or seen — anything unusual on his property lately?"

Slaney thought for a moment, gazing through the window. "He got a new dog." He shrugged. "That's all I can think of."

"Deborah mentioned he came over to the fence line to ask you a question."

Slaney shifted in his chair. "Frenchie didn't come to ask me a question. I had a question for him."

Rita kept her face impassive. "Oh, really?"

"We'd like to build a pool and carriage house. Our plans would make much more sense if Frenchie were willing to sell us a bit more of his acreage, rather than us blasting the hell out of the eastern corner."

"And you discussed this plan over the fence line?"

Slaney studied a fingernail. "He was concerned the carriage house would block his view." He chuckled. "View of what? It's goddamned flat everywhere."

"So you only discussed property matters?"

328

Slaney read a clock on the wall, then flicked his gaze back to Rita. "Yes."

"Hmm," Rita said. "That's not what Deborah said."

Slaney's gaze darted to the clock again. "Oh, no?"

"She said Frenchie mentioned UFOs. Or as we call them these days, UAPs."

Relief seemed to wash over the bank manager, and he laughed.

"Oh, my God, Sheriff, you wouldn't believe this guy." His smile spread naturally as he ran his hands over his head. "I didn't want to say anything — what would you think of me? — but that's all Frenchie talks about. He's always accosting Deborah about it. Worried that she's going to disappear like his mother."

"It's a legitimate concern, the welfare of women," Rita said with a smile. "Frenchie is only trying to look out for you and your wife, Mr. Slaney. He's a concerned citizen, that one." She leaned forward to pass him her card. "I'd appreciate you being in touch if you think of anything unusual you've noticed at his property. UAPs included."

"Will do," Slaney said, tucking her card into the top drawer of his desk. "And it's UAPs, Sheriff."

Rita pointed a finger. "That's right. UAPs." She got up and crossed to the door. Then paused. "That reminds me, do you own a drone?"

"Most likely," he said.

Rita raised a brow. "You're not sure?"

He gave a self-conscious laugh. "I'm a bit of a hoarder when it comes to electronics. Just ask my wife. She makes me keep my toys in the garage."

"Have you lost a drone this summer?"

"If you're asking if I've lodged them in trees before, yes. If you're asking when I last lost one..." He shrugged. "I couldn't tell you."

"Does anyone else have access to your garage?"

He shifted. "Possibly. I don't tend to lock it." He waved his hands in surrender. "I know, I know, you people are always telling us it's our fault if we don't keep our property secure. But hell, we live in the country. I moved out there to get some relief from stress."

"What kind of stress?"

He squared his shoulders. "Occupational, of course."

Rita looked round his office. "This place is stressful?" She whistled. "Have you tried working in New York City?"

He shuddered. "I can't imagine."

"Probably not," Rita said. "Well, thanks for your time, Mr. Slaney. I'll see you soon, to discuss my dad's affairs."

He gave her a thin smile. "I'll look forward to the pleasure."

Refraining from a smile of her own, Rita left his office, waving at Bev as she left the air-conditioned interior.

On the walk back she messaged Jason: *Please run a background check on Aiden Slaney.*

Then she checked her messages. The most recent was Mary Lou's: *Shannon Bachman found a note that Trevor left.*

Rita hurried to the parking lot behind the station. She unlocked the cruiser and got in, then messaged Mary Lou: *On my way.*

Chapter Forty-Nine

Rita sat on the sofa next to Shannon Bachman, pulling on a pair of nitrile gloves. Across the room, Shannon's mother Linda sat in the La-Z-Boy.

"Thanks for waiting for me," Rita said. "It must have been very difficult not to open that."

Shannon nodded, biting her lower lip. With quivering hands, she passed the sealed envelope to Rita.

"It was in the upstairs clothes closet," Shannon said.

"In the boys' room," Linda said, her voice lowered.

"Did they find it?" Rita asked.

"I did," Shannon said. "I was picking out clothes for them to wear to the funeral. I — I found it in their sock drawer." Then she burst into tears.

"He knew she'd be the one to find it," Linda said. "He left it there for her."

Rita looked at her. "What makes you think that?"

She broke off, strangling a laugh. "The boys hate wearing socks, and Trev never cared that they didn't. It was only me who nagged them and was always marching up to their room to get them each a pair whenever we were going anywhere." She cleared her tears. "It was a family joke."

"I can see Trev really loved you," Rita said. "And he had a sense of humor even in death. He must have been a really strong and resilient guy."

Shannon nodded. "He had a sense of humor, all right, but as to the other…"

Rita tore open the envelope and pulled out the papers inside. It contained four letters, each one folded in on itself and sealed with a dinosaur sticker, one letter for each of the three children and one for Shannon, each labeled in Trevor's handwriting.

The letter for Shannon was several pages long and sealed with two dinosaur stickers, touching snouts to suggest a kiss.

"This is Trevor's handwriting?" she asked, passing Shannon the letter.

Nodding, Shannon accepted the letter. Her hand shook. "I want to read it. But I'm also scared to."

Rita offered a smile. "This must be very difficult. I appreciate you having to read through it now in case it contains any evidence as to who harmed Trevor."

Shannon nodded and broke open the dinosaur stickers. Linda and Rita sat in silence as Shannon scanned the pages, her face growing paler, then flushing until her eyes filled with tears and overflowed.

She dropped the pages in her lap. "You said he loved me," she said, looking at Rita. "But this isn't a love letter."

Linda got out of the armchair and came over to Shannon. "What is it, pumpkin?"

Shannon's hands shook as she passed the pages to her mother. "It's a list of instructions — things he'd like the boys taught, places he'd like me to take them, traditions he'd like me to continue. And the last page is a set of instructions for his funeral, including the music he wants played."

"It must be a shock," Rita said. "My dad planned his own funeral and wrote his obituary before he died."

"At least it wasn't a bunch of orders to do!" Shannon's voice broke into a sob. "He's left me with three kids. I don't know how I'm going to do it by myself."

Linda passed Rita the pages, then perched on the end of the sofa to embrace Shannon.

"There's also a list here of when all of your bills are due," Rita said. "A list of account passwords and trustworthy tradesmen." She thumbed through documents for life insurance, medical insurance, house insurance, and car insurance. "I know this is difficult to understand right now, Shannon, but this is a sign of his love. He's taking care of you from the other side."

Still sobbing, Shannon nodded against her mother's chest.

"Trevor was very organized," Linda said. "He took very good care of her that way. He was a good husband and father."

Shannon cried harder.

"I'll leave you both now," Rita said, "so you can review these pages together." She got up from the sofa and moved towards the door. "As for the boys' letters, if there's anything in there that you think would be pertinent to the case, please let me know. And otherwise, I hope these documents will bring you a lot of healing."

"Thank you, Sheriff Jonas," Linda said. She patted Shannon's arm and said something softly in her ear, then left her propped up on the sofa cushions. "I'll walk you out, Sheriff."

Rita stepped out of the house and Linda followed her onto the stoop. "Sheriff, I wanted to mention that Trev did love Shannon very much. A mother can tell, you know. Sure, he screwed around with that Beth Winters a bit, but he was trying to sort out his feelings about his best friend who died. And when he got the diagnosis … well, he was almost out of his mind with terror and grief. It cut him up that he'd be leaving Shannon with three little kids dependent on Apex housing."

"Did he share these feelings with you?" Rita asked.

Linda nodded, her eyes filling with tears. "He confided in me a lot. Trev wasn't close with his parents, so he kind of imprinted on me." She smiled. "Called me 'Mom.'" So I leaned into it and loved him up as he needed."

"What things did he confide?"

A shadow fell across Linda's face. "He told me that he decided to stop doing chemo. It was just prolonging things. And he didn't want the kids to see him that way. He thought things would be easier for Shannon if the cancer took him quicker. But she would never agree."

"I'm glad he had you to talk to," Rita said. "Did he confide anything else? Do you know if he was involved in any kind of trouble?"

Linda shook her head. "Nope. I'm as surprised as anyone about that happened to him."

"Did Trevor ever mention Frenchie to you?"

Linda's face broke into a smile. "Of course. They were real close, too. The way I was like a mom to Trevor, Frenchie was like a dad. Frenchie brought Trevor a lot of peace."

"How so?"

"Well, a few weeks ago, he said, 'Everything will be all right, thanks to Frenchie.'"

"Do you know what that meant?" Rita asked.

"At first, I thought Frenchie might have had a place to rent on his property or something, since we're clearing out of this place. But when I asked Shannon, she said no, that Frenchie's place isn't suitable like that."

"What sorts of things did they do when they were together?"

"Cleaning up some dangerous goods on the property. Repairs around the place. Preventative maintenance. Usually Trevor simply referred to their 'projects.'"

"Had Trevor gone recently to help Frenchie with a project?"

"He went often," Linda said. "Sometimes Trevor didn't tell Shannon when he was going to Frenchie's. But I knew."

"Why did Trev keep quiet about his visits?"

"Because Shannon wanted Trev here all the time. To spend whatever time he had left in him with the boys." Linda's voice caught. "But he was a young man, Sheriff. He needed a shoulder to cry on, too. The guidance of someone older and wiser. A chance to be with the wind and the grass and the big skies." She shook her head. "I can't imagine what that poor man went through."

"I appreciate you sharing," Rita said. "If you think of anything else, please give me a call." She gave Linda her card. "Shannon is lucky to have you close by."

Linda smiled. "Even mothers need mothers. Maybe especially so."

Rita thanked her again and got in the cruiser. Before driving back to the SCSO, she called Tilda at Casper Forensics.

"Hey, Rita, I've got some updates for you."

"Me, too," Rita said. "We found a letter that the deceased left for the family."

"That's interesting," Tilda said.

"Yeah, personal messages to the family and some household information," Rita said. "It got me thinking about that plastic bag found in Trevor's pocket. Anything to update?"

"We found microscopic organic matter in it. But not enough to test. It would have been destroyed in the process."

"Ideas on what it was?"

"Honestly," Tilda said. "I think cookie crumbs. The plastic has slight grease smears."

"Fingerprints?"

"Plenty, only Trevor's. And that second set of prints in the car belongs to Shannon Bachman."

"Any prints match to Ken Saunders?"

"None. But we got a match for the lye," Tilda said. "Identical to the Apex sample. Though a common industrial chemical, it's not that common way out here in Still. Not exactly the epicenter of industry."

"True," Rita said. She thanked Tilda, then rang off. She drove back to the office there and ate a protein bar at her desk while reviewing the evidence. But it was sticky and dense and hard to swallow.

Someone knocked on her office door.

"Come in," Rita said.

Jason's head poked in. "You got a minute?"

"Definitely," Rita said. "What do you got?"

Jason took a moment to find his balance in the broken chair, then said, "The search is conducted, and so's the autopsy. Didn't find anything on the property that could be considered treasure. As for Frenchie, both he and his dog were beaten to death by the same shovel. They'd been dead about eight hours when we found them. There's also blood under Frenchie's nails, but we haven't got a match for it yet."

Rita chewed on her lip. "What do we know about Aiden Slaney?"

Jason opened the Notes app in his phone. "He and Deborah moved here recently, when Aiden took the position following Margot's death. He's worked in several branches, most recently in Cheyenne."

"Criminal record?"

"Nothing. But he's got his fair share of worries. The guy's mortgaged up to the hilt."

Rita said. "And yet he's ready to install a pool and a carriage house?"

Jason frowned. "What's a carriage house?"

"It's not what it sounds like. And the Slaneys aren't as rich as they look like, either, huh?" Rita said, tapping her fingers as she thought.

"They certainly don't have a stash of treasure," Jason said.

"Shannon's mom Linda said that Trevor said everything was going to be okay because of Frenchie."

"And so what does that mean?" Jason asked.

"Linda didn't know." Rita said, getting up from her desk. "But I have a feeling Irene might."

Chapter Fifty

While Jason drove, Rita checked her messages. A text had come in from Cash, letting her know that he was settling into Otto's and would acquaint himself with the kitchen before she came home for supper.

She closed her phone and looked out of the window. Her guts clenched. But it wasn't her digestive tract responding this time. It was the minnow, swimming in circles. Excited to go home to Daddy.

Daddy.

One father had just left Rita's life, and now here was another — a peer, but in some ways, so much like Otto. Later, he'd set a hot plate of food in front of her, oblivious to her morning sickness or the impending news that Rita had felt the minnow move for the first time, and yet no less eager to be a father in every way.

Rita let the feeling expand into her chest.

Jason turned into Irene's drive. He got out of the cruiser. "Nice fruit trees."

Rita got out and gazed up the rosy apples. "I didn't notice them last time." She looked around a noticed a plum and pear tree, as well. "Presumably she has a straw-berry patch, too."

"I wonder if she's had any offers," Jason said, indi-cating the Realtor's sign. "It's way the hell out here, but the house is in tidy repair."

"Maybe Frenchie lent a hand around the place," Rita said, mounting the front steps.

Irene met them at the door, not as cheerful as on their previous visit. Her white roots visibly showed.

"Have a seat," she said, plumping the throw cushions on the sofa. "Can I get you a strawberry iced tea?"

"That'd be great," Jason said.

"I'll have a water, please," Rita said, eyeing up the enormous bison tapestry on the wall.

"Certainly," Irene said. "Back in a jiff."

She disappeared from the living room. Rita and Jason settled side by side onto the couch. Rita counted the ducks in the needlepoint over the fireplace, while Jason studied the African violets from the comfort of the sofa.

"I bet she feeds those things," Jason said.

"Yeah," Rita said. "Strawberry iced tea."

Irene returned with two cups of pink liquid and one of water.

"We're to find out what you know about Frenchie's treasure," Rita said, accepting the glass.

Irene glanced between the two of them. "He told me to never tell no one about it." She shifted in the armchair, her fingers picking at the pin-tucks on her slacks. "It's not easy to tell a secret you've carried so long."

Rita smiled encouragingly. "Take your time."

Irene pressed her lips together, then pushed herself out of the scallop-shell chair. "You know what? It'll be easier if I show you."

Then she patted her thighs and headed down the

carpeted hallway. Drawers opened and closed. A few minutes later Irene returned, something fisted in her hand. She approached Rita and opened her fingers. In her palm lay a tarnished coin.

Rita picked up the silver coin, turning it in the light. Its faded engravings revealed a figure on one side and a barely legible denomination on the other, framed by intricate but worn borders. Rita passed the coin to Jason, then looked at Irene. "That's an impressive antique. Is this Frenchie's treasure?"

"Told me he had a collection of 'em," Irene said.

"Did he give you others?" Rita asked, as Jason snapped photos of the coin with his phone.

"He offered," Irene said, "when I listed the place. He thought I was selling because I couldn't afford the upkeep. But that's not the reason." She curled in her hands to look at them. "It's this damn arthritis. I'm going to go live with my daughter in Beaumont."

"Why did he give you this coin?" Rita asked, as Jason returned it to her.

"In case of an emergency." She shrugged. "Never needed it, though it was nice to know it was there."

"Have you had the coin appraised?" Rita asked.

"My daughter looked it up online. Worth about five hundred bucks." She gave a girlish giggle. "Not too shabby, huh?"

"I'm certain Frenchie would be very happy to know that you have still have this coin," Rita said in solemn tones. "In his final days, he seemed to be searching for his cash. His spirit can be consoled that it's not lost forever. A part of it's with you."

Jason bugged his eyes at her.

"What?" Rita hissed back. "My dad just died, okay?"

Jason finished his strawberry tea and set the empty

glass on the coffee table. "Thanks for the refreshment, Irene."

"Yes," Rita said, setting her empty glass next to his. "And for answering our questions."

"Anything to help catch Frenchie's killer," Irene said, clutching her coin.

Rita gave the bison a salute, then she and Jason followed Irene to the door. They bade her goodbye and got into the cruiser. Jason started the ignition, then lowered the windows to let out the hot air before closing them again and firing up the AC.

"Check this out," Jason said, swiping open to the photos he'd taken and passing Rita his phone. "That coin had traces of dirt on it." Then he pulled out of Irene's driveway.

Rita zoomed in to look at the dirt, packed into the grooves, obscuring the engravings. "So Frenchie's treasure really was buried."

"Given the number of exploratory excavations," Jason said, turning onto Frenchie's drive, "I'd say he forgot to mark down the 'X'."

"What's another way to explore the ground these days?" Rita asked.

As they rolled through the gates (now propped open by Forensics), Jason glanced at her sidelong. "Is this a riddle?"

"No, it's shop talk," Rita said. "Here's my point. Someone was using a drone, likely more than one, in recent months, to surveil his property in order to find the treasure. When Frenchie started digging holes, I bet this 'someone' started digging some holes of their own, assuming Frenchie wouldn't notice which ones weren't his own handiwork. This is why Frenchie reported that the drone was *following* him," Rita said. "It was monitoring his movements, allowing the operator to pinpoint spots for excavation later."

"It's not a difficult fence to scale," Jason said, pulling up to the outbuildings. "Would have been easy to access the property." He nodded towards the closest building. "Shovels and hoes layin' around everywhere."

"And Fang wasn't there till this week," Rita said.

Jason parked and turned off the ignition. "Poor guy." He blew out a breath. "Frenchie wasn't hurtin' no one."

"Nope," Rita said, looking out the window. "It's funny who gets to live and grow old and who doesn't." She shifted. "Thomas Gabriel's still kickin' strong. Is that fair?"

Jason didn't respond. For a moment, they sat in silence. Then he gave her a smile. "You know what you taught me about fairness?"

"What's that?" Rita asked.

"Solving crime is the best thing I can do for justice. Not writing tickets or enforcing the law. Just solving crime. Like it's a puzzle, in a thousand little pieces."

Rita nodded. "Flamingos."

Jason looked at her. "What's that?"

She shook her head, popping the door. "Nothing. Shall we go treasure hunting?"

She stepped out of the cruiser and took a breath.

Inhale.

The lowering sun flickered between the tree branches, the scent of ponderosa pines dancing on the breeze.

Exhale.

"It's nice out here, right?" she said.

Jason scanned Frenchie's scrubby expanse. "You mean out of town?"

Rita nodded. "Yeah. It's quieter. Not like Otto's place is a metropolitan neighborhood or anything. But folks have parties on the regular, and the bus tears through there a couple times a day."

Jason walked around to the trunk and popped it. "You don't like parties?"

"I don't like feeling like I have to do something about the illegal firecrackers or kegs while everyone else is having a good time." She rubbed her belly. "Besides, everything's changing."

Jason shrugged. "Probably can't go nowhere in a snowstorm."

"Would that be so bad?" Rita asked.

Jason looked at her. "You still a cop?"

Rita blew out a breath. "How the hell do I know? I'm trying to figure out if I'm even a mother."

"Well, you might not want to go into labor if you're out here in a snowstorm."

Rita frowned at him. "This bun ain't coming out of the oven in winter. Do your math."

Jason laughed and found two pairs of work gloves in the trunk. He passed one to Rita. "You sound local now."

Rita snorted. "If I'm gonna do this mother thing, here might not be such a bad place." She rapped the window. "Plenty of space to run around. No sirens going by."

"Hardly no one goin' by," Jason said, shutting the trunk.

Rita cocked her head. "Maybe bison."

"You thinkin' of moving?"

She pulled on the work-gloves. "Thinking of selling."

"Otto's place?"

Rita nodded. "Yeah, now that he's passed."

Jason stiffened. "Does that mean I need to move out now?"

"Move out? Not at all. I'm telling you in case you're interested."

He stared back at her, silent.

"You're not interested?" Rita said.

Jason's eyes grew moist. "I'm interested."

"Great," Rita said, "because I think you do a great job of looking after his place."

Jason nodded, swallowing his emotions. "I never thought I'd have a home of my own, you know, where I can just be myself and have everything how I like it." His smile wobbled. "I'm not sure I even know what I like. Not really."

"It'll be great," Rita said. "You can see the sunrise from the dining room and the sunset from the front porch. What more does a guy need?"

Jason laughed. "Exactly."

"Oh, and can you do me a favor?" Rita asked. "And answer a personal question?"

"Such as?" Jason asked.

"When you're on dating apps, do you ever see anyone you know?"

"Sure," Jason said, "I'm discreet though."

"I know," Rita said. "So I wouldn't ask if this didn't really matter. Have you ever seen Ken?"

Jason nodded. "Yep, I've seen him. I don't remember his profile name, though."

"That's okay," Rita said, "thanks for confirming." She slapped his bicep. "You're a vault. And you're gonna make an excellent sheriff one day."

"Thanks," he said, walking over to the nearest outbuilding and picking up two shovels leaning against the side. "But I hope you're not going anywhere yet."

Rita sighed. "Nope. Even though I seriously considered going back to New York several times in the past week." She accepted a shovel from him. "But I have a feeling this baby might have other plans for me."

Jason laughed and set foot across the field.

Rita fell into step with him. "So where the hell do we start, Deputy?"

"Well, considering me and Casper have already searched this whole property and didn't find a damn interesting thing, we're pretty much at the starting gate."

"Then maybe we should head that way," Rita said, pointing, "and start at the gates."

Chapter Fifty-One

"Goddammit," Rita said, throwing down the shovel. "I'm too fucking hot to dig anymore."

Slumped against a fence post, Jason slapped his neck. "And the damn mosquitos are swimming in my sweat."

Rita joined him at the fence. "Is this a fruitless pursuit? It's gonna be dark soon."

Jason surveyed the overgrown property. "One officer or another has already poked and prodded every bit of diggable dirt around this place. I'm having a hard time believing we're gonna find any coins."

"I have a hard time believing anything without food," Rita said. "Or water."

She pushed off the fence rail and waded into the grass, crossing the field towards the outbuildings. Jason followed and they walked in silence as the shadows lengthened across the field.

In Frenchie's house, Rita opened a kitchen cupboard and reached to the back to locate a glass.

Jason curled a lip. "You're not serious?"

Rita looked at him. "What?"

"That is one dusty-ass cup."

"Dust to dust and ashes to ashes," Rita said, managing a smile. "But not bacteria-laden. Anything organic on here's been mummified by now."

Jason failed to look convinced. "Whatever you say, Mommy."

She glanced at him. "Holy shit, I guess I am a mommy now. This is going to take some getting used to."

He grinned. "Not really like you to guess."

"Ha, ha." She turned on the faucet and hand-washed the cup, then shook off the excess, not trusting the stained kitchen-linens, and filled it with tap water.

With each swallow, her heartrate slowed. She drained the cup, feeling clear headed again.

"Not easy to search this place for treasure," Jason said. "Or evidence. It's falling apart around us." He gestured towards the dining room wall, where several rows of paper had been stripped. "Or rather, the place is being taken apart by Frenchie."

"Wait," Rita said, setting her glass on the counter. "Frenchie said taking down the wallpaper was his current project. And Shannon's mom Linda confirmed Trevor was helping Frenchie a recent project."

She walked up to the wall and tugged at one of the unfurled panels. "Look, there's another layer of paper here."

Jason came closer. "Maybe it's a map to the treasure."

Rita picked at the strip. "I think it's money." She tugged some more at the wall covering, then pulled out the bill. "Looks like a fifty." She flipped it over. "Nope, it's a hundred." She passed it to Jason. "Is this a fake?"

"Dunno," he said. "Looks more antique to me."

"Bag the bill," Rita said, "and let's head back to the office."

"Ten-four," Jason said, collecting the bill for evidence.

Back at the SCSO, Jason researched local coin dealers.

"Here's one in Cheyenne. I'll give them a call."

"Thanks," Rita said, pulling up Walter's chair. "Mary Lou, you got anything?"

Without a word, Mary Lou handed Rita a letter-sized envelope.

"What's this?"

"Open it," Mary Lou said.

Rita got up and went into her office with the envelope. She opened it sitting at her desk. There it was, in black and white: Otto's death certificate.

Now that she'd met with Alan Crawford, she no longer required accessing the copy in Otto's safe-deposit box. All the same, she got up and walked down the street to the bank, certificate in hand.

"Hi, Bev," Rita said, cutting the line to the teller's counter. "I've got my dad's death certificate here."

Pressing her lips together, Bev took the certificate. She shuffled to the Xerox machine, took a copy, then shuffled to the telephone mounted on the back wall. After a brief chat, she hung up the receiver and returned to the teller's counter.

Without meeting Rita's eye, she gave back the envelope. "Mr. Slaney will see you now."

"Thanks," Rita said, walking to his office.

She rapped on his door. "It's Sheriff Jonas."

"Come in," his voice said.

Rita entered. Slaney sat at his black particle-board desk. He smiled at her, then tugged on his shirt collar, his gaze drifting to her collar. "You have some dirt on your uniform."

"I don't doubt it," Rita said. Then she placed the envelope on his desk. "Investigating UAPs takes it out of me. Which is why I'd really like to clear up this matter of the lights."

Slaney stiffened. "Lights?"

"Yeah, what do you make of them?" Rita asked. "They were troubling Frenchie."

"I presume you're referring to our security lights. They respond to motion sensors, turning on at the slightest of movements. And there are quite a few critters out our way that can set them off at all hours of the night. Coyotes. Skunks. Owls, even."

"You got skunks out there?" Rita said.

"It's the wilds, Sheriff. So what can we do? It's not like we can shoot the damn pests. We've apologized to that lovely lady across the road — what's her name, Eileen?"

"Irene."

"Yes, Irene. I apologized for our security lights flashing at odd hours. For a while, we had a family of racoons scavenging in our trash cans. It was like a nightclub out there." He spread his hands and shrugged. "I must admit, Deborah and I are suburbanites, and still learning how to hack rural living. Like keeping our trash cans in the shed."

"I'm not sure if that's a hack or just common sense."

Slaney chuckled. "Have you come regarding some real business, Sheriff Jonas?"

Rita presented Otto's death certificate. "I have my father's paperwork."

"I see," Slaney said, picking up the document with lean fingers, each one tipped with a well-filed nail. His hands were nothing like Cash's. "Will you be keeping the box or closing it out?"

"Closing it out," Rita said.

"Very well," Slaney said, getting up. "Does Bev have a copy of the certificate?"

"Yes," Rita said.

"Great, we can head down now."

As they walked along the short corridor to the room with the safe-deposit boxes, Rita asked, "I'm also curious about flying lights."

Slaney gave her a sidelong glance. "Flying lights?"

Rita shrugged. "Drones, basically. My investigation at Frenchie's revealed two devices that have violated FAA regulations. A Phantom and…" Rita snapped her fingers. "Damn, I forget. But we've got the information for the make and model of both at the station. I'd like to ask you about these models, find out if they're the same as the ones you collect. Because you sound like a subject matter expert, and you might be able to assist with this case."

Slaney gave her a stiff nod. "Of course. Feel free to reach out when you have the information."

Rita grinned. "Oh, I will."

He unlocked a door and led Rita into a small room. The overhead fluorescent lights reflected along the rows of small, steel-fronted compartments, each secured with a keyhole.

"It's this one here." Slaney pulled out a box and set it on the small table in the center of the room.

"A double-wide," Rita said. "I didn't know Otto had so many secrets."

"I'll step out and wait," Slaney said.

When he was gone, Rita opened the box.

She stared.

It was full of cash.

Rita thumbed through packets of bills, all of them hundreds.

One packet at a time, she removed the money, lining

up the bills in neat columns on the table. She made a quick count. And took a sharp breath.

Close to half a million. What the fuck?

At the bottom of the drawer sat a copy of Otto's will, two envelopes, an old watch, and two loose rings — one a police academy signet, and the other his gold wedding band. Rita recognized the band instantly, though he hadn't worn it in years.

She slipped it onto her thumb, then picked up the first envelope. It contained additional photos of the woman she'd seen in the photographs at Otto's house. One was a formal portrait of Otto and the young woman in a studio setting with Roman columns. Whom had he loved before Carole so dearly that he'd sat with her for a professional portrait?

She set aside the photographs to take with her, then picked up the last envelope in the box, labeled 'Rita.' Her heart skipped at the site of her father's writing, the way he looped her R and turned the dot of her I into the cross of the T.

She opened the envelope.

But there was nothing inside.

She searched the box one last time, but there was no indication where the money had come from. Or what Otto had intended to do with it. Because his will certainly didn't mention it.

Steadying her breath, Rita opened her phone and took pictures of the serial numbers. As she worked, she returned the packets to the safety deposit box. Slaney must be wondering what was taking her so long.

Having returned everything to the box but the envelope of photos, she got up and poked her head through the doorway.

"Mr. Slaney?"

The bank manager stepped forward. "Yes, Sheriff Jonas? Is there anything you need?"

"Yeah," Rita said. "I'm gonna need a safe-deposit box for myself. And make it a double-wide."

Chapter Fifty-Two

Rita walked out of the bank, serial numbers running through her mind.

Half a million... What the hell had Otto been up to?

Not ready to go back to the SCSO, Rita walked to the Bledsinoes' memorial bench and sunk onto the seat. The boards had been warmed by the sun.

She unfolded the newsprint page in her pocket and read Otto's obituary:

Otto Bernard Jonas, beloved father and lifelong resident of Still, Wyoming, passed away peacefully on at the age of 74. A dedicated public servant, Otto served in the Still Country Sheriff's Office for over 30 years, and over 20 years as Sheriff, earning the respect and admiration of his community with his unwavering commitment to justice and integrity. Otto is survived by his daughter Rita Carolyn Jonas. Otto's legacy of service carries on in Rita, who followed in his footsteps and is Otto's greatest pride. His strength of love for his family will forever be remembered by those who knew him. Donations in lieu of flowers may be made in his name to the Casper City Hospital Oncology Ward.

. . .

RITA LOWERED THE PAPER.

Otto was known for familial love? Recently, she'd began to think he had a reputation for infidelity.

And she was his greatest pride? For following in his footsteps?

She pulled out her phone and texted Mary Lou. *Thanks for the obit.*

Mary Lou texted back right away. *Otto wrote it.*

Rita texted back: *All?*

OK part of it. He didn't know he had terminal cancer when he wrote it.

The part about me?

10-4, Mary Lou returned. *I chose the Oncology Ward. That okay?*

Rita sent a heart emoji. Mary Lou mirrored it with one of her own.

Rita refolded the obituary and returned it to her pocket. Then she looked up the online version on *The Casper Mountain Tribune* website.

She scrolled down to the comments, of which there were about a dozen. Mostly from veteran cops, and one from a sergeant who mentioned Otto had been his mentor as a rookie.

Rita thought back to her own days as a rookie in New York. And how, when she called Otto for advice, he always responded the same way:

"Dunno what to say, Honeybee, you city cops are different than my lot."

Had he really thought that? Were they really so different as cops?

Rita put away her phone and sat for a few moments. The fresh air did her head and heart good, and a few minutes later, she felt re-energized. She strolled across the street and jogged up the front steps of the station.

In the bullpen, Mary Lou and Jason quietly tapped on their keyboards. Jason looked up when she entered.

"I got some news," he said. "I spoke to that numismatist in Cheyenne."

"Oh, yeah?" Rita said, pulling up Walter's chair.

"Of course, he's only looking at a photo of the bill," Jason said. "But if it's what he thinks it is, it's very rare."

"Which is?" Rita asked.

"A one-hundred-dollar bill from 1880."

"And how rare?"

Jason folded his arms. "Currently, only ten are known to be in existence."

Mary Lou gave a whistle.

"And guess how much the last one sold at auction?"

Rita crinkled her nose. "You know I hate guessing."

"How the hell much?" Mary Lou said.

Jason rocked back in his chair. "Eighty grand."

Mary Lou whistled again.

"Wow," Rita said.

"Other denominations fetch hefty price tags, too," Jason said. "Fifties, twenties… What if the whole wall is papered with old bills?"

"That'd be a fucking fortune," Rita said. "Frenchie had already removed some of the paper. He must have gotten some of the bills, or he would have continued removing more. Instead he was out digging. Presumably looking for the coins, too."

"Once he was aware he was being scouted, I think he may have panicked and wanted to unearth everything. When I told Frenchie that there may have been a drone over his property, that probably spooked him worse than aliens." She shrugged. "He didn't want the aliens to take him, but he wouldn't have minded them bring back his ma. But the idea of theft? That was worse than contact."

"So where's the money he already found?" Jason asked. "Did he get it to Trevor already?"

"I don't think so," Rita said. "Maybe Frenchie first dug up some coins for Trevor. And when Trevor found out what they were worth, like Irene's daughter did, Frenchie decided to go for the bills, which meant peeling off the paper after had been there for God knows how many years."

"And this was the project Trevor was helping with?" Jason said.

"Yep," Rita said. "What Linda referred to as the solution to make everything all right."

"Financially, at least," Jason said. "So our murderer killed Frenchie for his treasure. The question is, did they abscond with it? Or did Frenchie take the secret to his grave?"

Rita sighed. "What have we missed?"

Jason took out a worn letter-sized map of the property. "Casper plotted all the outbuildings, boulders, and junk cars, things like that."

Rita leaned over Jason's shoulder to study the map.

"What's this?" Rita said, pointing to a rectangle.

"Old water heater," Jason said. "Outhouse is beside it." He paused. "A cop from Casper was supposed to search it."

"And do you think he didn't?" Rita asked.

"Well, it was hot," Jason said.

"Oh, Lord," Mary Lou said, waving a hand under her nose.

Jason cracked a smile. "I remember he was kicking up a fuss about it stinking to high heaven."

Jason picked up the receiver on his landline and placed a call. Connecting through to Casper, he asked to speak to

Deputy Hammond. Jason asked about the search and listed for a minute. Then he thanked Deputy Hammond and hung up.

"He only searched the structure because — and I quote — he wasn't paid enough to comb through shit."

"Go get your boots, cowboy," Rita said. "We're heading back out."

Jason pushed away from his desk and followed Rita to the back door. There, they grabbed slickers and overshoes and tools and went out to the parking lot. They tossed their gear into the trunk of the cruiser and headed back to Frenchie's.

As they passed Irene's, Rita noticed a sedan marked with a franchised Realtor's logo pulling into the drive.

"Looks like Irene's showing the place," Jason said.

"Looks like," Rita said, leaning forward to peer at Irene's front yard. An old elm tree shaded the north side. A dark shape caught her eye, fooling Rita's eye into thinking it a tire swing. I was only a broken bough hanging low, moving in the breeze.

But Cash could easily get his hands on a large tire to hang from one of the sturdier limbs. Maybe more than one tire. For more than one rider.

As Jason pulled into Frenchie's drive, Rita pulled out her phone. She texted Cash the address of Irene's house and the cell phone number for the Realtor, decaled on the back window of her vehicle.

Then she messaged: *Can you call now to book a viewing?*

Cash returned a thumbs up.

Jason parked the cruiser and popped the trunk. They got out and walked up to the outhouse, carrying shovels, slickers, and overshoes.

Side by side, they stood in front of it, staring at its time-worn door, splattered by mud and God knows what, its peeling gray planks leaning to the west.

"You know, it's probably easier if we knock the thing over," Jason said.

"Can you drive Frenchie's caterpillar?" Rita asked.

"Don't think we're gonna need one," he said, loping towards another out-building. From among the shovels and pickaxes, he picked up a sledgehammer and returned.

He swung it wide, driving it against the joists. A loud crack sounded as the entire structure shuddered. After three more blows, the outhouse toppled, and a cloud of flies exploded into the air.

Jason tossed aside the hammer and he and Rita approached the pile. They dragged aside the large boards, then kicked away the little ones. Then they stared into the pit.

"Looks pretty dry," Jason said. "Thank God."

"Yeah," Rita said, "and let's hope it hasn't been used in a while."

"Hm," Jason said, peering closer. "Not sure that's the case. But at least it hasn't rained in a while."

"Lucky day for us, I guess."

"You don't like guessing," Jason said, holding his nose.

"Thanks for reminding me," Rita said. "And for the record, that thing smells worse without the walls."

"Constable Hammond could probably have told us that," Jason said.

Rita pointed. "I see a glint of metal." She squatted to look closer. "Yep, there's definitely something in there."

She got to her feet and pulled on the slicker, boots, and gloves. "I'm going in."

She leaned over the pit and reached in.

"Not money," she said. She flicked the object, clearing

the excess goop, then laid the knife on the grass in the sunshine.

"The blade's broken," Jason said.

Rita looked at him. "Wanna bet this blade matches the broken tip pulled out of Trevor's back?"

Chapter Fifty-Three

Rita laid out Tilda's forensic photos on her desktop, reviewing the images of the knife. Then she placed the knife, in a clear plastic evidence bag, on top of the eight and a half by eleven printout. Though the scale of the actual knife was disproportionate to the zoomed-in image of its tip, it was clear by the breakage pattern that the two were a match.

Rita sat back in her chair. "What the hell? Trevor's would-be murderer?"

"Why would Frenchie try to kill Trevor?" Jason said. "Supposedly they were very good friends."

Rita chewed on her lip. "Exactly. Everyone said so." She tongued her cheek for a moment, "Maybe Trevor was stealing the money. Perhaps he'd found it on his own and then been sneaking it bill by bill."

"Frenchie finds out and he takes a knife to Trevor," Jason said.

"Except he was too elderly to do the deed," Rita said. "Or this was the project. Not the wallpaper. Trevor and

Frenchie staged the stabbing. And made to look like a murder. Because Trevor was soon to be dead anyway."

"So why didn't they go ahead with it? Frenchie was weak?"

"Maybe for moral reasons," Rita said. "Maybe because Frenchie viewed Trevor like a son. So he tried to talk Trevor out of it. Told him he would provide for Trevor instead. And ensure the well-being of Trevor's family by giving them his family treasure. So he started digging up the coins and peeling back the paper."

The phone rang and Rita scooped up the receiver. "Sheriff Jonas."

"It's Bill Lapinski at Apex. I've got information about the missing lye."

"Excellent," Rita said, "I'm on my way now."

She hung up and looked at Jason. "We've got to head on over to Genius HQ."

Jason got up and followed her out the door.

"Can you drive?" she asked. "I've got a growing thread of texts that I haven't been able to keep up with."

Nodding, Jason led the way through the back door and took the driver's side, while Rita buckled into the passenger seat.

She scrolled through her texts. There was a recent one from Cash saying he had an appointment to view Irene's property and that he was headed to Casper to meet with his insurance company about his house.

"Insurance," Rita said, suddenly remembering the letter Trevor had left for Jason.

"What's that?" Jason asked.

"There's something I've got to check out," Rita said. She dialed Mary Lou's number.

"What can I do for you, Sheriff?"

"Can you get in touch with Shannon, please, and find

out Trevor Bachman's insurance provider? He left all the pertinent details in that letter to her."

"Ten-four," Mary Lou said and hung up.

Then Rita returned Cash's text with a heart emoji as they rolled up to Apex.

Lapinski met them in the air-conditioned foyer and took them to his own office instead of the chemical storage building.

He sat at his desk, which held two large monitors. "Got some CCTV footage for you to look at."

Rita and Jason stood behind each of Lapinski's shoulders as he sat at his desk. Behind them, a large whiteboard on the wall displayed shift schedules and "0" incident reports (which Rita found impossible to believe).

"This happened on night shift last Thursday," Lapinski said, queuing up the reel. "One of our lab techs stole about a cup's worth of lye in a stainless-steel water bottle."

"The lab techs work graveyard shifts?" Rita asked.

"At times, yes. Right now there's a project running with slow chemical reactions that require around-the-clock monitoring to ensure completion." Lapinski indicated the screen. "It's rolling."

Rita watched as a figure moved across the warehouse and opened the chemical locker.

"Who's that?" she asked. "I don't recognize him."

"Me neither," Jason said.

Lapinski paused the video, then jerked his head towards the corridor. "Come with me."

Rita and Jason followed Lapinski out of the office and across the hallway to a small office. The man from the CCTV footage, wearing a lab coat, sat awaiting them in one of the visitor's chairs.

"He's detained here so you can arrest him for theft," Lapinski said.

Rita blinked at him. "Me?"

"Yeah. Saunders isn't here at the moment."

Rita gave him a look. "You're not wrong about that." Her gaze slid back to the employee. "I'm Sheriff Jonas and this is Deputy Perry. I'm not here to arrest you. We'd appreciate you answering some questions."

The man swallowed. He looked to be around Trevor Bachman's age. "Uh, okay."

"Can you give us your name, please, and your position here?" Jason asked, taking out his notepad.

The man gave a nervous nod and a half-smile. "Darius Palmer, Research Technician in the Chemical Testing Department."

"Why did you steal the lye?"

Palmer choked back a sob. "Trevor asked me to get it."

"That's a risky favor for a friend. You could lose your job, yes?"

Palmer's gaze flickered to Lapinski. "Yeah. But I felt bad for the guy."

"Were you and Trevor close?"

"Not really. We worked together. Went through that Personnel Optimization together. I took a job in the animal testing department. He took the severance package." Palmer's gaze darted between Rita and Jason. "After he left, I heard he got cancer."

"Did Trevor sound under duress when he asked for it? Or when you gave it to him?"

Palmer shook his head. "No. He seemed ... determined. Kind of in a hurry. Said he had some stuff to get done that day."

"Did he give you any indication of what that was?"

Palmer shrugged. "I figured he was doin' one of his projects."

"What do you mean by one of 'his projects'?" Rita asked.

Palmer rubbed some sweat from his brow. "There's an old guy he helps out sometimes. Bit of a hoarder, by the sounds of it. I figured he needed it to do a serious cleaning job. Like maybe get rid of some dog carcasses or something."

"That's rather gruesome, isn't it?" Rita asked.

"Dunno," Palmer said, shrugging again. "He said the old man uses an outdoor shitter half the time so he didn't have to walk back to the house from the scrapyard. And he eats tinned beans and cat food, so you can image how that smells. Rats around it all the time, Trev said. He said the old man never cleaned up the rat traps, so he'd go out once a week to clear 'em up. Said he buried 'em in a big hole out back the property."

"Trevor confided a lot in you," Rita said.

Palmer shrugged. "Hell yeah, he was having a shit-hard time. Er, pardon the French, Sheriff."

"Did you consider the dangers of this decision?"

Palmer licked his lips. "Of course. He swore me to secrecy. But Jesus Christ, I didn't think he was gonna kill himself with it."

"Who informed you of Mr. Bachman's cause of death?" Rita asked.

Palmer flashed a look at Lapinski. "Bill did."

Lapinski cleared his throat. "When Casper Forensics called, I put two and two together. That's all. There're rumors in town, of course. About the body that was found."

Rita looked at Jason. "How does this happen?"

"Dealing with the body *in situ* meant a lot of trades were involved." Jason gave a one-shoulder shrug. "Word gets around."

Rita sighed. "This doesn't happen New York. Not in the same way."

"Am I gonna lose my job?" Palmer asked. His hands shook.

"That's not for me to determine," Rita said. "At any rate, I'm not arresting you. This is Saunders' jurisdiction. He can figure it out. Thanks for your time, Palmer."

Rita led the way into the hallway, Jason at her heels.

"Well, what do you think, Deputy?" Rita asked as they walked back to the glass foyer.

"I think Trevor can't possibly have killed himself," Jason said, "not like that. He hated Apex. Why would he guzzle some of their property, instead of being with his family?"

"For the tragic poetry of it," Rita said, chewing on her lip. "His job had made him sick and then abandoned him with no recourse. So he decided to frame a representative of Apex for his death. Namely Ken Saunders. Because he knew the most likely way to get DNA was to have a physical altercation. And who better than one of the security staff?"

"Logical," Jason said. "And it helped that Trevor would have had access to Apex letterhead."

"Exactly," Rita said, giving Ginny a wave as they passed the reception desk. "Ken thought teenagers broke in, because he himself would never be able to climb through that window. But being in poor health, Trevor could have easily fit."

Jason pushed through the glass door and held it open for Rita. "So Ken's set up for murder and Shannon gets an insurance payout?"

Rita nodded. "And Trevor gets his vengeance, posthumously."

"But what about the knife wound in his back?" Jason asked. "Where does that fit in?"

"It's possible the original plan was the knife in the back, courtesy of Frenchie. But Frenchie was frail and couldn't do it. Or wouldn't. Not to his friend. So Frenchie pitched the knife in the outhouse and Trevor had to come up with a different idea. Without Frenchie's help, this time."

"So early that morning he gets Palmer to steal the lye."

Rita shivered. "Insurance adjusters wouldn't suspect someone would kill themselves that way."

Jason nodded, grave. "Suicide wasn't our first assumption, either."

Rita flicked through her message to find the contact information Mary Lou had sent. She called Trevor Bachman's insurance provider, Frontier Coverage. She navigated the menu until she connected with Camille Rodriguez, the adjuster for Trevor Bachman's policy.

"I have a few questions for you," Rita said after introducing herself. "Has Mr. Bachman's account been paid out yet?"

"No," Rodriguez said. "We're waiting on the cause of death. We'll need the death certificate within sixty days of his death."

"Right," Rita said. "Regarding the policy, can you tell me the terms for accidental death?"

"The policy pays a lump sum of $500,000 to the beneficiary if the policyholder's death is the direct result of an accident," Rodriquez said. "The accident must occur while the policy is in force, and the death must occur within ninety days of the accident."

"Exclusions?" Rita asked.

"Natural death, of course," Rodriquez said. "No benefits are payable if the policyholder's death is due to natural causes, including but not limited to heart attack, stroke, or disease."

"And suicide?" Rita asked.

"Another exclusion," Rodriguez said. "No benefits are payable if the policyholder take their own life, regardless of the circumstances or timing."

"Circumstances such as terminal disease?" Rita said.

"Yes," Rodriguez answered in a measured tone. "Such as terminal disease."

Rita thanked her and hung up.

She looked at Jason. "Trevor did this."

They crossed the Apex lobby and headed outside.

Rita glanced at Jason as they walked to the parking lot. "After giving him cancer, Apex laid him off and evicted his family. Soon to be dead, he wanted to leave Shannon with insurance money."

"But why carry through with the suicide if Frenchie had promised Trevor money?" Jason asked.

"Maybe Frenchie promised a great deal more than he was actually able to excavate and give to Trevor. Maybe his intentions were good, but in the end it wasn't enough. Like in Irene's case. And in desperation, Trevor acted."

Jason gave her a knowing nod. "It all seems to add up."

"Except Frenchie," Rita said. "Who the hell killed Frenchie?"

Chapter Fifty-Four

Rita broke her gaze from the quivering aspens flashing past the window to glance over at Jason in the driver's seat.

"What do you and me know about money?" she asked.

Jason tapped his thumbs on the steering wheel. "I know that life sure would be easier if we had more of it."

Rita made an affirmative sound. "There's that, yep. What else?"

Jason thought for another moment. "That we should probably be getting more of it for the things we do every day."

"I tend to agree with you and Deputy Hammond on that one," Rita said. "But basically, we don't know much."

Jason grunted.

"So when we don't know about money matters," Rita said, "where do we go?"

"The bank," Jason said.

"Right," Rita said. "And who works at the bank? Besides Bev?"

"Our friendly hometown bank manager, Aiden Slaney."

"Slaney said he talked to Frenchie over the fence line about property development. But maybe Deborah was being truthful about Frenchie having a question for her husband. They just kept the question a secret. I bet you anything Frenchie pulled a bill out of the wallpaper, walked over there, and asked the banker its value."

Jason glanced at Rita. "So now the banker gets a good look at it. Maybe even takes a photo and promises to get back to Frenchie."

"Uh-huh," Rita said. "He diligently goes and researches it and finds out it's worth a fortune. But what if he lied to Frenchie about them being worthless, because he wanted them for himself?"

"Then Frenchie's big promise to Trevor falls flat," Jason said, "and Trevor comes up with Plan B. And the Slaneys start to keep an eye on Frenchie."

"Literally spying on him with a drone," Rita said, looking up at the brilliant blue sky, where a single kestrel reeled. "I think it's time Mary Lou issues that warrant and we pick up Aiden Slaney for questioning."

Rita took out her phone and typed a brief message, requesting warrants. Then she messaged, *How's Ken?*

Mary Lou texted back, *Blue.*

Tell him to cheer up, Rita texted back. *His ordeal may be coming to an end soon.*

Jason drove past the station, then slowed, scanning for a place to parallel park.

"Busy day in downtown Still," he said.

Rita pointed. "What about here?"

"That's the loading zone."

"Yeah," Rita said. "You're loading me in and out of the cruiser."

"That's for the armored trucks."

Rita looked around. "How often does the cash truck come by?"

Jason thought for a moment. "I dunno. Once a week?"

"Exactly," Rita said as Jason passed the bank and turned the corner to circle the block.

But on his second time passing the bank, he pulled the cruiser into the loading zone. "You violate traffic regulations like this in New York, Sheriff?"

Rita rolled her eyes at him. "Where do you think I learned all my hot tips?"

"I'll keep looking for a spot," Jason said. "Text me when you're done and I'll meet you back here."

"'Fraidy cat. I saw how you told off Carole in her van at Otto's place. You could take on an armored vehicle driver."

Then she trudged up the steps to the bank, which felt twice as steep as the last time she'd been there. Inside, she scanned the tellers, looking for Bev. She spotted her, then waved.

Bev stepped away from the woman she was serving and waddled towards the end of the counter.

"I'm sorry, Sheriff Jonas," Bev said, "Mr. Slaney isn't in."

"I'm actually here to talk to you," Rita said.

Bev flinched and glanced over her shoulder to see who was within earshot. "Y-yes, Sheriff Jonas?"

"What time did Aiden Slaney arrive at work last Thursday morning?"

"Oh!" Bev said, startled by the question. Then she scrunched her lips together and moved them around, as though sucking up a spaghetti noodle. "Hmm. Now that I think of it, he wasn't in that day."

"Do you remember the reason?" Rita asked.

Bev's lips puckered some more. "He had a headache."

Rita smiled. "Perfect. Thanks, Bev."

Bev's eyes widened. "Did I say something bad?"

Rita shook her head. "Not at all. That's everything, thanks."

"Er — you're welcome, Sheriff Jonas." Wringing her hands, Bev returned to her teller's window.

Rita left the bank. She was pulling out her phone to text Jason when he pulled the cruiser pulled the loading zone. She popped the passenger door open and dropped into the seat, which was warmed by the sunshine.

"Thanks for the rock-star service, Deputy."

Jason pulled back into the lane. "I'm good for something around here."

"Well, if I ever change my profession, I'll hire you for a getaway driver."

Jason turned south, out of town, headed for the back roads.

"It's not feeling so remote out this way, anymore," Rita said.

Jason knit his brow. "It's not?"

"I recognize landmarks now." Rita said. "Like that gnarly old tree over there."

"Might not be a landmark much longer if a strong wind comes through."

"The point is, I used to feel lonely driving out this way. But now it feels like it's where I'm meant to be."

Jason pulled the cruiser into Aiden Slaney's driveway, their property now becoming as familiar to Rita as Frenchie's. She and Jason got out and silently walked up to the door.

Jason rapped the brass knocker.

"Damn," Rita said. "I thought you were going to hit the doorbell. I like the chimes."

Jason shrugged. "Chimes are nice. Especially since that knocker was a lot louder than I expected."

"Yeah," Rita said. She reached past him and banged the knocker a second time. The sound reverberated through the building. "That *is* impressive." Then she punched the doorbell, setting off the carillon. "You want to hear the chimes?"

Jason listened to the house toll. "Better than the knocker. Though if I had a house, I'd have a digital chime."

"Oh, like techno?" Rita said.

Jason shook his head. "Not necessarily. You can program anything you like."

"They're programmable?"

"Yep."

"So what would you program?"

Jason thought for a moment. "Post Malone."

Rita gave him a look. "I'm doing my best not to let you know that surprises me."

"Well, I don't think anyone's home," Jason said, stepping back from the door.

Rita pursed her lips. "I say we ring again to be sure." Then she hit the chime for a second time, depressing her finger until it played a full verse, then releasing it to echo.

A minute later, the bolt turned.

"See?" Rita said. "The second ring works every time. You gotta let the homeowner know you mean business." .

Jason cut her a look. "More hot tips from the beat in New York?"

The door flew open and Deborah Slaney stood in a silk bathrobe, hair wet. "Sheriff."

Rita smiled. "Hi, Deborah. Thanks for interrupting your activities to answer the door."

Deborah forced a smile. "I was having a bath."

"Apparently," Rita said, rotating her head to look at the giant peacock printed on Deborah's robe. The she looked at Jason. "Is it an obstruction to justice if you don't answer the door because you're bathing?"

"No," Jason said. "Obstruction of justice involves intentionally interfering with the investigation of a crime. Like hiding evidence. Or lying to authorities. Or tampering with witnesses."

"Hm," Rita said, glancing at Deborah.

She gave Rita a cold look.

"But it does mean that we can take actions to gain access," Jason said.

"Such as knocking loudly?" Rita asked.

Jason nodded. "I was thinking more like entering by force, if necessary."

"Hm," Rita said, looking him up and down. "New York might be the beat for you, after all." Then she flashed a smile at Deborah Slaney. "Must be nice to take a bath on a weekday afternoon." Rita looked own at her uniform. "I could use a bath right about now."

"Yeah," Jason said. "Considering you were fishing around in Frenchie's outhouse five minute ago."

Deborah flinched. "If you must know why I was showering in the middle of the day, Sheriff, I played a very vigorous game of pickleball this morning."

"Did Aiden play pickleball too?" Rita asked.

"Of course not," Deborah said, sounding offended at the idea. "He works on the weekdays."

"Not today, he's not," Rita said.

Deborah narrowed her eyes. "I beg your pardon?"

"Your husband isn't at work today," Rita said. "Do you know where he is?"

Deborah straightened her shoulders. "I'm sure he's in a meeting."

"Do you have a drone, ma'am?" Jason asked.

Deborah's gaze snapped to Jason. "I beg your pardon?"

"A drone," Jason said, "such as a Phantom."

Deborah's fingers fiddled with the gold-stitched sash of her bathrobe. "My husband does. Though I couldn't tell you the make or model. In fact, he may have more than one. He's a collector of gadgets."

"Why?" Rita asked.

Deborah shrugged. "They're expensive toys, aren't they? Why does a man collect anything?"

"That's a good question," Rita said. "Why collect anything useful that could be put to good use. Right, Jason?"

Jason nodded. "Yep. Never could figure out why folks collect coins instead of saving 'em."

"Are you a numismatist?" Rita asked.

Deborah fluttered her eyelids. "I beg your pardon?"

"Don't worry about it," Rita said. "I have a feeling you and Aiden prefer to spend your coins. Like on drones."

"Like I said, Aiden likes gadgets."

Rita indicated the diamond studs in Deborah's earlobes. "You do, too, by the looks of those earrings."

Deborah pushed a wet strand of hair behind her ear. "Is there anything else, Sheriff?"

"Not at this time," Rita said. "But I have a feeling we'll be back."

She and Jason turned on the stoop and walked back to the cruiser.

"So he's not at the Wyoming Valley State Bank and he's not at home," Rita said, tapping her lip. "Want to wager he's up to some shit that's shady as hell?"

"Can't help but think he's looking for more money at Frenchie's," Jason said. "Though we didn't see his car there, or at his own address."

"There's an old logging road that runs parallel to this one," Rita said. "It goes behind all the properties on this road." She pulled out her phone and opened a backroads map app. "I'll look it up."

Jason backed out of the drive and followed the app's instructions to access the logging road, slowing as the tires hit the gravel. Nearing the backside of Frenchie's lot, a vehicle sat parked on the shoulder.

"Nice Beemer," Jason said, parking behind it. "I'll run the plates."

"No need," Rita said. "I recognize the parking pass in the window."

Jason leaned forward to peer closer, then turned off the ignition. "Wyoming Valley State Bank."

"Hello, Aiden," Rita said to the parked car, as she stepped onto the dusty road. She circled to the trunk of the cruiser, where she and Jason put on their boots before entering the woods near the spot where the BMW was parked.

"Hear that?" Jason asked.

Rita paused. "Shuffling?" She listened, discerning the distance and direction of the sound. "Or scraping?"

"Or digging," Jason said. "After the last couple days, I know exactly what a shovel sounds like when it hits this packed dirt and shale."

He walked a few steps forward and pulled back a branch. Rita tucked closer to his shoulder and looked.

In a clearing in the cottonwoods, Aiden Slaney was digging a hole. On the ground by his feet lay a black duffel bag.

Jason advanced, his shoe snapping a twig. Slaney turned and glimpsed them in the trees.

Rita stepped out from the bushes. "Aiden."

Slaney threw the shovel at her and ran.

Chapter Fifty-Five

The shovel's blade hit Rita's knee and the handle struck her shin. She tumbled onto the ground, groaning.

"Fuck!"

"You okay?" Jason called back, running after Aiden Slaney.

Rita nodded, biting back pain. But Jason wasn't looking.

"Pursue!" she yelled after him. She rubbed her throbbing leg and pushed onto her feet. Hands on her belly. Protecting the minnow.

Inhale.

Then she flew into action, following Jason and Slaney through the trees.

Following the grunts and sharp inhalations of breath, she pushed through the foliage to find Jason and Slaney wrestling on the ground.

Jason had the upper hand, wrestling the manager onto his chest, then he snapped on the cuffs. He glanced up at her and Rita gestured for him to continue.

"Aiden Slaney," he said, before reading him his Miranda rights, "I'm placing you under arrest for murder."

"Murder?" Slaney sputtered. "Why the hell would I murder my neighbor? You've got no evidence."

"Well, that makes things easy," Rita said. "As soon as your blood doesn't match the blood under the victim's nails, you'll be released."

Slaney clamped his mouth shut and Jason hoisted him to his feet, while Rita dropped into a squat, her knee still throbbing, and retrieved the black bag. It contained a few handfuls of antique coins. Then she picked up the shovel along the way and walked alongside Jason and Aiden Slaney back to the cruiser.

They settled Slaney into the backseat, then pulled out of Frenchie's drive.

"Let's swing by home before heading to the station," Rita said.

"Huh?" Slaney said.

Jason pulled out of Frenchie's drive and drove the few hundred feet to the Slaneys' house.

Slaney sputtered in the back seat. "What the hell are we doing here?"

"Having a chat with Deborah," Rita said. "When it comes to your communication, the two of you aren't always on the same page."

Without waiting for his response, Rita got out of the passenger side. Jason lowered all four windows, then joined her in walking up to the house.

This time, Rita rang the bell twice, back-to-back, setting off a cacophonous carillon.

The door flew open, and Deborah stood there fully dressed in a gold shirt and shorts, her pin-straight hair brushed to a sheen.

"What is it now?"

"We've just arrested your husband for murder. Know anything about that?"

Deborah's eyes widened, then she tried to slam the door.

Jason's hand stopped it, pushing it open. Rita stepped inside. But Deborah was already in flight, running upstairs.

Rita gave chase, glimpsing her disappear into the master suite. Then Deborah closed the door behind her and locked it.

"Goddammit," Rita said, rattling the knob.

Jason caught up to her. "Now *that* is an obstruction to justice."

He pulled a shiv from his key ring and shoved it inside the doorknob. The lock popped and they entered the master bedroom. Behind the ensuite door, a toilet flushed.

Jason crossed to door, used the shiv in the knob, and popped the lock. But the door jammed when it hit something on the other side.

"She's pushed something in front of the door," he said.

"A literal obstruction this time," Rita said.

"How's your knee?" Jason asked.

Rita grimaced. "Still throbbing."

"Allow me then." He drew up his leg and kicked the door. Whatever was behind the door toppled with a loud crash and Deborah shrieked.

The door bounced back, and Rita helped Jason shove it open.

"Nicely done," Rita said, squeezing through the opening in the doorway, then stepped over the antique washstand that had barricaded the door.

Jason followed. "Thanks, that was my good leg."

Deborah stood before the toilet, clutching a handful of bills, also antiques.

In two steps, Rita was at Deborah's side, pulling her

hands behind her and snapping on handcuffs. Rita took the bills and passed them to Jason. "Bag them for evidence, please."

"Hang on," Jason said, leaning over the toilet bowl. "There's one in the bowl that didn't flush."

Rita grimaced. "Your turn."

Jason dipped in his fingers to collect it.

"It's not what it looks like," Deborah said.

"Really?" Jason said, shaking the dripping bill over the toilet bowl. "Because to me, it looks just like Frenchie's."

"Let's head downstairs," Rita said, leading Deborah through to the bedroom and into the hallway.

Jason bagged the bills and followed.

"I want to speak to my husband," Deborah said.

"No problem," Rita said. "He's already in the cruiser."

With measured steps, she navigated Deborah downstairs, mindful not to slip on the spiraling stone treads. "Wouldn't want to stumble down these things on a drunken night," Rita said.

Deborah made a non-committal sound.

"If you let me know where your housekeys are," Jason said, opening the front door, "I can lock up behind us. Since both you and your husband are coming down to the station."

Deborah's shoulder blades tightened. "The deadbolt requires a passcode. You'll need to uncuff me, Sheriff Jonas."

"No can do," Rita said. "Give me the code and I'll punch it in."

Deborah hesitated. "We have many antiques, Sheriff."

"Oh, yeah?" Rita said. "Well, then, we better lock up."

Deborah shuffled to position her back towards the door. She levered her elbows to elevate her hands. "Maybe I can feel my way through the keypad."

Rita laughed. "You don't trust me?"

Deborah tilted her chin. "Police corruption is a very real risk."

"So's bank fraud," Rita said. "But I still deposit my paycheck at Wyoming Valley State Bank. If my money goes missing, I know who to call — your husband. If your safety goes sideways, you know who to call — me. In the meantime, it's your choice if you want to leave your house locked or otherwise."

Deborah's lips turned white as she pressed them together. "Zero, seven, one, seven."

Rita entered the number and the bolt engaged with an electronic whirr. "July seventeenth?" she asked.

Deborah's pinched lips relaxed. "Yes."

Rita steered Deborah along the footpath. "Birthday?"

"Wedding anniversary," Deborah said, her voice as stiff as her spine.

They stepped off the footpath and crossed the large driveway, evenly coated in black asphalt. "How many years?"

Deborah set her jaw. "Thirteen."

"Lucky," Jason said.

"Who says?" Rita said. "I always heard thirteen's unlucky."

"Taylor Swift," Jason said.

"Oh," Rita said. "Well, if she says it's lucky, it probably is. 'Cause she's got some kind of luck."

Jason nodded. "Though she doesn't quite have what Post Malone does."

"I think thirteen's open to interpretation," Deborah said, craning to look into the rear seat of the cruiser. She spotted her husband and tried to rush forward, but Rita tightened her grasp, holding her back.

"This is all your fault, you half-wit!" Deborah snapped

at Aiden. "I told you to just buy the money off the old fuck!"

Jason opened the back door and moved to assist Deborah. But she'd already dove past him, into the backseat, giving Aiden an earful.

Jason pulled out his phone. "I'll put in the call to Forensics. And then I'm gonna call Beaumont for backup."

Rita shut the car door behind Deborah. "Good plan, since we've got two of them." Then she dusted her hands. "Jesus, they can fight."

"Thirteen years of practice," Jason said, walking around to the front of the cruiser. He leaned against the hood. "Let's hope they wind down by the time Beaumont arrives."

Rita joined him at the hood. For a moment, they listened to the interchange, one voice shrill and the other a rumble.

"This is what scares me about married life," Rita said.

Jason glanced at her. "What?"

"Talking in circles with the same person, year after year."

"Then you probably shouldn't get married," Jason said. "'Cause every year is a circle. Just circles and circles. That's all that life is."

Rita gazed up at the Slaney house, dripping in architectural features. It made Irene's place look like a lunchbox.

"Yeah, you're probably right. Although I don't know what Cash'll say about that, if we're already raising a kid together and putting our names on a mortgage."

Jason gave her an appraising look. "Hell, these days, a mortgage is more permanent than a marriage."

"Ain't that the truth," Rita said. She glanced sidelong at Jason. "You getting cold feet?"

He chuckled. "About Otto's place? Not on your life. You?"

Rita craned to see down the drive across to Irene's. But the house wasn't visible. "Probably," she said. "Though I think my feet are feeling chillier about the minnow than the move and marriage combined."

"I'd be the same," Jason said. "If I could have babies."

"Well, chances are you'll spend a lot of time with this baby," Rita said. "Because the only way I know how to raise this kid is on a shift rotation."

Jason nodded. "Deal."

Then they fell into silence, watching the shifting clouds. In the backseat of the cruiser, the Slaneys continued to argue.

Rita glanced at her watch. "Probably another ten minutes till Beaumont are here."

Jason adjusted his posture. "So what do we do about Ken Saunders? All the evidence seems to point to him."

Rita sighed and watched the last of the clouds drift behind a tall aspen. "It sure does."

Chapter Fifty-Six

Tilda walked out the front door of Slaneys' house onto the veranda, where Rita sat on the railing next to Jason.

"Well, that's a day's work done," Tilda said. "I've got you one broken drone, a bloody shirt and pair of jeans in the laundry room, and"—she showed a set of bills, spreading them into a fan— "five of these suckers." She tugged one out of the fan, which was missing its corner. "This is the one that went for a dip in the bowl."

Rita's stomach bunched. "Now I'm not gonna eat beef dip again."

"That'll be a good thing," Tilda said. "No offense to Ruby Joe's cooking, but even she'd agree you should cut back."

Rita gave her a look. "You're not my doctor."

"Nope," Tilda said, "nothing like Dr. Roseberg. But I plan on being your mother by proxy, since the one you got is nomadic. And for the health of the baby, would you eat some folic acid, already?"

"Shh," Rita said, giving her a look. "I don't want everybody around here to know."

Tilda swiveled her head, giving an exaggerated gander of the veranda. "I ain't saying nothing no one on this porch don't already know." Then she pointed at Jason. "Speaking of investigative acumen, your deputy here is gonna make one fine sheriff."

Rita smiled. "Don't I know it."

"He showed up for lunch after that autopsy with a way bigger appetite than you've ever displayed."

Rita glanced at Jason. "What?"

He straightened his shoulders. "Yeah, the autopsy wasn't so bad."

Rita chuckled. "This from the guy who usually pukes at every crime scene?"

"I discovered it's the element of surprise that's so upsetting to me," Jason said. "Not knowing what we're about to discover, but being able to smell it beforehand. But going into that autopsy where everything was clean, and smelled like formaldehyde, and my voice echoing off the stainless steel, and nothing sticky on my shoes...." He shrugged. "I don't know. It was easy."

Rita beamed at him. "I feel like a proud parent." Then she slid off the porch railing. "Speaking of parenting, we should take these two down to the station now."

Tilda glanced at the cruiser. "They haven't stopped arguing since I got here."

"Tell me about it," Rita said, heading down the porch steps.

"An officer from Beaumont's already at the station to meet us," Jason said.

"Perfect," Rita said as they approached the cruiser. "Since they can assist in processing the Slaneys, could you drop me off at Shannon Bachman's, please?"

"Ten-four," Jason said, getting in the driver's seat.

Rita buckled into the passenger seat and glanced in the backseat. "All okay in here?"

Aiden Slaney pullback his lips in a sneer. "That's my goddamned money," he said. "We're antique collectors."

"Then that means we won't find Frenchie's fingerprints on the bills then, will we?" Rita said.

Aiden stared back at her for a heartbeat, then pressed his lips together and leaned back in his seat, arms folded, mirroring the posture Deborah had already taken.

Rita gave Jason a satisfied smile. "There," she said. "Silence."

"Told you you'll make a great mom," Jason said.

Twelve minutes later, he pulled up to Shannon Bachman's house, dropping Rita at the curb. She walked up to the driveway and knocked.

Shannon's mom answered the door.

"Hi, Linda," Rita said. "Is Shannon here?"

"Yes. She's out back with the boys while Logan naps. I'll go call her in now."

Linda turned and headed to the back of the house, while Rita took a seat in the living room. While she waited, she studied a family portrait on the wall. The family was seated on a grassy lawn, casually dressed in matching chinos and white t-shirts. Trevor sat in the center with Shannon beside him, holding Logan as a newborn. Their two sons lolled in front of them.

Though signs of Trevor's illness were visible, he commanded the portrait with a silent strength, shoulders straight, smile broad, eyes twinkling. Death's jaws awaited, but he'd possessed an inner resilience borne of becoming a father, three times.

A love so great that it had inspired — and carried him through — his final actions.

Linda returned, leading Shannon by the hand. She looked gaunt.

"Hello, Shannon," Rita said.

Shannon lowered herself onto the sofa, still holding Linda's hand. "Sheriff Jonas."

Rita took a seat in the chair by the fireplace. "We have the answers we've been looking for in regard to Trevor's death."

Shannon gripped Linda's hand tighter. They glanced at each other. Then Shannon looked back at Rita and nodded, her lips pressed together.

"Trevor staged a murder," she said.

Shannon's face grew whiter, her eyes widening.

"He did it for an insurance payout," Rita said, "to provide for you and the kids. Before the cancer could take him."

Still gripping her mother's hand, Shannon nodded. But still she said nothing.

"He tried to frame someone at Apex," Rita said, "as a means of revenge for the injustices he and his family experienced."

A sob escaped Linda, and she dropped her head onto Shannon's shoulder. Shannon's gaze remained fixed on Rita.

"He killed himself," Shannon repeated, sounding more like a statement than a question.

"Yes," Rita said.

"Why would he put me through this? And why would he do it in such a horrible way?" Shannon asked. "We planned that me and the boys would be at his side, here in the house. And when we moved, we'd plant a tree over his ashes." Now her tears started to flow. Beside her, Linda was shaking. "We had prepared for everything all the way to the ugly end. And he ended it short! He suffered! He did it all by himself!"

"It is a terrible sacrifice to imagine," Rita said. She paused, holding space for Shannon's tears to ebb and flow. "Please consider that Trevor felt both betrayed and disempowered by Apex. By cancer. And he was guilt-ridden over errors he'd made in your marriage. All of these factors combined to create a strong desire — a need, even — to regain a sense of agency before death. To be heroic, in a sense. To provide for his family. Even if posthumously. And to avenge Apex, somehow."

Shannon nodded, again wordless, then crumpled into sobs. After a minute, she cleared her nose. "But now there won't be an insurance payout. And next month we'll still have to leave the house."

"The murder-suicide wasn't Trevor's first plan to provide for you," Rita said. "Originally, his friend Frenchie had hatched a plan."

"I don't understand," Shannon said.

"Frenchie planned to give you a gift. But someone lied to him and told Frenchie the gift was worthless. So Trevor devised an alternate plan on his own."

Rita set the torn corner of the bill on the coffee table in front of the sofa.

Shannon leaned forward to look at it, squinting through her tears. She wiped her eyes dry. "What's that?"

"The corner of an antique hundred-dollar bill, from 1880. The rest of the bill, along with the others, is currently in evidence," Rita said. "And alone is worth eighty thousand dollars, minimum. But I suspect the bills may be worth more because they're in excellent condition and the serial numbers are sequential."

Shannon and Linda stared at her. Then looked at each other.

"Hang on, Sheriff Jonas," Shannon said, getting up with a liveliness Rita hadn't yet seen in her. She ran up the stairs to the second floor, then returned a moment later, holding some pieces of sepia paper.

She walked up to Rita and handed her several antique bills. "These were in the Benny's and Corey's letters. I put Logan's away till he's older. There's probably five in there, too."

Rita counted out ten fifty-dollar bills, presumably from the 1880s like the hundreds.

She returned the money to Shannon. "So Frenchie did manage to give these to Trevor."

"In the letter, Trev says they're a gift from Frenchie. But that the money's old and not valuable anymore, so they can play with it. He goes on to request that I take the boys out to Frenchie's, to introduce them. Trev says Frenchie always wanted a son."

"It's evident Frenchie cared about Trevor like one," Rita said with a smile.

Shannon sniffled. "I suppose it's a blessing Trev'll never know what happened to his friend."

"As such," Rita said, getting up from the armchair, "when the money is released from evidence, I'll ensure it comes to you."

Again, Shannon and Linda swapped a look. Then looked at Rita.

Linda spoke first. "Are you saying this money is for Shannon and the kids?"

Rita nodded. "It'll be a while until you get it. But, yes, it'll come to you, Shannon. Keep me updated with your contact information when you move."

Shannon nodded. "Of course. Thank you. Thank you for everything." Then she hugged Rita, firm and brief. "I appreciate everything you did while you were mourning, too. I saw your dad's obituary in the newspaper."

"Thank you," Rita said. "I appreciate that. All the best to you and your family."

Shannon gave Rita a genuine smile, the first like it she'd seen. "Thank you. I'm so glad I'll be able to stay home with the boys now. At least till they're school age. Trev and I always wanted that."

Linda nodded, squeezing Shannon's shoulders. "Sure did. Everything'll be all right, now." Then she met Rita's eye. "In the end, we'll probably appreciate leaving Apex Hills and starting out new somewhere else."

Shannon sighed. "It'll feel strange, leaving this home. This town. These memories. But Trevor told me that his boys were going to need a dad. At first that was hard for me to hear, considering his infidelity. And I told him so. His answer was that, in those moments, Beth had needed a man in her household. And that one day I was gonna need a man in my household again, too. And I should make sure that happened."

Rita squeezed her shoulder. "You're going to raise some fine kids, Shannon Bachman. If any of you need short of any kind in the upcoming weeks, feel free to call down to the station."

"Thank you, I will," Shannon said.

Then Rita bade her goodbye and said she'd see herself out.

As she walked to the front door, she heard Shannon crying again and the soft murmurs of her mother.

Rita closed the door behind her and walked down the path.

And stopped short when she saw Otto coming up the sidewalk, carrying a trash bag.

But his gait was wrong. And the height was off, too.

"Arbuckle," Rita said, walking to meet him. "You look good in my dad's clothes."

"And I sure appreciate them," Arbuckle said. "But I think I put too many on today. It was hard to choose, so I layered 'em up." He unbuttoned his shirt to show a T-shirt underneath. "But I've been sweatin' like a skunk in rut." He shook the black trash bag he was carrying. "Not even sure I can finish my usual route. Think I might head to the Return-It Depot now."

"I'm walking into town, too," Rita said, falling into step with him. "Mind if I join you?"

Arbuckle tipped Otto's cap at her. "Don't mind at all, honey, be my guest."

But all Rita heard was "honeybee."

Chapter Fifty-Seven

Cash pulled into the parking stall marked *Reserved for immediate family.*

Rita pointed through the windshield to a silver Audi a few stalls away. "Ken Saunders is here."

She got out and walked around the back of Cash's pickup truck. Ken spotted her and got out of his car to come meet her.

"Rita."

"Hi, Ken."

"Sorry for showing up at your dad's funeral."

She nodded. "It's okay."

Ken adjusted his mirrored sunglasses. "I'm leaving town and wanted to say thanks."

"Of course." Rita offered a small smile. "And you're welcome. Good luck, Ken. New York never gets dull."

Ken put his hands in his pockets and rocked on his heels. "I'm actually going west. Gonna try starting out new. Maybe work in the fitness industry."

"That sounds like a good fit for you," Rita said.

"Look," he said. "I'm sorry for everything, you know, that ever happened between us."

Rita smiled. "Thanks, Ken. I believe you're sincere about that."

"One hundred percent," he said.

"Keep in touch," Rita said. "I mean it."

Ken grinned and held out his knuckles for a fist-bump.

"Goodbye, Ken," Rita said. Then she returned to Cash's side, who was chatting to some of Otto's neighbors. Hanging back, Rita gave a small wave.

He spotted her and broke away from the group, coming to her side. "Ready?"

She swallowed. "Ready."

Cash took her hand and escorted her into the funeral home. In the foyer, hushed voices exchanged salutations and handshakes. A large, framed photograph of Otto stood on a table surrounded by white lilies.

She pointed. "That's the photo Mary Lou sent along with the obituary. Dustin must have printed this one."

"Rita," a voice said.

Rita turned to greet Helen, accompanied by a woman of similar age and height. Helen's bleached hair had grown out two inched, the roots showing the same dark shade as her sister's.

"Helen," Rita said. "I'm glad you could come today." She met the other woman's eyes. "Thanks for bringing her, Susan."

Susan nodded. "I'm glad I can be here for her."

Helen blew her nose into a tissue, then took her sister's arm again. Susan led her though to the chapel, and Rita and Cash followed.

Inside the chapel, recorded classical music set a somber tone, as did the subdued pot-lights. On the benches sat approximately eighty guests, including some cops from Casper, mostly retired, plus the local firefighters, Otto's friends and neighbors, and other citizens of Still who liked to show up for milestone events, like the passing of notable townsfolk. Sitting among this set, Ruby Joe gave Rita a small nod.

They continued up the aisle, passing Rita's closest acquaintances, who sat on the first few rows of benches. Walter wore a charcoal polo shirt and sat next to Mary Lou, who'd tamed her hair into a small bun at the nape of her neck and opted to wear black, although her shirt was embroidered with roses and studded with grommets.

Spotting her, Mary Lou blew a kiss. "Way to stay strong, kiddo." Then she winked. "I see you're taking a page out of my book."

Rita blinked at her. "Huh?"

Mary Lou leaned forward to tug Rita's black t-shirt. "You're wearing fan apparel in the direst of moments."

Rita looked down at the ABBA screen print. "I don't actually like ABBA. I'm wearing it for Otto."

Mary Lou blinked. "Otto liked ABBA?"

Rita shrugged. "Apparently. Someone gave him this shirt for his birthday. And seeing as it's black..." She shrugged again.

"It looks good on you," Jason said, seated on the bench across the aisle.

Rita had also never seen Jason in head to toe black before. He looked smart, sitting between Blaze Wright (also in a well-cut suit) and another man who exuded a strong pong of Old Spice.

Then Rita recognized him: Arbuckle. Showered and shaved, he looked about ten years younger.

He gave her a wink. "You got this, honey."

Rita bit her lip. "Thanks, Arbuckle. Otto's shirt looks good on you, by the way."

Arbuckle sat up straighter. "Thanks. Now go knock 'em dead."

Rita smiled. "Don't think you're supposed to say that at a memorial service."

He matched her smile. "Then knock some life back into 'em."

Rita laughed, and several mourners turned to look at her. Gripping Cash's hand, she pulled him into the first row.

"You okay?" he asked, quiet.

"Yeah," she said. "This is surreal."

He squeezed her hand, then they fell silent as Dustin Ashbury approached the podium.

"Greetings," he said into the small microphone. "Today, we gather to remember and honor Otto Bernard Jonas. I invite you to find comfort in the reflections and memories shared during this service as we come together to celebrate Otto's life and legacy."

"Oh, shit," Rita said, pressing her cheek to Cash's shoulder.

"What is it?" he whispered.

"My guts," she said. "I feel queasy."

"Shit," Cash said. "You got anything for that? What do pregnant ladies take? Tums?"

"No Tums," Rita said. "Dr. Roseberg's orders. And I'm not a lady. But I might have something in my purse." She found the sample of Vita-Boost Bubble Yum, ripped open the packet, and popped the stick in her mouth.

Cash blinked at her. "You're chewing bubble gum?"

"It's homeopathic."

"That good for the baby?"

"It's supposed to be good for everyone," Rita whispered. "I'm hoping it's gonna be good for my stomach."

"I can smell it, you know," Cash said.

"What? My stomach?"

"No, the bubble gum."

"It's seaweed. I promise not to blow any bubbles."

"—invite Rita to come up," Dustin said.

Then the music filtered through the speaker again.

Cash elbowed her. "It's your turn."

"I know," Rita said, jumping up. She walked onto the dais, then paused, scurried back, took out her gum, and held it out to Cash. "Psst!"

He leaned in to whisper. "What?"

She flapped her hand. "Take it."

He held out his palm and she dropped in the pink wad. "That's gross."

"What d'you mean, it's gross? I let you put your sperm inside me."

"Jesus Christ, would you keep it down?"

"They're all gonna figure it out in eight months anyway."

"Here." A hand thrust over the back of the bench.

Rita took the small plastic packet. "If that's a pack of condoms you got for me this time, Edith Mae, you're too late."

"It's Kleenex," Edith Mae said.

Rita looked closer at the miniature set of facial tissues printed with flamingos. "Otto might have liked flamingos."

Edith Mae winked. "I know."

Rita passed Cash the Kleenex. "Here, put my gum in this." Then she hurried back to the podium.

For the eulogy.

Her legs shook.

She licked her lips.

Then cleared her throat.

"What can I say?" Rita said. She splayed her hands on

the podium, pressing her fingertips to the wood. "I haven't prepared anything to tell you."

Her gaze traveled to Cash. He shifted on the bench, chewing on a thumbnail.

"But don't worry," Rita said. "It's not because I have nothing to say about my father. But the last few days, the local SCSO has been investigating two suspicious deaths."

She paused to crack open the bottle of water Dustin had placed there for her. She took a sip, then continued.

"Otto would be proud of me working at a time like this. Not because it is venerable to work through a period of bereavement." Her gaze flicked to Mary Lou, then found Jason, and returned to Cash again. "Or to put work before family." This time she looked at Cash. "But because I, like Otto, have dedicated myself to upholding justice in a small town. And this position requires me to take leadership even during the storms in my own life. The past week has taught me what it truly means to be sheriff in a small town."

Rita took another sip, then carried on as though Otto stood at her side with an encouraging hand on her back.

"Society would have us believe that compartmentalizing our work and personal lives makes us better at the job. That may be true in New York, where the heartbeat of the city never stops. But in a rural county, the people who need help are neighbors, friends, family, loved ones. And when duty calls, I answer. And though I was working this week, I often thought of Otto. Even felt his presence." She cracked a wobbly smile. "And I don't even believe in ghosts."

Several guests obliged her with a laugh, Mary Lou offering up the greatest enthusiasm.

"Yesterday I was reminded of Otto's nickname for me," Rita said, seeking Cash's eyes. "*Honeybee*. And I realized how dearly I missed hearing Otto say it, even though for a long time I resented the nickname." She laughed. "He always used to say I was as sweet as honey, but I could sting like a motherfucker. Pardon my language." She shrugged. "I'm a cop's daughter."

She took another sip of water.

"The reason Otto used to say I could sting like a bee harkens back to when I was eight. He was teaching me how to use a shiv to release a pair of handcuffs, during which I cut my thumb. I remember being frozen with fear as I stared at the blood welling up, and thinking that he should be running for the iodine and bandages, like I always did for Carole when—"

Rita broke off and took another swallow of water, this time a big one. She needed to stay on track. She capped the bottle and continued.

"Anyways, he never went and got the iodine and bandages. Instead, he praised my pain threshold, then used the shiv to slit his own thumb and pressed it to mine. Then he said, 'Jesus, that's stings,' as if it'd been my suggestion he cut himself."

Some attendees chuckled, and someone cleared their throat. Cash.

"Oh, come on, Rita," he said, "that's not why Otto used to tease you for having a sting."

The room grew even quieter and stiller. Rita stiffened. Then whispered back to him in the front row, her voice hoarse: "What the hell are you talking about?"

Cash got up and came to her side at the podium. "I'd like to share a story too," he said into the microphone. "The story of how Rita earned that nickname." He gave her a sidelong wink. "I knew Otto well, too." Then he addressed the guests again. "He was like a dad to me, since for most of my life my dad hasn't been around."

Rita felt for Cash's hand and threaded her fingers through his.

"So, the sting that Otto liked to tease her about was that she once stabbed him with a paring knife."

Rita frowned. "You're gonna tell *this* story?" She sighed and pulled the microphone from him. "I stabbed Otto for a very good reason, I'll have you know," she said to the guests. "I thought he was Cash."

"You make that sound like a good thing," Cash said.

"Well, you'd been bothering me." Rita said. "Coming up to my window because you knew I used to sneak out at night. And you were trying to get me to sneak out with you."

"Sure was," Cash said. "You were very resistant to the idea, though."

"Exactly," Rita said. "I kept a paring knife in my bedside table, in case you didn't fully get the message.

Cash tugged the microphone toward him. "So one night Otto comes home and he's drunk, right? Because he used to tipple at the end of a shift. And he knew that Rita kept that window unlocked, 'cause she was sneaking in and out all the time."

"We've already been over that part."

"We all snuck in and out in those days, didn't we?" Cash said. "She was sixteen, I was—"

"I was?" Rita said. "How do you remember all these details?"

Cash gave her a look. "Could you stop interrupting?"

"You should consider going into my profession," she said.

"So this window's unlatched," Cash says, addressing the attendees, "and Otto's gotta use it, right? 'Cause Carole's passed out downstairs, and if anyone wakes her, it's hell to pay."

Rita stiffened. Memories of the night came rushing back, now richer, brighter, bolder. She remembered Otto had smelled different. Like flowers. She had told him so. To which he had chuckled and said that he got tangled in a bush while chasing down a perp.

Of course, it was probably the years that he was cheating with Helen, laying in another woman's scented bedsheets. Although was it really considered cheating when Carole would come and go without notice, for weeks at a time?

At the back of the chapel a figure moved towards the door. It was Carole slipping out, her face ashen. Rita's gut twisted. Cash, like Rita, had assumed she wasn't here.

"—and even though she stabbed him," Cash concluded, "Otto never held it against her. Rita was always his greatest pride. He and Rita sincerely loved each other, and I loved him too, and Otto will be missed."

"Hear, hear," Ruby Joe said.

"Although shortly before he passed," Cash said, "he told me if I ever mistreated Rita, he was gonna come back as a bison and mow me over."

Rita's heart skipped a beat. "That's enough," she said into his ear.

Then she stepped back from the podium, clutching the bottle of water with one hand and taking Cash's with her other.

Leading her to the bench, Cash gave her hand an encouraging squeeze. She squeezed it back.

And finally, Rita cried.

Chapter Fifty-Eight

At a table in the corner, Rita blew her nose into the last flamingo-printed tissue.

"These things are so small, I can only empty one nostril per tissue," she said.

Edith Mae gave her a grim nod. "The boxes don't fit in my pockets. Or sleeves for that matter." From her flowered pocket — she'd forgone black to wear a dress constructed of Carole's fabric scraps, flowers being a symbol of memorial — she withdrew another packet of Kleenex. She passed it to Rita.

"Thanks," Rita said, taking a tissue patterned with ice-cream cones.

Cash approached with a paper plate piled with pastries. He extended the array. "Another lemon square or date bar?"

Rita shook her head. "I already ate half a dozen, and that was on top of the sausage rolls."

"There are sausage rolls?" Edith Mae said, getting up.

"They're in the warming trays," Cash said as she beelined for the buffet.

Cash set the plate on the table and pulled up a chair next to Rita. "Guess you got your hunger back."

Rita blew out a breath. "Guess so."

Ruby Joe approached, wearing a black dress and pair of heels. A gold cross hung in a chain around her neck. Rita had never seen her in anything aside from jeans and sneakers.

She pulled out the chair on the other side of the table and sat. "How you holding up, honeybee?"

Rita nodded. "Okay. Though I'm not used to so many people calling me 'honeybee.'"

Then Rita noticed Ruby Joe's cheeks streaked with tears and her nose red and swollen. She extended the packet of ice-cream cone Kleenex.

Ruby Joe took a tissue and blew her nose, then fixed her teary eyes on Rita. "I'm sorry for not being around much lately. I've had a lot going on."

Rita nodded. "I figured. Me, too."

Ruby Joe gave a resigned nod. "Double homicide is no small undertaking."

"Yep," Rita said. "Thank God for Jason."

Ruby Joe leaned in and gave Rita a rough hug. "Take care, honeybee." Then she broke away, and pushed back from the table, leaving as abruptly as she'd arrived.

Rita glanced at Cash. "She's really cut up."

Cash made an affirmative sound. "I never knew they were so close."

"Maybe she was one of Otto's dalliances?" Rita said.

Cash gave her a look. "With Ruby Joe? Never."

Rita sighed. "You're right. But I couldn't stop thinking about the possibilities, looking at the women in attendance. Maybe I've got more half-siblings out there, like Lisa."

Cash squeezed her shoulder. "You don't need to be thinking about that right now."

Rita forced a smile, then turned to Cash. "I'm really not feeling well. I'd like to get some fresh air."

"Was it the lemon squares or the sausage rolls?"

Rita stifled a burp. "I think the culprit's a mini quiche."

Cash stood up from the table, taking Rita's arm. "Come on," he said, leading her from the reception hall.

Outside in the parking lot, a shrill voice shouted in anger.

Carole.

She and Cash turned to look. Across the lot, Ruby Joe and Carole were arguing.

"What the hell's going on?" Cash asked Rita.

Carole's arm shot out, taking a swipe at Ruby Joe, who stepped back, dodging the slap.

"Whoa, whoa, whoa," Rita said, charging across the lot, "hold up." Within five paces of Carole, she could smell that she'd been drinking. "What the hell's going on here?"

"Oh, Jesus Christ," Carole said, rolling her eyes. She squinted at Rita. "And why the hell are you wearing an ABBA T-shirt?"

"Probably because Otto was a die-hard fan in the 70s," Ruby Joe said, her voice tight. Her gaze flickered to Rita. "He used to sing you 'Honey, Honey' for a lullaby." She gave Cash a look. "That's where the nickname really comes from."

Carole snarled. "Here we go again, singing praises to Otto."

"Let's not talk here," Rita said, putting a hand on Carole's arm. "Not now. You've been drinking."

"Ha!" Carole barked. "You're shaming me for raising a glass to the man who sired you?"

"Come on, Carole," Cash said. "We'll give you a ride home. I'll drive your van out to Sunny Daze and Rita can follow in my truck."

But Carole ignored him, boring her gaze into Rita. "Do you know your dad was a drinker when I met him?"

Ruby Joe set her jaw. "That's old history, Carole."

"Blotto," Carole said. "That used to be his nickname. Blotto Otto. The guys at the cop-shop all used it." Carole burped and Rita's guts responded in kind. "But I'm the one who came up with it."

"I'm sure you did," Rita said. "Just like you called me—"

"Shush now, everyone," Ruby Joe said. "Rita, you don't need to listen to any of this. It's water under the bridge. Your dad stopped coming into The Shaft when you were about ten."

Rita glanced at Ruby Joe, surprised at her detailed knowledge of Otto's past. And Rita's childhood.

Carole sputtered. "Sure, he gave up binge-drinking when you born. But he started smoking twice as hard."

"Let's go, Carole," Cash said, taking her arm.

Carole shook him off, glaring at Rita. "And why the hell can't I stay for the reception?" She thrust a finger towards Ruby Joe. "When she is?"

Rita set her jaw. "Why the hell would you have a problem with Ruby Joe attending today?"

Carole spat on the ground. "Because he wanted nothing to do with his sister!"

A chill ran up Rita's spine. She blinked at Carole. "Ruby Joe is Otto's sister?"

Carole burst into bitter laughter. "I should have guessed you didn't know. You really don't know anything, do you, Rita?"

Rita looked at Ruby Joe. "Ruby Joe?"

"We had a falling out years ago," she said, her voice tight.

"And everyone in this stupid little town went right

along with it," Carole said. "Pretending they weren't family. Pretending there wasn't no bad blood between 'em."

Ruby Joe set her jaw. "Those were Otto's wishes, not mine."

Rita stared at her again, recognizing the younger woman she had seen in the black and white photographs. Beside the picket fence. Leaning against the Buick. Of everyone at the funeral, she probably knew Otto the best.

But did she also know about the half-million in his safe deposit box? Or was the money a secret, too, like his step-daughter, Lisa and estranged sister?

"Please forgive me," Ruby Joe said, treating for Rita's hand. "I was only trying to keep the peace."

Rita blinked at her. "Peace? Is that what you call all these secrets?" She turned back to Carole. "I've had enough. Please go."

But it was Rita who turned to go, leaving Cash standing with Carole and Ruby Joe as she marched across the parking lot, blinding walking ahead.

Her phone vibrated in her pocket. Probably more condolences. But trained by the job, she glanced at the caller ID.

And stopped walking to answer it. "Hello, Angela."

"I heard your dad passed. I'm calling to offer you my condolences."

"Thanks," Rita said.

Angela made a satisfied sound "Now you can now focus on yourself again. You give any more thought to my offer?"

Rita dried her eyes. "You get straight to business, huh?"

"You and I are career women, Rita," Angela said.

Rita stayed silent, unable to disagree.

"So is the timing better?" Angela asked.

Rita's hand rubbed her belly. "Well, not entirely."

"Then maybe it's time for a change," Angela said. "Maybe it's time to come work for me."

Rita chewed on her lip, thinking. "About that…"

The End

About the Author

Lauren Street has always loved a mystery. As a kid growing up in bible belt country she devoured every whodunit book she could get her sticky little hands on and secretly investigated all of her (seemingly) normal boring neighbors. Sometimes their pets and farm animals too. All grown up now and living in the UK with her thoroughly unsuspicious (and often unsuspecting) husband, she writes domestic psychological thrillers about families torn apart by secrets and lies. And she sometimes still peers over garden walls to check up on the neighbors.

Also By Lauren Street

The Nanny Problem

The Nanny Problem

The Still County Thrillers

Still Here

Still Buried

Still Burning

Still Hidden

The Bishop Smoky Mountain Thrillers

Hide Me Away

Fuel To The Flame

Closer By The Hour

A Gamble Either Way

Calling My Children Home

Too Far Gone

Here You Come Again

A Friend Like You

The Company You Keep

One By One

Come Back To Me

The Only Way Out

Replaced with Nolon King

Replaced

In Her Place

Irreplaceable

The Salazar Redwood Forest Thrillers

The Girl Who Couldn't Stop Dying

The Girl Who Couldn't Get Out

The Girl Who Couldn't Be Found

Standalone Novels

Postpartum